FLIRTING WITH THE BARONESS

Patience impulsively touched his arm. "You cannot kill him!" she protested. "His uncle is a rich and powerful man. Would you not hang for it?"

He covered her hand with his own. "No harm will come to *me*, I do assure you."

Patience had no doubt that Mr. Broome would prove more than equal to the nefarious Mr. Purefoy. She felt as though a terrible weight had been lifted from her shoulders. She could almost pity Mr. Purefoy.

Reluctantly, she withdrew her hand. "If we don't return soon, Mr. Broome, your cousin will think we've made off with his horses."

"Nonsense," he said lightly. "Freddie will think I am making love to you, that's all."

"Now why would he think that?"

"Having met you, how could he think otherwise?"

Books by Tamara Lejeune

SIMPLY SCANDALOUS

SURRENDER TO SIN

RULES FOR BEING A MISTRESS

THE HEIRESS IN HIS BED

CHRISTMAS WITH THE DUCHESS

THE PLEASURE OF BEDDING A BARONESS

Published by Kensington Publishing Corporation

The Pleasure Of Bedding A Baroness

TAMARA LEJEUNE

ZEBRA BOOKS
KENSINGTON PUBLISHING CORP.
http://www.kensingtonbooks.com

ZEBRA BOOKS are published by

Kensington Publishing Corp.
119 West 40th Street
New York, NY 10018

All Kensington titles, imprints, and distributed lines are available at special quantity discounts for bulk purchases for sales promotion, premiums, fund-raising, educational, or institutional use.

Special book excerpts or customized printings can also be created to fit specific needs. For details, write or phone the office of the Kensington Special Sales Manager: Attn. Special Sales Department. Kensington Publishing Corp., 119 West 40th Street, New York, NY 10018. Phone: 1-800-221-2647.

Zebra and the Z logo Reg. U.S. Pat. & TM Off.

ISBN-13: 978-1-4201-0874-3
ISBN-10: 1-4201-0874-3

First Printing: November 2011
10 9 8 7 6 5 4 3 2 1

Printed in the United States of America

Chapter 1

No one who saw Miss Patience Waverly when she first came to London would ever have believed that, mere weeks before, she had been thought one of the prettiest girls in Philadelphia. Eight weeks at sea had been more than sufficient to reduce her from a vibrant young woman of twenty to a weak and bloodless bag of bones. Her cheeks and eyes were sunken, her skin was an unhealthy gray, and her body was lost in clothes that no longer fit her. For propriety's sake, she had clapped a bonnet over her hair, which hung in thick black snakes down her back, but she was really too exhausted to care about her appearance. Only the ever-present nausea, which somehow seemed worse on land than it had been at sea, kept her from falling asleep in the yellow hackney as it made its way through the busy streets of the city of London.

Her sister had fared much better on the voyage from America. Miss Prudence Waverly's eyes still sparkled like enormous emeralds. Her shiny, jet black hair was arranged in soft curls, and her skin was like milk and roses. In her royal blue cloak and silk-covered bonnet, she bore a striking resemblance to the Parisian fashion plate she had so meticulously copied.

Now no one would ever have guessed that Patience and Prudence were sisters, let alone identical twins.

Sleek and healthy, even a little on the plump side, Pru Waverly stretched her arms over her head in the yellow hackney coach and yawned ferociously. "Can't you do this tomorrow, Pay?" she said plaintively. "There are some very nice hotels here in London. I'm sleepy!"

"Hotels are a waste of money," Patience replied, sounding very brusque as she fought back another wave of nausea. "I asked the attorney to find us a small house in a quiet, respectable neighborhood, assuming there is such a neighborhood in London," she added darkly.

One heard such unpleasant tales of the fleshpots of Europe.

"It's only one night," said Pru.

"No," Patience said firmly. "It's foolish to pay for a hotel room when we are renting a perfectly good house. At least, I hope it is a perfectly good house," she added. "For what we are paying, it ought to be!"

Distracted by the view from her window as they passed a row of shops, Pru gave up the argument, and the chaise continued on to the offices of Bracegirdle, Bracegirdle, and Pym, in Chancery Lane.

Upon hearing that the Miss Waverlys had come to see him, Mr. Horace Bracegirdle first exclaimed, "At this hour?" for it was nine o'clock in the evening. While it was by no means unusual for attorneys to keep such late hours in the city, they did not usually receive clients—and most especially not *female* clients—after dark. Despite his misgivings, however, Mr. Bracegirdle tugged his best wig over his shaved skull and hurried out to the lobby to meet the two young ladies from America.

Pru greeted him, smiling, and swiftly introduced herself and her sister. To her surprise, the attorney gave all his attention to Patience.

"But you are ill, my lady," he exclaimed in dismay, hurrying to support her frail body. "Smithers, fetch the brandy!"

"I'm perfectly all right," Patience said faintly, fending off Smithers. "I was seasick on the journey—and no better now that I am on land, it seems. But I shall be all right in a day or two, I daresay."

Murmuring his sympathies, Mr. Bracegirdle ushered Patience into his gloomy, paneled office, gently helping her to a chair of oxblood leather near the fireplace. Not at all pleased to be so completely ignored, Pru followed in consternation.

"Really, my lady! You are very pale," Mr. Bracegirdle fussed, hovering over Patience like a devoted nurse. "If you will not take brandy, perhaps you will take a little water?"

"There's nothing really wrong with me," Patience insisted. "I was in excellent health when we left Philadelphia. I'm a little tired, that's all."

Pru, unused to being relegated to the background, said resentfully, "We're both tired. It was a very long journey. You may have been sick, Patience, but *I* had to nurse you."

"The sooner we take possession of our house, the sooner we can rest," said Patience. "Shall we get down to business, Mr. Bracegirdle?"

The attorney seated himself at his desk. "Of course," he said, taking up a document. "As you know, your uncle, Lord Waverly, died very suddenly six months ago."

"You mean he committed suicide," Patience said bluntly.

He blinked at her, surprised and a little offended.

Patience smiled briefly. "We Americans are deplorably forthright, I know. Never mind the spoonful of sugar, Mr. Bracegirdle. Just give us the medicine. My uncle committed suicide. Bankrupt and hounded by creditors, he jumped off a bridge and drowned himself."

Mr. Bracegirdle looked shocked. "Quite," he murmured in dismay.

"We don't pretend to mourn his passing," Patience went on. "We never even knew of his existence until we received your letter."

"I think we *should* pretend to mourn him," Pru protested. "After all, Pay, he was our father's brother. Our father never spoke of his native land, Mr. Bracegirdle, but somehow I always knew, deep in my heart, that we were descended of royalty. Father had such an elegant profile."

"Oh. Did he?" Mr. Bracegirdle said rather helplessly, venturing into the silence that followed Pru's disclosure.

"I understand there is no will to be read," Patience prompted him.

"His lordship does not appear to have had the time to make out his will before his unfortunate demise," Mr. Bracegirdle said, stubbornly clinging to his euphemisms. "Your father, Mr. Arthur Waverly, being dead, the two of you represent his lordship's only living relatives. As the eldest, Miss Patience Waverly is next in line. Therefore, she inherits. Congratulations, my lady."

"You mean *Patience* gets everything?" Pru said, frowning. "I get nothing?"

"I'm afraid so, Miss Waverly."

"Not fair!" Pru exclaimed. "When our grandfather died, we each got half of his money. I'm just as much Lord Waverly's niece as *she* is."

"The European system is inherently unfair and corrupt," Patience explained. "That's why we got rid of it in America. Don't worry, Pru! I'll sell off all the assets and split everything with you, fifty-fifty. Assuming there's anything left after the debts are paid."

"Split?" Mr. Bracegirdle repeated in astonishment. "I'm afraid you do not understand, my lady. One does not *split* a barony."

"Of course not," Patience said brusquely. "Try to keep up, Mr. Bracegirdle. I mean to sell the land, and split the *money* with my sister. I understand there's an estate of about twenty-six thousand acres. I can sell those acres, can't I?"

"The property is not entailed," he admitted. "But, my lady! You would not sell Wildings, surely? It has been in your family for generations. I believe it was the prospect of having to sell his beloved home in order to pay his debts that drove Lord Waverly to despair."

"Well, it won't drive *me* to despair," said Patience. "It's only dirt, Mr. Bracegirdle. I'm not sentimental."

"Well, *I* am," said Pru. "I'm extremely sentimental. I'd like to *see* the place where our father was born. Then we can sell it."

"Of course we must see it," said Patience. "I'd be a fool to sell it before I know what it's worth, and I won't know *that* until I see it. Do you have any idea what it's worth, Mr. Bracegirdle?"

"Some might say it is priceless, my lady," he said, in a rather reproachful tone.

"Nothing is priceless," Patience replied. "You must have some idea."

"Perhaps ten thousand," he said very reluctantly.

"Pounds or dollars?"

"Pounds, of course," he said stiffly.

"So . . . about forty thousand dollars?" Patience said, rubbing her temples. "I haven't checked the rate of exchange since I left Philadelphia, but I don't suppose it's changed all that much in two months. And what is the debt against the estate?"

Mr. Bracegirdle consulted some figures. "Five thousand, seven hundred, sixty pounds, four shillings, and thruppence."

Patience was obliged to rub her temples a bit longer.

"Let's see . . . That's about twenty-four thousand dollars. Forty thousand, less twenty-four thousand—that's sixteen thousand dollars. Not bad, Pru."

"No, indeed," said Pru.

"But, surely, my lady," Mr. Bracegirdle interposed, "with your maternal grandfather's fortune at your disposal, there can be no need to sell Wildings."

"But my grandfather's fortune is not at my disposal," Patience told him. "We are his heirs, of course, but I'm afraid the money has been placed in trust. We can't touch the principal until we are thirty."

"Thirty!" Pru repeated with bitter emphasis.

"I am aware of the terms of your grandfather's will, my lady," said Mr. Bracegirdle. "I have been in communication with your American trustee."

"Oh, Mr. Gordon!" Pru exclaimed. "How I hate him! I once asked him for an advance on my allowance, and all he gave me was a very stern lecture. I desperately needed new stockings, but he would not budge!"

"You never learned to darn properly," Patience said, shaking her head.

Pru rolled her eyes. "Darn! One does not darn silk stockings from Paris!"

"Er, yes," said Mr. Bracegirdle, looking a little flustered. "Quite. However! Notwithstanding the excellent Mr. Gordon, there is nothing, my lady, in your grandfather's will to prevent you from borrowing against your expectations."

"I beg your pardon?" said Patience.

He smiled, showing his yellow teeth. "Indeed! I've taken the liberty of drawing up the papers for you. With a stroke of the pen, your uncle's debt can be cleared away and, with it, all your embarrassment. So you see, my lady, there is no need to sell the estate. You can borrow as much as you like now, and pay it back in ten years, when you come into the fullness of your inheritance."

"It is not my ambition to live beyond my means, sir," Patience said coldly. "I prefer to sell the estate."

"What does he mean, Pay?" Pru whispered to her. "Can he really get us as much money as we want? Give *me* the papers, Mr. Bracegirdle. I'll sign!"

"I'm afraid we must have your sister's signature," Mr. Bracegirdle told her regretfully. "You are not yet twenty-one, Miss Prudence."

"Neither is she!" Pru said indignantly. "We're the same age."

"Yes, but *she* is Baroness Waverly of Wildings," Mr. Bracegirdle explained, "and, as such, she is your legal guardian, Miss Prudence."

"What?" Pru gasped.

"It *is* unusual for a female to assume a peerage in her own right, and not at all desirable, to be sure, but, in this case, I'm afraid it could not be prevented," Mr. Bracegirdle apologized. "Your uncle's title is as ancient as it is noble, but, sadly, when the papers were drawn up in the twelfth century, no one thought to exclude the female line! A shocking oversight, it seems to us now, but, in those days, they did not perceive the danger, perhaps, of modern women putting themselves forward as the equals of men."

"Never mind all that!" Pru cried impatiently. "What do you mean *she* is my guardian? We're twins! We came into the world together."

"As I said before, one cannot split a barony, Miss Prudence. My lady preceded you from the womb by some twenty-seven minutes."

"My lady!" Pru exclaimed, outraged. "What is she? A duchess? I thought you were just being English with your 'my lady' this and your 'my lady' that. Are you telling me *she* is royalty?"

"Oh, no," Mr. Bracegirdle assured her. "Some royalty *are* nobility, of course, but not all nobility are royalty, you understand."

"No," Pru said, frowning.

"Your sister is a baroness, Miss Prudence, a Peeress of the Realm. But she is not a member of the royal family."

"What about me?" Pru demanded.

He smiled. "Rejoice, Miss Prudence, for you are the *younger sister* of a Peeress of the Realm."

Pru scowled at him.

"The title is of no consequence, Pru," Patience said quickly. "I didn't come here to claim the title. I came here to claim the estate. The estate is what matters."

"You *knew* about this!" Pru accused her. "Why didn't you tell me? My lady!" she added spitefully.

"Pru, these silly European titles don't mean anything," Patience declared, oblivious to Mr. Bracegirdle's reddening face. "There is no substance to them. They are obsolete, like the monarchy itself. People of sense and education are perfectly capable of ruling themselves. America has proved that to the world. We don't need a rigid class system to maintain order."

"If titles and royalty are so obsolete, *Your Majesty*," Pru shot back, "why don't you abscond?"

"I think you mean abdicate," Patience calmly replied. "If I were to refuse the title, everything would go to *you*, and then *you* would be *my* guardian. *That*, of course, would be ridiculous."

"*This* is ridiculous! I don't need a guardian."

Patience winced as her sister's voice became shrill. "It's just a title, Pru. It doesn't mean anything. It's just business. As for being your guardian, I have always given you the benefit of my advice, and, in any event, you'll be twenty-one next year, and no longer a minor."

"*Then* can I sign the papers?" said Pru. "And get as much money as I want?"

Patience flinched. "Well, yes," she admitted. "When you are twenty-one, you'll be free to enter into any contract you choose. Just remember, the bank will want its money back, plus interest, when you are thirty. Don't come crying to me if there's no money left in ten years."

"Thank you for the vote of confidence, Your Majesty!"

Patience turned back to the attorney. "I'm sorry you went to the trouble of drawing up papers, sir," she said crisply. "But I won't be borrowing against one inheritance to pay off the debts of another! Wildings will have to be sold, along with any other assets my uncle left behind."

"It shall be as Your Ladyship commands, of course, but selling the estate will take time."

"Yes, Mr. Bracegirdle," said Patience. "I'm in no hurry to cross the Atlantic again any time soon, believe me! We are prepared to stay for a year. That is why I instructed you to find us a house in London. You did so, I believe?"

"Yes, my lady," he replied. "In Clarges Street. I think you will find the rent very reasonable."

"Ha!" said Patience, looking over the lease.

"Your American trustee has already approved the amount," said Mr. Bracegirdle, producing another document. "London, Your Ladyship must understand, is an expensive place. Your Ladyship would not want to be in a questionable part of town. Mayfair is very quiet and respectable, very safe, and, of course, fashionable."

After looking over the documents very carefully, Patience signed, but muttered, under her breath, "Highway robbery."

Mr. Bracegirdle gave her the latchkey to the house, and Patience tucked it into her reticule. "As your attorney, my lady, I must beg you to reconsider. At the very least, if Your Ladyship would consent to pay off Lord Waverly's debts of honor . . . ? Tradesmen, of course, may be put off for months, but—"

Patience snorted. "Debts of honor? Gambling debts, you mean?"

"It is one thing to make a shopkeeper wait for his money, my lady. But it is quite another to delay payment to a gentleman with an IOU!"

Patience climbed to her feet. "You're quite right," she said. "The shopkeepers will be paid as soon as I can manage it. The gentlemen with IOUs can wait."

"My lady!" he protested, quite shocked.

"Is that everything?" she asked.

"Heavens, no, my lady," he said, rising from his desk. "There is a great deal more to go over. I have a great many papers for Your Ladyship to sign."

"Then I'm afraid it will have to wait," said Patience. "I'm much too tired to read any more documents tonight."

"But there is no need for Your Ladyship to *read* any documents," he protested. "Here at Bracegirdle, Bracegirdle, and Pym, we read the documents *for* you. All that is required is your signature."

"Thank you, but I never sign anything without reading it," Patience said firmly. "My grandfather taught me that. It served him well."

"I trust you, Mr. Bracegirdle," said Pru. "When I am twenty-one, I'll sign anything you put in front of me."

"No, you won't," Patience said. "You're just needling me! You may call on me in a day or two when I have caught up on my rest," she went on, turning to Mr. Bracegirdle. "You know the address, of course."

"Of course, my lady. Smithers will see you to your carriage."

Prudence fell asleep in the hackney. Patience also

wanted very much to sleep, but every time she closed her eyes, queasiness overwhelmed her, and she was obliged to open them again.

At last they arrived in Clarges Street. The driver stopped his vehicle in front of one of the neat Georgian houses.

"Are you sure this is Number Seventeen?" Patience called up to the driver, looking at the house with the gravest misgivings. At this late hour, while the rest of the street was dark and quiet, this one house was ablaze with light. Human shadows danced in every window, and strains of music and raucous laughter could be heard clearly from the street. "Quiet, respectable street, my eye!" she muttered under her breath.

Pru's eyes fluttered open. "Are we here?" she asked, her voice thinned by sleep.

"Prudence, I want you to wait in the carriage," Patience said in her firmest voice.

Pru yawned. "Why? What's the matter?"

"Just wait in the carriage until I come and get you!" was the only reply she received.

Patience slipped out of the carriage, told the driver to wait, and went up the steps. Taking out her latchkey, she unlocked the door and went inside.

Maximilian Tiberius Purefoy opened one bloodshot eye and with supreme disfavor, regarded the servant who had awakened him. Bare-chested, wearing only black hosiery and a red satin cape, Max had come to the masquerade in the guise of Mephistopheles, complete with horns and a tail. Every exposed inch of skin, including his face, had been painted with scarlet greasepaint.

"What do you want?" he growled at the servant. "Can't you see that I am busy?"

For the occasion of his twenty-fifth birthday, Max had

invited two hundred of his closest friends to help him celebrate. For the venue, he had chosen an empty house in Mayfair—of which there were many, this being late October and out of Season. The drawing room had been converted into an opium den with cushions covering the floor and Chinamen teaching the neophytes how to smoke. Everyone was drunk or worse, and, needless to say, women were as plentiful as they were available. At the moment, Max was perfectly sated, floating on a cloud of opium, a nameless female snoring in his arms. At one point she had been dressed, one supposed ironically, as an angel. Her white feathers had stuck to his paint, and she was smeared with red grease.

"What do you want?" he repeated, pushing his angel away and tucking his sleeping member back into the slit that ran down the front of his pants. At the beginning of the evening, a huge black codpiece had adorned his costume, but that was long gone.

The servant looked vaguely familiar. "Who are you?" he asked curiously, momentarily forgetting that he was quite angry with this person for waking him up.

"I am Briggs, sir. The butler. Begging your pardon, sir, but there is a lady here."

Max laughed. "It's my birthday," he said happily. "Look around you. There are lots of ladies here. She'll have to get to the back of the line."

"But she says she is *Lady Waverly,* sir!" Briggs protested.

Max frowned in confusion. "What sort of a costume is that?" he slurred amiably.

"Costume, sir?"

"Costume, Briggs," Max roared, suddenly full of righteous anger. "It is a costume party. I am, of course, Mephistopheles. But what I want to know is what sort of costume is a Wady Laverly?"

"I don't believe her ladyship is wearing a costume, sir."

"Lady Godiva! Excellent," Max approved. "But she should have gotten here sooner. I am spent. Too bad! There aren't as many as one might think who will do Lady Godiva properly."

"Lady Waverly says she is the tenant, sir. She has a lease, sir, and a latchkey."

"Don't be silly," said Max, climbing unsteadily to his feet. "I borrowed this house for the night from a very good friend whose name I cannot recall at the moment."

"Mr. Broome, sir," said Briggs, who always made a point of remembering his employer's name.

"Yes, Freddie," Max agreed. "Freddie is my very good friend. He is also my cousin. He would have told me if there was a tenant coming. Ask him. He'll tell you."

"We did not expect Lady Waverly tonight, sir."

"That," said Max, poking him in the chest with a greasy red finger, "is quite your own fault."

Wrapping his cloak around him, he stumbled off in the direction of the sunken ballroom, which had been flooded for the occasion. Two mermaids waved to him from the water. Suddenly feeling quite energetic again, Max unclasped his cloak and plunged down the steps into the pool, roaring as the ice-cold water slapped against his skin.

The mermaids, one blue haired, the other green haired, swam away from him screaming, but it was all in fun, and he soon had them out of the water. Making his way up to the balcony with his catch, he flung them down on one of the sofas and buried himself between them. With screams of drunken delight, they pretended to resist as he struggled to get them out of their costumes.

"Have a care with our tails, sir! These costumes must go back to the theater in the morning, and there will be hell to pay if you tear them."

"Oh, you're *actresses,*" he said, enlightened. "Well, I don't need a *tear,* my sweet. All I need is a tiny little hole."

"Sir!" protested the green-haired naiad. "We're not prostitutes."

"But it's my birth-night," he pouted. "Can't you wriggle out of it?"

"Sorry, sir," the blue-haired one answered, laughing. "It takes a buttonhook and an awful lot of grease to get us out. And even then, you know, there's our reputations to consider."

"I won't tell a soul," he swore solemnly, freeing a breast from a corset decorated with shells.

He was thus agreeably engaged when a long shadow fell across him. "Mr. Purefoy, I presume?" enquired a fierce female voice.

Looking up, Max beheld a terrifying face with baleful green eyes gazing down at him with murderous contempt. He was deeply impressed with her costume; usually females were far too vain to make themselves ugly for a masquerade. They always did themselves up like angels and fairies and Cleopatras and shepherdesses and, well, mermaids. This female was truly repulsive.

"Medusa, is that you?" he asked, rising to his knees.

Patience gasped as his cloak fell open to reveal his near nakedness. "How dare you expose yourself to me!" she said furiously.

"I'm not ashamed of my body," he answered loftily. "I get plenty of exercise, as you can see. I must say, I like your snakes," he went on, struggling to a standing position and reaching for her hair.

Patience slapped his face, wishing she had the strength to punish him as he deserved.

"There's no need to shout," he said, shouting in her face. "Heavens! Is that your breath or mine? Who painted your face, love? 'Tis a bloody masterpiece."

"You're drunk," Patience said in disgust. "How dare you! Get away from me."

Max frowned at her. "Are you trying to spoil my party?"

"Yes!" she said angrily. "That's exactly what I'm trying to do."

"Well, I'm sorry, my dear, but I simply won't stand for it," he said. And, easily overcoming her struggles, he picked her up, lifted her over the balcony, and threw her into the pool below.

Chapter 2

Flailing wildly, Patience hit the icy water, her screams drowned as she went under. From the balcony, Max watched with drunken detachment as her heavy cloak and skirts dragged her down to the marble floor of the pool. A most unpleasant, sharp-tongued shrew, he decided.

"Will she drown, sir?" the green-haired naiad asked curiously, sidling up to him.

"Don't be silly," Max scoffed. "No one ever drowned in a ballroom. Of course she can sw—" He broke off as he realized with a hard, sickening jolt, that the sour-faced female had not resurfaced. Through the clear water, he could see her dark, unmoving form. Panicking, Max threw off his scarlet cape and flung himself over the balcony railing into the water.

The frigid water shocked him into clearheaded sobriety. His heart pounding, he swam to her and heaved her bodily to the surface. She was only a slight, bony thing, but her drenched cloak and skirts made her shockingly heavy. Gasping for air, Max dragged her halfway up the ballroom steps and out of the water. All around them, the inebriated gaiety of his birth-night celebration continued unabated, but Max now felt far, far removed from it all.

For one terrifying moment, he was certain that he had killed her. Then she suddenly came to life, croaking horribly. Spluttering, she spewed out a stream of water. As relieved as he had ever been in his life, Max hauled her up to her feet and threw her over his shoulder. She was as unresisting and limp as a rag doll as he carried her up the stairs. Pushing through the crowd on the balcony, he made his way to Briggs, who was wringing his hands at the entrance to the ballroom, dithering as though he dared not come any farther.

"Come with me," Max barked, carrying his dripping burden past him out into the relatively quiet hall.

Briggs hurried to keep up with him. "I'm sorry, Mr. Purefoy, sir! Her ladyship insisted on speaking to you."

"Never mind!" Max barked over his shoulder. He was heading for the stairs. "Lady Waverly is unwell. We must get her to a room—a quiet room. Where—?"

Quickly, Briggs jumped ahead of him, leading him through the hall, up the main staircase and into one of the bedchambers. "Where is her ladyship's maid?" Max asked, after depositing Patience onto the bed. "For that matter, where is her husband? If he is a man, he will challenge me to a duel, I shouldn't wonder!"

"Her ladyship has no husband," Briggs answered, busily lighting candles. "I suppose her maid is still waiting in the carriage outside," he added.

Max could hardly bear to look at the pale crumpled figure lying on the bed. "I'll fetch her maid," he said quickly. "In the meantime, find a maidservant to look after her—get her out of those wet clothes and dry her off and so forth. And send a boy to fetch the doctor—Wingfield, in Harley Street. Tell him Max Purefoy wants him. I—I must find some decent bloody clothes! And, for God's sake, build a fire!" he snapped as he strode from the room.

In another room, he toweled off, removing all of the

scarlet paint from his face and most of it from his body. A servant found him some clothes that fit him passably. By the time he had returned to something like his normal appearance, the house had been largely abandoned by his guests, though here and there a few stragglers lingered. Some, as was always the case at Max's entertainments, would have to be carried out.

Smoothing back his hair, Max went outside to the yellow hackney chaise that still waited at the curb. The driver was assisting one of the house servants with his fare's trunks. Max went up to the door of the vehicle, but discovered it to be locked. Knocking, he said, "Open the door, girl! Your mistress wants you."

A white, frightened face appeared at the window.

After the departure of her sister, Pru had sat in the carriage, torn between a genuine desire to stay in the comfort and safety of the carriage while Patience dealt with the problem, and an equally genuine desire to defy her sister and go up to the house. Her mind had been made up for her when the doors of the house were suddenly flung open and what seemed like hundreds of bizarre-looking characters came running out. The hackney carriage was an attractive object to them. They clustered around it, hammering on the doors, shouting drunkenly and pressing their sweaty faces against the glass to leer at Pru.

The driver, fortunately, had the presence of mind to lock the doors, thus protecting his passenger. Taking out his club, he began beating them back. Terrified the mob would break the glass, Pru flung herself down on the seat with her arms over her face. After what seemed like an eternity, they appeared to give up, and drifted off into the night.

"Unlock the door," Max repeated, giving her a smile of encouragement. She was a very pretty girl, he had noticed, with big green eyes, fine skin, and black curls.

Pru stared at him through the glass. He seemed normal

enough, if a trifle disheveled. His skin was very brown, in sharp contrast to his eyes, which were a pale gray. His hair was very black and unruly. He wasn't handsome, she decided. His mouth was too wide and his nose was too big. But he was tall and well-built with broad shoulders and long legs. He had an attractive smile. Hesitantly, she unlocked the door. He had it open immediately.

"Wh-who are you?" she asked, staring at him.

"I'm Purefoy," he told her simply. Taking her around the waist, he set her on the ground.

His manner was so forthright that she instinctively trusted him. "Were you caught in the riot, sir?" she asked.

He glanced down at her. She wasn't just pretty, he realized. She was truly a beauty. A trifle small, perhaps, but well-formed. And those eyes! A man could lose himself in their brilliant green depths. "Riot?" he said, amused. "I suppose it *did* look like a riot, everyone running away at once. People are such cowards," he added, but without rancor. "At the first sign of trouble, off they go."

"What did the mob want?"

"What mobs always want," he said, drawing her smoothly up the steps to the house. "Something for nothing! Anyway, they are gone now. We need not concern ourselves with them. I'm sorry if they frightened you, Miss . . . ?"

"Waverly," she said promptly. "Miss Prudence Waverly."

"Good God!" Max uttered. "I thought you were Lady Waverly's maid! You are her relation?"

"Well, of all the nerve!" cried Pru, stamping her foot. "Did Patience tell you I was her *maid*? Oh! She may be my guardian for the moment, but I'm not her servant! I'm her *sister*!"

Max bit his lip. At that moment he would have preferred dealing with an irate husband or an angry tiger, for that matter. Anything but the tears of a distraught sister would have been less of a blow to his conscience. "I'm very sorry, Miss Waverly," he said contritely. "I don't want you to worry, but it seems that your sister has—has been—has been taken ill. Well, not ill exactly. It is all my fault!"

To his surprise, she laid a comforting hand on his arm. "Oh, no, sir!" she said softly. "You mustn't blame yourself. My sister has been ill for two months. She was horribly seasick the whole time we were on the ship, and she's still very weak."

"You've just arrived from—from America?" he guessed, correctly identifying her clipped, mid-Atlantic accent.

Pru nodded. "Well, Philadelphia, Pennsylvania, anyway," she said. "Look, Mr. Purefoy, I don't see how you are to blame. I'm very grateful to you for your assistance, I'm sure."

"Assistance," he muttered under his breath, hating himself. "I've sent for the doctor, of course. Dr. Wingfield is the best physician in London. He has attended my family for years."

"That's very kind of you, sir," Pru said appreciatively.

"No, it isn't. I'm not kind. I'm the most selfish, thoughtless ass!"

"Well, *I* think you're rather wonderful," said Pru, smiling up at him.

Suddenly, he felt no need to confess to this lovely girl the full extent of his guilt. Let her hate me tomorrow, he decided. "Come," he said. "I'll take you to your sister."

By this time, Briggs had found a female servant to look after Patience. A nightgown had been found for her, and her wet clothes had been taken away. Warm and dry, Patience lay still in the bed, her breath shallow. Pru kissed her on the forehead and stroked her hair.

"How peaceful she looks! All she really needs now, sir, is rest, I'm sure," Pru said confidently. "She hasn't been eating very well or sleeping, you see. The sea voyage was very hard on her."

"I hope you're right, Miss Waverly," he said uneasily. "I hope it is nothing that won't soon mend." Leaving the sisters alone, he went downstairs to meet the doctor.

James Wingfield had known Max since the latter was a small boy. "What the devil have you done now?" the physician greeted him, not mincing words.

Max quickly gave him the facts. "It was a harmless prank," he added defensively. "How was I to know she couldn't swim?"

"You might have enquired, sir, before you drowned her!" Wingfield snapped. "These damned parties of yours! Someone's going to get killed one of these days."

"I've learned my lesson," Max said contritely. "No more wild parties. My friends will be disappointed, of course, but my mind is quite made up. Look here, Wingfield!" he went on as the doctor started up the stairs to his patient. "Lady Waverly's sister is with her now. She's a mere child. It would only upset her if she knew—knew what I have done. Surely, there's no cause for that?"

"You should have been beaten regularly," Wingfield said grimly. "Your uncle indulges you too much. And so do I," he added roughly. "No, I won't tell the child you tried to drown her sister."

While the physician examined his patient, Max sat with Pru in the hall outside the room. "He's just going to tell us she needs her rest," Pru said. Rather sleepy herself, she suppressed a yawn.

Dr. Wingfield, however, came out of the patient's room looking very grave. "I'm afraid your sister is suffering from severe anemia, Miss Waverly," he told her. "It is very serious."

"You mean she doesn't remember anything?" Pru said, puzzled.

Wingfield had no patience for ignorance, and he spoke rather brusquely. "Anemia, Miss Waverly, not amnesia."

"Can't she have both?" Max murmured.

"Let us hope not, Max," Wingfield said coldly. "Her ladyship is suffering from a deficiency of iron in her blood. She's also severely undernourished. Has she lost a great deal of weight recently?"

"Well, yes, of course she has," said Pru. "She used to be quite healthy."

"The Waverlys have just come over from America," Max explained. "Lady Waverly suffered greatly from mal de mer."

"Mal de mer?" Pru repeated, pronouncing it "moldy mare." "The ship's doctor said it was only seasickness!"

"A long voyage without proper nourishment can lead to all sorts of difficulties," the doctor said. "Your sister is very weak, child. When is the last time she ate any solid food?"

"This morning," said Pru. "She ate a very good breakfast. But then she was carriage-sick," she added, grimacing. "We kept having to stop on the way for her to be sick on the side of the road. It was very unpleasant. But Patience was bound and determined to reach London today. She kept saying she was all right. I—I didn't know she had moldy mare!"

"Miss Waverly, have you anyone else to look after you?" Max said. "Besides your elder sister, I mean?"

"No," Pru replied. "Our parents are dead. We've been on our own since we lost our grandfather. We have a trustee in America, and that is quite enough for us, let me tell you."

Dr. Wingfield frowned. "What about your sister's husband? Lord Waverly, is it? Where is he?"

Pru stared at him. "Oh, no!" she said. "Lord Waverly was our *uncle,* sir. Patience inherited the title from him."

"Oh, yes, of course," said Dr. Wingfield. "I read about it in the papers. A suo jure baroness—and an American, besides. I thought the name was familiar."

"I see," said Max, who rarely bothered with newspapers. "Well, Miss Prudence, we must find someone to stay with you until your sister is better."

"Will you stay with me?" she asked him, with sweet, trusting simplicity.

Although he was a man of notorious personal habits, Max was deeply shocked by her suggestion. At the same time he was touched by the girl's naiveté, which he judged to be quite genuine. "That will not be possible, Miss Prudence," he said gently. "You must have a respectable *lady* to look after you. I would not make you a creditable chaperone."

"Oh," said Pru, crestfallen.

Dr. Wingfield cleared his throat. "As for the patient— if anyone is interested in her, that is—she's going to need constant nursing for the next few weeks if she is to make a full recovery."

"Weeks!" cried Pru. "Is it as bad as that? She can't still be seasick! Not on land."

"It will take time for her to regain her strength," said the doctor. "She must have a nurse."

"I can't!" cried Pru, clinging to Max. "I can't do it! I stayed with her the entire time we were on the ship! I never left her side! But I can't do it anymore! I'm simply exhausted! I hate the sickroom! The smell!" She lifted her face to look at the doctor. Tears stood in her green eyes. "You must think I'm horrible. But I just can't do it anymore!"

Max's heart went out to her. "No one thinks you're horrible," he said, patting her shoulder. Searching his pockets, he was mortified to discover that he had no handkerchief to lend her. "Of course you can't do it. You can barely keep your eyes open. Dr. Wingfield is not suggesting that you become your sister's nurse."

"Indeed I am not," Dr. Wingfield promptly agreed. "Despite what you may think, young lady, I have no desire to have *two* patients in Clarges Street, which is what I will have if you ruin your health while looking after your sister's. I was thinking of a professional nurse, someone who is used to dealing with sick people."

"I know just the person," said Max, brushing away Pru's tears with his hand. "My old nurse, Mrs. Drabble. She's very capable, Miss Prudence. There is no one I trust more."

"You needed a nurse, Mr. Purefoy?" Pru asked him shyly.

He smiled at her. "Long ago, when I was a child. She lives here in London now, an independent lady, but I believe if I ask her, she will come."

"Would you, sir?" Pru said gratefully. "We don't know anyone in London, except the attorney. Patience would know what to do, of course, but she—!" She broke off, her lip trembling. "I—I shall have to depend on *you*, sir," she managed, after a slight pause. "I *do* depend on you."

Max exchanged an uneasy glance with Dr. Wingfield. The girl was terrifyingly naive.

"I will go and fetch Drabble now," Max said quietly.

Pru squared her shoulders bravely. "I will sit with Patience until you return, sir."

"No," Dr. Wingfield said firmly. "*I* will sit with her. You will go to bed, Miss Waverly."

Pru made no protest, but meekly followed the maidservant to the room that had been made up for her.

* * *

Mrs. Drabble, roused from her comfortable bed in Wimpole Street, received him in her parlor with a heavy shawl thrown over her nightgown. Years before, as a young widow, she had been his wet nurse. Now well into her middle years, she still regarded Max as an incorrigible child. Years of intimacy had erased much of the class barrier between them, and she never hesitated to speak her mind to him. "I ought to box your ears," she said angrily, when he had made his full confession to her.

"I ought to let you," Max said ruefully. "I am stung all over with remorse. I vow I will never do anything so foolish ever again in my life. Why, I might have killed the woman. Please, Drabble, for old times' sake, for my sake, will you go to Clarges Street? I know you're comfortably retired, but I need you. I know she'll be in good hands with you. There's no one I trust more!"

"Wait downstairs, you scoundrel!" she said grumpily. "I'll get dressed."

When Pru woke up the next morning, the house was filled with hothouse flowers. Eagerly, she snatched the card.

Most abjectly, it said, in heavy black scrawl, *I am sorry for the events of last night. No lady should ever be exposed to such rude behavior. When I think that you may have come to grievous harm, I am deeply ashamed. Drunkenness, of course, is no proper excuse for offering violence and insult to a lady of quality. I beg you will accept my profoundest apologies. Please believe that I am, now and forever, your most obedient servant to command.*

It was signed, simply "Purefoy."

Pru, dazzled by the elegance of the gentleman's language, and delighted with the gallantry of his thoughts, tucked the card into her jewel case.

Later, that afternoon, Max called at Clarges Street. He had taken great pains with his appearance, or, at least, his valet had, and he was looking every inch the prosperous gentleman as he rang the bell. He did not come alone.

Of uncertain age, Lady Jemima Crump had nothing but her title and her charms to recommend her, but, then, there was nothing more she needed to fulfill the role of chaperone to Miss Waverly. Taffy haired, dirt poor, and rather too fond of wine, Lady Jemima nonetheless enjoyed an excellent reputation. Launching young ladies into society was her main source of income, occasionally augmented, but more usually diminished, by her passion for cards. When Mr. Purefoy came to her door, she was already committed for the forthcoming Season to three sisters from Brighton, but one does not say no to a Purefoy.

Briggs led Pru's callers up to the drawing room, where all traces of the previous night had been meticulously removed. Instead of opium pipes, the room was filled with lilies. Pru appeared in a few moments, looking quite fresh and rested in a gown of pale pink muslin. The gown, while quite avant-garde by Philadelphia's standards, was quite passé for London. Lady Jemima, who was not familiar with Philadelphia fashion criteria, regarded it as an utter waste of muslin, but Max thought it became her very well.

"Mr. Purefoy!" she said, greeting him with outstretched hands. "How nice to see you again. Thank you for the flowers, and your beautiful note!"

Max found her warmth and exuberance endearing, while Lady Jemima observed it rather doubtfully. The girl was very pretty, of course, but, as Lady Jemima knew very well, beauty was no guarantee for a successful Season, unless it was accompanied by a large fortune, good breeding, and excellent manners—fortune—of course, being the most important quality of all.

Max bowed over Pru's hand, and quickly asked after her sister's health.

"Thank you, sir. I believe she is a little better," Pru answered, looking at Lady Jemima with great curiosity. Violently clashing colors were in fashion at the moment, and, with her bright, pinkish orange hair combined with a violet and yellow ensemble, Lady Jemima fully represented the idea.

Max hastened to make the introductions, and Pru offered the Englishwoman her hand. Lady Jemima's smile froze in place. "If I might just give Miss Waverly a hint," she said gently. "It is not correct for one to shake hands upon an introduction. One shakes hands only with one's most intimate acquaintances, and then, only with discretion. I remember when my dear brother returned from India after an absence of some twenty years, he and I very cordially shook hands."

"That's terrible!" said Pru. "Poor thing! I bet he turned around and went straight back to India!"

Max stifled a chuckle. "I have brought this lady to live with you, Miss Prudence. Lady Jemima has all the necessary credentials to present a young lady at the Court of St. James."

Pru's eyes widened. "The Court of St. James!" she gasped. "You mean the queen and all that? The princes and the princesses?"

"Of course," he said, amused by her excitement. For him, an evening at court was a long, giant yawn, to be avoided at all costs. "No young lady can enter society until she has been presented at court. Once she has her majesty's seal of approval she is free to go out into society and find a husband. In your case, of course, the husband will find *you*."

Pru laughed. "Do you think so?"

"Of course," he said warmly.

"Let us not get ahead of ourselves, Mr. Purefoy," Lady Jemima pleaded. "First, Miss Prudence, we must get you ready for your presentation."

"I'm ready now," said Pru, tossing her black curls over one shoulder and twirling one long lock around her finger.

"You most certainly are not," Max said bluntly. "Unless, of course, it is your wish to be laughed at by everyone in the throne room!"

Pru's cocky smile vanished instantly. "W-what?" she stammered.

"I'm sure no one will laugh at Miss Prudence," Lady Jemima said quickly.

"I'm afraid we English are quite stubbornly scrupulous when it comes to etiquette," Max said firmly. "Especially where the royal family are concerned. Listen to Lady Jemima and do as she tells you, and I'm sure you'll do fine. Ignore her teachings at your peril!" he added, only half jokingly.

"I promise," Pru said humbly. "I suppose I have a lot to learn."

"The first drawing room is not until January," Max went on. "Your sister, as a peeress in her own right, probably shall be invited to that one."

"I would say so," Lady Jemima agreed. "A baroness in her own right! And an American! There will be a good deal of interest in her debut—especially if she is as lovely as her younger sister."

Pru frowned. "What about me?"

"Perhaps the fourth drawing room," said Lady Jemima.

Max frowned. "We must do better than that, Lady Jemima. Why, she'll miss half the Season!"

"Of course, with *influence,* anything is possible," Lady Jemima said innocently.

Max understood her meaning perfectly. "Don't worry,

Miss Prudence," he said. "One way or another, we'll wrangle you an invitation to the first drawing room."

Pru wriggled happily. "Thank you, Mr. Purefoy!"

Quite charmed by her unfeigned gratitude and delight, Max stayed much longer than he had intended, promising Pru invitations to any ball or entertainment she wanted once the Season began. He promised her vouchers to Almack's and a box at the theater, and she, in turn, promised to dance with him at every assembly. Lady Jemima began to wonder if Mr. Purefoy had taken more than a passing fancy to the American.

When at last he rose to take his leave, Pru pouted. "Must you go so soon?"

Max smiled at her. "I will come again tomorrow," he promised, "and, if your chaperone approves, I will take you for a drive in the park. The fresh air and sunshine will do you good. You must not stay shut in all day, Miss Prudence, just because your sister is unwell."

Lady Jemima, her thoughts fixed on marriage, even if the gentleman's were not, did not hesitate to give her approval for the scheme.

"Mr. Purefoy would never distinguish a young lady with his attentions if he were not thinking of marriage. You have made a conquest of him, my dear," she said excitedly to Pru, when Max had gone.

"So it would seem," Pru said languidly, going over to the mirror to preen. "Men are always falling in love with me. It's very tiresome. I sort of collect them, you see. They are like moths to the flame."

To Lady Jemima, it was an odious, conceited reply, but, as her livelihood depended on pleasing her charges, she protested only mildly. "Surely you would not compare Mr. Purefoy to a moth! He is one of the most eligible gentlemen in England."

"Is he?" Pru said idly. "If he's so eligible, why doesn't he have a title? Even you have a title."

Lady Jemima was so shocked by this piece of ignorance that she completely overlooked the insult to herself. "My dear child," she whispered in a tone of awe, "do you not know that Mr. Purefoy is *nephew and heir* to the *Duke of Sunderland*? The lady he marries will be a duchess one day!"

Pru pricked up her ears. "Duchess? Is that as good as a baroness?"

"As good as a—!" Lady Jemima was now flabbergasted. "I can see we shall have to study the Order of Precedence, Miss Prudence! I had not thought you Americans as backward as this! The Duke of Sunderland is the *first* duke in the Order of Precedence, saving only the Princes of the Blood, of course."

"Never mind that," Pru said impatiently. "Is a duchess better than a baroness?"

"Yes, of course."

Pru smiled. "I'd like that," she said simply.

That evening, as Pru was reading the Order of Precedence aloud to Lady Jemima, Mrs. Drabble came into the room. Patience was awake and asking to see her sister.

"You must not stay long, however," Mrs. Drabble warned, as she left the sisters together. "I shall be back in ten minutes."

Pru knelt beside the bed and took Patience's hand. As much as she sometimes chafed under Patience's sisterly guidance, it was frightening to see her brought so low by illness. "How are you feeling, Pay?" she whispered.

Patience's eyes fluttered. "Thank heaven you are safe," she breathed. "I was so worried. I told the nurse I wouldn't drink my barley water until I saw you with my own eyes. I kept imagining you in the carriage all by yourself. I should never have left you alone."

Pru was instantly nettled. "For heaven's sake! I'm not completely helpless without you, you know. Did you really think I'd still be sitting in the carriage waiting for you to come and get me?"

Patience smiled faintly. "I just wanted to see for myself that you're all right."

"You're the one who's sick, not me."

"Sick?" Patience's voice rose an octave or two. "I'm not sick! I nearly drowned."

"Drowned? Pay, what are you talking about?"

Now quite agitated, Patience tried to sit up. "The devil was here—a big red devil. He threw me over the balcony. He tried to drown me. I could have died."

"That's quite a nightmare you had!" Pru said sympathetically.

"It was not a nightmare," Patience insisted. "The devil tried to drown me, I tell you! He was here in this house."

"I think you might be delirious, Pay," Pru said, patting her hand.

Patience threw off the coverlet and started to climb out of bed. "I know what happened, Pru. I'll prove it to you. Help me!"

"You should not leave your bed," Pru replied, "but, if you promise to remain calm, I will take you over the house myself and prove to you that it was only a dream."

"I shall be very calm," Patience promised, and Pru helped her down the stairs to the ballroom. Tiled in white marble, it was surrounded on three sides by a wide balcony, from which spectators could watch the dancers below. Patience tottered down the steps of the grand staircase, utterly confused.

"This was all flooded," she whispered. "There were mermaids in the water."

"Mermaids?" Pru echoed in disbelief. "Patience, you sound like a madwoman! Let me get you back to bed."

"No!" said Patience, clinging to the marble banister. "I was here last night. I walked up to the devil. He was with two mermaids on a couch, right over there. He exposed himself to me. Then he picked me up and threw me over the railing."

Pru stared at the marble floor of the ballroom. "Dearest," she said gently, "you're not making any sense. If the devil threw you over that balcony, you would be dead. You would have broken your neck. You must have been dreaming."

"Good heavens!" Mrs. Drabble called from behind them. She was running as fast as she could on her short legs, her plain, kindly face red from exertion. "You should not be out of bed, Lady Waverly!" Bustling up to her patient, she firmly led her from the room.

"I wasn't dreaming," Patience insisted. "It really happened."

"Of course it did, my dear," Mrs. Drabble said soothingly as she helped Patience up the stairs. "And Mr. Purefoy, is very sorry for it, too. I wanted to box his ears when I heard what he had done. But he gave me that little boy look, and my heart melted as it always does." She clucked her tongue.

"Purefoy! That's the devil's name," said Patience, growing agitated again. "I couldn't remember it before. I knew it was peculiar. He was the devil! And those were *his* mermaids!"

"Please don't distress yourself, Lady Waverly," Mrs. Drabble crooned.

"I don't know how he did it, but he flooded the ballroom. He did!"

"Of course he did," Pru said, adopting the nurse's soothing tone. "But he's gone now, Pay. Please don't get upset again! You must rest and get better. Isn't that right, Mrs. Drabble?"

Together, they ushered Patience back to bed. She was asleep before her head hit the pillow.

Pru went back to the drawing room wringing her hands.

"What is the matter, dear?" Lady Jemima cried.

"Patience has gone mad!" said Pru. "She thinks Mr. Purefoy is the devil, and that he tried to drown her in the ballroom! She is out of her head."

"Oh, dear," Lady Jemima murmured. "How distressing for you!"

"It is," said Pru, glad that someone, at least, cared about her feelings. "It's very distressing for me. She became so agitated! A vein was pulsing in her neck. And I could not even defend poor Mr. Purefoy from her outrageous assertions! Mrs. Drabble seems to think we must humor the patient. And, I suppose, we must," she added. "At least until she is stronger. Perhaps it would be better if I didn't see Mr. Purefoy again."

Lady Jemima gasped. "What, child? And ruin your chance of becoming a duchess? Go for your drive tomorrow. Make of it what you can. Your sister need not know."

"If she sends for me, and I am not here—" Pru began.

"I will make her some excuse," Lady Jemima promised. "I am on your side, Miss Prudence. I want you to succeed. I will do anything I can to help you."

Pru smiled. "I'm glad you're here, Lady Jemima! I'm glad there's someone here who cares about *me* and what *I* want. Patience loves me, of course, but she doesn't understand that I'm not like her. I don't want to be independent. I want to be taken care of."

Impulsively, she hugged the Englishwoman. Lady Jemima felt an odd warmth in her chest. She opened her mouth to explain to the American girl that English people did not hug, but somehow the words did not come. It felt rather wonderful to be hugged.

Perhaps we *should* hug, she thought, trying to imagine hugging her stern father, or perhaps her cold mother. The warm feeling in her chest vanished.

Perhaps not, she decided.

Chapter 3

For the next three weeks, while Patience slowly regained her strength, Max devoted himself to Pru's amusement. He liked Pru. He enjoyed her company. She wasn't like English girls, who so carefully preserved an air of cool detachment, even boredom. Nothing ever bored Pru. With shining eyes and parted lips, she threw herself wholeheartedly into every new experience. As Max showed her the sights of London, he was charmed to see the city through her eyes.

Every day brought something new and wonderful to Pru. Max could not have bestowed his generosity on a more grateful recipient, and her obvious delight spurred him to greater and greater generosity.

Besides long drives in London's many beautiful parks, there were shopping excursions to Bond Street, and trips to Gunter's for pastry and flavored ice. He took her to the museums, to Astley's Amphitheatre, and together they rode Mr. Trevithick's engine in Euston Square. On one memorable, rainy day, he treated her to a tour of Sunderland House, his uncle's vast London mansion. The servants were quite surprised; Max had never brought a young lady to his uncle's house before.

There were no evening entertainments, however; these would have to wait, he explained, until after her presentation. Then there would be balls at Almack's, concerts at Covent Garden, countless plays and private assemblies, weekends in the country, midnight suppers, and Venetian breakfasts.

"But, Max, who will invite me anywhere?" Pru fretted, as these delights were dangled before her on one of their morning drives through Hyde Park. "I don't know anyone in London!"

His answer was as simple as it was arrogant. "You know me."

Without prompting of any kind, he pledged to give her every assistance in society. He would introduce both Pru and her sister to all the most important people in London, thus ensuring that the Waverly sisters would be deluged with invitations. He even promised to give a ball at Sunderland House, specifically to launch Pru and her sister into society; *that,* in and of itself, surely would be enough to make any young lady's Season a runaway success. By doing so, he hoped to ease the guilt he felt for nearly drowning Lady Waverly, though he certainly did not reveal to Pru the true motivation for his extraordinary generosity.

November gave way to December, and Max, engaged to spend Christmas at Breckinridge, the Duke of Sunderland's country estate, was obliged to leave London. He would stay if he could, as he explained to Pru, but, while he could very easily dispense with anyone else's claim on his time, he had a firm duty to his uncle. He would have invited the Waverlys to Breckinridge (he said), had Lady Waverly not been in such poor health. Giving Pru a pretty gold case for her visiting cards as an early Christmas present, he took his leave and drove off in his curricle, with no plans to return to London until after the first of the new year. Immensely pleased with his own kindness to the little

American, Max arrived at Breckinridge with a conscience almost totally clear.

Pru did not miss Max very much at first. The preparations for her presentation at court and the social Season that was to follow so occupied her in the days after his departure that she hardly had time to think of anything else. Besides numerous dress fittings, there were dance lessons—which Pru adored—and French lessons, lessons in deportment, lessons in penmanship and etiquette—all of which she despised. Very soon, the routine of lessons, lessons, lessons began to wear on her, and, as the weeks passed and no other young man with plenty of money and a fast curricle came to take Max's place, she began to miss her old playmate very much indeed. She even thought it possible, as she turned over the little gold card case in her hands, that she had fallen in love with him, even though he was not as handsome as she would have liked him to be.

In love or not, the idea of being in love was sufficient to relieve an afternoon of boredom. Hurrying to the desk in the drawing room, she sat down to write Mr. Purefoy a letter of blazing passion. She had just snipped off a lock of her glossy black hair with her penknife when the door opened, and Patience trudged into the room on weak legs. Mrs. Drabble followed her as though fearful that her charge might collapse at any moment.

Patience had only recently felt well enough to leave her room. For weeks her only exercise had been walking the floor of her room, from her bed to the fireplace, from the fireplace to the window, and back again in a dreary circuit. In the evenings, she would sit up in bed while Pru read to her. The drawing room, with its big windows overlooking Clarges Street, was a refreshing change of scene for her. For a moment, she stood blinking in the strong sunlight streaming through the windows.

Hastily, Pru tucked the lock of hair into the envelope

and sealed it. "I was just coming to sit with you," she lied, jumping to her feet as Patience crept over to the sofa and sat down. Though she was still pale and thin, and obviously weak, her head was clear and her green eyes were bright. Mrs. Drabble wrapped the shawl she carried around Patience's shoulders, then began stirring up the fire with the poker.

"I think it's time I wrote another letter to Mr. Broome," Patience said, her voice clear and strong. "He has not replied to my first."

"Mr. Broome?" Pru repeated innocently, hiding her own letter behind her back. "Oh, the landlord. Has he not answered your letter?"

Patience's eyes narrowed with suspicion. For weeks, she had been prone to a fatigue and foggy-headedness that were quite unlike her. She had been obliged to dictate her letters to Pru. "You know he hasn't," she said. "Pru! You did send the letter, did you not?"

"Of course I did," Pru assured her. "Though I do not see how the riot could have been Mr. Broome's fault."

Patience rubbed her temples. "For the last time," she said petulantly, "it was no riot! It was a bacchanal—in our house! Whether Mr. Broome permitted Mr. Purefoy to use this house for his disgusting orgy or not, I do not know. Either way, I must protest. Respectable people should not be subjected to such lurid sights. And I certainly won't be held accountable for any damages caused by that man and his nasty friends!"

Pru flinched to hear her sister hurl insults at her friend, but did not quite know how to defend him without exposing her secret. For Patience knew nothing at all about Mr. Purefoy's attentions to Pru, and Pru was glad to keep her in ignorance. It was not lying, exactly. Indeed, it was for Patience's own good that she remain in ignorance, for had not the doctor said that nothing should be done to upset or

excite the patient? Luckily, she had been confined to her
bed for the most part while Max remained in town, or she
would have been very upset indeed. She would have made
a horrible stink, in fact. As it was, Patience knew nothing
of the outside world but what she was told. In the house,
Mr. Purefoy's name was never mentioned, and, even if she
had glanced at the society columns in the newspapers Pru
sometimes brought her, the doings of Mr. P—— and Miss
W—— would not have interested her in the least.

"You must be careful, Pay," she warned. "Mr. Purefoy
comes from a very powerful family. We can't afford to
offend him if we are to get on in society."

"I am not afraid of this man," Patience declared. "I'm
not going to kowtow to a villain just because his uncle is
some big lord. We fought a war so we wouldn't have to,
remember? We are not servants. We are free people. And
if the man doesn't like criticism, then he should behave
himself!"

"His uncle is a duke, not a lord," Pru corrected her.

The tinge of awe in her tone only served to irritate
Patience further. "His uncle may be a *king,* for all I care!
In any case, *he's* nothing but a knave. I *will* write my com-
plaint to the landlord," she went on stubbornly, pulling herself up from the sofa, "if you are quite finished at the
desk?"

"Oh, yes," Pru said quickly, yielding her place. "I was
only scribbling."

"Scribbling? Scribbling what?"

Pru shrugged innocently. "Must you interrogate me?
I'm just practicing my handwriting. Lady Jemima says I
shall be quite busy writing thank-you notes and that sort of
thing once the Season begins. A lady's handwriting must
be perfect."

Patience settled into the chair. "Lady Jemima," she repeated. "Oh, yes! The chaperone. We must talk about that.

Now that I am feeling better, we really should give her notice."

"What?" cried Pru. "But, Patience, we *must* have a chaperone. If you dismiss Lady Jemima, who will sponsor us at court? We have to be presented. We can't just show up. The guards would never let us in."

Patience chuckled. "Would that be such a terrible thing?"

"Yes! It would!" Pru said angrily. "*I* want to go to balls and parties, even if you don't, Patience Waverly! And we won't be invited anywhere unless we have been presented at court."

Patience rolled her eyes, but said, almost tolerantly, "If it means so much to you, I will write to the American embassy. I'm sure Mr. and Mrs. Adams would be glad to present us to the English court."

Pru's eyes widened in horror. The very last thing she wanted was to be presented at court alongside a host of American bumpkins dressed, no doubt, in their hideous homespun fashions. "But we can't send Lady Jemima away," she quickly protested. "She gave up her place with another family to come to us. We are very lucky to have her. Her father was the Earl of Shrewsbury. What is *Mrs. Adams* compared to that?"

Patience's eyes flashed. "What, indeed? Her father-in-law was our second president, may I remind you. I happen to think that is far grander than a mere earl."

"Not at the Court of St. James, it isn't," Pru argued sullenly.

Patience sniffed. "This tells me all I need to know about the Court of St. James!" she declared. "It is silly to *pay* Lady Jemima to present us at court when our ambassador will do it for free."

Pru frowned. "*Pay* Lady Jemima? What are you talking about?"

"Yes, child," Patience told her. "Her ladyship is charging us a hefty fee for her . . . ahem! . . . services. Not to mention the expense of feeding her. Didn't you know?"

Pru tossed her head. "I don't care! And don't call me child!" she added petulantly. "I am keeping Lady Jemima."

"If you do, you will bear the expense," Patience warned her.

"You mean to say I *shall* bear the expense, I suppose," Pru sniffed.

"Shall, will. What is the difference?" Patience said crossly.

"It's no use explaining it to you," Pru said loftily. "But I am keeping Lady Jemima. Some things are worth paying for, you know—even our old miser of a grandfather knew that. If Mr. Adams charges nothing for his assistance— well, then perhaps he knows best what his assistance is worth!"

"You may do as you like, of course. You always do! But so will I."

"So *shall* I."

"I shall and will go to the Court of St. James on the arm of my ambassador," Patience said coldly. "Or I shan't and won't go at all! I shall and will keep my money in my purse. You can pay for the honor of being presented by Lady Jemima all by yourself."

"I shall!" said Pru. Flouncing from the room, she banged the door shut.

Blowing out her breath, Patience snatched a fresh sheet of stationery from its pigeonhole and began to write an angry letter to Mr. Broome.

The following morning, Patience at last met Lady Jemima. With Mrs. Drabble hovering over her, she managed to walk down the stairs to the breakfast room. In this cheerful, sunlit, yellow room, Pru and Lady Jemima were gorging themselves on scones lathered in Devonshire clotted cream and topped with damson plum jam.

"Good morning," she said clearly, as they looked at her in surprise.

"Patience!" Pru exclaimed. "Do come and have some of these scones. They are delicious."

"Dear Lady Waverly! We meet at last," Lady Jemima murmured as Mrs. Drabble helped Patience to a chair.

Patience eyed the middle-aged lady a little doubt-fully. Pru's chaperone looked an odd, almost freakish creature with her bright pink orange hair. Her morning gown of rust-colored silk trimmed with black and green ribbons was far and away the ugliest garment Patience had ever seen.

"Lady Jemima, I presume?" she said, drawing her napkin across her lap while Mrs. Drabble filled her a plate at the sideboard. "My sister tells me you are a necessary evil, though, I must say, I don't think you are either."

Lady Jemima hardly knew what to say to this, but, suddenly, she did not feel that her position in the household was as secure as she had believed.

"I never said any such thing," Pru said crossly.

"I couldn't possibly eat all this," Patience said faintly, eyeing with dismay the mounds of sausages and bacon and eggs Mrs. Drabble had brought to her.

"My lady, you'll never get your strength back if you don't eat," Mrs. Drabble told her firmly.

"You must have something, too, Mrs. Drabble," said Patience, pushing her eggs with her fork. "You haven't had your breakfast yet, have you? Why don't you join us?"

Mrs. Drabble blushed with embarrassment, Lady Jemima bristled with indignation, and Pru explained in a very loud whisper, "Mrs. Drabble takes her meals in the kitchen with the other servants, Patience."

"Mrs. Drabble is hardly a servant," Patience said indig-nantly. "She is a very skilled professional nurse, and, I hope, my friend. I know I'm very grateful to her for all she has done for me. Please, Mrs. Drabble, I would be honored if you would take your meals with us."

"Your Ladyship is very kind," Mrs. Drabble murmured, curtsying. "But I—I have already had my breakfast. Please excuse me."

"Yes, do go on," Lady Jemima said airily. "We will look after Lady Waverly."

"You see," Pru said airily, when the nurse had left the room, "Mrs. Drabble knows her place. You only make them uncomfortable when you encourage them to get above themselves."

"It was your cold looks that made her uncomfortable," Patience said angrily. "It's not for you to say who I can and can't have at my table."

Pru shrugged. "Well, now that you are better, I'm sure you will be giving Mrs. Drabble her notice anyway. What you need now, instead of a nurse, is a lady's maid. You should hire one at once. Mine is French. She is called Yvette."

"A lady's maid? We never had a lady's maid in Philadelphia," Patience objected. "We always looked after ourselves. I can brush my own hair and darn my own stockings, thank you."

"That was all right for Philadelphia," Pru told her. "But it won't do in London, I'm afraid. I don't think you realize, Pay, that, once the Season begins, we'll be far too busy to do any mending. And we'll be changing our clothes five and six times a day. You wouldn't be able to keep up. As for your hair—you really ought to have yours cut and styled like mine. Well, perhaps not exactly like mine," she added. "I have a book of heads. I will let you borrow it."

"Don't you mean you *shall* let me borrow it?" Patience said waspishly.

Pru made a face at her.

"Anyway, I don't need a maid. I shall never be too busy

to do my own mending. And I shan't be changing my clothes five times a day. That's just silly."

"Of course, you will have to change your clothes!" Pru protested. "You must have morning gowns, carriage gowns, walking habits, riding habits— Well, I don't suppose *we* need riding habits, since we don't actually ride, though Lady Jemima says we ought to learn. But in any case, we shall need afternoon dresses, tea gowns, dinner gowns, evening gowns, ball gowns, and, of course, court dresses."

"I have my everyday dresses and my Sunday best," Patience stubbornly replied. "That has always been sufficient. I don't aspire to be a fashion plate."

"No! You aspire to humiliate me—and yourself, if you only knew it!" Pru shot back. "You must have new clothes, Patience, and a lady's maid to keep you in fashion. People will think you are a backward American bumpkin if you do not dress properly. I can arrange for you to have an appointment with my modiste—Madame Devy is the best in London. And I'm sure Lady Jemima would be glad to help you find a maid."

"Indeed, I would, Your Ladyship—" Lady Jemima began, eager to ingratiate herself with the baroness.

"That will not be necessary," Patience said shortly. "There must be a hundred servants in this house. Some one of them must be capable of ironing a dress and mending a hem. If I find I need a new dress or two, I will—I shall make them, as I have always done."

"This economical streak of yours is so unbecoming!" Pru complained. "You can't be seen in London wearing your home-sewn atrocities. You must remember that you are a baroness now, Pay. People will expect you to look the part."

Patience laughed. "And play the part, too, I suppose!"

"Well, yes," Pru said insistently.

"As if I were a character in a play?" Patience scoffed. "I am no such thing."

Pru looked at her slyly. "And if you are busy sewing for yourself, when will you have time for your charity work? Or do you mean to abandon the poor little orphans completely?"

Patience gasped indignantly. Mrs. Drabble was part of a charity organization that attempted to provide warm clothing for London's myriad orphans. In her free time, she was forever knitting hats, mittens, and scarves. Patience, who hated to be idle, had put herself to work as soon as she was able, producing many admirable woolen shawls. "Of course not," she said. "If it comes down to a choice, I am adequately clothed; they are not."

Pru let out a groan. "And while we are on the subject," she went on after a short pause, "we must have a carriage. We cannot do without one."

"No, indeed," Lady Jemima echoed, drawing a look from Patience that effectively silenced her.

"While we are on the subject!" Patience repeated. "I'm quite sure we weren't anywhere *near* that particular subject. A carriage! What's next? A yacht?"

"We were on the subject of things we must have," Pru said coldly. "We must have a carriage. Yachts, as nice as they are, can't really be considered essential—at least not in London."

"We don't need a carriage," said Patience. "I know one thing about London: it is full of hackney coaches. They'll take you anywhere you want to go, and, what's more, it's cheaper than keeping horses and grooms and drivers. Think of it this way: the less you spend on transportation, the more money you will have to spend on clothes."

"Yes, but, Patience, one cannot go to a ball in a hack! A yellow hack with a number plate on the door?" Pru howled. "I'd rather die! Why, the person who sits on the seat before you could be anybody! And one cannot go to the Court of St. James in a hack!"

"No, indeed!" Lady Jemima could not help exclaiming.

"We must have a carriage with our coat of arms on the door," Pru said confidently.

"We have a coat of arms?" said Patience, momentarily distracted.

"Of course we do; we are the nobility," Pru replied.

"What does it look like?" Patience asked.

"Oh, it's very grand," Pru assured her. "Three golden lion's paws on an azure field."

Patience made a face. "Rather gruesome, don't you think? Anyway, shouldn't a lion have four paws? What happened to the fourth?"

"Never mind!" Pru snapped. "The point is that we are aristocrats and aristocrats do not go around in hacks! We simply must have a carriage. Surely even you can see that. Everyone will be laughing at the stupid Americans in their hack! Is that what you want?"

"No," Patience said quickly. "You're right. We must have a carriage. I'll write to Mr. Gordon. He has the authority to release funds from the accrued interest of the trust."

"Yes, but he never does," Pru said darkly.

"He does when I ask him," Patience said simply.

Pru shook her head. "It will take too long—months!—to get anything out of Mr. Gordon. We must have a carriage as soon as possible. Certainly, we must have it when the Season begins."

"I'll ask Mr. Bracegirdle to inquire about hiring a carriage," Patience promised.

"A hired carriage!" cried Pru. "Why, that's hardly better than a hack! No, we must have our carriage built to order. I know just how I want it. I've already selected the upholstery for the cushions."

"Nonsense," Patience said flatly. "Buy a carriage?

Prudence, may I remind you that England is not our permanent home? Our first business here—our only real business here—is to settle our uncle's estate."

"But it wouldn't be all that expensive, really. The carriage maker's already given me a very good estimate. How much, do you suppose? You will never guess, so I'll tell you. Only two hundred dollars! Only two hundred for the sweetest town carriage you ever saw with all the amenities! London, you see, is not as expensive as Philadelphia," she went on quite smugly. "Though I very much doubt we could find anyone to make us such a carriage in Philadelphia. Wait until you see it!"

Patience set down her fork. "Two hundred dollars?"

Pru nodded eagerly. "You stare! But everything in London is too absurdly cheap! And of such quality! We'd be fools not to buy everything in sight!"

Patience's eyes widened in alarm. "Is that what you have been doing?" she said slowly. "Buying everything in sight?"

Pru laughed. "What do you suppose my ensemble cost?" she asked, pronouncing the French word just as it was spelled. Full of her own cleverness, she stood up and turned slowly in a circle so that Patience could take in the full glory of one of her newest gowns.

"Your ensign bull?" Patience repeated, frowning. "What do you mean?"

"My ensemble!" Pru explained, twirling. "It is French for—for—well, for clothes, I suppose, for lack of a better word. I told you I had been taking French lessons. You should have lessons as well," she went on, ceasing to twirl. "In English society it is de rigueur to speak French."

"De rigueur" was pronounced emphatically as "day rigger."

"In just a few weeks, I have learned ever so many useful phrases from Mamselle. Nest paw. Silver plate. Mares-ey.

Mares-ey bow coop. And . . . ensign bull. So? What do you think I paid for my ensemble?"

Patience did not think the morning gown of grass green and canary yellow stripes became Pru at all, but she reserved the full force of her loathing for the short, sky blue spencer worn over the striped gown. Cut much too small to meet over Pru's chest, it was by no means lacking in very large buttons, two on each side—but, of course, no buttonholes. It offended practical Patience in every possible way.

"Whatever you paid, it was too much!"

"That is what you think!" Pru exclaimed in triumph. "Only thirteen dollars for all of this! In Philadelphia, it would have cost me at least fifteen!"

Patience groaned. "Pounds, Prudence! Pounds, not dollars. Thirteen pounds for a perfectly stupid, tiny, little jacket."

"It is called a spencer," Pru informed her coldly.

"Why have buttons on a jacket that obviously can never be fastened? Why have buttons and no buttonholes? Why have a jacket at all, if the point is to leave your bosom exposed?"

"It is the fashion," Pru explained.

Patience frowned. "How many of these little ensign bulls have you bought?" she demanded.

"It was necessary!"

Patience closed her eyes. "How much have you spent?"

"I don't know exactly," Pru answered.

"Approximately then!"

"A lot," Pru admitted.

"I would say," ventured Lady Jemima, in an attempt to be helpful, "not more than a thousand pounds."

Patience paled to the roots of her hair. "A thousand pounds!" she gasped. "On clothes? Pru, you bought all new clothes before we left Philadelphia!"

"But they were the wrong clothes," Pru explained.

"Philadelphia is at least two years behind the rest of the world. And I needed a dress for court. That cost over two hundred all by itself."

"Almost enough for a carriage!" Patience said furiously. "Two hundred pounds for one dress? That's nearly eight hundred dollars!"

"Well, I can't very well go to St. James's Palace dressed in rags, can I?"

"No, indeed," Patience said angrily. "But you will be going in a hack! Oh, I beg your pardon! You *shall* be going in a hack!"

"I hate you!" cried Pru, bursting into violent tears.

"Perhaps it is not my place to say this, Lady Waverly," Lady Jemima began tentatively. When Patience did not immediately respond, she went on, "But a thousand pounds is not so very much to spend on a London Season. Miss Prudence will make a brilliant marriage, you'll see. And then, of course, the outlay will have been worth it all." She smiled benevolently.

Patience shot her a swift glance. "Marriage!" she exclaimed. "What on earth are you talking about? We haven't come here to find husbands."

Lady Jemima stared at her, quite shocked. "Lady Waverly! Don't you want to be married?"

"Certainly not, and neither does my sister. If she did, she could have had her pick in Philadelphia."

Pru scowled, her tears drying up as suddenly as they had appeared. "Oh, who could marry any of those yokels? I *do* want a husband, as it happens. I would very much like to get away from *you* and set up my own house!"

"You don't mean that," Patience said, wounded.

"Did you think I would be content to live with you forever?" said Pru.

"It had occurred to me," Patience answered, "that one

day you might fall in love and get married, but . . . Well,
you make it sound as though you want to escape from me!"

"I do," said Pru.

Patience was deeply hurt. Tears pricked her eyes. "Well,
if that is how you feel about it," she murmured. Climbing
to her feet, she dragged herself toward the door.

Almost immediately, Pru was stung by guilt. "I'm
sorry!" she cried, overtaking Patience and kissing her
hand. "I didn't mean it. Oh, I hate it when we fight. Whatever happens, we will always be the closest of sisters."

"Of course we will," Patience said. "Or is it 'shall'?"

"I haven't the slightest idea," Pru admitted.

Patience hugged her. "Bring me your bills, and we'll
figure something out."

Pru drew back. "You won't make me send my new
dresses back?"

Patience smiled ruefully. "I doubt they can be sent back.
But why don't I buy the dresses you had made in Philadelphia? You don't want them anymore, do you? Some of
them I quite liked, and you know I don't mind being two
years behind the rest of the world."

"I knew I could count on you! And the hack?" Pru went
on anxiously. "You won't really send me to St. James's
Palace in a hack?"

Patience sighed. "No. I'll speak to Mr. Bracegirdle
about a carriage. If it makes sense to buy one, I will. But
I'm fairly certain it will be cheaper to hire the thing."

Pru recognized that this was the best offer she was going
to get from her frugal sister. "Thank you, Pay," she said
humbly, kissing her cheek.

Within the hour, Pru had delivered both her entire
American wardrobe and her entire collection of London
bills to her sister's room. Once they were safely in Patience's hands, Pru thought no more about them.

Chapter 4

The Honorable Mr. Frederick Broome, faultlessly turned out in evening dress, sidled up to his cousin, who was watching the dancers in the ballroom at Breckinridge with a marked lack of interest. "Nothing like your little entertainments, eh, Max?"

Max glanced at his slim, boyishly handsome cousin, envying him the easy elegance with which he wore formal dress. "There is nothing little about my entertainments," he replied. "We missed you at my birth-night," he added.

"Forgive me. I was visiting a sick relative," Freddie replied, smiling as he told the obvious lie. "But no matter! I have had a full account of the orgy from the tenant. The lady doth not mince words. I'm surprised the letter didn't combust as I read it. She seems to think she is owed some recompense. She wants half her rent returned to her."

"Return all of it," said Max. "I'll give you a banknote for the full amount."

Freddie hid a smile. "Was it as bad as all that? I'm sorry I missed it."

"It was not an orgy," Max said defensively. "It was a harmless costume ball."

"How original," drawled Freddie. "And the lady wearing only black shoes and gloves? What was she meant to be?"

Max frowned. "The shoes and gloves were red. It was Miss Sally Sugar, as the five of hearts. Rather clever, I thought."

Freddie's brows rose. "Have we established, then, that Miss Sugar is indeed a natural redhead?"

Max shrugged. "It could have been a red merkin, I suppose. I don't know."

Freddie sighed. "Then I suppose we'll never know. As for Lady Waverly—"

"I neither know nor care. A most unattractive female."

"Indeed? And her ladyship's sister? Also unattractive?"

Max stirred uncomfortably.

Freddie grinned broadly. "May one assume at least that *she* is the Miss W—— upon whom Mr. P—— has lately been lavishing his attentions?"

"I may be in some trouble there," Max admitted sheepishly.

"Oh, dear."

"It was all very innocent," Max protested. "The circumstances were extraordinary. Miss Waverly's sister was ill—injured by me. I only meant to be kind. I was sure she regarded me as nothing more than a friend, looked up to me as an elder brother, almost. But it seems she was in love with me the whole time. She has sent me a letter . . . and, Freddie? Freddie, there was a lock of hair in the envelope."

Freddie's long, elegant nose wrinkled in disgust. "Not from her monosyllable?"

"No, thank God," Max said violently. "From her head. But that is quite vile enough."

"Oh, yes. Perfectly vile. What did you do with it?"

"Do with it? I was so shocked, I threw it on the fire."

Freddie shook his head. "Idiot! Now you'll never be rid of her. She'll always think you've got her revolting lock of hair hidden away somewhere as a treasure. You should have sent it back to her. Now you have a problem."

"I paid too much attention to her."

"Indeed you did, Mr. P——! I shouldn't be surprised if Miss W—— thinks you are engaged."

"But I never made love to her," Max protested. "She has nothing to accuse me of. I treated her as a kindly elder brother treats a younger sister, that is all. If I had known her true feelings—which, believe me, she hid quite well!—I should never have made her so many promises."

Freddie pricked up his ears. "Promises? Oh, dear! Is Max ensnared at last?"

Max shook his head impatiently. "I promised her my assistance in society, that is all. I promised to give a ball for her and her sister at Sunderland House."

"How dreadful. You might as well marry the girl. As it is, everyone will think you are engaged. Ah, well!" Freddie yawned. "I shouldn't worry about it too much. If it gets too thorny for you, we can always take the necessary precautions."

"It won't come to that, I hope," said Max.

"We can all hope," Freddie replied. Excusing himself, he went to ask a very pretty young lady in sea green satin to dance.

Left behind, Max resumed leaning against one of the marble pillars. For the first time in his life, he was not looking forward to the new year.

For Patience, the new year began with the loss of Mrs. Drabble, of whom she had grown quite fond. But she had not gone very far, and Patience, now perfectly restored to health, found she could walk to Mrs. Drabble's house in quiet, respectable Wimpole Street very easily. While she very properly had refused to engage in any familiarities with Lady Waverly in Clarges Street, Mrs. Drabble was only too happy to receive Patience in her own parlor.

Pru hardly noticed her sister's frequent absences. The carriage had been hired! At Pru's insistence, the Waverly coat of arms had been painted on the doors. Every afternoon, she and Lady Jemima made a slow progress through Hyde Park. As London began to fill up, in preparation for the social Season, these afternoon drives became increasingly important. And no matter how strong the winds of January, the top was always down. For what is the point of driving in the park if one cannot see and be seen? Only on the most inclement days would Pru consent to forego her drive in the park.

Invitations arrived from St. James's Palace. Snatching them up from Briggs's tray, Pru ran to find her sister poring over her accounts in the drawing room. Together, they opened the large, cream-colored envelopes. Pru's face fell immediately. "The fourth drawing room!" she said plaintively, tossing the card away. "Did you get the fourth also?" she asked her sister.

Patience hastily stuffed her invitation into a drawer. "It doesn't matter."

"You got the first, didn't you?" Pru accused her. "Didn't you?"

"You're perfectly welcome to come with me to the American reception," said Patience, going back to her balance sheet. "Mrs. Adams will be delighted to present us."

"No, thank you!" Pru retorted, thoroughly out of temper.

"Then, perhaps Lady Jemima can help you," Patience suggested. "It's what you're paying her for, isn't it?"

To her relief, Pru hurried off to Lady Jemima's room. "You can get me an invitation to the first drawing room, can't you, Lady Jemima?" she said, her hand on the door handle.

Lady Jemima was at her escritoire writing letters. "What, my dear?"

Pru frowned. "I have been invited to the fourth drawing room," she complained. "I want to go to the first drawing room. You are always boasting about your friends at court. Can't you do something? It's what you're paid for, after all!"

Lady Jemima blinked at her. "I have many friends at court," she said, "but none as powerful as your Mr. Purefoy."

"Max!" Pru exclaimed. "Yes, he did promise to help me. I'll write to him at once."

"Heavens, no!" cried Lady Jemima. "That would be most improper!"

"Improper?" Pru echoed.

"Well-mannered young ladies do not write letters to gentlemen," Lady Jemima said firmly. "At best it would be seen as an insufferable presumption. At worst, the gentleman may think you are *fast*. Either way, it will give him a disgust for you."

"What?" Pru gasped, pale with horror. "Why didn't you tell me that before?"

"I did not think it necessary. Do not say you have written him a letter?" Lady Jemima's eyes were round, and her thin, painted brows had risen to the middle of her powdered forehead.

Pru hung her head.

"Did he write back? Or did he return the letter?"

"No," said Pru.

Lady Jemima heaved a sigh of relief. "Then he has decided to pretend he never received it. *We* shall pretend you never wrote it. And perhaps it really did go astray. We must hope so."

Pru was not one to linger over the mistakes of the past. "How am I to ask for his help if I cannot write to him?" she inquired.

"As your chaperone, I shall write to Mr. Purefoy on your behalf," said Lady Jemima, taking out a fresh page of cold-pressed paper.

"He promised me a ball," said Pru. "And tickets to Almack's."

"Vouchers," Lady Jemima corrected her gently.

Pru frowned over the letter when it was finished. "You don't even mention the ball or Almack's," she pointed out.

"A gentleman does not forget his promises," Lady Jemima assured her. "It would be impertinent to remind him."

Pru trusted her to know her business. Her faith was rewarded when, in less than a week's time, the invitation to the first drawing room had been secured. Moving a china shepherdess out of the way, Pru set the card on the mantel in the drawing room, where she could admire it every day.

Max returned to London with his uncle a week before the opening of Parliament.

In his early sixties, the Duke of Sunderland suffered from crippling rheumatism, and his digestive system was notoriously delicate. Needless to say, his grace was not a good traveler. Upon arriving at his London house, his grace went straight to bed, leaving Max at leisure. Max's digestive system was as notoriously robust as his uncle's was delicate, and the hour was ideal for a late luncheon, but, as the servants had plenty to do already, he decided to go out. Resisting the lure of his club in St. James's Street, and yearning for nothing more elegant than gooseberry tarts, he left his uncle's mansion and walked to a quiet little house in Wimpole Street.

Mrs. Drabble received him in her sitting room upstairs.

"How well you do look, my dear Max," she greeted him, swelling with pride. "The last time I saw you, I confess you were looking a bit seedy. But that is what happens when a young man drinks to excess. You'll have gout before you're thirty, I shouldn't wonder!"

Max bristled. "I'm as fit as ever I was. *This* is all muscle," he added, slapping his belly in an angry demonstration.

"You certainly do look fit now," she congratulated him. "You should spend more time at Breckinridge. Clearly, country life agrees with you."

Max sighed. "As you know, his grace is on a very restricted diet . . . which means that, when I am with him, I too am on a very restricted diet! And, of course, when one is in the country, one gets so much exercise, what with all the hunting, shooting, riding, walking, and dancing."

"Dancing?" said Mrs. Drabble, pricking up her ears.

"We had three balls. The Hunt Ball. The Christmas Ball. And, of course, New Year's Eve Ball. My uncle threw every girl in Christendom at me in the hope I might marry one of them," he added. "I think he is becoming rather anxious on that score."

"Dancing, you know, is very dangerous exercise. It often leads to marriage."

"Marriage, then, represents the end to dancing?" he teased her. "But I like dancing."

She snorted. "You like changing partners."

"If I do *not* change partners, I am reliably informed, I shall be *obliged* to marry."

"Was there no one at Breckinridge to tempt you?"

"No one. I wish you would come back to us," he added. "Breckinridge is not the same without you."

"I like my little house," she said firmly. "I like my friends. I like my independence. And, anyway," she added, "it is my gooseberry tarts you miss, not me."

"That is not true, and you know it. You have been like a mother to me."

Mrs. Drabble blushed with pleasure, but said gruffly, "If I *had* been like a mother to you, I would have spanked you. The Lord knows you needed it. You do not regret giving me a pension?" she added, with a touch of anxiety.

"No, of course not!" he said, horrified. "I regret not having you with us. I don't like the new nurse, and I'm quite sure my uncle doesn't either. She lacks your warmth."

"I'm sure Miss Steele is very efficient."

"He's very sorry, you know, that he pinched your bottom," Max added softly. "He has given me his word that he will never, ever do anything like that again, if you will just come back."

Mrs. Drabble was scarlet to the roots of her gray hair. "He dared to tell you that? Oh!"

"Was it really so terrible? I often pinch your bottom."

"It is one thing," she said, shaking with anger, "for *you* to pinch my bottom, sir! It is quite another matter when the Duke of Sunderland pinches my bottom! He ought to know better. I am a respectable widow! What would Mr. Drabble say if he were here? There was nothing to do but resign my post at once. He would not pinch Miss Steele's bottom," she sniffed.

"No, indeed," Max agreed. "Nor would I. Miss Steele is not a woman to be trifled with."

"Nor am I!" she flashed.

"Very well," Max said hastily. "We will say no more about it."

"More tea?" she asked, still fuming.

"Yes, thank you," he said meekly. "And . . . about those gooseberry tarts . . . ?"

"I'm very sorry," she said. "I cannot offer you any gooseberry tarts today."

"But I could smell them halfway down the street!" he protested.

"I baked those for my sewing circle, not you," she said primly.

"Bugger your charity ladies," he growled. "I have been yearning for your gooseberry tarts since I left London over a month ago. I have been dreaming of them every night."

"Maximilian!" she said angrily. "Language!"

"Sorry," he muttered. "But you must be able to spare one or two!"

"No, I can't," she retorted. "I only baked a dozen, and, since Lady Waverly joined our group, we are exactly twelve."

"Lady Waverly!" he exclaimed, after a pause. "You would give *her* my gooseberry tarts?"

"She is an excellent needlewoman," said Mrs. Drabble. "Look! She netted me this beautiful lace collar for Christmas."

No expert on lace, Max frowned at the collar fixed to Mrs. Drabble's dress, which was otherwise of unadorned brown bombazine. "You don't like the clock I gave you? It's French. How well it looks on your mantel!"

"It is a very beautiful clock, my dear," she told him. "But, you know, there is something very special about a gift that is handmade. It comes from the heart."

"From the hands, you mean," he muttered. "And when I was seven I whittled you a little horse out of wood."

"Don't sulk. I still have it. It is one of my treasures."

"It ought to be. I nearly cut off my finger! I notice it is not on the mantel with my clock," he added in strong reproach.

"No, it is a private treasure. I keep it hidden safe from robbers in a box at the very back of a drawer in my bedchamber."

Max made a face. "What? Not buried in the garden?"

She laughed. "You had better go now, Max. I expect the

ladies to begin to arrive at any minute. You know what a fuss they make over you."

Max got to his feet. "I daresay Lady Waverly is none too eager to see me again," he said ruefully.

"No, I don't suppose she is," said Mrs. Drabble. "After what you did to her! I don't think she will ever forgive you."

"I'm sure I don't blame her," he said ruefully. "And now, if I promise not to pinch your bottom, will you allow me to kiss you good-bye?"

"Incorrigible rogue!" she said, offering him her cheek. "Jane will show you out. Jane!"

"No need," he said quickly. "I daresay Jane is busy. I'll let myself out."

He did so, collecting his hat and gloves from the little cloakroom at the foot of the stairs. As he was leaving, Jane herself started up the stairs with a plate piled high with tarts. Deftly, Max liberated one, giving poor Jane a wink. Then he left the house, strolling back the way he had come.

As he drew near the intersection of Oxford Street and Bond, he suddenly saw Miss Prudence Waverly hurrying up the street toward him. Until that moment, he had not appreciated just how much he had been dreading seeing her again. The desire to get away undetected was very strong. Bolting down the last of his gooseberry tart, he hastily retreated to the other side of the street, shielded, he hoped, from her view by a passing carriage. To his relief, she did not seem to see him, but continued on her way with quick steps. Max did the same.

Halfway down Bond Street, he found Freddie Broome looking into a shop window. "I'm afraid you have jam on your face," Freddie greeted him.

"Gooseberry tart," Max corrected him. Taking out his handkerchief, he quickly removed the evidence.

"How is Mrs. Drabble?" Freddie asked cordially. "With

you it is a gooseberry tart. With me it is a baked egg. There is something very comforting about a baked egg."

"There is indeed," Max agreed very gravely.

"I suppose there is something very comforting about a gooseberry tart, too," Freddie said civilly. "*Chacun à son goût,* as the Frogs say."

"Precisely," said Max. "Now what's all this I hear about you selling my grays?"

"I think you'll find they are mine," Freddie replied. "You lost the bet, remember?"

"I'll buy 'em back!" said Max.

"And so you may," Freddie replied, "at Tattersall's! They're in the Monday sale."

"You should have offered them to me first."

"Didn't know you were in town," Freddie replied, "and I'm in a hurry. I'm off to St. Petersburg on Tuesday."

"You can go to the devil for all I care!" said Max. "Take them out of sale. They're mine! I'll give you five hundred guineas for them on the spot!"

"Now, you know I can't do that," Freddie said mildly. "I would if I could, Max. But you know I can't. Besides, didn't you just buy Bassington's chestnuts?"

"Not a patch on my grays!" said Max.

Freddie suddenly gave a low whistle. "I say! That's a damned fine-looking girl!"

Max immediately turned to catch a glimpse of the damned fine-looking girl. All the color drained out of his face. He cursed under his breath.

"Max!" she shrieked, waving exuberantly. "Oh, Max! Yoo-hoo! Over here!"

She must have seen him, after all, as he was crossing Oxford Street. She must have doubled back in pursuit of him.

"Miss W——, I presume?" Freddie drawled, raising his quizzing glass.

Max did not bother to answer. Turning quickly, he ran, leaving Freddie staring after him in astonishment. Willing in that moment, to do anything to escape Pru, Max darted into traffic, jumped onto the running board of a passing carriage. Opening the door, he flung himself inside, rolling on the floor.

One of the passengers, a severe-looking middle-aged female, instantly began beating him with an umbrella. "Forgive me!" Max pleaded, raising one arm to fend off the blows. "There's someone after me. I'll be gone in a moment. I mean no harm! I just had to get away!"

"I quite understand," said the other passenger, a handsome, self-assured young woman with auburn hair and pale blue eyes. Her pale blue hooded cloak exactly matched her eyes. "When a girl is that pretty the only thing to do is run away! Porson, you may stop beating Mr. Purefoy now."

Max looked at her gratefully. "Thank you, Miss . . . er . . . ?"

Her neatly plucked brows rose slightly. "Lady Isabella," she said, with a slight emphasis on the "Lady." "She is remarkably determined, whoever she is," she went on quite calmly, looking out the window. "Perhaps she has a genuine claim on you, Mr. Purefoy?"

Max shuddered. "Certainly not! I throw myself on your mercy, Lady Isabella."

She smiled. "You are quite safe now, Mr. Purefoy. The beautiful girl is gone. You may take a seat. Porson! Give Mr. Purefoy your seat."

Lady Isabella's maid quickly moved to join her mistress, leaving the opposite seat for Max. "Thank you," he said. "You know my name. Have we met?"

If Lady Isabella was hurt that he did not remember her, she gave no sign. "My brother and I were fortunate enough to be invited to Breckinridge at Christmas," she replied. "We danced together twice at the ball, Mr. Purefoy."

Max was embarrassed. He ought to have recognized the sister of one of his oldest acquaintances. He blamed the American girl; she had wreaked havoc upon his equilibrium. Why, she must have flown from Wimpole Street to overtake him in Bond Street! And how had she known he would be in Wimpole Street? No one knew he liked to visit his old nurse.

"Are you quite all right, Mr. Purefoy?"

Isabella's genteel voice pulled him out of his thoughts. "Forgive me!" he said. "How are you? You are coming out this year, I believe?"

"Last year," she laughed. "Thank you for noticing."

"Yes, of course," he murmured.

"I was just on my way home. May I set you down somewhere? I believe the danger has passed," she added with an arch smile. "Or has it? Indeed, your face is very red. I think perhaps I should wish you joy."

"Good God, no!" he said violently. "A slight entanglement, nothing more. I have been foolish, but not so foolish as to offer marriage. No! I merely promised to give a ball in that young lady's honor at Sunderland House."

"I see. The beautiful girl is a relation, perhaps?"

"She is no relation of mine. She is, in fact, an American."

Her eyes widened. "Not the American baroness everyone is talking of?"

Max frowned. "No. Miss Waverly is the younger sister. I won't bore you with all the details," he added impatiently. "Suffice it to say that her elder sister nearly drowned because of me. While her ladyship recovered, it was only natural that I call on them in Clarges Street from time to time."

"Certainly. To inquire after Lady Waverly's health."

"Just so! But I could not ignore Miss Pru—Miss Waverly, I mean. Perhaps it was wrong of me to show her a little of London, but I only meant to be kind. I did not realize that she was falling in love with me until it was too late. Now she is pursuing me in Bond Street! What am I going to do?"

"It's seems quite hopeless," said Lady Isabella, her eyes twinkling with amusement. "You will have to marry her."

"Don't joke!" he pleaded.

"Poor Mr. Purefoy," she murmured. "Shall I set you down here? If we go any further, I shall be taking you home with me. I don't think my brother would approve."

"May I call on you sometime?" Max asked, as he left her carriage.

"Sometime?" she said coolly.

"Tomorrow," he said. "Are you in Grosvenor Square again this year?"

"Yes," she answered, holding out her hand to him. He kissed it, then closed the door.

"What a piece of luck!" Isabella cried, as her carriage moved swiftly on. "Fate has dealt me a very promising hand. If I play my cards right, I might be a duchess. They say the Duke of Sunderland will not last another year."

"Yes, my lady," said her maid.

Isabella scowled at her. "And the next time a gentleman jumps into my carriage," she said angrily, "you must hit him harder!"

Chapter 5

Max strolled to his club, enjoyed an excellent late luncheon, and strolled back to Sunderland House, quite recovered from the shock he had sustained in Bond Street. Venable, the steady, dignified butler, let him in.

"Is his grace still in bed?" Max asked, handing the parlor maid his hat and gloves.

"No, sir," Venable replied. "His grace is in the drawing room with Miss Waverly."

Venable spoke without inflection, but his doubts were betrayed by a slight lift in the brows and a slight question in the eyes.

"What?" Max echoed in disbelief. "She had the audacity to come here?" Without waiting for any reply, he started up the stairs, taking them two at a time.

"Max! There you are at last!" cried Pru, jumping to her feet as he burst into the room. "I have been keeping your uncle company, as you can see."

If Venable had seemed a little doubtful, the Duke of Sunderland seemed amazed. "Miss . . . er . . . Waverly tells me she has been here before . . . ?"

"Oh, yes," Pru said eagerly. "Max gave me the grand tour! It makes our little house in Clarges Street look like a mean little hovel! I won't tell you what it makes our house in Philadelphia look like."

Max looked at her coldly, but Pru took no notice of that. "I thought I saw you in Bond Street!" she went on happily, seizing Max by the hand. "Did you not see me? Well, no matter! I knew you must come home eventually. I have been getting to know your dear, dear uncle! He kept you away from London so long that I was afraid he didn't approve of me. You *do* like me, don't you?"

"I like all of Max's friends," the duke answered, casting his nephew a look of appeal.

"Miss Prudence," Max said coolly, "what are you doing here?"

She blinked at him. "I told you: I saw you in Bond Street. At least, I thought I did. That was my first inkling that you were back in town. Perhaps I didn't see you at all. Perhaps it was a sign from heaven!" She giggled.

"It most definitely was not a sign from heaven," said Max.

"No, I suppose not. I just wanted to thank you," she went on, "for the invitation to the first drawing room. You just don't know what it means to me! You haven't forgotten that you promised to give a ball, too?"

"I have not forgotten," he said coldly. "The ball will take place the night after your presentation. That is the done thing, I believe."

"Oh, heavenly!" said Pru. "I don't mean to remind you of your promise," she added quickly. "Lady Jemima says I should not remind you of any of your promises to me. But I did want to make sure that you had not forgotten. I wondered why you did not arrange for me to be included in the first drawing room before the invitations were sent out. You did say you would give me every possible assistance in society."

"It must have slipped my mind."

"I would not have minded the fourth drawing room," she

went on. "But Patience is invited to the first drawing room, and it hardly seemed *fair*! Especially when she doesn't even want to go."

"Miss Prudence, my uncle is very tired. Please allow me to show you out."

Pru smiled angelically at the duke. "Of course! I can come back tomorrow, when you are feeling better. Goodbye! Parting is such sweet sorrow, don't you think?"

"It would be better, Miss Prudence," said Max, "if you would allow us to call on you in Clarges Street. My uncle's health does not always allow him to receive visitors."

"Of course. I understand," Pru whispered. Startling them both, she backed out of the room in a series of deep curtsys better reserved for the throne room at St. James's Palace.

"There's no need for all that, Miss Prudence," Max told her curtly. "A simple curtsy would have sufficed."

"I know, but I need the practice," she replied. Outside, she drew his attention to the Waverly coat of arms painted on the door. "Isn't it handsome? Patience calls it 'the mystery of the missing lion's paw'! She's so impertinent. Honestly, I wish she would abdicate and let me be the baroness. I'd be so much *better* at it than she is."

With a curt bow, Max put her in the carriage and closed the door. Then he went back to the drawing room to face his uncle.

"What a pretty girl," the duke congratulated him. "Lively, too. She has such ebullience! Such joie de vivre! I—I quite like her. The two of you might have been made for each other!"

Max was not in the least bit deceived. "Don't worry, Uncle. I have no intention of marrying her."

The Duke of Sunderland heaved a huge sigh of relief. "Oh, thank heavens!" he cried weakly. "Twenty minutes in her company and I'm quite done in! I like conversation as much as the next fellow, I'm sure, but there is such a thing as overdoing it."

"I am sorry she imposed on you."

The duke drew his shaggy gray brows together. "I rather got the impression, from the young lady's conversation, that *you* had been imposing on *her*! Long, romantic rides in the park. Trips to the museums, the circus, Madame Tussauds."

"I didn't see the harm," said Max. "Not until it was too late."

"Well, you have promised her a ball," said the duke, "and a ball she must have. I suppose we will have Soho to make the arrangements."

"No, no," said Max. "You must leave everything to me. You are not to lift a finger."

"I wouldn't mind arranging an engagement party," grumbled the duke. "I would not have you marry without love, dear boy—you know I would not! I quite learned my lesson with your poor father, God rest his soul! But I'm not getting any younger, you know. I would like to see you married before I go. I do not mean to pressure you in any way. Only consider! If you were a married man, this young lady would not be bothering us."

Max's gray eyes twinkled. "Wife as shield," he mused. "Why did I not think of it before?"

"There must be someone you like," the duke said, exasperated.

"Oh, dozens," Max said lightly. "But in all seriousness, you have been very good in allowing me to choose my own wife. No, you have," he insisted as the duke protested feebly. "I do appreciate it. And, I think, it would be churlish of me to keep you waiting much longer. Do you remember a tall, auburn-haired girl at our Christmas Ball?"

The duke's eyes lit up. "Dear boy! It is enough for me that you remember her. Has the lady a name?"

"Isabella Norton. The Earl of Milford is her brother."

The duke made a face. Endowed with a set of features not unlike those of a toby jug, he was quite good at making faces. "Toady Norton?" he said incredulously. "If *he* has a sister, why, she must be seventy at least!"

"You are thinking of *old* Lord Milford," Max told him. "I was at school with young Lord Milford."

"Indeed? My, how time flies! It seems like only yesterday I was sending you off to school. Well, well! My nephew, in love with Toady Norton's girl! What a small world it is."

Max shook his head, alarmed. "I did not say I was in love with her, sir! Don't order the wedding breakfast just yet! But she may suit. She has birth, breeding, and manners. She is not a beauty, perhaps, but she is handsome enough. She *looks* like a duchess. More to the point, she *behaves* like a duchess! I make no promises, but I am engaged to call on her tomorrow."

"An excellent beginning!" said the duke.

After Pru's invasion of Sunderland House, Max found the quiet serenity of Lady Isabella's drawing room enormously attractive. The lady herself was very cool and polite and, after Pru's histrionics, Max had a new appreciation for the cool and the polite. He felt that life with Isabella could not fail to go smoothly, and he even envied her brother a little.

"How odd my behavior must have seemed to you yesterday, Lady Isabella," he began. "I believe I owe you an apology as well as an explanation."

"You owe me neither, sir," she answered. "I trust my maid did not hurt you? Porson can be a little overzealous in defense of her mistress, I fear."

Max touched his scalp briefly. Under his black, curly hair there were some sore spots, but nothing too painful. "It was no more than I deserved," he said. "I had no right to enter your carriage, but my situation was truly desperate. If need be, I would have taken a dozen beatings from your excellent Porson."

"A dozen beatings?" she said lightly. "The young lady frightens you that much?"

Max shuddered. "Yesterday I was only frightened," he said. "Now I am terrified."

Lady Isabella listened attentively as he described returning to Sunderland House, only to find his uncle in the clutches of the exuberant Miss Waverly.

"I am amazed!" said Lady Isabella, shaking her head. "Is there no one to check the young lady? Has she no guardian? No chaperone?"

"She has both," said Max. "Lady Waverly is her guardian, and I myself engaged Jemmie Crump to act as duenna."

"And yet Miss Waverly runs wild in the streets," Lady Isabella said, clucking her tongue.

"Quite literally."

"It is most improper. It is one thing for a young lady to *pursue* a gentleman," Isabella added, with a glint of humor in her steel blue eyes. "It is quite another to chase him down Bond Street! She must have been quite out of breath!"

"And so was the gentleman," he said, as the servant brought in the tea.

Isabella prepared his tea exactly the way he liked it: black with a little lemon. "Would you care for a gooseberry tart, Mr. Purefoy?" she asked, handing him his cup. "I believe they are still warm."

"My favorite!" Max exclaimed, in surprise. "Ever since I was a child. How did you know?"

"But I had no idea," Isabella exclaimed in delight. "They're my favorite, too!"

"What a happy coincidence," he said.

"Your poor uncle," she murmured presently. "How

shocked his grace must have been! And how incredibly callous of Miss Waverly to insist on your giving her a ball, when his grace is not in the best of health! Could you not make her some excuse?"

"I have no intention of breaking my promise," Max said firmly. "My uncle shall not be inconvenienced. May I hope," he went on, "that Your Ladyship will attend? I'd be most grateful."

"Of course I shall go, if you are good enough to invite me. But I must protest! Surely, you must realize, Mr. Purefoy, that, if you give Miss Waverly a ball at Sunderland House, everyone will assume you are engaged to her!"

"Not if I am engaged to another lady," said Max.

"Oh?" said Isabella, raising her pale blue eyes to his pale gray ones.

At precisely that moment, the doors of the drawing room opened and a short, rather heavyset gentleman with a large, handsome head, and thin, sandy hair came into the room.

"You remember my brother, of course," said Isabella. If she was annoyed by the interruption, she gave no sign.

Max and Lord Milford had attended all the same schools, but they had always moved in different circles, Milford being four years older.

"My lord," Max said.

"Nice to see you again, Purefoy," Milford said, taking a cup of tea from his sister. "I have just come from the park. Not one in three of the women I passed were worth looking at! If that is any indication, it is going to be a very dull Season indeed!"

"My dear Ivor," Isabella murmured repressively.

"You should have been in Bond Street yesterday," said Max.

Lord Milford looked interested. "Bond Street? Why? Did you see many beauties there?"

"Only one," Max replied. "But, then, how many do you need?"

"Only one," said Milford. "Well? And who was this beauty? Do you mean to keep her all to yourself?"

"No, indeed," said Max. "She is Miss Prudence Waverly, a great heiress from America."

"You did not tell me she was an heiress!" Isabella exclaimed.

"Oh, yes," said Max. "She and her sister have something like a hundred thousand pounds each."

"I don't believe it!" Isabella said incredulously. "I was sure Lord Waverly died bankrupt."

"He did," Max acknowledged. "The money comes from their maternal grandfather. He made his fortune in shipping, I believe."

"Beautiful *and* rich," Isabella said lightly. "No wonder you ran away from her, Mr. Purefoy!"

"And the sister," Milford interjected, "this baroness everyone is talking of—rich, too? Are you quite sure about this, Purefoy? I had not heard that they were rich."

"Quite sure," Max assured him. "But, I think you will find that the elder sister is not as pretty as the younger, if that matters to you."

Milford sighed. "I should like to find rank, fortune, and beauty all united in one person. Isabella tells me I must lower my standards or die a bachelor! But I will not compromise. She must be rich and beautiful and well bred, or I will have none of her!"

"Very commendable, I'm sure," Max said. "One should always aspire to achieve perfection, I suppose." Rising, he quickly took his leave of Isabella, saluted her brother, and quit the house.

No sooner had he gone than Isabella turned on her brother with cold fury. "*Why* did you have to come in at just that moment, pray?" she demanded.

Unconcerned, Milford picked up a gooseberry tart, then flung it down in disgust. "Gooseberry! You know I loathe gooseberry tarts!"

"As do I," she snapped. "But *he* likes them. That is what matters."

He snorted. "You think he will marry you if you feed him gooseberry tarts? You're a damn fool!"

She glared at him. "We were just beginning to discuss marriage when you interrupted us! He was just about to speak. Did the servants not tell you who was with me?"

Milford snorted. "You told me Purefoy would marry you if I took you to Breckinridge for Christmas, but nothing came of it. I spent a fortune on your wardrobe, and he scarcely looked at you!"

"He danced with me twice!" she protested.

"Danced with you twice," he mimicked. "For the amount I spent, that is quite a handsome result, I must say! Only five hundred pounds per dance! Let me tell you, Izzy, this is your last chance. If you can't get Purefoy this time—and I don't see how you can with that long nose of yours and no fortune to speak of—then you will have to take Sir Charles Stanhope—*if* he will still have you, that is! You'll take anyone who asks you, in fact. You won't get a third Season."

"It is your fault we are poor," Isabella said bitterly. "You gamble too much! You should have married Miss Cruikshanks!"

His lip curled. "I? Marry the daughter of a draper?"

"A very rich draper!"

"I am the Earl of Milford," he informed her loftily. "I do not marry with tradesmen's ugly daughters. I care not how rich they are."

Isabella's eyes glinted. "What lady of birth, beauty, and breeding would *stoop* to take you?" she sneered. "Let's face it, Brother, you will always come up short."

Lord Milford glared at her. "Was that, perhaps, a reference to my height?"

"No, Brother," she answered. "It was a reference to your lack of height!"

"Napoleon was not a tall man," Milford said coldly, "and yet the Princess of Austria married him."

She laughed. "Depend on it, Brother! When you have conquered all of Europe, you may have your pick of the royal ladies."

"You were a fool to refuse Sir Charles," he shouted at her, red in the face. "Who are you to turn up your nose at a rich baronet? You may never receive another offer of marriage. You are on the shelf! Stale goods!"

"I *shall* marry Mr. Purefoy," she said quietly. "I *shall* be a duchess. Have a care how you speak to me, sir."

"You?" he sniggered. "A duchess? You have nothing but your name to recommend you! Do you think you are handsome enough to tempt *him*? He has bedded the most beautiful women in Europe."

"And has married none of them," she replied. "The Duchess of Sunderland must be a lady above reproach. Beauties, however virtuous they may be, always attract gossip. I would be a credit to him. I tell you, he was on the verge of proposing to me."

"Nonsense. You have no dowry."

"It isn't necessary for *him* to marry for money," she said. "He wants a well-bred, quiet wife. Is that so strange? I shall be expected to nurse the old duke, of course, but I won't mind that."

"Nurse him? Help him into his grave, you mean!" he snorted.

Isabella quietly and firmly changed the subject. "Miss Waverly is rich and beautiful and well bred," she said.

"Well bred?" he scoffed. "She is American!"

"Her grandfather was a baron."

He snorted. "And so was her uncle! I have an IOU from his lordship, but when I presented it to the attorney, he said there was no money to pay it. 'Speak to the baroness,' he said."

"If you were clever, Brother, you would call on her ladyship and forgive the debt."

"Forgive the debt! Are you mad? Lord Waverly owed me a monkey."

"You would be a simpleton indeed to let a mere five hundred pounds stand between you and a fortune," said Isabella. "You heard Mr. Purefoy! A hundred thousand pounds!"

"I heard him say she was not pretty," he said, after a brief silence.

"I have never set eyes on the baroness," Isabella answered. "But her younger sister is a remarkably beautiful young lady. The blackest hair, the greenest eyes. She also has a hundred thousand pounds."

"Two heiresses? In one family? And neither is married?"

"It does seem rather unfair," said Isabella. "But shall we not call on them? They are in Clarges Street. No one knows about them yet. If you could get to them first . . ."

He jumped up. "Don't just sit there! Get your bonnet on!"

Patience sat at her desk studying the latest installment of Pru's bills. "What is it, Mr. Briggs?" she called over her shoulder as the butler slid into the room.

"Your Ladyship has a visitor," he said, gliding toward her with a single card on his large silver tray.

Patience sighed. "Mr. Briggs, how many times have I asked you not to call me 'Your Ladyship'?"

"More than once, my lady. What shall I tell the gentleman?"

"I suppose that depends on who it is," said Patience.

He stood silently before her with his tray.

Impatiently, Patience picked up the card. "Sir Charles Stanhope," she read, frowning. "He called yesterday while I was out, didn't he?"

"I believe so, my lady."

She sighed. "Persistent! I suppose I'd better see what he wants. Send him in."

Rising from her desk, she turned to face her visitor, a portly, red-faced gentleman, well past middle age, with yellow teeth and more hair growing out of his ears than he had on his head. He stared at her as if he had never seen a woman before.

"Sir Charles Stanhope?" she said politely.

"Are *you* Lord Waverly's niece?" he demanded in astonishment.

"Yes, sir," Patience answered, extending her hand to him. "I am Patience Waverly."

"My lady!" he said gruffly. Seizing her hand, he planted his wet mouth on the back of it. "You don't look a thing like him, your uncle. Lucky for you," he added, with a coarse laugh. "You have the look of your father, Arthur Waverly. Now *he* was a handsome devil. Black-haired with eyes as green as glass. The ladies loved him."

Patience quickly drew back her hand. "Were you acquainted with my father? Do please sit down," she added. "I'll ring for some refreshments."

"Thank you," he said, settling into a chair.

"I have not had the pleasure of meeting any of my father's friends," she went on, seating herself on the sofa. "Did you know him well, sir?"

"I belonged more to the older set, Miss Waverly," he told her. "But I knew your uncle very well." Taking out his quizzing glass, he put it up and looked at her hungrily. "I must say, you are a monstrous pretty girl—though a bit on the thin side, if you don't mind my saying so."

Patience minded a good deal, but said nothing.

"I'll come straight to the heart of the matter," said Sir Charles. "Your uncle, God rest him, died owing me five thousand pounds."

"I'm afraid you must take that up with the attorney," said Patience.

He scowled. "I've seen Bracegirdle already. Impertinent wretch! He says I haven't any proof of the debt. He sent me away with a flea in my ear!"

"I'm very sorry to hear that," said Patience. "I have never had a flea in my ear, but I imagine it's quite a nuisance."

"You mock me?" he growled.

"Sir, if Mr. Bracegirdle refuses to acknowledge the debt, I see no reason why *I* should honor it."

He stared at her in disbelief. "But your uncle and me had a wager! He lost, so he did, but, before I could get his IOU, the dirty rotten scoundrel threw himself off Westminster Bridge! When they pulled him out of the Thames, the fish had eaten his face. There was nothing to identify him but his watch and chain. Serves him right, too."

Patience was on her feet. "How dare you! You should be ashamed to come here asking me for money! You led me to believe you were a friend of my uncle."

His eyes popped and a vein pulsed in his greasy forehead. "I don't want money!" he said. "I want Wildings. I want the land. And I want you, too."

"Excuse me?" she gasped.

"Sit down, girl," he said impatiently. "I am asking you to be my wife, not my mistress, if that's what you think. I'm a rich man. It's a good offer."

"Get out!" she said, almost choking.

"Don't be missish," he told her. "It's the only way

you have of canceling the debt. I admit, I did not come here with marriage in mind. But now that I have seen you, my dear—!"

He bounded up to her with shocking speed, and would have taken her into his arms, but Patience forestalled him by slapping him hard across the face. A white handprint appeared on his red cheek.

"You are not very civil," he complained. "Is this the only answer I am to receive?"

"I have another hand, sir, if you would like another answer!"

His eyes narrowed. "You shall marry me," he said. "The debt must be paid. I have no IOU, madam, but I do have witnesses."

Patience was seething. "Get out, before I have my servants throw you out!"

"Take care, my lady," he huffed. "If you persist in insulting me, I may be tempted to withdraw my offer of marriage. I will leave you to think about *that*." Shaking his fist at her, he added, "If I were your husband at this moment, I would beat you."

"If you were my husband, sir, I'd throw myself into the river like my poor uncle!"

Running to the door, she tore it open. Briggs stood there, this time with two cards on his tray. "Lord Milford and his sister to see you, my lady."

"Show them in, Mr. Briggs," Patience said quickly.

A handsome young lady swept into the room, dressed in a smart emerald green costume. Black cockerel feathers decorated her bonnet, framing her long, patrician face. Looking at her, Patience, who normally gave little thought to the style of her clothes, was suddenly very glad that she was wearing one of Pru's old gowns, a dotted muslin trimmed with blue ribbons.

"Lady Isabella!" Sir Charles exclaimed, bowing. "I did not expect to see you here."

"Sir Charles," she replied coolly, sketching a curtsy. "How do you do? You remember my brother, of course."

Lord Milford, hat in hand, stood behind his much taller sister, staring at Patience.

"Of course, my lord," Sir Charles gushed. "Come in, my lady! Do come in! I'll send for some tea. And plum cake! That is your favorite, I know. How good of you to call on me! It is indeed an honor!"

In his enthusiasm, he seemed to forget that he was not in his own home.

Isabella quickly reminded him. "We have not come to see you, Sir Charles. We have come to see Miss Waverly." She smiled warmly at Patience, whom she, naturally, had mistaken for her twin sister.

"I shall return, Lady Waverly," Sir Charles snarled at Patience.

"You will not be admitted," Patience answered. For emphasis, she tore up the gentleman's card and flung the pieces at him.

Sir Charles stalked from the room, his face as red as a turkey's neck, but he did not forget to bend over Isabella's hand. "My lady! May I call on you tomorrow?"

"Certainly not," she said coldly, snatching away her hand.

Lord Milford returned the baronet's bow with a cool nod, and Sir Charles passed out of the room. Presently, they heard the front door bang shut.

Isabella smiled at Patience. "How do you do, Miss Waverly?" she said, sinking into a graceful curtsy.

"I beg your pardon," Patience said quickly. "I am not Prudence. I am Patience Waverly."

"You are Baroness Waverly?" said Isabella, staring. Mr. Purefoy had said the baroness was not as pretty as her sister. She could not understand it. Why would he lie? Perhaps the young lady was playing a joke.

"I am the baroness, but only because I was born twenty-seven minutes before my sister," Patience explained. "We're twins."

"Good heavens!" Isabella exclaimed. "I had no idea."

"I'm afraid my sister is not here at the moment. She is at her dancing lesson. Or is it her French lesson? I forget. She will be back soon, if you would care to wait, Miss . . . ?"

"Forgive us for staring," said Isabella, driving her elbow into her brother's ribs. "I am Lady Isabella Norton. This is my brother, Lord Milford. He seems to have been struck dumb by your beauty," she added.

"No! Not at all," Milford protested.

Patience barely suppressed a laugh. "Please, sit down. I'm very happy to meet some of Pru's friends. May I offer you some refreshment? Some cherry water?"

Isabella sat down on the sofa, dragging her brother with her. "My brother adores cherry water," she said. "Don't you, Milford?"

"Oh, yes," he said quickly. "Cherry water. It's my favorite."

Patience smiled. "Cherry water for our guests, Mr. Briggs."

"Very good, my lady."

Patience sank into a chair. "I have asked him not to call me that. I confess I find it a little disconcerting. The title, I mean."

"Why should it be disconcerting?" Isabella asked.

"In America, we do not have titles. We believe that all men are created equal. Even our president is Mr. Madison."

"How very interesting," Isabella said politely. "Our estate agent is Mr. Madison. Perhaps they are related?"

Briggs returned with a tray and, grateful for the interruption, Patience began pouring a suspicious pink liquid into glasses.

Lord Milford accepted his glass with trepidation. Isabella sipped hers cautiously.

"It reminds me of our beautiful cherry trees back home," said Patience.

"Oh, yes? Are there many cherry trees in America?" Isabella inquired, pronouncing it "Americker."

"America, you must understand, is a great big place," Patience replied, hiding a smile. "But we have a great many cherry trees in Pennsylvania."

"Ah! Pennsylvania! What a perfectly charming name for a country estate," Isabella exclaimed. "You must miss it dreadfully. When do you think you will see it again, Lady Waverly?"

Patience's eyes widened. "Country estate? Oh, no. Pennsylvania is not a country estate. It's a commonwealth. Pru and I are from the city of Philadelphia, in Pennsylvania."

Isabella had never heard of either, but she smiled politely.

"It *was* the capital of the Unites States at one time," Patience told her. "Washington, of course, is the capital now."

"Oh, *dear*. I thought *he* was the prime minister," said Isabella.

"Mr. Washington was our first *president,*" Patience said, beginning to frown, for not only was Isabella ignorant, she was condescending. "The capital city was named in his honor. You'll be glad to know we're rebuilding Washington since it was burnt down two years ago by the British army," she added tartly.

"Oh, I'm sure it was an accident," said Isabella very quickly.

"How exactly do you know my sister?" asked Patience, abruptly changing the subject, which was not doing her temper any good.

"I'm afraid we don't, Lady Waverly," said Isabella. "We

came here to see you. That is, my *brother* has something he would like to say to you. Don't you, Ivor?"

"Oh? Did my uncle die owing you money, sir?"

"Yes. A monkey," said Milford.

"A monkey!" Patience repeated in astonishment.

"Yes, a monkey," he replied. "I have presented my IOU to the attorney to no avail."

"But my brother has come to forgive the debt," Isabella added quickly.

"Yes, that's right," said Milford, after only a slight hesitation, for the baroness quite obviously met two of his requirements in a wife. The only doubt he entertained concerned his most important requirement: fortune. Without corroborating evidence, Purefoy's word on the subject could not be trusted. After all, Purefoy himself might have been deceived.

"You're very kind, sir, but I—" Patience began.

"Good," Isabella interrupted her. "It has been troubling my poor brother a great deal." She leaned forward, and before Patience could form a reply, went on, "And, I confess, dear Lady Waverly, that there is something troubling *me* a great deal. I must beg to speak to you alone. Ivor, will you be good enough to call for me in, say, twenty minutes?"

Milford frowned. "What am I to do for twenty minutes? It is not long enough for anything! In any case, you can have nothing to say to Lady Waverly that I cannot hear."

"Would you care for more cherry water, sir?" Patience asked him.

"I would not put you to any trouble, my lady," Milford said, and hastily took his leave, just as Patience had hoped, for she was very curious to hear what his sister had to say.

Chapter 6

Patience could not help but notice that, despite her claim, Isabella did not seem troubled in the least. "Yes?" she said simply, when Lord Milford had gone.

Isabella folded her gloved hands neatly in her lap. "It concerns your sister, I'm afraid. Miss Prudence Waverly."

"You said you did not know my sister," Patience said sharply.

"We have never met," said Isabella. "But when I saw her yesterday in Bond Street, I felt it was my duty to come to you, and just give you a hint before her behavior sinks you both."

"I don't know Bond Street. But if it is so dreadful to be seen there, why were you in Bond Street?"

"Lady Waverly, my interference is of the friendliest nature!" Isabella protested. "Your sister is very young—you both are—and perhaps things are different in Pennsadelphimore, but *here* young ladies do not chase young men down the street, no matter how great the temptation."

"I beg your pardon," said Patience.

"Not only is it unseemly, it rather defeats the purpose," Isabella went on. "Such wild behavior can only give the gentleman a disgust for your sister. And you, Lady Waverly! If you do not take the trouble to check your sister, you very well may be tainted by the association!"

"You are mistaken," Patience said coldly. "My sister would never do such a thing. No need! Men are perfectly happy chasing after *her*."

"Not this man," said Isabella. "Mr. Purefoy has only to snap his fingers, and he can have any girl he wants."

Patience's eyebrows shot up. "Purefoy!" she gasped, two livid spots of color blotching her cheeks. "*That man!* You speak to me of *that man*? I will not have his name spoken in my house!"

Isabella found this response both amazing and interesting. "I see you are acquainted with the gentleman," she murmured.

Patience's eyes flashed. "I certainly am not! And he is no gentleman! He is the devil. He is wicked, vile, degenerate, loathsome, lewd, drunken—!" She stopped, having run out of breath as well as adjectives. "The night I came to this house, *he* was here . . . cavorting with his disgusting friends. I saw such sights—sights too shocking to relate."

"He is quite famous for his parties, I believe," said Isabella.

"Famous! He should be notorious. And it was not a party! We have parties in Philadelphia. *This* was an orgy! If this man is imposing himself on my sister, I will have his guts for garters. Why has nothing been done about him?"

Isabella shrugged helplessly. "He is the Duke of Sunderland's heir. Everyone—everyone knows he is a villain, but no one will stand up to him. He is too powerful. A man like that can do whatever he pleases with a girl, without consequence. Your sister, Lady Waverly, does not apprehend the danger. Perhaps she thinks he will marry her."

"You saw my sister with—with him?" Patience said anxiously. "You are certain?"

"Oh, yes," said Isabella. "Unless, of course, it was Your

Ladyship whom I saw in Bond Street," she added, with a faint smile.

"Was there blood?" said Patience.

"Heavens, no!" said Isabella.

"Then it wasn't me," Patience said darkly. Rising to her feet, she went to the fireplace, where Pru's invitation to St. James's Palace had pride of place on the mantel.

"You will take steps to protect your sister, I trust?"

"Oh, yes," Patience said grimly.

"I fear he is very skilled in the art of seduction, my lady, having practiced it from a very early age," Isabella said sadly. "He began with the servant girls at his uncle's estate, I believe, throwing them away when he was done with them."

Patience stared, very white around the mouth.

Encouraged by the effect her revelations were having on the gullible baroness, Isabella went on with her wholly fictitious account of the rake's progress. "Unchecked by his uncle, he soon progressed to innocent maids in nearby villages. Farmer's daughters, then tradesmen's daughters. Finally, he raped the vicar's child!"

"The man is a fiend! In America, we know what to do with men like that. Not that we have men like that in America," Patience said hastily.

"No one can touch him here, because of his uncle. Every day he grows bolder in crime. Not very long ago, he forced his way into a lady's carriage and—and ravished her—right in front of her maid! She, of course, could not say a word to anyone, for fear of retribution."

Patience stretched out her hands to Isabella. "Was it you, Lady Isabella?"

"I?" cried Isabella, jumping to her feet. "Certainly not! How dare you! I came here to warn you, and you—you insult me!"

"I beg your pardon most humbly," cried Patience, now

completely convinced that Lady Isabella had been one of Mr. Purefoy's many victims. "I'm most grateful to you for coming to me with this information. I was very ill when I first arrived in England, and, I'm afraid, I was not able to watch over my sister. But, now that I am better, I will keep her safe. I *shall* keep her safe."

"If I were you, I would send her away from London."

"I should like to," Patience said. "But I'm afraid my sister would never consent. She is to be presented at court."

"Oh? Which drawing room?"

"The first."

Isabella stared. "The *first* drawing room? How, may I ask, did you manage that?"

"I didn't," Patience told her. "It was all Lady Jemima's doing."

Isabella knew better. Silly old Jemmie Crump could never have managed it in a hundred years. It must have been Mr. Purefoy. "Do you know that he means to give a ball for her?"

"My God! Is there no end to his wickedness?"

"Apparently not," said Isabella, who would have killed for a ball at Sunderland House. Gathering up her reticule, she rose gracefully to her feet. "I think I hear my brother returning from his drive. I will meet him downstairs."

To her surprise, the baroness hugged her. "Thank you for telling me all this," said Patience. "It can't have been easy for you. I won't forget your kindness. I'm sorry if I was a bit prickly at first," she added awkwardly. "I see now that you only meant well. I hope you will come again. I do want to make you known to my sister."

"I will certainly call again," Isabella promised. "As for my brother, I believe he is smitten."

Patience was taken aback. "Oh! Then perhaps you would be good enough to give him a hint, Lady Isabella. I—I am not interested in marriage at present."

"Poor Ivor! He will be very sorry to hear that," Isabella murmured.

As smug as any criminal who has gotten away with his crime, she took her leave, glowing with triumph, and went down to meet her brother.

Lord Milford's tiger hopped down from the groom's seat to open the door of the curricle for Lady Isabella, barely getting back in time before the earl let his horses go.

"Well?" Milford said to his sister. "I suppose you put in a good word for me?"

Isabella hid a smile. "Did you like her, Brother? I couldn't tell. You were so quiet."

"She's very pretty, of course, though, perhaps a bit thin," he said stiffly. "And a baroness in her own right. That is pleasing, too. If she is as rich as Purefoy says, I am willing to overlook her deplorable American accent. Did she speak well of me when you were alone?"

"Speak well of you?" Isabella mocked. "How could she, with her deplorable American accent?"

"Never mind that. What did she say about me?"

"You're in luck, Brother. She likes men who stare at her like perfect imbeciles and never open their mouths."

"That's all right then," he said, pleased. "I shall stay at home tomorrow, for tomorrow her ladyship will return our call. That's the way it's done. I want the house looking its best for her, too. And we'd better get some of that disgusting pink water in, too."

"No!" Isabella said, alarmed. "Tomorrow you must call on Lady Waverly again, Brother, for Mr. Purefoy has promised to call on me. He may have something particular to say! No, Brother, you must go to *her* in Clarges Street."

"It will look very odd if the Earl of Milford calls on the same lady two days together," he protested. "People will talk."

"Indeed, they will, Brother!"

"Oh, yes," he said, after a moment. "I see what you mean. We *want* them to talk. Very well. I shall call on her tomorrow and stare at her without speaking."

Isabella sighed. "No, you must talk to her tomorrow."

He frowned. "But you said she likes men who stare at her."

"You must show her some variety. Oh, for heaven's sake! Take her for a drive in your curricle," Isabella said impatiently. "Must I think of everything?"

"I shall take her for a drive in my curricle," he announced. "That, certainly, will get the *on-dit* going!"

"What an excellent idea, Brother," Isabella said dryly.

Patience confronted Prudence the moment her sister returned to the house that afternoon, before Pru had a chance to remove her cloak and bonnet.

"Where have you been?" she demanded.

Pru paused at the hall mirror, while Lady Jemima slipped quietly upstairs to eavesdrop.

"I was at my French lesson, of course," Pru answered, removing her bonnet and rearranging her crushed curls. "Would you like to hear me conjugate some irregular verbs?"

"No," said Patience, her arms folded. "I would like to know what you were doing in Bond Street yesterday!"

"I was only window shopping! I didn't buy anything!"

"I don't care about that," her sister said impatiently.

"No?" Pru said sweetly. "In that case, I bought a fan."

"I am very worried about you, Pru," Patience began again, trying to sound less accusatory. "I know you have been seeing—seeing *that man*."

"What man?" Pru said, laughing. "Who, Max?"

"No, Mr. Purefoy," said Patience, surprised into speaking the dreaded name. "Who the devil is Max?"

"Max is Mr. Purefoy," Pru told her. "It's short for Maximum. In Latin, that means *the most*. And he is, Patience; he is the most."

Patience's eyes glittered. "Yes, that is what I hear," she said coldly.

Pru sniffed. "Who is your spy? Lady Jemima?"

"No. A—a friend. Someone who is as worried about you as I am. Someone who knows what this man is capable of."

"Well, your spy is misinformed! I was not with Max in Bond Street yesterday. I saw him, but I couldn't catch him."

Patience caught her breath. "Pru, you must promise me never to see him again. He is dangerous, Pru. Dangerous."

Pru rolled her eyes. "You're not going to tell me again how Mr. Purefoy tried to drown you in the ballroom, are you?"

"I'd be wasting my breath," Patience said.

"Yes, you would," Pru said angrily. "I'm glad you know! I'm tired of keeping secrets. For your information, Mr. Purefoy has been everything kind! While you were sick, he devoted himself to me. He showed me all the sights of London. We were together every day. He was most attentive. We did not mean to fall in love. It just happened!"

"Good God! I had no idea! How could you be so foolish?"

"It was delightful," Pru said defiantly. "I was quite sad when he went away to spend Christmas with his uncle. But he is back now, and everything is just as it was. He is as much in love with me as ever."

"This has gone far enough! He is not in love with you, you—you fool."

"He is," Pru insisted. "Yesterday, I met his uncle. I was afraid his grace would not approve of me, but in no time at all I had him eating out of my hand! He is going to give a ball for me."

"That will not be possible, I'm afraid," said Patience.

"As your guardian, I will not permit it. You will have nothing more to do with that family, and they will have nothing more to do with us."

"Max will have something to say about this!" cried Pru.

Patience pressed her lips together. "If you ever go near him again, I will dismiss Lady Jemima, and you will not go to St. James's Palace. I will send you back to Philadelphia under armed guard! You will not see him again."

Her face white as a sheet, her eyes glittering with rage, Pru stared at her.

"Do you think I am bluffing?"

"No," Pru said sullenly. "I don't suppose it would do any good to tell you how much I hate you."

"None whatsoever," Patience said cheerfully. "But, then, I know that this is for your own good. One day you will thank me for it."

"Ha!"

Patience sighed. "Do I have your word?"

Pru glared at her. "I will not seek him out," she said, "but if he—I should say, when—he seeks me out, I will not be rude to him."

"No," Patience agreed. "I will. And since the servants are under strict orders never to admit him to this house, and, since you will not leave this house unless I am with you, I think you will be safe."

Turning, she started up the stairs to the drawing room. Pru followed her, howling indignantly. "You can't hold me a prisoner!"

"Oh, yes, I can," Patience returned, as Lady Jemima, who had been listening on the landing, hurried away from them. "Unlike America, this is *not* a free country. I am your guardian. I can and I will lock you up if that is what it takes to keep you safe from harm."

"But my lessons!" Pru protested. "You can't keep me

from my lessons! You wouldn't do that, surely?" she added, beginning to whine.

Patience assumed a conciliatory tone. "I'll go with you to your lessons, and I will take you home afterward. I might even hire a gig, and drive you around town myself. Would you like that?"

Pru wrinkled her nose. "A gig?"

"Yes, a gig! I drove a gig in Philadelphia, and you never complained."

"I didn't know any better," said Pru. "Nobody drives a gig in London."

"All right, then," Patience said pleasantly. "What do the fashionable people drive here in London?"

"Mr. Purefoy drives a curricle. It's ever so fast! And then you have the high-perch phaeton. I suppose that's very fast, too." Suddenly she scowled. "You can't buy me off with a town car, you know!"

"I'm not trying to buy you off," Patience lied. "I miss driving my little gig. It would be fun. I could take you for a drive in the park every afternoon."

"Five o'clock is the fashionable hour," Pru told her eagerly.

"I'll be sure to avoid it," said Patience, though she instantly regretted her levity. "Only joking! We can go at the fashionable hour. But we mustn't count our high-perch phaetons before they are hatched."

Pru sighed. "Oh, what's the point? You're not really going to do it. You'll just say it's too much money like you always do!"

"Yes, that does sound like me," Patience admitted. "But, look, if you promise me that you won't see this man again, I will promise to do something nice for you. Something you want, even if it is expensive."

"Really? Then I want a high-perch phaeton," said Pru. "I won't give him up for anything less!"

Patience could barely contain her happiness. It could hardly have been true love, she reflected, if Pru was willing to give him up for something so trivial! "You shall have it," she promised. "I'll borrow the money if I have to!"

"I get to choose it!" said Pru.

"Certainly," Patience agreed readily. "I'll begin making inquiries tomorrow."

"Max buys his horses at Tattersall's," said Pru.

"Very well. We'll go tomorrow, if you like."

Pru scoffed at her sister's ignorance. "Sales are on Mondays."

"Then we'll go on Monday," said Patience. "That will give me time to arrange for a letter of credit from the bank. Would you like to go to the bank with me tomorrow?"

"Lord, no," Pru said crossly. "May I go to my room now, Baroness? Or would you like me to scrub the floor on my hands and knees before I go?"

"Don't be silly. Of course you may go to your room."

"Without my supper, I suppose." Pru was on her way out of the room, when Patience suddenly called to her. "Yes, milady?"

Patience grimaced, but did not allow herself to be provoked. "I was just wondering," she said, "if you knew where I might find a monkey?"

Pru lifted her brows. "A monkey?" she repeated doubtfully.

"I know it sounds funny, but one of our uncle's creditors came to see me today—an earl, as a matter of fact. He has an IOU for a monkey. He offered to forgive the debt," she went on, frowning, "but I—I think I'd better pay it. I'm afraid his lordship took a bit of a shine to me, and I don't want there to be any misunderstanding there. When you were out shopping, did you ever happen to see any monkeys for sale?"

Pru hid a smile. She knew, as her sister evidently did not,

that "monkey" was merely slang for five hundred pounds. Wouldn't Patience look a perfect fool if she sent a gentleman a live monkey? And no one, in Pru's view, deserved it more than her officious, interfering, tyrannical sister.

"I would like to settle the debt as soon as possible," said Patience.

"Well, there's a monkey shop in New Oxford Street," said Pru, "but I never went in."

Patience went to the desk to consult her guidebook, murmuring, "New . . . Oxford . . . Street . . ."

Pru burst out laughing.

"There's no such thing as a monkey shop," Patience said, closing the guide to London.

"I'm sorry," said Pru, not sorry at all. "Just tell Briggs you want a monkey, and he'll send out for one."

"Mr. Briggs, you mean," Patience corrected her.

"No, just Briggs," Pru insisted. "He doesn't like it when you call him 'Mister.' It's customary to refer to one's butler by his surname only. He thinks you're making fun of him when you call him Mr. Briggs."

"Oh!" Patience said, horrified.

"You have a lot to learn, don't you?" Pru said. "May I go to my room now, milady?"

Patience sighed. "Yes."

"Shall I ring the bell for Briggs on my way out, milady?"

"Thank you."

Briggs glided into the room a few minutes later. "Yes, my lady?"

"I have a rather strange request, Mr. Briggs," Patience told him. "I need a monkey. Do you think you can get one? I would like to send it to Lord Milford, in Grosvenor Square," she went on, reading the address from his lordship's card and grossly mispronouncing "Grosvenor."

"Pardon me, my lady?" he said, with brows slightly lifted.

"Oh, I'm sorry," Patience said quickly. "What I meant to say was, I would like a monkey, *Briggs,* if you please."

"Very good, my lady," answered Briggs. "How should Cook prepare it?"

"No!" Patience said quickly. "It's not to be cooked, Mr. . . . er . . . Briggs. I want a live monkey."

"Very good, my lady. What sort of monkey?"

Though she had not expected the question, Patience had an easy answer. "The cheapest you can find."

"Very good, my lady. Will there be anything else?"

"No," said Patience. "Thank you, Mr.– " Once again, she caught herself saying the dreaded word. "Thank you, Briggs."

The butler certainly did not smile, but there was a serenity in his eyes as he said, "Very good, my lady."

The monkey was delivered to Lord Milford the following morning in Grosvenor Square, while the earl and his sister were still at breakfast. Milford regarded the tiny capuchin in astonishment as his butler carried it in.

"Compliments of Lady Waverly!" he repeated in disbelief.

Isabella giggled. "You did say her uncle owed you a monkey!"

The monkey bit the butler, thereby securing his release. Quick as lightning, it scampered down the length of the table, stole a peach from the silver epergne, and jumped onto Isabella's shoulder. Isabella stopped laughing and caught her breath as the monkey's tail curled softly around her neck.

"I think he likes me," she whispered, after a moment.

"You're very welcome to him, I'm sure," said her brother. "Most unsanitary! What does Lady Waverly mean? I'm sure I have a sense of humor, but this is gross impertinence!

She must know I meant five hundred pounds! Why should her uncle owe me a monkey-monkey?"

"Don't you see, Ivor?" said Isabella. "Lady Waverly is *flirting* with you!"

"Flirting with me!" he exclaimed, eyeing the capuchin doubtfully. "D-do you think so?"

The clever little creature flung the peach pit at the earl.

"Of course," said Isabella, brushing the monkey's tail away from her face. "What else can it be? She is teasing you, Ivor."

"Teasing me! Well! That's all right then, I suppose," said her brother.

"It means she likes you."

"Yes, thank you, Izzy! I know what it means when a female teases me!" he snapped. "I ain't stupid, you know."

"You will have something to talk about when you call on her," said Isabella. "Besides my headache, I mean. Don't forget to make my excuses to her."

"I won't forget," he said angrily. "Why do you always think I will forget? I was endowed by my Creator with an excellent memory."

After breakfast, Isabella arranged herself in the drawing room where she intended to wait, until the end of time, if necessary, for Mr. Purefoy to call. The monkey sat with her, and she could not have imagined a more prettily behaved creature. Before leaving for Clarges Street, Lord Milford stuck his head in the door.

"Come here," she commanded, frowning. "Your neck cloth wants adjusting."

As Lord Milford approached, the monkey suddenly jumped onto Isabella's shoulder and hissed at him, baring its teeth. The earl, naturally, drew back.

Isabella laughed. "How sweet!"

Milford scowled. "Sweet! He nearly took off my finger."

"I don't think he likes you."

"The feeling is entirely mutual!"

"You frightened him," Isabella said indulgently. "He was protecting me."

Milford grunted. "I won't have to worry about Purefoy taking liberties!"

Later, that night, as she cried herself to sleep, Isabella wished she had taken this little incident more seriously, as the omen it was.

Mr. Purefoy had called very soon after the earl's departure. "What's this?" he'd said, smiling, as he came into the room and saw Isabella's animal companion. The little capuchin sat on her shoulder, playing with her pearl earring. "A rival?"

Isabella had laughed. "A gift to my brother from Lady Waverly," she said. "But I think he likes me best. Don't you, monkey?"

Max raised his brows. His gray eyes flashed with curiosity. "A gift from Lady Waverly, you say? I didn't know your brother was acquainted with the baroness."

"We called on her yesterday. Ivor was quite taken with her, and I think she likes him, too."

Max frowned. "What?"

"I said Ivor was quite taken with her—"

"I heard you," he said curtly. "But why would *you* call on Lady Waverly?" he demanded.

"After what I saw of her sister in Bond Street," Isabella answered, "I was concerned. As I suspected, the baroness knew nothing of her sister's behavior. She was very grateful."

"I'm sure you meant well," he said stiffly, "but you should not have interfered."

"I could not help it," she said, looking down at her hands. "Perhaps I care too much."

His mouth twitched. "And so Ivor was quite taken with her ladyship? Is he that badly dipped?"

Isabella blinked at him. "You imply that my brother is a fortune hunter?"

"What else could he see in Lady Waverly?"

"But the baroness is very beautiful," Isabella protested.

Max gave a short laugh. "Beautiful!"

"She is, perhaps, a little thin," Isabella admitted. "Her sister has the better figure."

"Upon seeing the baroness for the first time, I mistook her for the Medusa!" said Max.

"The Medusa!" Isabella said. "But Lady Waverly and Miss Prudence are twins, you know. Identical twins."

"Who told you that?" he laughed.

"I have seen them with my own eyes," she said. "I don't pretend that my brother is sorry that Lady Waverly is an heiress, but if money were his only consideration, you know he would have married Miss Cruikshanks last year."

"True," Max admitted.

Isabella smiled sadly. "She would have been better off, perhaps, if he had married her. Lord Torcaster mistreats her, from what I hear. It's almost enough to make me glad I have no fortune," she added. "When I marry, at least I shall have the happiness of knowing that I am loved for myself alone."

She looked at him expectantly.

"I simply cannot believe," Max said, "that they are twins! Lady Waverly was ill when I met her, but— Even so! Miss Prudence never said a word. She spoke only of her elder sister. Her much, much elder sister, I thought."

Isabella felt that the interview had gotten off track. "Ouch, monkey!" she said, to draw Max's attention back to herself. "Let go of my earring, monkey!"

Startled by her outburst, the monkey, which had merely been toying with her jewel, suddenly pulled harder, and would not let go.

"Oh, Mr. Purefoy! Help me!" Isabella cried, in real distress.

Max immediately crossed the room. Avoiding the creature's bared teeth, he grasped it by the scruff of its neck, allowing Isabella to pry its tiny fingers from her earring.

"Thank you, sir," she said prettily, when she was free.

Still holding the monkey by the scruff of its neck, Max rang the bell. A footman appeared to take the animal, but the capuchin would not go quietly. Uttering an unearthly howl, he sprayed his captor with urine. Cursing loudly, Max released the creature, which promptly escaped up the drawing room curtains. From this vantage point, it began with great enthusiasm to fling its feces at anyone who ventured near him.

Horrified, Isabella ran from the room, and Mr. Purefoy, without once mentioning marriage, immediately left the house.

Chapter 7

"How do you do, Lord Milford?" Pru said politely as the earl bent over her hand and kissed it fervently. Privately, she thought him rather ridiculous, with his big head, short legs, and pompous manners. His collar points helped to conceal his weak chin. On his feet were tall, high-heeled boots trimmed with silver tassels.

"Lady Waverly," he murmured. "Do forgive me for calling again so soon, but I did want to thank you for the little monkey you sent me. Such an adorable, clever little creature!"

Pru saw no reason to tell the man that her sister had gone to the bank. With a gracious gesture of her hand, she offered him a seat next to her on the sofa. He accepted, parting his coat tails to sit down. "I'm so glad you came, sir," she said, in a soft, breathless voice. "I wasn't sure how you'd take my little joke. Not everyone has a sense of humor."

"I dearly love a laugh," he assured her. "Isabella and I laughed and laughed. What a good joke, we said. She has the headache."

Having seen the lady's *carte de visite,* which Patience had left carelessly on her desk, Pru knew already that Isabella was his lordship's sister. "From laughing?" she asked innocently.

"What?" he said blankly, too slow to catch her meaning.

"Was it the laughing that gave her the headache?"

"Oh, no. She woke up that way."

Pru decided it would be a very good joke—better than the monkey, even—to persuade this thickheaded ass that Patience liked him. Lightly she touched his hand. "Would you care for some tea?" she asked. "I was just about to have some myself."

His lordship returned home in excellent spirits. He had sat with Lady Waverly for twenty minutes, or so he reported to his sister. The baroness had received him very warmly, and he had every reason to believe that her ladyship favored him. Better yet, he had come away with the impression that the rumors of the lady's large fortune might very possibly be true.

"Her ladyship seems most anxious to buy a high-perch phaeton, too," he told Isabella, putting his feet up on the little table in his sister's boudoir. "Frightfully expensive, I warned her. But she said, and I quote: 'Price no object, my lord!' The three sweetest words in the English language, even when spoken within an American twang. I'm to take her to Tattersall's on Friday to look for something suitable. Most anxious she was to have the benefit of my taste and judgment. Really, she implored me with those great green eyes of hers. And, do you know, I believe there is not a speck of hazel in them?"

Isabella, who had been seated at her escritoire writing in her journal when her brother had intruded upon her, said coldly, "*Kindly* get your Hessians off the table!"

"Mind your tone, madam," he warned her.

"I think only of you, Brother," she said, changing her tone.

"I need hardly remind you that we lease this house, and you know how particular Lord Torcaster is of his furnishings."

Reluctantly, he moved his feet.

"Didn't you hear what I said, Izzy? I'm to escort her ladyship to Tattersall's on Friday."

"I did not think ladies were permitted at Tattersall's," she said. "Hallowed ground and all that, what, what?"

"Don't be snide. Ladies are allowed on the premises on Fridays—properly escorted, of course. It is a new rule. They still are not permitted to attend the sale on Monday. Her ladyship has asked me to be her agent, should she see anything she likes."

Isabella frowned. "Why did you never take me to Tattersall's?"

He gaped at her. "My sister! Making a show of herself at Tattersall's? Being ogled by all the men? I should think not. Who would marry you then? I'd never get rid of you."

"What about Lady Waverly? You're taking *her*."

"She is a baroness," he explained loftily. "And very rich, I do believe. Besides, she is American, and we cannot hold them to the same standards."

"Definitely not," Isabella agreed.

"For example," her brother went on, "if an English girl had sent me that monkey, I would not have been amused in the least! Quite the reverse, I should think. But Americans are always amusing, I think."

"I take it you have not yet seen your drawing room," she said dryly.

"There was quite a flurry of activity as I was going past," he said.

"Weren't you curious?"

He shrugged. "I daresay the servants know their business."

"Your amusing little monkey made a terrible mess in there," she informed him.

"Did he? Cheeky little monkey," Milford said indulgently. "Never mind. The servants will clean it all up."

"I should not have cared in the least," she snapped, "except that Mr. Purefoy was here! Just as he was going to propose, your monkey went berserk! He ruined the curtains."

Milford snorted. "Oh, yes, of course! Mr. Purefoy is forever on the verge of proposing to you! How dare you blame my monkey for your failure? Where is the dear little creature now?"

"The dear little creature swallowed my earring," Isabella answered sourly. "The servants are retrieving it now from the creature's bowels."

"I say! Won't that hurt?"

"I'm sure it would," she replied, "if the dear little creature were still alive."

He stared at her, his pale eyes bulging. "You killed monkey?"

"Well, I can't go about with only one earring! Great-aunt Hester's amethysts, too!"

"Bugger Great-aunt Hester! What am I supposed to tell the baroness?"

Isabella shrugged. "Tell her it choked on a peach pit. Tell her it ran away."

He frowned. "She will think I was careless with her gift."

Isabella sighed impatiently. "Then, by all means, place an advertisement in the *Times* for a lost monkey! Offer a reward of a hundred pounds."

"A hundred pounds!"

"Slow-coach! As no one will ever find that particular monkey, you won't be called upon to pay."

"I quite realized that," he lied angrily. "And don't call me slow-coach!"

And, just to show that he was not a slow-coach, when he placed his advertisement, he offered a reward of *five* hundred pounds. A monkey for a monkey, in other words. Lady Waverly, he was sure, would enjoy the joke.

On Friday, he called again in Clarges Street, and this time both sisters were at home. Patience, standing in the hall when Briggs opened the door to the earl, could hardly pretend she was not at home.

"Lord Milford," she said civilly as he lingered over her hand, she thought, a bit too long. "I fear you have come at a bad time. I was just on my way out." Dressed in a bright purple walking habit—one of Pru's castoffs—as well as her bonnet and gloves, she was merely stating the obvious.

"Dear lady! I am not late, am I? This was the appointed time, surely?"

Patience looked at him blankly. "The appointed time?"

"I have come to take you to Tattersall's," he explained. "You are still interested in a high-perch phaeton?"

"There must be some mistake," Patience said firmly. "My sister and I are going to Tattersall's."

"I fear there is only room in my curricle for one passenger," said his lordship.

Pru chose that moment to make her entrance. "Hello!" she said, gliding down the stairs very slowly, giving them time to appreciate the full effect of her gentian blue walking habit trimmed with puce and pea green ribbons.

Patience hardly noticed Pru's latest ensemble. "What have you done to your hair?" she gasped.

Pru shook the cropped curls bunched over her ears. "Yvette cut it for me," she said proudly. "It's the very latest style. Do you like it?"

"No. You look like a cocker spaniel," Patience said

brutally. "Hurry and put on your bonnet. You have kept me waiting long enough."

"Aren't you going to introduce me to your beau?" Pru said coyly.

"My what? Oh, I beg your pardon, sir!" Patience said, flustered as she turned to Lord Milford. "This is my sister, Prudence."

"Charming!" he pronounced, bending over Pru's hand. "If Miss Waverly would like to come with us to Tattersall's, I shall be only too glad to dismiss my groom. You may have his seat, Miss Waverly!"

"Thank you ever so!" said Pru. Dashing to the mirror, she arranged her bonnet over her curls very carefully, tying the silk ribbons under her chin.

"That is very kind of you, my lord," Patience said firmly, "but I have already sent for the carriage."

"But we cannot go alone, Patience," Pru said gaily. "Tattersall's is a private club. We must be escorted by a member, or they will not let us in."

"It would be my honor," Lord Milford said unctuously, "to escort two such lovely ladies. Shall we?"

"Oh, yes!" said Pru, seizing his lordship by the arm, leaving an exasperated Patience to follow them out.

From the groom's seat, Pru could easily hear and participate in the conversation between the driver and his passenger. "Did Your Ladyship happen to see my little advertisement in today's paper?" Lord Milford began as his curricle started down the street at a sedate pace.

"No, sir," said Patience, observing with disapproval that the heads of his lordship's horses were cinched much too high.

Milford looked disappointed. "No? But it was worded so cleverly. 'Reward offered. A monkey for a monkey.' What, what?" He laughed at his own joke, accidentally jobbing the mouth of one of his horses. The beast skittered to one side. In retaliation, Lord Milford angrily yanked the reins, pulling the horse's head back even further. "No, you don't you, you blackguard! Not a bad joke, eh?" he asked, prompting Patience.

"What joke?" Patience asked, her hands itching to snatch the reins from him.

"A monkey for a monkey," he repeated. "You know!"

"Is there something *wrong* with the monkey I gave you?" Patience said, puzzled.

"No, no!" he cried. "It's perfectly fine! In the pink of health! It ran away, of course, but, other than that, there's nothing wrong with it."

Behind them, in the groom's seat, Pru laughed immoderately.

"There!" said Milford. "Your sister thinks it's funny."

"Prudence will laugh at anything," Patience said, annoyed not to be in on the joke, but much too proud to ask to have it explained to her. "I wish you would not pull at their mouths so!" she added. "Their necks are almost bent in half."

"That is the fashion," he informed her. "A high, arched neck has such an elegant appearance, would Your Ladyship not agree?"

"I don't think the horses like it," Patience said coldly.

"They do let their lines collapse if you give them the chance," he admitted. "But I will teach you how to keep them under control."

Patience looked at him incredulously. "You? Teach me? Sir, you are very presumptuous!"

He gaped at her. "But Your Ladyship begged me to teach you how to drive!" he protested.

"I most certainly did not," Patience said angrily. "I'll have you know, sir, that I am an excellent driver! Furthermore, if I were in need of lessons, you would be the last person on earth I'd ever ask to teach me! For heaven's sake, mind where you are going!"

While perfectly sound, her advice, unfortunately, came too late to assist him. Whilst he was staring at her slack-jawed, Milford's team veered to avoid a pedestrian. Before the earl could get them back under control, the side of the curricle had scraped against another curricle.

"Mea culpa, my lord!" cried the other driver, even though the Earl of Milford was clearly at fault. "I beg your pardon! Do please send me a bill for the damage."

"I should think so, indeed," said Lord Milford.

"Nonsense!" said Patience. "Sir, it was entirely your fault!"

The other driver turned his head, and, with a little gasp of dismay, Patience recognized him. It was Sir Charles Stanhope.

Coldly, he touched the brim of his hat. "Lady Waverly is mistaken," he insisted. "The accident was entirely my fault. I do apologize, my lord."

"Don't let it happen again," Milford said coolly. "I daresay a hundred pounds will do the trick. Not here, man!" he added angrily. "Send it to my house."

Chastened, Sir Charles hastily put away the wallet he had reached for too precipitously. "Certainly, my lord. With your lordship's permission, I shall call tomorrow."

"Today would be better," Milford replied, eager to get his hands on the money. "Go now. You will find my sister at home. Leave it with Isabella."

"Yes, my lord!" Sir Charles said easily. "Thank you, my lord!"

Thoroughly disgusted by this demonstration of the in-equities of the class system, Patience had little to say for the rest of the drive to Grosvenor Street.

"You live in Grosvenor Street, my lord, do you not?"

Pru asked him, imperfectly recalling the address on his lordship's card. "Which house is yours?"

"I live in Grosvenor *Square,* Miss Waverly," he corrected her.

"Then you must know Mr. Adams," said Patience, breaking her silence. "He is at Number Nine."

"Mr. Adams?" he sniffed. "I have not had the honor. I know of no one who has."

"Mr. Adams is the American ambassador," Patience said indignantly.

"That certainly does explain it," said his lordship.

"Explain what?" Patience said, her eyes narrowed.

"Why no one ever goes there, of course," he replied.

Patience laughed bitterly. "You English think yourselves so superior! But, don't forget, sir, we have bested you twice in as many wars, and, if you are ever so foolish as to make war with us again, you will be bested a third time."

He smiled tolerantly. "I fear Your Ladyship's speech is riddled with so many errors that it would take a man with more patience than I possess to correct them all."

"Name one," Patience said.

"There is no such word as 'bested,'" he informed her. "The correct word, if, indeed, I understood Your Ladyship's meaning, is 'worsted.'"

"Is that so?" Patience said hotly.

"Furthermore, Your Ladyship would do well to consult a dictionary on the difference between 'will' and 'shall.' I recommended it to my estate agent, and he found it most instructive. Why, he speaks almost like a gentleman now. As for England making war on her colonies, Your Ladyship is mistaken. Quite the reverse, I should say. You Americans keep making war against England. Biting the hand that feeds you, what? And, as for besting us, or, rather, worsting us, twice, nothing could be so absurd. We are better off without America. Better to cut the cancer out than allow it to spread through the body politic. In the end, we judged, quite rightly, that the colonies were not worth the trouble of keeping them."

Patience laughed scornfully. "Is that what you tell yourselves?"

"In the second conflict," he added, "America achieved nothing but a return to the status quo. That, my dear Lady Waverly, hardly can be called a worsting."

"As the victor of two wars, sir, I believe we Americans may assert our superiority over England in whatever terms we choose! Let us say we *bested* you the first time, and *worsted* you the second! Do you like that better?"

"Patience!" Pru cried in horror. "You are being an ugly American. Lord Milford, I do apologize for my sister. She forgets that we are half English."

"No, I don't," Patience retorted. "Our father had the good sense to leave England."

Lord Milford could hardly believe that Lady Waverly was the same sweet creature who had received him with such pleasure a mere two days before! Never in his life had he been so deceived in a woman's character. Probably she is not even rich, he decided. If, at this point, they had not been within sight of Tattersall's in Grosvenor Street, he would have been tempted to make some excuse and take the sisters home. As it was, the street was so crowded it would have been nearly impossible for him to turn the curricle around.

After handing the reins to the attendant, Milford jumped down and helped Prudence from the groom's seat. Not content to wait for him, Patience opened her door and climbed down. "This way, Lady Waverly," he said sharply. "No unescorted female will be permitted inside."

"That's ridiculous," she grumbled.

"Indeed," he said coldly. "If it were up to me, women would not be permitted in Tattersall's at all!"

"If that is how you feel, why did you bring us here?" Patience asked.

Milford made no answer. With his lips pressed tightly together, he led them swiftly into the main room, where sunlight streamed in through the glass roof. Patience bought a sale book from one of the pages hawking them in the sawdust enclosure.

Pru could not be bothered to look in a book. "I like that one!" she cried, pointing.

"That is a saddle horse," his lordship told her knowledgeably. "Do you ride, Miss Waverly?"

"No, my lord," she admitted. "But I have always wanted to learn."

"Nonsense," said Patience, turning the pages of the sale book impatiently. "The only time you ever sat on a horse, you nearly died of fright."

"I was only ten," Pru said angrily. "You didn't much like it either!"

"No," Patience admitted. "I prefer driving."

"And she has the calluses to prove it," Pru sneered. "May we look at the saddle horses, my lord?"

"Of course," he said amiably.

"Oh, I wish I had brought some sugar lumps," Pru murmured.

Patience, her nose in the sale book as she walked after them, inadvertently stepped on a young man's foot. "Excuse me, sir!" she said, red faced with embarrassment. "I'm so sorry! I wasn't watching where I was going."

The young man touched the brim of his hat. "Not at all," he said, at almost the same time. "I saw my chance and I took it."

She blinked at him. "Sir?"

"I saw that you weren't looking where you were going, and I deliberately placed my foot where you were sure to step on it," he explained.

"Why would you do that?" she asked, bewildered.

"To make you look, of course," he replied. "How else could I hope to make your acquaintance?"

He was rather handsome, with a boyish face and angelic blue eyes, but, unfortunately for him, she had always preferred the rugged type. He was just a bit too beautiful for her. "I seem to have become separated from my companions," she murmured.

Instantly, he offered her his arm. "Allow me to escort you to them," he said.

Patience hesitated. "But I don't even know you," she protested.

His blue eyes twinkled. "But I know you," he said. "You are Miss Prudence Waverly."

Patience frowned. "I am Patience Waverly, sir," she corrected him coldly. "How is it you know my sister, sir?"

He gave a start of surprise. "You are Lady Waverly?" he repeated incredulously. "I could have sworn you were Miss Prudence Waverly."

"You did not answer my question, sir. How do you know my sister?"

"I don't really," he conceded. "I have seen her but once, and then only from a considerable distance. Perhaps," he went on tentatively, "Your Ladyship would permit me to introduce myself?"

"I insist that you do!"

"I am Broome. Mr. Frederick Broome, your landlord."

"Oh!" said Patience. "How do you do, Mr. Broome?"

To his surprise, she stuck out her hand, and, to her surprise, he shook it.

"I have written you two letters, sir," she went on rapidly. "As yet, I have received no reply from you."

Freddie lifted his well-groomed brows. "No? How very odd. I instructed my man of business to write to Your Ladyship without delay. In any case, allow me to answer you now. There is no question of Your Ladyship's being responsible for any damage caused by the dastardly Mr. Purefoy."

Patience beamed at him. "At last! Someone who understands that he is dastardly. Everyone else is awed by his wealth and rank. His uncle's wealth and rank, I should say. You are not afraid of him, Mr. Broome?"

"Certainly not. Believe me, I have had words with the man. I shall have more words with him, too, after meeting you. Why, the things he said about you! I am tempted to call him out!"

"He is by no means worth it," she said. "I do not care in the least what he says about me."

"He told me you were the most unattractive female he ever saw in his life."

Patience's face slowly turned crimson. "It is of no consequence," she choked. "I didn't like him either!"

"It is clear that you were more than inconvenienced by the man," Freddie said sympathetically. "In light of your suffering, I am quite prepared to refund the full amount of your rent. I really must speak to my man. You should already be in possession of the funds."

Patience was taken aback. "That is very generous, Mr. Broome," she stammered. "But I'm afraid I cannot accept! We cannot stay in your house rent free."

"I insist," he said. "After your ordeal, I could not possibly charge you rent."

"Could we not split the difference?" said Patience.

His brows rose. "By all means, let us split the difference," he said gamely. "If Your Ladyship would be good enough to tell me how?"

Patience laughed. "I have just agreed to pay half the rent, sir."

"Shall we say a third?"

"Deal," said Patience, sticking out her hand again.

Before the bargain could be sealed, however, Prudence, with Lord Milford in tow, came bounding up to them. "Patience!" she scolded her. "We thought we'd lost you."

Patience quickly introduced their landlord.

"Good heavens!" said Freddie. "There are two of you! Why are there two of you?"

"We are twins, Mr. Broome," Patience told him.

Milford greeted Freddie with stiff civility, returning the latter's bow with a slight nod.

"Come, Lady Waverly," he said. "Mr. Broome is nothing more than the younger son of a baron. He should know better than to put himself forward in this shocking manner."

Patience's eyes flashed with anger. "You forget, sir, that my father was the younger son of a baron! Sir," she went on, turning her back on the earl, "I understand that a lady must have an escort in this place. Would you be good enough to lend me your arm?"

"I'd be delighted to give it to you outright," he replied.

Milford, acutely aware that his rejection was being observed by dozens of interested acquaintances, bowed stiffly. "I am obliged to you, Broome," he said angrily.

"Your servant, Milford," Freddie replied carelessly. With a cheery wave, he led Patience away. "And, so, my lady! What can I show you? A hunter, perhaps? I know just the one."

"You're very kind, sir," she murmured. "I hope I'm not taking you away from your own business."

"Not at all," he assured her. "I was just waiting for my cousin. But he is very late, and not half as pretty as you are. I am completely at your disposal. I have a friend selling a lady's hunter. If you had worn your habit, we could mount you."

"Oh, I'm no rider," she told him quickly. "I want something to drive, Mr. Broome."

He looked down at her in surprise. "What?" he said. "With those soft little hands?"

"I am stronger than I look, sir," Patience told him. "I drove a gig in Philadelphia, and I never met with an accident."

"Oh, you don't want a gig," he said instantly. "A pony phaeton would be better."

"My sister suggested a high-perch phaeton," Patience said doubtfully.

He shook his head. "Let me give you the *verbum sap,* Lady Waverly. A high-perch phaeton is good for two things: breaking your neck, and breaking your horse's neck."

"Oh!" said Patience. "I wish to do neither, Mr. Broome."

"I have a friend selling a pony phaeton." Taking her sale book from her, he flipped through the pages. "Here. Lot twenty-seven. Shall we go and have a look?"

"It seems a good place to start," Patience agreed, allowing him to guide her.

As they walked, Freddie began to extol the virtues of his friend's pony phaeton, but broke off suddenly. "There is my cousin now. Would you mind awfully . . . ? I particularly want to introduce him to you."

"Of course I don't mind," said Patience, as they changed course. "But why should you particularly want me to meet him?"

Freddie had no time to reply, however, for a gentleman came striding up to them at that moment. Without so much as a glance at Patience's face, he said, "I think, sir, that you have kept me waiting long enough!"

Patience stared at him, hardly able to believe her ears. He sounded, but did not look at all English. His hair was very black and curly. His skin was very brown, in sharp contrast to his light gray eyes. His mouth was wide and his nose was hooked. He was remarkably tall, with wide shoulders and very long legs encased in fawn-colored riding breeches.

"You're the one who was late, cuz," said Freddie, not in the least cowed by the larger man. "Did you think you were the only one interested in my grays, sir? I've half sold them already to Sir Charles Stanhope."

"Oh, I wish you wouldn't, Mr. Broome!" Patience said impulsively. "They're much too good for *him*."

At the sound of her voice, the dark gentleman's eyes swung to her face. Patience caught her breath. He was too harsh-featured to be considered handsome, but there was an intensity to him that she found enormously attractive. Her pulse quickened instinctively, and, for all his good looks and charm, Freddie Broome was instantly eclipsed. She was hardly aware of his existence.

The gentleman stared back at her incredulously. *"You!"* he spat, his gray eyes glittering with inexplicable rage and loathing. "How dare you come here? Is there no place on earth where I am safe from you? Would you hound me to my very grave? Damn you! Damn you to hell!"

Chapter 8

Patience stared at him in shock, for a moment quite unable to speak.

"I say, cuz!" Freddie protested. "I think you owe the lady an apology. In fact, I'm quite sure of it."

Max Purefoy shot his cousin a look of furious contempt. "Did you bring her here, Freddie? I am obliged to you, sir."

"This is nothing but the silliest, male prejudice," Patience said, finding her voice. "Why should women not be allowed to look at horses? What are you afraid of? What do you think we're going to do to you? I have as much right to be here as you, sir!"

His eyes narrowed. "Oh, I doubt that very much," he said quietly. "I am a member of the Jockey Club."

"And I am a guest of a member," she told him curtly. "Who is this gentleman, Mr. Broome?" she demanded, giving the word "gentleman" a scathing emphasis.

Freddie's brows rose. "You have met him already, surely!"

"I have never seen him before in my life," Patience declared.

"But I thought everyone knew him," Freddie murmured,

mischief glinting in his angelic eyes. "He's positively ubiquitous."

"I have not been in London very long," said Patience. "I have not had a chance to see all its fixtures. But I'm sure I would have remembered meeting such a rude, disagreeable man."

"I'm afraid the offensive fellow is my cousin."

"Well, your cousin is very rude, Mr. Broome!"

Freddie's mouth quivered with unspent laughter. "He is, isn't he? Cousin, I really must insist that you apologize to Lady Waverly. Her ladyship has done nothing to deserve such treatment."

"Her ladyship!" Max repeated in astonishment, looking again at Patience. "No, it cannot be," he added under his breath, even though he had already noted a few slight differences between this lady and her sister. Patience was thinner, she wore her hair differently, and her purple habit was quite plain, lacking those garish embellishments that all too often marked Prudence's style.

"I don't wonder at your astonishment, cuz," Freddie chirped on. "Anyone who heard that devil, Max Purefoy, describe this delightful lady could not help but be astonished to meet her in the flesh! Why, she is nothing like the Medusa!"

"No, indeed," Max said faintly. His embarrassment was excruciating, much to Freddie's amusement. Abruptly, he offered Patience a bow. "I do beg your pardon, my lady, most humbly."

Patience's cheeks were flushed. "You do not think that women should be permitted in Tattersall's at all, do you? Not even in the company of a member?"

He managed a weak smile. "I am happy to make an exception in your case, my lady."

"I see. In that case, I accept your apology, Mr. . . ? Mr. Broome, is it? Like your cousin?"

"A fine name, is it not?" Freddie said, beaming.

"I see very little family resemblance between you," Patience said curiously.

"How extraordinary," Freddie remarked. "Most people see none. He's a bit of a black sheep, I'm sorry to say."

Max frowned at his cousin. "Freddie, if you should suddenly feel the need to be elsewhere, no one will miss you, I'm sure."

"Lady Waverly will miss me," Freddie protested. "I have promised to help her find a horse."

"I wish you wouldn't," said Max. "The last lady you mounted broke her neck."

"That is a lie! It was only a bad sprain. Anyway, her ladyship don't ride. She wants a pony phaeton."

Max raised his brows. "Do you want a pony phaeton?" he asked, looking at Patience.

"I don't know what I want," she admitted. "I drove a gig in Philadelphia. I am from Philadelphia," she added a little awkwardly.

"Oh, I love the mountains," said Freddie, but the others did not seem to hear him.

"My sister likes the idea of a high-perch phaeton," Patience went on, "but your cousin has advised me against it. Lord Milford drives a curricle."

"If you call that driving!" Freddie snorted, and this time he was rewarded with a quick smile from the lady.

"It was his curricle I admired," said Patience.

"Why don't I take you for a drive in mine?" Freddie suggested. "I'm selling my team, as it happens. They're in the Monday sale. But I can have them put in the traces in a flash. We'll be sailing through Hyde Park before you know it."

"I would like that," said Patience.

"I do hate it when people take me out and try to sell me

things," Max said lightly. "He will do nothing but talk up his horses, all the while hiding their flaws. I'll take the lady."

"Flaws?" said Freddie. "As I recall, they had no flaws when you lost them to me."

"Yes, but you have been driving them these three months," Max replied. "I was going to take them out myself, anyway, to make sure you had not ruined them. Lady Waverly may as well come along."

"Oh," said Patience. "Are you thinking of buying your cousin's horses?"

"He won't pay me what I want," said Freddie.

"What do you want for them?" Patience asked.

"Only a thousand guineas," he answered. "But my cousin swears he will not give more than five hundred."

"A thousand guineas!" cried Patience. "That puts me out of the running, I'm afraid."

"Come for a drive anyway," said Max. "I'd like a woman's opinion on how they handle."

He offered her his arm, and, without hesitation, she took it. Freddie trailed behind them, feeling and looking quite superfluous. Max half turned his head, saying, "Why don't you go ahead and make the arrangements, Freddie?"

Muttering under his breath, Freddie lengthened his stride, disappearing into the crowd.

"Do you always do that?" Patience asked.

"Do what?" he said, glancing down at her.

"Your cousin," she said. "It wasn't very nice of you to cut him out like that. After all, he saw me first. It's not fair play. It's not—what is it you English say? It's not grasshoppers?"

"Cricket," he corrected her, chuckling. "It's not cricket. But, you know I could not have cut him out if you hadn't liked me better."

Quite discomfited, Patience quickly turned her head so that when he looked at her he would see only the crown of her bonnet. Pleased with himself, Max led her swiftly through the room to the outdoors. Patience had the impression that the crowd parted around her companion, but, perhaps, that was just her imagination.

"Are those your cousin's horses?" she asked presently, as she caught sight of Freddie ahead of them in the cobbled yard. He was talking to a groom holding a tall, splendid set of grays.

Max noted the lack of enthusiasm in her tone. "You don't like them?" he said, surprised.

"I know it is the fashion," she said, "but I wish they would not force their heads up like that! I'm sure it must be painful."

"Look again, please. There's no need to force their heads into position. They do it quite naturally. Do you see?"

Patience looked again, and as they drew nearer, she could see that the grays had been blessed with naturally high, arched necks. "Yes, I do see," she said, feeling a little foolish.

"It is necessary only with inferior stock to ratchet up their heads," he went on. "I don't approve of it, but one cannot stop people from trying to achieve the look. Not everyone can afford the very best, after all."

"Is that why your cousin wants so much money for them?" Patience said incredulously. "Because of the way they hold their heads?"

"It is certainly one of the reasons," he replied.

"A handsome pair, are they not?" Freddie hailed them.

"They're beautiful," Patience told him. "I wonder you can bear to sell them."

"My cousin has been appointed to a diplomatic post," Max explained. "He leaves England next Tuesday for the frozen steppes of Russia."

"For the marble steps of St. Petersburg, anyway," Freddie said. "My mother thinks it will be good for me to learn a profession. Poor woman! But don't worry, Lady Waverly. I have not forgotten my tenants. If you should need anything, my cousin is at your disposal."

"There's no need to state the obvious," Max said, looking very warmly at Patience.

"You're very kind," Patience murmured.

"I am not kind at all," Max replied.

Freddie sniffed. "I thought there was no need to state the obvious."

Dismissing the groom with a swift, "Shan't need you," Max opened the door of the curricle and offered Patience his hand.

Taking his hand, she stepped up into the car and took the reins. Max climbed up the other side. The car was so narrow it was almost impossible for two people to sit in it without touching, as she knew all too well from her experience in Lord Milford's curricle. This time, however, she felt not the slightest desire to shrink against the side of the car.

"Do you think you can handle them?" he asked her, arranging the rug over her knees.

"Why not?" she said. "If they have been well trained?"

"I trained them myself."

"Then you should not be afraid."

His mouth twitched. "No, indeed. If Your Ladyship will condescend to drive us *to* the park, I shall endeavor to drive us back."

"Yes, of course," said Patience, suddenly quite flustered.

"Is something wrong?" he inquired presently.

"I can't seem to find the brake," Patience confessed, pink with embarrassment. "Where is it, please?"

"It is beside my right thigh," he answered. "It is always here beside my right thigh. I would be happy to disengage it for you. But, perhaps," he added delicately, "it would be better if I drive, after all."

With one hand, he seized the reins. With the other he disengaged the brake. In one graceful movement, he turned the horses, and the curricle shot off in the direction of Hyde Park so swiftly it took Patience's breath away. She was quite sure that Lord Milford could not have managed such a tight turn. Indeed, she was not entirely sure she would have been able to manage it herself.

"You're not going to get carriage-sick, are you?" he asked sharply, glancing at her white face.

"No, indeed," she said, hastily knotting the ribbons of her bonnet under her chin. "It feels like we're flying."

"That is just how it should be," he said, pleased. "Too fast? Too much wind?"

"Oh, no!" she said breathlessly. "I'm not afraid! You can go even faster if you wish."

He did. The stately mansions in Park Lane passed in a blur. The curricle flew around Hyde Park Corner and sailed through the gates into the park. Avoiding the riders in fashionable Rotten Row, Max turned north onto a small lane leading toward the Serpentine, where he was obliged to slow down. The swans gliding over the water glanced at the intruders, but did not fly away. Patience looked at them with pleasure.

"Swans in January!" she exclaimed.

"Their wings are clipped," he told her.

"Oh!" she said, dismayed. "I wish you had not told me that."

"Are you cold?"

"Not at all," she answered. "Compared to winter in Philadelphia, this is quite temperate. And the sun is shining." She had lowered her veil over the brim of her bonnet as he was driving, but now she folded it back, and lifted her face to the sun.

"These horses have not had their wings clipped!" she said.

"No, indeed. Tell the truth! You've never driven before, have you?"

Patience flushed hotly. "I have so! I have been driving since I was fourteen, sir, and I am now twenty."

He raised his brows. "And yet, you could not find the brake!"

"In America, sir, the brake is on the left, not the right," she told him.

"I see!" he said, laughing.

"No, really, it is," she insisted.

"Why?"

"I don't know," she said crossly. "I am not a carriage maker. I can tell you don't believe me, but it's perfectly true!"

"I shall, of course, take your word for it," he said gravely.

"You shall, or you will?" she muttered.

"I beg your pardon," he said. "I mean, of course, that I *will*. I *will* take your word for it, with the greatest of pleasure. I meant no offense."

"No offense was taken, Mr. Broome," she said, shrugging. "I'm afraid I can't tell a glimmer of difference between 'shall' and 'will.' In America, we're not so fussy!"

"I don't mean to be fussy," he apologized. "In my youth, I had a tutor who was a bit of a stickler. 'Shall' may be used to indicate some sort of obligation, a lack of choice, or a fait accompli. Will is used to indicate desire. Will you marry me?"

Her head turned swiftly, and she looked at him. "I beg your pardon?"

"I'm giving you an example," he explained. "It is the example my tutor gave. The gentleman says, 'Will you marry me?' He never says 'Shall you marry me?' The lady may answer 'I will,' or 'I shall,' according to her feelings. Both are perfectly acceptable."

"And if the answer is no? Does the lady say 'I shall not' or 'I will not'?"

"I never heard of such a thing," he said. "The lady always answers in the affirmative."

"What?" she said, laughing.

"I know of few men brave enough to propose to a lady, fewer still who would propose when the lady's answer is in doubt. If there is the least chance the lady might refuse, we men are base cowards, I fear."

"But American men are very different," said Patience. "They are not afraid, certainly, of the women they hope to marry."

Max frowned. "But you are not married."

"No," she said.

"Did no one in Philadelphia have the courage to ask you?"

"Yes," she answered, after a moment. "He was from Boston, however."

"Was he ten feet tall?"

Patience laughed. "I had no opportunity to measure him."

He glanced at her briefly. "Did you not? I rather think you measured me with a glance. But, perhaps, I flatter myself?"

"Perhaps you do," she said primly.

"And what did you tell the bold fellow from Boston? 'Shall not' or 'will not'?"

"In America, we simply say yes or no."

"Yes or no? How does the poor fellow know which it is?"

Patience laughed. "I told him no."

"How cruel! And yet, I can't help but think he deserved it."

"If anything, I was not cruel enough," said Patience. "The very next day, he proposed to my sister! She has never quite forgiven me, I don't think."

"Would she have accepted him if he had asked her first?"

"I hope not," said Patience. "He was a fortune hunter, and he had a mustache."

He chuckled. "Which was the more objectionable?"

"It is difficult to say," she answered. "It was quite a vile combination."

"Indeed," he said gravely. "We have our share of fortune hunters, of course, but none, I think, wearing mustaches."

"Are you a fortune hunter, Mr. Broome?" she asked.

He raised his brows. "If I were, do you think I would admit it?"

"No, but I thought, perhaps, I might catch you off guard. The look on your face then might tell me all I need to know."

He smiled slowly. "How did you get on?"

"Not very well, I'm afraid," she admitted. "Your face told me nothing. If you are a fortune hunter," she went on, "I think it only fair to tell you that, in spite of what you may have heard, I am *not* in possession of a great fortune, and neither is my sister. We do not come into our inheritance until we are thirty."

"But in ten years you will be rich?"

"Yes. Very."

"I suppose it is possible that I shall be quite penniless in ten years," he said. "I'll be only too happy to marry you then, if you would be good enough to wait."

"I don't think so," she said, trying not to laugh. "Thank you all the same."

"Yes or no would have sufficed," he rebuked her, and then she did laugh.

"If only you had laughed like that when first we met," he said sadly.

"What do you mean?" she said, surprised. "How could I laugh when you were cursing me?"

"I am very sorry for that," he said quietly. "Sorrier than

I can say. I think it would have been quite something to have known you."

"But, surely," she said, "we will see each other again. You are not going to Russia with your cousin?"

"I might do that," he said. "I leave the matter in your hands."

"In my hands?" she repeated, bewildered. "I can't tell you where to go."

"You will," he said grimly.

"I don't understand you, sir," she said.

"We have met before," he said. "I am glad you do not remember. You will remember soon enough and then it will all be over."

She laughed faintly. "You are very cryptic, sir. I am certain we have never met before."

"Are you?"

"Quite sure."

"Not even in a dream?"

"Oh, I don't have those sorts of dreams," she said quickly.

He raised his brows. "What sort of dreams?"

"Never mind," she said primly. "Isn't it time we went back?"

"Not yet," he said. "Let us go a little farther."

Patience suddenly felt nervous. He had driven her, she realized suddenly, to quite a secluded area of the park. "I would like to go back now, sir," she said quietly.

"First I must speak to you," he said. "It's about Purefoy."

Startled, she swung her eyes up to his face. "What? I do not wish to speak of him! The mere mention of his name is enough to spoil the beauty of the day. Please take me back."

"I shall . . . presently. You have already heard from my cousin that I—that he has said some things not very flattering to your person. His behavior, certainly, has been inexcusable. But, perhaps, he is not as bad as you think. Perhaps, given a chance, he may yet redeem himself."

"You are his advocate!" she accused him. "His friend?"

Max shook his head. "His friend? No. But I am obliged to see something of him. I cannot escape the acquaintance, as they say."

"I am sorry for you. You say he is not as bad as I think. Let me tell you, he is worse than you could ever imagine. There is not a shred of decency about his character. He is a thorough villain. An ugly customer, as we say in America!"

"Come now," Max said mildly. "I know something of his wild parties, Lady Waverly. I know how you came to meet him. There is no excuse, of course, for what he did. But it was his birth-night and he'd had rather a lot to drink."

"You say there is no excuse for his behavior, and then you try to excuse it!"

"I know he is ashamed of himself. He has been a different man since that night. You would not recognize him if you saw him again. You might—you might even like him a little."

"You are mistaken, Mr. Broome! His is one face that is burned—burned—into my memory. As for shame, he has none. I count myself quite fortunate that he merely tried to *drown* me! I understand that his other victims have not been so lucky!"

Considerably shocked, Max brought the curricle to a complete stop. "Other victims!" he repeated. "What can Your Ladyship possibly mean?"

Patience shook her head. "Please! Let us not discuss the matter further. You know what he has done to me, but I am not at liberty to tell you anything more about his crimes against the less fortunate members of my sex."

"What crimes?" he demanded.

"Sir! I beg of you—!"

"You *shall* tell me," he said roughly. "If he is guilty of some crime, I should like to know about it."

She glanced up at him. "Why? When nothing can be done to stop him! You know, I suppose, that he is the nephew of a duke. Apparently, that counts for a great deal in these parts. In America," she added with a sneer, "a man would be ashamed to be somebody's nephew."

"For your information, I am uniquely qualified to stop Purefoy—if indeed he must be stopped."

"He must be stopped! But what makes you so uniquely qualified?" she asked curiously.

"I have no fear of him," said Max. "He fears me."

She stared at him, her cheeks quite pink. "D-does he?" she stammered, shivering.

"Oh, yes. But I can't do anything unless you tell me what he's done."

"Then you will punish him?"

"If he is guilty, he will be punished, certainly. And I will not be merciful."

Patience bit her lip, hesitating. "It means betraying a confidence."

"Think of the greater good," he encouraged her. "Really, you can trust me. Nothing you say will ever be repeated."

"I believe I can trust you," she said. "It is an ugly tale."

"I gathered as much. Go on."

"It is my understanding that he began his sordid career by forcing himself upon innocent servant girls."

"That is a damnable lie!" he roared.

"It is quite true," said Patience. "The lady who told me knew everything about it. According to her, he has ruined scores of young women—too many to count. No woman is safe from him. And if he could not seduce his victim, he did not scruple to ravish her."

Max was gray around the mouth. "Who told you this?"

"One of his victims. I won't give you her name, so don't ask!"

"A servant?" he said angrily.

"What difference would that make?" she demanded. "You would not take the word of a mere servant, I suppose?"

"I am not inclined to take anyone's word for it!" he said. "Perhaps, in your hatred for the man, in your thirst for revenge, you have invented this sordid history?"

"You accuse me of lying, sir?" she gasped. "I fear I lack the imagination, having never been exposed to such cruelty! I could not have conceived of such iniquity. I had supposed him no worse than the average corrupt European, content to pay for his pleasures."

"You have a low opinion of the species, I see!"

"My grandfather warned me about the dangers of the fleshpots of Europe."

"Indeed," he drawled. "My grandfather warned me about the dangers of tooth decay."

"Would you be more inclined to believe me if I told you my informant was a lady? The sister of a nobleman, in fact. She had no reason to lie to me, and every reason to keep it a secret."

"Then why didn't she?" he retorted. "And what secret am I to believe she is keeping? What does she say the fell fiend did to her?"

"He assaulted her in her carriage in broad daylight. He simply jumped in! Her maid even beat him with an umbrella but nothing could stop him from slaking his lust. Any other man would be hanged. But because his uncle is a duke, nothing can be done about it. You do not believe me," she added unhappily, after a short silence. "You think I am making it up."

"No," he said slowly. "The brave little maid with her umbrella lends your story just that touch of authenticity it was lacking."

Patience felt that he was mocking her. "I'm sorry I told you as much as I did, if you're not going to do anything about it," she said primly.

"Oh, but I shall do something about it," he told her softly. She looked at him swiftly. His gray eyes were hooded but the hardness of his mouth made her shiver. "What are you going to do?"

The hard mouth twisted into a smile. "I rather think a swift and terrible justice is in order, don't you?"

Patience impulsively touched his arm. "You cannot kill him!" she protested. "His uncle is a rich and powerful man. Would you not hang for it?"

He covered her hand with his own. "No harm will come to *me,* I do assure you."

Patience had no doubt that Mr. Broome would prove more than equal to the nefarious Mr. Purefoy. She felt as though a terrible weight had been lifted from her shoulders. She could almost pity Mr. Purefoy.

Reluctantly, she withdrew her hand. "If we don't return soon, Mr. Broome, your cousin will think we've made off with his horses."

"Nonsense," he said lightly. "Freddie will think I am making love to you, that's all."

"Now why would he think that?"

"Having met you, how could he think otherwise?"

Quite pleased with his answer, Patience lifted her face expectantly, but he made no attempt to kiss her. Instead, he turned the curricle around. More than disappointed by the snub, she was puzzled. Clearly, he liked her, and she certainly had made no attempt to hide her own attraction. And yet he did not kiss her. In her experience, American men were not so reticent.

Perhaps, she thought, European men are not as suave as they would like us to believe.

"Would you care to take the reins, Lady Waverly?" he asked, laying them across his wrist.

"Thank you," she murmured. Taking the reins from him, she clicked her tongue at the grays. The sheer power of their first plunge caught her off guard, and she was lifted out of the seat. Max instinctively caught her waist in his hands; had he not, she very well might have been plucked bodily from the car.

"Thank you," she said again, resuming her seat, her cheeks pink with embarrassment.

There was little conversation on the way back, Patience being obliged to concentrate on her driving. "Don't be nervous," he said, untangling the reins for her for the second time. "You're doing fine. You have a nice, light touch."

She glanced at him. "I feel so clumsy," she confessed.

"Just relax. Horses can sense when you are anxious. It makes them anxious as well. If anything should happen—"

She turned round eyes to him. "Why?" she wanted to know. "What's going to happen?"

"Just don't panic, if anything should happen. That is all I meant. *They* will know what to do, even if *you* don't."

"Thank you for the vote of confidence!"

"You're doing quite well, really."

"For a woman, you mean?"

"You are doing well for a *person,* shall we say. Exceptionally well for a person who has never had more than one in hand before."

Patience sighed. "Is it so obvious?"

"Yes."

She laughed ruefully, and accidentally jogged the reins, inadvertently setting the horses to a faster pace. "They're so sensitive," she complained, getting them under control. "I daren't breathe, for fear they will take off. It's like trying to rein in a pair of lightning bolts! My horse in Philadelphia had a nice, hard mouth. You practically had to beat him to get him going. Perhaps you are thinking I don't deserve the honor of driving such splendid creatures?"

"Not at all. I was thinking you are much too good for a gig."

Patience felt absurdly pleased. It was almost as good as a kiss, that compliment. Almost.

"Why not let them go?" he said lazily. "It's what they want. It's what you want, too, I suspect. Give them a touch of the whip."

Making sure she was firmly in her seat, Patience did so eagerly, and the curricle shot off like a rocket. Max's hat set off in the opposite direction.

"Too much wind, Mr. Broome?" she called out, glancing at him.

"Mind the tree!" he cried, perhaps regretting giving her the reins.

"Don't be silly," she shouted back. "There aren't any trees in the middle of the road!"

In the next instant, the horses had carried the curricle off the road, however, and Patience was very much obliged to mind the tree. Remembering his advice, she did not panic. Her trust in him was entirely vindicated when, at the last possible second, the horses turned aside as one, avoiding the tree, and carrying the curricle back onto the road as smoothly and neatly as anyone could wish.

To her chagrin, she discovered that hers were not the only hands on the reins. "You helped me," she complained.

His breath was coming in short gasps. "You're welcome," he said, reaching for the brake.

"You've lost your hat," she observed, frowning at him. "Shouldn't we go back for it?"

"Never mind my hat," he said angrily. "You just took ten years off my life!"

"I think I must have overcorrected at the bend," she mused.

"You certainly did! You're lucky the horses didn't go off in two different directions. The tree would have split us down the middle!"

"Oh, I knew they wouldn't do that," she said, laughing. "They're a team, and, besides, you trained them, didn't you?"

He stared at her. "Are you mad? We might have been killed!"

"Oh, don't be such a baby!" she said impatiently. "You were never in any danger! I had the situation well in hand. You said not to panic, that they would know what to do. Well, I didn't panic, and they *did* know what to do. So it was just as you said, wasn't it?"

Max stared at her in amazement. "You, Lady Waverly, are a daredevil!"

"What are you complaining about?" she said, annoyed. "You're still alive, aren't you? Your heart is beating. Your lungs are full of air. What more do you want?"

"Quite a bit, as it happens," he said, and bringing his mouth down on hers quite roughly, he kissed her. He kissed her until he was out of breath. "It has always been my ambition to die in the arms of a beautiful woman," he murmured. Crushing her against him, he kissed her again.

When he released her, her green eyes were stormy. "You certainly took your time!" she said. "Are you always so slow off the mark?"

Max raised his brows. "Actually, I'm quite fast for an Englishman," he told her, "but then I am half Italian. In England, we do not kiss, as a rule, before the engagement."

"What?" she said incredulously. How can you possibly know if you want to marry someone if you haven't kissed him?"

"An excellent question," he conceded. "In America, you kiss *before* the fact, then?"

"I think it best, don't you? Why, it's just like driving these horses before you decide whether or not to buy them."

"You have shocked me, Lady Waverly," he said, only half joking, "and I do not shock easily, being the average corrupt European male. Are all American girls as fast as you?"

Patience laughed. "Actually, I'm quite slow for an American. But then I am half English," she added, with a wicked twinkle in her green eyes.

Chapter 9

When they returned to the yard at Tattersall's some thirty minutes later, two people were waiting with Freddie. Because of the crowd, Patience was obliged to slow the grays almost to a crawl. Catching sight of Pru, Patience waved. "There is my sister," she said, pointing out the lively young lady in pea green and gentian blue to Max. "And that is Lord Milford with her. I'm afraid I've kept them waiting. They will be angry with me, and I don't blame them."

"Are you sorry?" he asked quietly.

"No!" she answered firmly.

Max managed a weak smile. He had hoped to continue the deception a bit longer, but, it seemed, fate had other plans.

And so did Prudence.

"Max!" she shrieked, recognizing her sister's companion as the curricle rolled toward them. "Over here, Max! Yoo-hoo!"

Patience frowned. "Is my sister addressing *you*, sir?" she asked, puzzled.

"With great enthusiasm."

She stared up at him. "Do you know my sister? Is your— Is *Max* your Christian name?"

Lifting his hand, he beckoned to his cousin's groom. "I was christened Maximilian," he said. "In Italian: Massimiliano."

"And . . . how do you know my sister?" she asked, with an edge of suspicion to her voice. "Why did you not happen to mention that you knew her?"

The groom, a wizened little man with a leathery mask for a face, had made his way to them. "Take your seat, Hawkins," Max commanded him, "and look to the lady."

"Yes, sir!" The groom climbed nimbly onto the folding seat behind the car.

At the same time, Max turned the handle on the outside of the door and jumped out.

"Where are you going?" Patience cried, reining the grays to a stop.

Carefully, he closed the door. "I am very sorry," he said softly, looking at her with one gloved hand on the door. "You will never forgive me, I know. But I am sorry."

"Forgive you for what?" she asked, bewildered. "Mr. Broome!"

"Try not to hate me too much," he said. Turning, he walked away, and again she noticed how quick the people were to get out of his way. It was not her imagination. There could be no doubt that Mr. Broome was an important man. But where was he going?

Not content to wait for her sister to come to her, Pru was pushing her way through the crowd, followed by a reluctant Lord Milford.

"Patience! Where is Max?" Pru said, as she looked for him in vain. "He was here! I saw him! What did you do with him? What did you say to him?"

"Get in," Patience said, vexed. "Stop making a spectacle of yourself."

Pru bristled, but evidently thought better of making a verbal protest. Instead, she opened the door of the curricle, kicked down the steps, and climbed up. "He was here," she exclaimed happily. "I can still smell his scent. He smells like the cedars of Lebanon, don't you think?"

"How would you know how he smells?" Patience demanded.

"How do you think I know?" Pru said smugly. "I've smelled him, of course."

"Pru! How do you know Mr. Broome?"

"Mr. Broome? Why, you were there when I met him," Pru answered carelessly. "Are you going to buy his curricle? Lord Milford says they are not half as good as his."

"Does he?" Patience said curtly. "I'm not talking about Mr. Frederick Broome. It is his cousin I mean."

"But I don't know Mr. Broome's cousin," Pru said petulantly.

"Of course you do. You were shouting his Christian name just now."

Pru stared at her. "Max Purefoy is Mr. Broome's cousin? Good Lord! I had no idea. I wish now I had been nicer to him. But how was I to know? Lord Milford told us he was nothing more than the younger son of a baron! Oh, I do wish there were a pocket edition of *DeBrett's Guide to the Peerage*! Heavens, Patience! Are you all right?"

Patience was quite pale. Her hands shook violently on the reins. "Thank you," she said, just managing to choke out the words. "I'm quite all right. Do you mean to say that *that* was Mr. Purefoy?" she went on, color flooding back into her face.

"Yes. Does this mean that you have changed your mind about him?" Pru said eagerly. "I knew you would. I knew if you gave him a chance you would find him just as charming as I do. Where did he vanish to? Didn't he see me?"

"He told me his name was Broome," Patience fumed.

"On top of everything else, he is a liar, too! No, Prudence! I'm afraid I do not find him charming. Quite the reverse!"

"Oh, you are impossible!" Pru complained angrily. "I see now that you were rude to him, and that is why he left without speaking to me. Did you— *Patience,* did you *dare* tell him to stay away from me?"

Patience laughed shortly. "If he ever comes near you again, or me, I will shoot him with my pistol!"

Pru gasped. "Patience, if you shoot Max, I will never speak to you again!"

"So be it," Patience said grimly, and the vehicle resumed its slow crawl back to its owner.

"I expect my cousin was called away suddenly," Mr. Frederick Broome began cheerfully, as he came forward to open the door for Patience.

Patience refused to take his hand as she stepped down. Freddie had the grace to look ashamed. "Ah," he said. "All has been revealed, I see."

"What a clever pair of jokers you are," Patience said softly. "You and your cousin—if indeed that lying coward is your cousin."

"Well, of course he is," Freddie said sheepishly. "What do you take me for?"

"Do you really want me to answer that, Mr. Broome?"

Freddie jammed his hands in his pockets and looked down at his feet. "I suppose not," he mumbled.

"I will tell you anyway," said Patience. "You are not worthy of the name Broome. Unlike yourself, a broom is an honest, useful tool. You, sir, are merely a tool. 'Tool' should be your name."

"I say!" he protested weakly. "That's a bit harsh."

"You must forgive my sister," Pru said, as Lord Milford appeared to help her down from the curricle. "She belongs in a cage."

"Lord Milford, would you be good enough to take us home now?"

He bowed. "Certainly, my lady," he said. "And if Your Ladyship is interested in making a purchase, I should be delighted to act as your agent in the Monday sale."

"That will not be necessary," Patience said coldly. "There is nothing here I want."

"I knew you wouldn't buy anything," Prudence grumbled. "I knew you would not keep your word."

Lord Milford, enjoying the attention he was receiving from his acquaintances as he escorted the American beauties to his own curricle, said soothingly, "Never mind, Miss Prudence. We did not find what we were looking for today, but we shall come again. We must not settle for anything less than perfection. I shall help you."

On the way home, Patience insisted on taking her turn in the groom's seat. As a Peer of the Realm, Milford did not like it—it could not possibly be correct to put a suo jure baroness in the back seat while her younger sister sat in the front—but as a man he was not sorry to have Prudence seated next to him. Although titled and beautiful to behold, the baroness was a prickly, opinionated female. Pru was more agreeable. What she lacked in rank, she made up for in warmth. And if the sisters were equal in wealth, as rumored, Lord Milford decided Miss Prudence would make an admirable second choice, should he not succeed with her elder sister.

It was now quite necessary for him to establish, beyond all doubt, that they were rich.

While his lordship was thus engaged, his sister sat home all day, but no one came to see her except for Sir Charles Stanhope, and Isabella was not as yet so hopeless as to be at home to *him*. Upon returning to Grosvenor Square that afternoon, Milford found her sitting exactly where he had left her that morning.

"You are very dull today," he observed, as he watched her prepare the tea.

"Thank you, Ivor."

"You should have come to Tattersall's with us," he told her as she poured out his tea. "Though I do not know where I could have put you, for Miss Waverly had the groom's seat. We might have gone in the carriage, I suppose, but then Lady Waverly would not have been able to admire my driving skills."

"Respectable females do not frequent such places," Isabella said firmly. "I know not why the rules were changed to allow it, but I am persuaded they will be changed back, as soon as this madness for feminine equality passes. I blame Lady Viola Devize. Why must the Jockey Club change its rules to accommodate *her*? She will want them to allow female *members* next! I loathe all females of that kind. Duke's daughter she may be, but she is not good ton."

"You are in quite a pet," he said, frowning. He himself was quite pleased with the world and everything in it, and he could not help feeling that Isabella was attempting to spoil his happiness. "Purefoy was at Tattersall's today, and, as far as I could tell, he made no objection to women being there."

Isabella's mouth fell open. "You saw Mr. Purefoy?" she said sharply.

"I did not see him, no," her brother admitted. "That is, I think I glimpsed him in the crowd, but he was walking away and I could not be sure. My fair companions saw him, however. In fact, he took Lady Waverly for a drive in Freddie Broome's curricle. His team is not half as good as mine, and so I told him, but he only smiled back at me in the most impudent manner. Of course, he won them at cards from Purefoy. The younger son of a baron has no business with such an equipage. A gig would be quite good enough for *him*."

"*She* went for a drive with my Mr. Purefoy?" Isabella said, almost with savagery. "Lady Waverly? Why, that sly, deceitful little slut! You won't credit it, but that hussy had me persuaded that she loathed Mr. Purefoy! And all the time, she was scheming to catch him herself. No wonder she is so desperate to keep him from her sister!" Her thin lips curled in a sneer and her eyes hardened to cold, blue diamonds. "I suppose they fought for his attention like common streetwalkers?"

"No, indeed," said her brother. "I never left Miss Prudence's side. Lady Waverly went off with Freddie Broome, which I did not like, but she is headstrong and nothing would stop her. When we looked for her again, Mr. Broome told us she had gone off to the park with Purefoy. They are cousins, you know, though I'd be ashamed of my aunt if she married so far beneath her as Lady Helen did. I wonder Purefoy acknowledges the connection."

Isabella was not listening. She could not believe how easily Lady Waverly had beguiled her. What an actress! "She is cleverer than I thought," she murmured to herself. "I thought Miss Prudence Waverly was my competition, but here is a more serious threat. I have seen the true face of my enemy. I only hope it is not too late. Oh, why did you let Lady Waverly go off with Freddie Broome?" she burst out in frustration, glaring at her brother. "Was *she* not your object? Why did you relinquish her?"

He frowned. "If you must know, I did not find her ladyship quite as agreeable today as I did when I saw her last. She has a rebellious nature, which, I can only suppose, she hid from me at first. I was glad that she sat in the groom's seat on the drive back. Miss Prudence is a far more pleasant companion. *She* does not presume to advise me on my driving."

"Artful trollop! Do you not see what is happening? The baroness has set her cap for Mr. Purefoy and she seeks to fob you off on her younger sister! Why else would she give up her seat in the curricle to her inferior."

"They are sisters," he protested. "Twins! They would share equally in life's pleasures. It was Miss Prudence's turn to sit beside me."

Isabella shook her head. "You were cozened, Brother."

His face was red. "Was that not nobly done? I did think it strange that she would give up her rightful place," he said thoughtfully. "You would not have done so, no matter what affection you felt for your sister."

"No, indeed," said Isabella.

"And I do not think there is much affection between them at all!" he said. "They argue so violently. I think you are right, Sister! She did try to fob me off! Well, I shan't be fobbed off! Not by her or anyone else. I shall marry her, whether she likes it or no!"

"Oh, yes?" she said doubtfully. "And what of Mr. Purefoy?"

Milford scoffed. "What of him? I am sure he did not like her."

Her eyes lit up. "Why do you say that?" she said eagerly.

"He left her so abruptly," Milford answered. "He could not be bothered even to return her to her friends. He left her with a groom and simply vanished."

Isabella actually smiled. "She must have offended him."

He snorted. "How could she not with that vulgar American accent? I daresay she presumed to tell him how to drive his cattle! Their heads are too high for her ladyship, I suppose. He must have been very angry indeed to abandon her like that."

"Serves her right! Of all things, I hate deceit." Isabella

gave a deep sigh of contentment. "I believe I shall call upon her ladyship tomorrow, and triumph over her in person. More tea, Brother?"

Lord Milford accepted. "What have you ordered for my dinner?" he asked presently. "Mutton, I suppose. Could we not have lamb now and again?"

"You are dining at your club tonight," Isabella informed him.

"Am I?" he said, pleased. "Who invited me?"

"You must dine at White's this evening," she told him patiently. "Or Brooks's. Wherever Mr. Purefoy dines. Then you may gently inquire in a brotherly fashion after his intentions toward me. He did promise to call on me. I do not count as a visit the day the monkey chased him out. Why, he was not here above a minute. You must remind him to keep his promise."

Milford liked dining out, but he could ill afford to pay for the privilege. And, unlike grocers' bills, one's account at one's club must be kept in good order. "How do you know Purefoy ain't dining at Sunderland House with his uncle?" he said belligerently.

"From what I hear, his grace is on a very restricted diet," Isabella replied. "Barley water and pudding."

Milford shuddered. "I'd rather be dead."

"The lady who marries Mr. Purefoy will not have to wait long to be a duchess, perhaps!" said Isabella. "But you may depend on it. Mr. Purefoy will be dining out. He likes his red meat and his claret. Dine with him tonight and I shall order you a lamb for tomorrow. I shall make the mint sauce myself."

Lord Milford went first to White's, where he was detained for several minutes by Lord Torcaster, who had seen him at Tattersall's with Lady Waverly and her sister. In the previous season, Torcaster had been on the verge of bankruptcy, but he had restored his family to preeminence by marrying Miss Cruikshanks, the daughter of a wealthy merchant.

"I wonder you do not bring your American friends to dine with us at White's," Lord Torcaster drawled as he met Milford on the stairs.

Milford continued on to the dining room. "You know as well as I do, my lord, that females are not allowed in White's."

"I would be tempted to make an exception for two such attractive young ladies," Torcaster leered. He belonged to the older generation, and his ivory teeth looked very yellow against his powdered skin and wig. "Heiresses, too, from what I hear, and one an hereditary baroness!"

Milford was not deceived by his lordship's derisive tone. Lady Torcaster was cross-eyed and dull as a cow. Torcaster, no doubt, wished that he could have held on for another year.

"Who told you they were heiresses?" he asked. "Was it Purefoy?"

"Purefoy? No, it was my barrister. The man has a nose for money. A million pounds between them, by God!"

Milford frowned. "I heard it was dollars."

"Dollars, pounds," snarled Torcaster. "It is more than I got for Cruikshanks's fat daughter."

Milford smiled tranquilly. "How is dear Lady Torcaster? Breeding, I hope?"

Torcaster flushed under his maquillage. "Fortunately, my last countess furnished me with both an heir and a spare. I hear Purefoy deprived you of the baroness today. It will not be long, I trow, before some handsome young buck steals the other one, too!"

"What has Purefoy to say to anything?" Milford returned, considerably nettled. "I have already fixed my interest with Lady Waverly."

"I rather doubt it, my boy," said Torcaster.

Milford stiffened. "You doubt my word, my lord?"

Torcaster laughed. "Perhaps it is the lady whom I doubt."

"I tell you, I do mean to marry her," Milford said hotly.

Torcaster lifted his painted brows. "Mean to, sir? I meant to read the Bible cover to cover. However, I did not. Anyone can mean to marry anyone."

"I shall marry her," Milford declared.

"Ah! Yes, of course. But will *she* marry *you*?"

"Of course."

"You speak with such certainty!" Torcaster marveled. "Shall we open the betting book?"

Milford hesitated.

"I thought not," Torcaster said smugly.

By this time, the conversation had attracted some notice from the other gentlemen in the room. Milford heard derisive laughter, murmurs of ridicule.

"*I* am as good as engaged to Lady Waverly," he announced, red with anger. "I will bet you what you like, my lord! I am not afraid."

Torcaster snapped his fingers for the betting book. "Shall we say ten thousand pounds, my lord?"

Milford paled, but said resolutely, "Certainly."

The bet was duly entered into the book. Torcaster smiled broadly. "My Lord Banville," he called across the room to a handsome young man. Lord Banville had not been paying attention to the fracas between the Earl of Torcaster and the Earl of Milford, but he turned his beautifully barbered head at the sound of his name.

"My lord?" he said languidly.

"Did not Lord Waverly die owing you a little money?" Torcaster asked, trying to pull an innocent face and managing a droll one.

The viscount shrugged. "A mere trifle. But two or three thousand. Why?"

"You should call on the new baroness, sir. Forgive the debt, and see what happens."

"That would be poaching, sir!" Milford protested, outraged.

Torcaster only laughed. "Lord Milford forgave a debt of a mere five hundred pounds, and he has been living in the lady's pocket ever since."

"Let him live there, then," Lord Banville said indifferently.

"To fortune, my lord, I know you are perfectly indifferent," said Torcaster. "But the lady is uncommonly beautiful, my lord, and she has a twin sister. And then, of course, there is Wildings. Twenty-six thousand acres of unspoiled wilderness. Are you a sportsman, my lord?"

"Wildings, did you say?" Lord Banville murmured.

"Now just a minute," Milford protested. "I saw the lady first! Forgiving the debt was my idea!"

Banville's lip curled. "What would *you* do with twenty-six thousand acres of prime wilderness?" he said scornfully. "You must be the worst shot in the kingdom."

"But I am practically engaged to the lady," Milford protested weakly.

A smile played on the viscount's lips. "Then what are you afraid of?"

As Isabella had foreseen, Max did indeed dine out, though it must be said he had little appetite. He had sent a note to Freddie Broome, inviting him to dine, but his cousin had not shown up. Max could not blame him. Glancing up at the clock for the hundredth time, he saw the Earl of Milford bearing down on him.

"Ah, Purefoy! I was hoping to dine with you. All alone?"

"As you see," Max said coolly.

Milford took this for an invitation and sat down. "Isabella

particularly wanted me to dine with you," he went on, signaling to the waiter.

"Isabella?" Max repeated blankly, as if he had never heard of the lady.

Milford looked surprised. "My sister, you know."

"Oh, yes," Max murmured. "She is in good health, I trust?"

"Excellent health, sir. Sound as the pound. The women in our family are remarkably healthy, sir. Excellent breeders."

Max lifted his brows. "Your mother died in childbirth, did she not?"

"Well, yes, but both her children were perfectly healthy," Milford said quickly. "That is the important thing. Isabella pretends to have the headache, of course, but it is nothing serious. An excuse to stay home, nothing more. In case you should care to call on her, Purefoy."

"Perhaps I will call tomorrow," said Max. "Will you ask her to stay at home?"

"She shall stay at home," Milford assured him. "Poor Isabella! She has been fretting for nothing. She was sure Lady Waverly had poached you!"

A shadow fell across the table, and Max was pleased to see his cousin.

"Sorry, Max! I did not get your note until quite late."

Max smiled broadly. "My dear fellow! I thought you would never speak to me again. Take my chair," he added, hurrying to get another, beating out the efficient waiter.

"Don't mind if I do," said Freddie, sitting down and reaching for the claret. "Mind you, it was a mean, dirty trick, leaving me to face the bloodthirsty virago by myself!"

"She would have ripped me limb from limb," Max protested.

"Coward!"

Max sighed. "Quite so."

Freddie shook his head. "If you aren't careful you will

wake up one of these days married to that female. Then there will be no escaping her. I don't suppose you will be careful, however. Shall I wish you joy now, or will it keep until I return from the frosty bosom of the Romanovs?"

"You jest!" Milford accused him.

"No, my lord," Freddie replied. "I'm off to Russia on Tuesday."

"You jest about marriage, sir," Milford said testily. "You know very well that Purefoy can be in no danger from Lady Waverly."

"Quite right," said Max. "There's not the least chance of my getting her now."

"No, indeed," said Milford, "for I have just bet Lord Torcaster ten thousand pounds that I will marry her."

Max regarded him with his brows drawn together. *"You?"* he fairly snarled. "You marry that—that magnificent creature? I *don't* think so!"

Milford stared at him. "Why not, sir?"

"Because *I* am going to marry her, that's why!" Max said fiercely. "Shall we wager on it, sir? Ten thousand pounds, again? What's more, I will give you odds of five to one."

"Five to one?" Milford gasped. "But that is fifty thousand pounds, sir!"

"Only if I lose," Max replied. "I don't intend to."

Freddie chuckled. "You would do well, my lord, to get out of my cousin's way. There is a decided scent of orange blossom about his person that does not bode well."

"I will take your bet, Mr. Purefoy!" Milford said, glaring at Freddie.

It was, perhaps, not the wisest thing he had ever done, but Milford's pride would not allow him to be mocked by the younger son of a baron. He regretted the words as soon as they left his mouth, but there was nothing to do but insist on having the betting book brought out.

But, then, as he thought more about it, he began to think it would have been foolish of him to pass by the opportunity to enrich himself. If he married Lady Waverly, he stood to gain sixty thousand pounds, over and above the fortune she would bring to her husband.

Even if he failed to marry her, he might yet win *fifty* thousand pounds, if he could but prevent Mr. Purefoy making her his wife. With fifty thousand pounds, he could pay off his bet with Lord Torcaster very easily.

And, even if Purefoy *did* marry the baroness, all was not lost! He, Milford, could always marry Prudence.

By the time he returned home, he firmly believed he had been clever.

And, yet, for some reason, he said nothing about it to his sister when he saw her the next morning at breakfast. Isabella, he felt instinctively, would not understand.

Chapter 10

"Lord Banville!" Lady Jemima exclaimed, snatching the gentleman's card from the silver tray. "And his mama, dear Lady Mortmaigne! Straighten your lace, Miss Prudence. One never gets a second chance to make a first impression, you know."

Pru glanced up from her novel, slowly twisting a lock of her hair around one finger. "Never mind my lace. He won't be looking at my lace."

"The countess will be looking," Lady Jemima retorted.

"I suppose that is my cue to leave," said Patience, rising from the escritoire where she had been attempting to balance her accounts. "You look very nice, Pru."

Pru pointedly looked away.

Patience sighed. Pru had not said a word to her in twenty-four hours. Perhaps her visitors would put her in a better mood. She herself regarded purely social calls as tedious interruptions, but Pru always seemed eager for more.

"My dear Lady Waverly," Lady Jemima protested as Patience started for the door. "Lady Mortmaigne and her son represent the uppermost circle of English society! Would you skulk away without meeting them?"

"Why? What have you got against skulking?"

"What excuse am I to give?"

Patience glanced down at the bill in her hand. "Tell their excellencies that I must speak to the housekeeper about green peas. I don't remember eating any. At three shillings a pound, I think I should remember eating them."

"How can you talk such nonsense?" Pru said angrily, forgetting that she had decided to punish Patience with silence. "She is a countess! And her son is a viscount! One cannot talk to the nobility about green peas."

"Then I had better go," said Patience, but, before she could make her escape, Briggs opened the doors, and she was obliged to stop short. An elegant middle-aged lady and a handsome young man, both with chestnut hair and blue eyes, stood looking at her.

"How do you do?" said Patience, sticking out her hand.

Lord Banville bowed over it, and would have kissed it, but his mama elbowed him in the ribs, and said, under her breath, "Don't be daft, Lawrence. Shake the lady's hand. That's how they do it in America. Isn't that right, Lady Waverly?"

Patience's eyes lit up. "You've been to America, ma'am?"

"Heavens, no," Lady Mortmaigne replied, "but I met Mr. Adams once at a reception—oh, years ago, when I was first married. And now his son is the American ambassador. My, how time does fly! I daresay, Mr. John Quincy Adams will become your president one day, too, like his father before him?"

"That will depend on the election, ma'am," Patience replied. "Won't you come in? This is my sister, Miss Prudence Waverly. Perhaps you know Lady Jemima already?"

"Everybody knows Jemmie," Lady Mortmaigne said, sailing past Patience to greet Lady Jemima like an old friend. "Er . . . will you not shake hands with me, Miss Waverly?"

"No, ma'am," Pru said. "I will curtsy. I have been practicing for the queen."

As she demonstrated the deep court curtsy, Patience quietly slipped out of the room. She was partway down the stairs when she heard a voice behind her.

"You are not leaving, I hope, Lady Waverly?"

Patience smiled at Lord Banville. "I beg your pardon, sir, but I really must speak to my housekeeper about this bill for green peas."

To her annoyance, he trotted down the stairs to her. "Would this help you at all, Lady Waverly?" he asked. Taking out his billfold, he presented her with a card.

Patience looked at it, puzzled. "This is one of your cards, sir. I have one like it already."

She would have handed it back to him, but he said, "Your uncle was good enough to place his vowels on the back of it, my lady. Pray, accept it with my compliments."

Patience turned the card over and gasped. "Twenty-five hundred pounds! Sir, I can't—! Sir, it will take me some time to raise such a sum."

"You misunderstand me, my lady," he said quickly. "I have not come to collect. As far as I am concerned, the debt died with your uncle. Take it, please. Tear it to bits, burn it if you like, but make no attempt to pay me."

Patience shook her head, albeit reluctantly. "I can't accept such generosity, sir. If you will but give me time, I shall square all my uncle's debts."

"Why on earth should you be obligated to pay his gambling debts?" he said. "I shall be very much offended if you try to pay me. I won't take a penny." Taking her hand, he firmly closed her fingers around the card.

Patience flushed. "If you insist, sir."

"I do insist." Smiling, he offered her his arm. "Shall we return to the drawing room?"

Patience hesitated, but felt that she could not very well refuse.

In the drawing room, he led her over to the fire. Taking the bill from her hand, he tossed it into the flames.

"Sir!" Patience protested.

"What are you burning, Lawrence?" his mother demanded.

"I believe it was a bill for green peas," he replied. "It's the only thing to be done with a troublesome bill."

"I would be happy to pay it," Patience protested, "but I do not remember eating any green peas."

"Lady Jemima? Miss Waverly? Do either of you remember eating any green peas?"

Both ladies shook their heads.

"Obviously a mistake, then," said his lordship. "I'm glad I burned it. Perhaps," he went on, lowering his voice so that only Patience could hear him, "Your Ladyship would care to burn the little card I gave you?"

"I think I shall keep it in case you change your mind, sir," she answered, placing the card on the mantelpiece, next to Pru's invitation to St. James's Palace.

"Lawrence! What are you whispering to Lady Waverly?" Lady Mortmaigne's voice carried across the room to them. "Come and drink your tea."

"I always make the tea," Pru was saying as her sister and the viscount joined the rest of the group. "My sister, for all her accomplishments, has not yet learned to make tea. How do you take it, my lord?"

Lord Banville took his cup, thanked Pru briefly, but then turned to Patience. "I see you are to attend the first drawing room, my lady. You will see me there—and Mama, too."

"You will see my sister there," Patience told him. "Mrs. Adams very graciously has agreed to present me to her majesty at the American reception at the end of the month."

"How extraordinary!" Lady Mortmaigne murmured.

"My sister has a strange aversion to pomp and circumstance," Pru said.

"I'm sure Mama can wrangle us some invitations to the American reception," Lord Banville said.

"I shouldn't think they'd be very hard to come by," replied Lady Mortmaigne. "Nothing like invitations to the Duke of Sunderland's ball! I understand it is to be held in your honor, Lady Waverly."

"No!" Pru said angrily, before Patience could make any reply. "It is to be held in *my* honor, Lady Mortmaigne! Of course, you shall be invited, both of you."

Patience held her tongue, but, as soon as their visitors had gone, which they did promptly after twenty minutes of tea and polite conversation, she said quietly, "Prudence, you know there isn't to be any ball. You must not promise people invitations to an event that will never take place. I have already written a letter to the duke."

Pru was on her feet. "You had no right to do that!" she cried, thrusting out her jaw pugnaciously. "It's my ball! It's nothing to do with you."

"I'm sorry, Pru, but I can't allow you to accept favors from the Duke of Sunderland."

"Why? Because you don't approve of Max?"

"You shouldn't call him by his Christian name," said Patience, coloring. "And, no, I certainly do not approve of him. If you only knew the things he's done!"

"Yes, I know! He tried to drown you in the ballroom," Pru sniffed. "What of it? I'm tempted to try it myself! I daresay he is not as *perfect* as Lord Banville," she added coldly. "How cozy the pair of you seemed! And how *manly* of him to follow his mother around."

"We are indebted to Lord Banville," said Patience. "He has forgiven a debt of two and a half thousand pounds!"

"Is that why you kept him all to yourself?" Pru said

sourly. "One could hardly get a word in edgewise! Thick as thieves, you were."

"Why should you care if you did not like him?" Patience asked reasonably.

"I don't care," Pru declared unconvincingly. Tossing her head, she flounced from the room.

On Monday evening, when Lord Milford called, he could not help but notice the viscount's card on the mantelpiece.

"It is rather late for a visit, is it not?" Patience greeted him. "My sister and Lady Jemima are already dressing for dinner."

"I called three times today, but you were not at home," he answered, sounding rather peeved. "Did Lady Jemima not tell you?"

"I accompanied my sister to her lessons today," Patience explained. "I was not aware, sir, that you expected me to sit at home all day waiting for you to call."

He looked shocked. "I see Banville has been here," he muttered resentfully. "I suppose he offered to forgive your uncle's debt?"

"If he has, how does it concern you, sir?"

He frowned. "Obviously, the man is a scoundrel. He means to place you under an obligation to him, my lady! He had the insufferable presumption to copy my idea!"

"Indeed, sir?" Patience said politely. "Was it your idea to place me under an obligation to you?"

"No, of course not," he said angrily. "You wound me deeply! I am nothing like Lord Banville, I hope! You have nothing but Banville in your head! Admit it! You are thinking of him now!"

"No, indeed," said Patience. "As a matter of fact, I was wondering if you happened to go to the sale at Tattersall's today."

"Why? Was I supposed to go?" he said defensively. "You gave me no commission."

"I was merely curious to know who bought Mr. Broome's curricle horses," she said.

He shrugged. "Purefoy, of course. No one would dare outbid him."

Patience sighed. "Too bad. I *did* like driving them."

"I wish I had known you wanted them," he said fervently.

Patience hid a smile. "Would you have dared to bid against the great Mr. Purefoy?"

He drew himself up. "I'm not afraid of Purefoy," he declared. "I am one of the few people in London who would dare oppose him. For your sake, I would do it, too."

"I'll bear that in mind," said Patience, not sure he was to be believed.

Milford felt he had found favor with the lady. Considerably pleased with himself, he would have settled into a chair, but Patience forestalled him. "Forgive me for keeping you so late, sir," she said firmly. "I won't keep you any longer. Do please give my regards to your sister."

Outmaneuvered by the lady, there was nothing Milford could do but leave.

Returning home, he found his sister in raptures because Purefoy had been to see her. Milford thought it rather disloyal of her to be in raptures when her brother was feeling glum.

"Did he propose?" he asked rudely.

"No," Isabella admitted, "but he was extremely attentive and he did ask me to go for a drive with him tomorrow afternoon."

"Now why should he do that?" Milford wondered aloud. "I suppose he means to make Lady Waverly jealous."

Isabella glared at him. "Is it so strange that Mr. Purefoy should desire my company?" she demanded. "Why don't you invite Lady Waverly for a drive in the park tomorrow? Then we shall *see* who is jealous!"

* * *

On Tuesday morning, Patience visited Mrs. Drabble in Wimpole Street. When she returned to Clarges Street that afternoon, a leathery faced groom was walking a curricle drawn by two splendid grays up and down the street. Patience recognized them at once. Hurrying past the servant who opened the door to admit her, she ran up to the drawing room without stopping to take off her bonnet, her cloak, or her gloves. Her eyes darted around the room.

"Where is he?" she cried, panting a little from running up the steps.

Pru looked up from her novel. "Who, Patience?" she asked innocently.

"You know very well who!" Patience said furiously. "I know he's here! His horses and his curricle are outside! Where is he hiding?"

"You mean those splendid grays? They *used* to belong to Max," said Pru, closing her book over her finger. "But he lost them in a bet to Mr. Broome. He drives a team of chestnuts now. As for the grays, Mr. Broome sold them at Tattersall's yesterday."

"Yes. To Mr. Purefoy!" said Patience. "No one would outbid him."

"Mr. Broome outbid him," Pru told her.

"What?" Patience said incredulously. "Who told you that?"

"Mr. Broome told me so himself."

"He bought his own horses?"

Pru shrugged. "That is what he said. He wanted to tell you all about it himself. He waited for you for over an hour, but he could not wait for you any longer. He's off to Russia now. I don't suppose we'll ever see him again."

"He seems to have forgotten his horses!" said Patience.

"He wants *you* to have them."

Patience was horrified. "What? I cannot accept such a gift!"

"I know. That's why I accepted it for you," said Pru.

"Pru!" Patience said angrily.

Pru burst out laughing. "I'm only joking. It's not a gift. He wants you to look after them while he's away, that's all. 'Anything to keep them out of Max's hands,' he said. Why should he say such a thing?"

"Because Mr. Purefoy would not pay a fair price for them," said Patience. "And no one dared to outbid him—except, of course, Mr. Broome. Well, I'm glad Mr. Purefoy did not get them! It's good for him not to get *everything* he wants! Good for you, Freddie!"

Pru's eyes were round. "Does this mean you're going to keep the curricle?"

Patience hesitated. "I would never accept such an expensive *gift,* of course," she said. "But I suppose it would be all right if I were to look after the team while Mr. Broome is away. The horses will need exercise, and—and he *does* owe me an apology, after all."

Pru could hardly believe her ears. "May we take them out now?"

Patience glanced out the window. "They do look rather fresh," she said. "Hawkins has been keeping them warm. It would be cruel to put them away without letting them go a little."

"I'll get my bonnet!" cried Pru.

In less than five minutes—a record for Pru!—she returned, and the sisters set out for Hyde Park, with Hawkins in the groom's seat, and Patience holding the reins.

"I wonder if they remember me," Pru murmured as Clarges Street passed in a blur.

"Who?" Patience asked curiously.

"The horses, of course!" Pru said. "You do know they

used to be Max's, don't you? He used to drive them on Mondays."

Patience rolled her eyes. "Does the man have horses for every day of the week?"

"He did," Pru replied. "But then he lost his Monday horses in a bet or a card game, I forget which it was."

"Only a fool would risk such splendid horses on a bet or a game of cards," Patience said.

"Don't call Max a fool. We shall quarrel," said Pru.

Patience bit her lip. "I don't want to quarrel with you, Pru," she said. "But there is something I must know. Did he kiss you?"

Pru stared at her. "Who? Mr. Broome? Certainly not."

"Not Mr. Broome! Mr. Purefoy! You can tell me if he did. I won't—I won't think any less of you, if he did. Only I must know."

Pru laughed. "All this anxiety! Patience, you goose! Englishmen are not like Americans! There's no kissing until *after* the engagement. And, of course, no respectable girl would allow a man to kiss her unless he were her affianced."

Patience could feel her face grow hot. Undoubtedly, Mr. Purefoy did not think she was a respectable girl! "I understand Mr. Purefoy is half Italian," she said, as they came within sight of the park's gates.

"You should not listen to such ugly gossip!" Pru said angrily. "Just because a man is a little tanned doesn't mean he's Italian."

"He told me so himself," Patience said mildly.

Pru was no longer listening. They had entered the park by means of a road thronged with elegant vehicles. "How smart we look!" Pru said happily, as they passed through the gates and joined the throng of vehicles on Carriage Drive. "Everyone is looking at us! I do believe we are the only two ladies in a curricle. And, Pay, you are the only lady driver—oh, except for Lady Caroline Lamb! She has her high-perch phaeton. There! Do you see her? She has daringly short hair. She is in love with Lord Byron, you know. 'Tis rumored that she sent him a lock of her hair— and 'twas not from her head!"

"Prudence!"

"What?" Pru said innocently. "*I* didn't do it!"

Patience was forced to slow down the grays, matching their pace to that of the other vehicles. "It's too crowded here," she complained. "There are some lovely, quiet paths down by the Serpentine, if we could just find a way out of this traffic."

"No," Pru protested. "No one will see us on a quiet path. I think you miss the whole point of going for a drive in the park."

With a frown, Patience negotiated around two ladies who had stopped their barouches in the middle of the road so that they could chat. There seemed to be two circuits; one traveling clockwise, the other counterclockwise, both deplorably slow. Stops were frequent as friends and acquaintances met. Patience longed to get away.

Before long, Pru began to stir with dissatisfaction, too. Everyone was staring, she noticed, but no one was looking at her. No, they were all looking at Patience; Patience who sat high in the driver's seat, wearing a veil of very fine netting over her face to keep out the dust. It gave her an air of mystery. As a woman driver, she stood out. Gentlemen tipped their hats to her. Dowagers put up their eyeglasses. Young ladies whispered enviously as she went by.

Bits and pieces of conversation drifted to Pru's ears.

". . . American . . . very rich . . ."

"Green eyes, my dear . . . not a speck of hazel in them . . ."

"Invited to the first drawing room . . . declined . . . queen furious . . ."

"Prinny wants to meet her, of course . . ."

"Oh, of course!"

"Oh, look! There he is!"

Pru's head swivelled around so quickly she made herself dizzy. But the Prince Regent was nowhere in sight. She did see Lord Milford, however, driving his curricle, a pretty, golden-haired woman beside him.

"There is Lord Milford," she said, nudging Patience in the ribs. "*That,* I suppose, is his sister. You did not tell me she was so pretty," she added testily.

"I don't know who she is," Patience replied. "Lady Isabella has auburn hair."

"You are betrayed!" Pru said dramatically. "This is Lord Milford's revenge on you for carrying on with Lord Banville!"

"Pray, don't be absurd," Patience murmured.

"Lord Milford!" Pru called out, waving to the earl before her sister could stop her. "Yoo-hoo! Over here!"

At the sound of her voice, the earl gave a start. His face turned bright red. To Patience's astonishment, he pretended not to see them, and drove off in a hurry.

"Just as I suspected," Pru said smugly. "*That* was his mistress."

"Surely not!" Patience exclaimed.

"Isn't it obvious? Why else would he run away like that?"

Patience's face was scarlet with embarrassment. "His mistress? No, I don't believe it."

"They all keep mistresses here," said Pru. "In European society, everyone turns a blind eye. It's all very civilized. But then, Europeans are much more sophisticated than we are."

Patience grimaced. "Sophisticated! Is that what you call it? I call it sin."

"Don't be so naive, Patience! Men have needs—even

Lord Milford, apparently. You're not jealous, are you? You're far prettier than she is. Younger, too."

"Jealous! Pray, don't be absurd. I pity the woman with all my heart."

Pru giggled. "So do I! I don't think he is attractive at all."

"I would pity her even if he were attractive," Patience declared.

"Really? Why?"

"Imagine how she must have felt when he drove off like that," said Patience. "She must have felt he was ashamed of her."

"I'm sure she knows her place," Pru said carelessly. "You think too much, Pay. She's probably an actress or something."

Patience pressed her lips together. "Perhaps we need not go to the theater after all."

"Oh, for heaven's sake!" Pru said impatiently. "If you insist on associating only with people of the very purest character, you will end up a lonely old woman, and you will never have any fun!"

Patience shook her head. "I suppose Mr. Purefoy keeps a mistress," she said.

Pru scowled. "Don't be ridiculous," she said sharply. "Of course he doesn't. He thinks only of me."

"Now who's being naive?"

Pru shifted in the seat. "If he does have a mistress, I'm sure he will give her up when he marries," she said defiantly. "Anyway, I would never allow it!"

"How provincial of you," Patience said lightly.

"Oh, shut up!" Pru snapped.

Patience could see that Pru was thinking about what she said, however. Good! Now, if only Mr. Purefoy would drive by with his mistress . . . That, surely, would put an end to Pru's infatuation with the man.

"Our father did not keep a mistress," she said quietly.

Pru made no reply, forestalled, perhaps, by Sir Charles Stanhope, who overtook them at that moment in his gig. "Lady Waverly!" he cried, drawing alongside her. "What are you doing with Mr. Broome's horses?"

"I don't see what business that is of yours, sir," Patience said, annoyed.

"It ain't modest!" he said. "And it ain't safe! A little thing like you. A female! You'll do yourself an injury. I'm strong as an ox, and I can hardly keep my cattle under good control!"

"So I see," Patience said coolly.

"I insist that you pull over. Let your tiger drive. You there!" He actually called out to Hawkins.

"Damn your interference!" said Patience, now angry. "You have no right to insist on anything! Go away!"

"I have every right," Sir Charles retorted. "You know I have! I warn you, madam, when I am your husband, I won't tolerate such rank insubordination!"

"This conversation is at an end," she said, speeding the grays with a slap of the reins.

Pru was laughing as the curricle easily outstripped Sir Charles's gig. "Why didn't you tell me you had such a handsome young suitor!"

"Don't even joke about it!"

"He's following us now," said Pru, glancing over her shoulder.

"I'll get rid of him."

Spying a barouche in conference with a landau up ahead, Patience headed straight for it, skirting it neatly at the last moment. Sir Charles, intent on his quarry, did not see the obstacle until it was too late. He panicked, dragging at the reins. Unfortunately, the gig, a heavier, more cumbersome vehicle than the two-wheeled curricle, did not quite clear the side of the barouche.

"What do you think you're doing, sir?" the barouche's

passenger, a grandam in a towering green turban, demanded.

"Oh, well done!" Pru congratulated her. "Max could not have done it better."

Patience blushed with pride, but said, with sarcastic inflection, "High praise indeed."

Pausing just long enough to make sure there were no bones sticking out, she continued on her way, weaving deftly through the traffic. She was in sight of the park gates when she suddenly saw Mr. Purefoy driving his curricle. He was traveling in the clockwise circuit; she was in the counterclockwise circuit.

He was not alone. A lady sat beside him in the curricle, wrapped in a beautiful silver fox fur. The lady was looking up at Mr. Purefoy adoringly, laughing and chattering madly. He seemed equally pleased with her. His white teeth flashed in his dark face as he smiled.

His mistress, she decided, a sour taste in her mouth. A few minutes before, she had wished for this, but now, suddenly, she felt nauseated.

Clicking her tongue at the grays, she started to move them to the far side of her lane, pulling alongside the vehicle ahead.

"Do you think *he* keeps a mistress?" Pru asked suddenly. "Sir Charles, I mean?"

"I neither know nor care!"

Pru began to laugh. "If I were his wife, I would insist upon it!"

Patience managed a weak laugh. She had lost sight of Mr. Purefoy and his companion.

Tucking back into traffic behind an open carriage, Patience was dismayed when the open carriage suddenly came to a dead stop, right in front of her, forcing her to do the same. The grays did not like it and whinnied their disapproval. Patience's hands tightened on the reins.

"My dear Max!" said the lady in the open carriage, her voice ringing clear as a bell.

Max seemed not to hear her, but drove past her vehicle, intent on meeting Patience.

"Well, I never!" the lady in the open carriage said angrily.

"Good afternoon, Lady Waverly!" said Max, touching the brim of his hat.

"Max!" cried Pru, then fell silent as she saw his female companion.

"You did that on purpose, Mr. Purefoy," Patience said hotly, the words falling from her lips impulsively. "You knew I was behind that lady in the landau! You knew she would stop to speak to you! You could have caused a collision!"

His mouth twitched. "As you did to Sir Charles a bit further back? Is that not a trifle hypocritical, Lady Waverly? May I present my companion?" he went on smoothly, without waiting for her to reply.

"No, thank you!" said Patience. "If it's all the same to you, I would rather not meet your—your mis—"

She broke off, staring in blank amazement as she recognized his companion.

"You remember Lady Isabella Norton, of course," said Max.

"How do you do, Lady Waverly," Isabella said with perfect equanimity while Patience stared, openmouthed. "And this can only be Miss Prudence! How delightful to see you."

"I don't understand," Patience said, frowning as she looked from one face to the other.

Isabella looked at her quite blankly. "What do you mean, Lady Waverly? What is there to understand? A beautiful day for a drive, is it not?"

"I see you decided to take Freddie's grays," Mr. Purefoy remarked.

"I'm only minding them for him while he's away,"

Patience said, her cheeks flushed behind her gauzy veil. "I'm glad *you* didn't get them," she added.

"Even if they match my eyes?" he said lightly.

"They are too good for you," she said angrily.

Max raised his brows. "You see, Isabella? Lady Waverly and I are not the best of friends. She does not approve of me."

Isabella tightened her grip on the gentleman's arm. "We need not care for *her* good opinion, surely."

"I shall endeavor not to care," Max replied, pulling a face, "but I doubt I shall succeed. I do so wish to be liked by everyone."

"That is not possible for anyone, Mr. Purefoy," Patience said sharply.

Isabella was enjoying her rival's discomfiture immensely. "Come, now, Lady Waverly! Jealousy does not become you!"

Patience turned white. "Jealousy!"

Isabella sighed. "Such bitterness! Mr. Purefoy, I must tell you something very unpleasant. This lady told me that you were in the habit of ravishing serving maids. Of course, I gave no credence to her scurrilous lies. Nor did I repeat them to anyone. But if you should hear of it, from anyone else, here is the source."

"You lie!" Patience gasped. "'Twas *you* who told *me*!"

Isabella shook her head sadly. "Exposed, all she can do is point the finger at someone else. Pathetic, is it not, Mr. Purefoy?"

"It certainly is!" Patience snapped.

Finding an opening in the traffic, she drove away as quickly as she could. Isabella's thin mouth curved in triumph as she watched her rival quit the field.

"I'm so sorry, Pru," Patience said, glancing at her sister's pale, strained face.

"Did you do that?" Pru asked. "Did you say those vile things about him?"

"No, of course not! How would I know his habits? She told me."

"She lied," Pru said fiercely.

"Of course she lied. I see that now. And I was only too willing to believe her!"

"We must tell Max he is nursing a serpent in his bosom," said Pru.

"Rather hard to say which is the serpent," Patience said dryly. "In any case, I told him on Friday what Isabella had told me about him. I didn't tell him her name, but he must have guessed. Today, he proved to me that she was lying. I would not change places with that lady for anything," she added.

"Nor would I," said Pru. "I can't wait to see the look on her face when she realizes she's not half as clever as she thinks. Oh, Pay! Does this mean you approve of Mr. Purefoy now?"

Taken aback, Patience made no immediate answer.

"You were wrong about Max," Pru insisted. "Admit it! He's not the devil."

"Perhaps not," Patience returned, "but that doesn't make him an angel!"

"Good," Pru said, smiling. "I don't want an angel. *I* want a man."

Chapter 11

On Thursday, Patience left Pru at her dancing lesson at Miss Godfrey's Academy for Young Ladies, then drove on to Mrs. Drabble's house in Wimpole Street. Jane opened the door for her, bobbing a curtsy as she recognized the baroness.

Slipping into the house, she hurried to the little cloak-room off the hall. There she took off her bonnet and placed it on the shelf before hanging up her cloak. Judging by the number of cloaks and shawls hanging on the hooks, she was almost certainly the last to arrive. She hastened up the stairs to make her apologies to the other ladies.

"I'm so sorry I'm late, Mrs. Drabble," she began breathlessly.

"That's quite all right, dear," said Mrs. Drabble, coming forward to kiss her. "We are just getting started. Miss Haines brought us some of her famous currant buns."

"Mr. Purefoy has had three already," Miss Haines said proudly.

"Forgive me, Lady Waverly," Max said quickly, as her startled eyes swung up to his face. "I've taken your seat."

He had risen from his chair when Patience entered the room. Looking quite large and out of place amid the petticoats, he stood surrounded by an assortment of seated ladies, most of whom were elderly. A fox among hens!

"What are you doing here?" Patience demanded. "How dare you!"

"It's only a chair, Lady Waverly," Miss Haines said mildly. "We'll get you another one."

Mrs. Bascombe pursed her lips in disapproval. "Mr. Purefoy has as much right to sit in that chair as she does. More, too, for he is our patron!"

"Our what?" Patience said incredulously.

"Who do you think pays for our buttons, Lady Waverly? Our cloth, and our notions? Mr. Purefoy, that's who."

"I have always been interested in helping orphans," Max said, assuming a cloak of virtue Patience was certain he had no right to wear. "I am myself something of an orphan, you know. My father died before I was born. My mother, poor woman, did not know what to do with me. She gave me to my uncle to raise, and went back to her own country. You are also an orphan, I think, Lady Waverly? Perhaps we are kindred spirits?"

"Kindred spirits!" she exclaimed in astonishment.

"Of course, you have the companionship of a sister," he went on amiably. "I have often wished for the comfort of a brother or sister."

"You have your uncle," she said primly. "Perhaps you should go home to him."

"Well!" said Mrs. Bascombe. "I'm sure it is not up to you, Lady Waverly, when Mr. Purefoy goes home!"

"Her ladyship thinks me a bad nephew," Max said sadly. "But, actually, I am here on my uncle's behalf. He desires me to speak to you, Lady Waverly. May I?"

"You may use Jane's little sitting room," Mrs. Drabble offered. "No one will disturb you there."

"Oh, it is nothing private," Max assured her. "My uncle has undertaken to give a ball for Lady Waverly and her sister. They are to be presented at court next week. What could be more splendid than a ball at Sunderland House? It sets just the right tone for the Season, don't you think?"

"Any young lady would give her eyeteeth to be launched from Sunderland House," Mrs. Bascombe said, a little resentfully.

Patience glared at Max. It was most unfair of him to bring up the subject in company—or at all. He ought to have accepted her refusal like a gentleman. "As I explained in my letter to your uncle, Mr. Purefoy," she said coldly, "as grateful as we are for your uncle's kind offer, my sister and I can't possibly accept."

"You mean to say you refuse, Lady Waverly?"

"I must, Miss Haines," said Patience. Looking around the room, she saw that everyone was looking at her with a mixture of astonishment and disapproval. "I did not ask him to give me a ball!" she said defensively.

"No, I did," Max said ruefully. "I made a promise to your sister, which I am bound to keep, Lady Waverly."

"I hereby release you of your promise, sir," Patience said tartly.

Mrs. Bascombe loudly clucked her tongue.

"If only it were that easy," said Max, as the circle of ladies whispered amongst themselves. "But I'm afraid the arrangements have already been made. The banquet ordered. The musicians hired. The flowers on their way from our hothouses at Breckinridge. Invitations sent."

"I'm very sorry," said Patience, "but you should have asked me first. I am Prudence's guardian, you know. How would it look if your uncle—a stranger to us—were to give a ball in our honor?"

Max shrugged. "Like kindness, I suppose. But how will it look if the ball is suddenly canceled?"

"My dear," put in Mrs. Drabble, "you can have no

conception of the sort of gossip that would ensue—none of it flattering to you or your sister."

"That is preposterous," said Patience. "Why should there be gossip?"

"There is always gossip," Max told her. "Very likely it would be enough to ruin all your chances in society. You do not care about that, perhaps, Lady Waverly, but think of your sister. Don't let your dislike for me cloud your judgment."

After a moment, Patience said ungraciously, "Very well. You may have your ball."

"Very handsome of you, I'm sure," Mrs. Bascombe said sharply.

Mrs. Drabble looked tremendously relieved. "Good! It's all settled. Do sit down, Lady Waverly, and try one of Miss Haines's currant buns. More tea, Mr. Purefoy?"

Max smiled apologetically. "I fear Lady Waverly has long desired my absence."

"You are mistaken," she said crisply. "I'm completely indifferent as to whether you stay or go. I don't regard it in the least."

He raised his brows slightly. "Then I need not leave on your account?"

"No," she said, seating herself on a wooden stool brought up from the kitchen by Jane. "There is little here for you to do, however. I'm sure you will be quite bored."

"Bored? You astonish me," he said, resuming his seat between Mrs. Bascombe and Miss Haines. "How could I be bored with such charming companions?"

"I see," Miss Haines said tremulously. "She thinks that we are boring!"

"No!" Patience said quickly, horrified that she had hurt the feelings of a sweet-natured, elderly spinster like Miss Lavinia Haines. "Indeed, I do not, Miss Haines. I meant only that an afternoon of sewing probably is not the gentleman's idea of entertainment. By the way," she went on as Miss Haines glowered at her, "your currant buns are delicious."

"At last! Something upon which we can agree," said Max, making Miss Haines blush radiantly with pleasure.

"Pshaw! An old family recipe, nothing more."

He smiled warmly. "But those are the very best kind of recipes, Miss Haines."

"Indeed, they are," said Mrs. Bascombe. "You should taste my cherry tarts, Mr. Purefoy."

"I should be delighted," he said. "And you, Lady Waverly? Do you think we two shall agree on cherry tarts as well?"

"Oh, Lady Waverly likes anything with cherries," said Mrs. Drabble.

"I do," Patience admitted. "I miss the cherry trees back home. I shan't be there to see them bloom this year, but, God willing, I'll see them next year."

Max frowned. "You mean to return to America, then?" he said sharply. "I—I assumed you would make your home here."

Patience shook her head. "As soon as my uncle's estate is settled, Pru and I will go home, of course."

"And if your sister does not wish to leave England?"

Patience frowned. "Prudence and I have never lived apart."

"We will lose our fastest darner when Lady Waverly leaves us," said Mrs. Drabble. "She can make the rattiest old stocking look new again in mere minutes!"

"A rare talent indeed," Max said gravely.

Patience had the distinct impression that he was laughing at her. To hide her annoyance, she opened her mending basket and took out a little jacket with several torn seams. "And you, Mr. Purefoy?" she said, locating a reel of black cotton. "Have you any talents that might be of use to our circle?"

"I have been known to sort buttons and wind cotton," he replied. "I'm surprisingly good at threading a needle, too. Shall I— Shall I thread your needle for you, Lady Waverly?"

Somehow, he made the offer sound slightly indecent.

"You may certainly thread mine, Mr. Purefoy!" Mrs. Bascombe said, rather suggestively. "My poor old eyes! Here, Mr. Purefoy. I'll hold the needle for you. Now you must lick the thread, sir. Moisten it between your lips to make it nice and stiff. Or you'll never get it in!"

She regarded him over the tops of her iron-rimmed spectacles. "Dear me! I thought you said you'd done this before."

"Really, Hyacinth," Mrs. Drabble chided the enthusiastic widow.

"My dear Mrs. Bascombe," Max protested, laughing. "You've got to hold it still! Stiff or not, how am I supposed to get my thread through the eye of your needle if you keep moving it about?"

"Poke away, Mr. Purefoy! Poke away," she said cheerfully.

Miss Haines's eyes were round. "Would you mind threading mine, too, sir?"

"Certainly, Miss Haines. Such a tiny little needle yours is, too! Lady Waverly?"

"I'll thread my own, thank you," Patience said, red faced.

Mrs. Drabble felt it was time to change the subject. "Are you at all nervous about your presentation, Lady Waverly?" she asked, expertly pulling her thread through a tiny button on a little girl's dress. "I'm sure I wouldn't blame you if you were."

"I'm not in the least bit nervous," Patience answered.

"Nor should you be," said Max. "You will have at least two friends in the room when you make your curtsy to Queen Charlotte. I always attend the first drawing room with my uncle."

"I don't curtsy," she said, frowning at him.

"Never?" he said, raising his brows.

"I'm American," she explained. "We don't believe in—"

"Good manners?" he suggested.

"We believe in equality, Mr. Purefoy. I would gladly shake her majesty's hand—"

He laughed out loud. "Now *that* would cause quite a stir!"

Patience bent her head to bite her thread. She worked steadily with one eye on the clock. At the end of the second hour, she put away her mending and rose to take her leave. To her annoyance, Max, who had been keeping up a steady stream of conversation with the other ladies, rose with her. "Pray, do not go on my account, Lady Waverly," he said quickly.

"No, indeed," she said crossly. "I must go and collect my sister from her dance lesson."

To her annoyance, he followed her into the cloakroom, closing the door upon them as she was putting on her cloak. "How dare you! Get out!" she snapped.

She might as well have not spoken. "You were not driving in the park yesterday," he said. "Those horses should be exercised every day, you know."

"I did drive in the park yesterday," she answered. "Not that it's any concern of yours. But it was Green Park, not Hyde Park. It's just as beautiful and far less crowded."

"And, of course, it is nearer to Clarges Street," he said thoughtfully. "Very well. I'll take Hyde Park, and you can have Green Park."

"I will drive where I please, Mr. Purefoy," she answered. "You may do the same."

"Thank you," he said gravely. "I thought perhaps you were trying to avoid me. If that is your desire, you will have a better time of it if I assist you."

"I would like to avoid you now," she told him. "You may assist me by moving away from the door."

He was very big and the room was very small, scarcely bigger than a closet. He took a step forward, pressing her against one wall. "Is this better?" he inquired solicitously.

"Stand aside, Mr. Purefoy, or I will call for Jane," she threatened.

"If you call for Jane I will kiss you," he replied.

"If you kiss me, I shall scream!"

"If you scream, the whole household will come running," he said. "You would be compromised. I'd have to marry you."

Infuriated, Patience struck him across the face.

"What was *that* for?" he asked, pressing his hand to his cheek.

"You know perfectly well what it's for!"

"Perhaps I do," he conceded. "It's because I kissed you, isn't it? Not today, but before, in the park. I didn't mean to kiss you. It just happened. We'd nearly wrecked the curricle. My pulse was racing. My heart was pounding. And there you were! You seduced me with your fine eyes."

Patience glared at him, her chin balled up like a fist. "And my sister?" she said. "Did she also seduce you with her fine eyes? They are the same eyes, after all!"

He frowned. "I never had the honor of kissing Miss Prudence," he said coldly. "If she told you I kissed her, then she is lying."

Aware that she wanted to believe him more than was good for her, Patience frowned back at him. "She would not admit it, of course."

He relaxed. "No?" he mocked her. "Perhaps you should

torture her. I understand that people will confess to anything—to killing Christ, even—if they are tortured."

"If I am going to torture anyone, Mr. Purefoy," she snapped, "it will be you."

"Would you be good enough to start now?" he murmured. Taking her roughly by the shoulders, he kissed her mouth. The deep, rich warmth of his mouth shocked her, and she fell against him, her knees buckling. When he released her some time later, she was quite breathless and extremely disappointed in herself. His gray eyes laughed at her as she struggled to gather her wits.

"Oh, Mr. Purefoy," she gasped, her eyes round with wonder.

He favored her with a smug grin. "Please, call me Max," he invited her.

"I—I—I—!" she gasped, panting desperately for breath. "Oh! Oh! Oh! I am all a-flutter!"

"Well, of course you are," he said.

"I melt, sir! I melt! I melt like butter beneath the torrid rain of your hot, manly kisses. I surrender to you utterly!"

Max was beginning to look a little doubtful. "Steady on! It was only a kiss. It wasn't even my best work."

"Only a kiss?" she gasped, her beautiful eyes wounded. "How can you say that? How can you be so cruel? You have rocked me to my foundation, sir! I am toppling, sir! Toppling! I swoon! I die!"

Trembling, she fell backward into the cloaks hanging against the wall.

"No, no!" he said, hastening to catch her in his arms. "You mustn't do that!"

Taking hold of his lapels, Patience buried her face in his broad chest and began to sob wretchedly, her shoulders shaking. Perhaps she overdid it a bit. He seemed to think so.

"Very funny," he said coldly.

Quite dry-eyed, Patience looked at him, smiling rather

nastily. "You conceited ass!" she said. "I suppose you think that is all it takes to make me swoon!"

"I have no idea what makes you swoon," he said.

"Get out of my way," she said angrily, snatching her bonnet from the shelf.

"Oh, come now! It's a bit late to be missish," he said impatiently. "I already know you've been kissed before me—quite often, too, I should think!"

"When *I* choose to allow it," she retorted. "I'm afraid you don't quite measure up. I only allow gentlemen of sterling character to kiss me."

"So just my humble self then, after all," he said lightly.

"They do exist," she told him. "In America they are quite plentiful."

"No wonder you want to go home!"

"Yes!"

He drew his dark brows together over his gray eyes. "You do realize, of course, that Isabella was lying?" he said sharply. "I am no saint to be sure, but I am not—I am not as bad as that."

"Still you are quite bad enough!" she said. "You forget, sir, that I saw you with my own eyes participating in that disgusting orgy!"

"Here we call it a birth-night," he said mildly. "Hardly an orgy. You'd almost have to go to the Continent for that sort of thing. Really, I'm no worse than the average fellow."

"And no better either!"

"Quite so," he agreed.

The door opened, and Jane stood there. Behind her were several interested ladies.

Without missing a beat, Max handed Mrs. Bascombe her kerseymere cloak. Red-faced, Patience left the house. She had arranged for Hawkins to return for her with the curricle in two hours, and much to her relief, he was not late. Climbing up, she took the reins, while he scrambled into the groom's seat.

"You're late," Pru said grumpily to her sister as Hawkins raised the curricle top over their heads. A cold light rain had begun over Miss Godfrey's Academy for Young Ladies, but, to Patience's surprise, the streets of London remained as crowded as ever. Everyone, it seemed, carried an umbrella. There was even one kept under the seat in the curricle.

"I did not want to risk coming early," Patience replied, urging the grays to a trot as they headed home to Clarges Street. "I know how much you like your dancing lesson. What was it today, the waltz?"

Pru pulled her cloak tightly around her. "The *boulangère*. I shan't be allowed to waltz unless the patronesses of Almack's grant me permission." She made them sound like the goddesses of Mount Olympus.

"You have your tickets to Almack's, don't you?"

"Vouchers, Pay," Pru corrected her wearily. "Vouchers, not tickets. Yes, of course we have our vouchers, but that is no guarantee that the patronesses will allow us to waltz."

"Us?" Patience echoed. "Don't imagine I'll ever accompany you to Almack's, Pru. Why, it's nothing but a marriage market! As for asking *permission* to dance—permission to dance at a ball, for heaven's sake!"

"Only the waltz."

"Lady Jemima will accompany you to Almack's. The carriage is yours whatever evening you wish. But you know I have no patience for such foolishness!"

Pru smiled suddenly. "Father always used to say that we were very badly named, for *you* had no patience, and *I* had no prudence."

"Quite right he was, too. Do you seriously suppose you

will not be permitted to waltz?" Patience asked curiously. "How does that work exactly? Will you be called before the court and examined? Will the patronesses look at you through their lorgnettes and say: 'Forsooth, her forehead is too wide; she shall not waltz?'"

Pru frowned. "If my forehead is too wide, so is yours."

"Never mind, Pru. You can always waltz at home. I won't tell anyone."

"If only you had not canceled my ball at Sunderland House!" Pru lamented. "Then my success would be assured."

Patience sighed wearily. "I'm afraid I was too late to cancel the ball," she said, shaking her head sadly.

Pru stared at her. "Don't— Don't tease me," she faltered.

Patience shrugged helplessly. "The arrangements have all been made. The invitations have gone out already. To cancel now would be to commit social suicide. People would talk. So . . . despite my misgivings, the ball must go on."

"Never mind your misgivings," said Pru, hugging her sister so fiercely that the horses on the other end of the reins rolled back their eyes and whinnied. "I always knew you would relent! You would not be so cruel. Not to me. I cannot wait to tell Max! He has promised me the first two dances, you know."

"I've already told Max," said Patience. "I saw him today at Mrs. Drabble's house. It's all settled. It was he who told me the ball could not be canceled—not without doing a good deal of harm to your reputation, that is. And to mine as well."

"You saw Max at Mrs. Drabble's house?" Pru repeated incredulously. "Oh, yes, of course," she murmured before Patience could reply. "I'd forgotten she was his old nurse. Awfully nice of him to visit an old servant, don't you think?"

Patience frowned. "I didn't realize Mrs. Drabble had been Mr. Purefoy's nurse."

"Oh, yes. He was the one who brought her to Clarges Street to attend you. Dr. Wingfield, too. And Lady Jemima, of course. I would not have known what to do, but Max did, of course."

"Why did you never tell me?" Patience asked.

"Tell you? The doctor said not to do or say anything to upset you. Even after you were better, I thought it best to keep mum. You'd boil over even at the mention of his name. But you like him now, don't you, Patience?"

Patience parked the curricle at the curb outside their house. "Tell me the truth, Pru. Has he kissed you? Because if he has—"

"He has not," Pru insisted. "At all times, he has treated me with the utmost respect. He's an English gentleman, and that is a very different thing than what we are used to. Remember the man from Boston?" Pru shuddered eloquently. "Max has English reticence. He would never dream of kissing a girl—not a nice girl anyway. Not unless he had quite made up his mind to marry her. I think," she went on dreamily, as Hawkins jumped down to open her door, "I shall let him kiss me at the ball."

The door opened and Briggs came out with an umbrella. Pru was up the steps before she realized that Patience was not with her.

"Aren't you coming?" she called out, surprised.

"I think I'll take the grays for one last jaunt before I put them away," she answered, nodding to Hawkins to resume his seat behind her.

"Patience! It's raining!"

"The horses don't care, and I—I—"

Patience drove off without finishing her sentence.

She needed to think.

Chapter 12

The next morning, Patience woke up with streaming eyes and a sore throat. Pru showed her no pity. "It serves you right for going out in the rain," she declared when she looked in on her sister after luncheon. Patience was just getting out of bed.

"It was only a light drizzle," Patience protested. "Anyway, it gives me some excuse for not appearing at court on Monday. If anyone asks, you may say I have a bad cold."

"There is no question of your going to meet the queen with a swollen nose," Pru vehemently agreed. "We could not risk you sneezing on her majesty! Shall I send for Dr. Wingfield?"

"I'll be quite all right in a day or two," Patience assured her. "There's no need to send for the doctor. No one ever dies of a trifling little cold."

"No one ever dies of seasickness either," Pru retorted, "but *you* nearly managed it."

The next day, Patience was improved, and on Monday, as planned, Pru and Lady Jemima set off for St. James's Palace in the carriage. Dressing for such an event was a long, arduous process, and Pru had been up before dawn. She was advised to eat little and drink less; no facilities would be available to the young ladies. Along with all the other debutantes making their first court appearance that day, Pru would be required to sit in her carriage with her chaperone until the master of ceremonies sent for them. The wait could be two hours or ten, depending on her majesty's pleasure, and Pru would be among the last called, for the girls were to be presented by strict Order of Precedence.

Patience, who could not understand why anyone willingly would put themselves to so much trouble for so little result, kissed her sister good-bye, and spent a leisurely afternoon exploring Bullock's Museum, where she saw, among other charming artifacts, Oliver Cromwell's skull and the big green campaign coach of Napoleon Bonaparte. In Hatchards book shop, she bought a copy of Mrs. Godwin's *A Vindication of the Rights of Woman*.

Prudence returned home, well after midnight. Patience was waiting up for her, reading her new book, but, too exhausted to talk, too exhausted even to eat, Pru went straight to bed.

Letting her go, Patience detained Lady Jemima very briefly. "All went well, I trust?"

"Oh, yes, my lady," the chaperone assured her, biting back a yawn. "Her majesty received Miss Prudence with every appearance of pleasure. She made a very pretty curtsy, and, of course, it did not hurt that she was wearing the Sunderland diamonds."

Patience frowned. "The what? You must be mistaken, Lady Jemima. I gave Prudence leave to hire some jewels. She told me she had done so."

Lady Jemima could not look Patience in the eye. "Well, but one cannot hire such jewels, you know. Mr. Grey had nothing left but topaz! And, of course, Miss Prudence could not be presented in topaz!"

"Heaven forbid," Patience said with heavy sarcasm.

"In any case," said Lady Jemima, glancing up with a hint of defiance, "there's nothing to be done about it now. The duke's man comes to collect them in the morning."

Patience angrily started down the hall to her sister's room, but Lady Jemima stopped her. "Let the child sleep, Lady Waverly, I beg of you. Mr. Purefoy offered the jewels; she did not ask for them. Did you expect her to refuse diamonds, when the alternative was topaz?"

"No," Patience answered, with a sigh. "I suppose not. But *he* should have known better than to send them! He did it behind my back, too!"

"It was just the touch we needed for a complete success," Lady Jemima said happily. "It gave Miss Prudence a little something extra. She'll be mentioned in tomorrow's paper, I daresay. The queen spoke to her for a minute at least—oh, an eternity!"

Patience bit back a sarcastic remark. "As you say, there is nothing to be done about it now. Good night, Lady Jemima."

The older woman curtsyed to the younger. "Good night, Lady Waverly."

The next morning, Lady Jemima wisely pleaded the headache and took her breakfast in her room. Patience went down to breakfast to confront Prudence, only to find her sister in the very best of spirits, dividing her attention between a plate of food and a pile of invitations.

She glanced up as Patience walked in. "What's eating you?" she asked. "Never mind! I don't care! There's nothing you can do or say to spoil my perfect happiness! I expect you will try anyway," she added with a sniff. "But you won't succeed."

Patience sat down and drew her napkin across her lap.

"I don't mean to spoil anything," she said, uncomfortably aware that she was being defensive. "But I must point out the folly of accepting favors from Mr. Purefoy."

Pru stared at her blankly. "What on earth are you talking about?"

"The Sunderland diamonds, of course! Lady Jemima told me you borrowed them."

"Oh, that! I thought—" She broke off, chuckling.

Patience's suspicions were aroused. "You thought what?" she demanded.

"I suppose I might as well tell you," Pru said airily.

"Tell me what?"

Pru handed Briggs a folded newspaper. "Take this to her ladyship. I'll let you read it for yourself," she told Patience as Briggs bore the news down the length of the room.

"What have you done?" Patience demanded, snatching the newspaper from the butler's tray. Pru had folded it so that the society page was on top.

"You needn't thank me," said Pru as Patience scanned the lines. "I confess I did it as much for myself as I did it for you. But we will both benefit from it, you'll see."

"'The American, Lady Waverly, made her curtsy to the queen as if she had been doing it all her life,'" Patience read in outraged disbelief.

"'And her ladyship's sister, Miss Prudence Waverly, was no less graceful,'" continued Pru, having committed the pertinent lines to memory already. "'It is to be hoped that the raven-haired beauties will grace the Court of St. James with the perfume of their presence on many more occasions.'"

"You impersonated me!" Patience said hotly.

"It wasn't easy," Pru said proudly. "First, I was presented as you, then I had to hurry to the back of the line to be presented as me. Is it any wonder I was exhausted when I got home?"

"How could you? You curtsyed! I swore I never would."

"Then I have spared you some unpleasantness," Pru said. "There would have been a great scandal, you know, if you had refused to curtsy. And I would have been tainted by the association. It was for the best, Patience."

"You planned this behind my back!" Patience accused her. "You and Lady Jemima—and Max Purefoy!"

Pru blinked at her. "Max? Max had nothing to do with it. It was all my own idea. You really must stop trying to blame him for everything," she added sanctimoniously.

"How can you say he had nothing to do with it? He gave you diamonds to wear!"

Pru smiled happily. "Wasn't that ever so thoughtful of him?"

"You had no right to pretend to be me!" Patience shouted.

"But it would have looked so very strange if I came out and you didn't," Pru protested. "What are you complaining about? I did you a favor. You are out—with no trouble to yourself, I might add. I did all the work! Already the invitations are pouring in! I must ask Max which ones I ought to accept and which I should decline."

"I'd decline them all if I were you," Patience muttered.

"I'll be better off without you, I'm sure!" Pru retorted. "You should not go out into society at all if you are so determined to disapprove of everything you see."

"Believe me, I won't! You will have to tell Mr. Purefoy what you did," Patience went on grimly. "I won't have him thinking that I accepted this favor from him. I daresay he thinks me a hypocrite, to criticize him one minute, and then accept diamonds from him the next!"

Pru laughed. "You need not worry about *that*! When I was presented as you, I wore the topaz we hired from Mr. Grey."

Patience stared at her. "You what?"

"I knew you wouldn't want to wear *Max's* diamonds," Pru explained. "I think his feelings were a bit hurt, actually."

Patience gasped in dismay. "You mean he was there? You spoke to him—as *me*?"

"Oh, yes; he was there with his uncle. I hardly had time to talk to them, however; I had to rush back to the carriage to put on my diamonds. Then I had to wait three more hours to be presented as myself."

"What did you say to him?" Patience asked, dreading the answer.

"I don't remember exactly what I said, but I was extremely rude to him, and to his uncle, too, of course. I may have just mentioned to the duke that the French had the right idea about what to do with the aristocracy. Off with their heads!"

"What?" Patience squawked. "Pru! Tell me you didn't!"

"I was pretending to be you," Pru said innocently. "Isn't that what you always say?"

"I have never said 'off with their heads!'"

"True. You are content to call them leeches and parasites, but I have always thought that rather hypocritical of you. Everyone knows that the quickest way to get rid of the aristocracy is to kill 'em."

Patience's cheeks were hot. "You did *not* say that!"

"No, of course not; there wasn't time."

"What he must think of me!" Patience said, leaving the table without touching her food.

"If it's any consolation," Pru called after her, "I'm sure they don't think of you at all!" Quite unconcerned about her sister's embarrassment, she went back to her breakfast and her invitations.

Isabella Norton read the same society column that morning at breakfast. "Personally," she sniffed, "I should be ashamed to be presented at court wearing borrowed plumes!"

"Your gown was hired," her brother reminded her. "Do you think I have hundreds of pounds lying about to buy court dresses for my sister?"

"I have my own jewels," she said coldly. "That is the main thing."

"No one need ever know your pearls are glass," he agreed. "But . . . are you quite certain the girl was wearing the Sunderland diamonds?"

"Quite sure," Isabella said coldly.

"And it was the younger girl, you say, not the baroness?"

"How keenly disappointed her ladyship must have felt!" Isabella said, but, since Lady Waverly's disappointment could hardly have been greater than that of Isabella herself, she spoke without triumph. "I pity her! To be outstripped by a young sister—albeit a younger sister only minutes her junior—must be a very bitter pill to swallow."

"I wonder what he is playing at," Milford said thoughtfully.

"Isn't it obvious?" said Isabella. "He lent the younger sister the diamonds to put an end to the elder sister's pretensions! Or, perhaps he is trying to make *me* jealous," she went on hopefully. "He is testing me. But I shall be dignity personified. I shan't create any scenes. He may play with these Americans as much as he likes. I shall bide my time."

Milford grimaced. "I think it only fair to tell you, my dear, that Mr. Purefoy has made a bet. He has hazarded fifty thousand pounds."

His sense of fairness did not require him to reveal his own part in that bet, however. In fact, he was as determined as ever to keep Isabella in ignorance.

"What of it?" she shrugged. "I would not interfere in any of his pleasures. With a fortune such as his, fifty thousand pounds is but a drop in the ocean."

"But Lady Waverly was the subject of his wager," Milford explained. "I'm sorry to have to tell you this, Izzy, but Purefoy has vowed to marry her."

"What?" Isabella cried, her face pale and drawn.

"I'm afraid it's true. Imagine how I feel," he went on quickly. "I made a wager with Lord Torcaster the same day that *I* would marry Lady Waverly. He goaded me into it. It's your fault," he added petulantly, "for making me go out that night. If you had but given me lamb chops at home, none of this would be happening."

"You must have misunderstood," said Isabella, her voice shaking. "Mr. Purefoy, and—and Lady Waverly! I cannot believe it. Perhaps he wagered to bed her, but not *wed* her, surely! Why, the only way he could win a bet like that would be to *marry* her—*actually marry her.* He would not do that, surely."

"I notice you don't seem very concerned about your brother!"

"I hope your wager with Lord Torcaster was not a very large one," she said dutifully.

"Ten thousand pounds," he said. "A mere trifle to his lordship!"

"Quite!" she said furiously. "Because *he* had the sense to marry Miss Cruikshanks!"

His face turned red. "I have my pride, you know. Torcaster is shameless. But I do wonder at Max playing up to the younger sister when he has vowed to marry the elder," he went on quickly, before Isabella could retort. "What can he mean?"

Isabella's brow furrowed in thought. "Could it be Lady Waverly has refused him?" she murmured at last. "He sent the diamonds to her, perhaps, but she passed them on to her sister?"

"Passed them on?" he repeated incredulously. "Passed them on, and then wore topaz herself?"

"It doesn't seem very likely, does it?" Isabella agreed. "I might *just* believe that Lady Waverly prefers you to Mr. Purefoy, but no one could prefer topaz to diamonds!"

Milford scowled at her.

"Far more likely that Lady Waverly is playing some deep game."

"Perhaps she doesn't like him, as she pretends," said Milford.

"Perhaps," said Isabella. "We must keep them under close surveillance at the ball tomorrow night."

"What ball? You said we were not engaged tomorrow night. I cannot escort you. I made . . . er . . . plans."

"You will see your mistress another time," Isabella told him. "Tomorrow night, you must bring me to the ball at Sunderland House."

"Oh! Did you receive an invitation, after all?" said her brother.

"A strange oversight, I'm sure, nothing more," Isabella said.

Milford was horrified. "Are you suggesting that we gate crash?"

"Don't be such a mouse," she told him contemptuously. "Faint heart never won fair maid. Do you want to win your bet or not?"

Milford flinched, and Isabella knew that she had won.

Sunderland Square was already crowded with vehicles by the time Lady Waverly's carriage arrived. Prudence had decided to arrive at the ball fashionably late, the better to make her entrance, a decision she now bitterly regretted. "Why did you not tell me there would be such a crush?" she berated poor Lady Jemima as the driver inched slowly toward the lights and music spilling from the open doors of the Duke of Sunderland's mansion. "At this rate, we're going to miss everything!"

Lady Jemima patted her pink hair. "I tried to tell you," she murmured. "But you would not listen. Of course, everyone who is anyone will be here tonight."

"But Max promised me the first two dances," Pru pouted. "You don't suppose he would start the dancing without me?"

She need not have worried. Before Lady Jemima could make any reply, the carriage door opened and Max himself stood there with a gloved hand outstretched to Pru. "It is not far, Miss Prudence, if you would care to walk," he said, helping her down the steps. "Or, if you prefer, I can offer you one of our chairs."

Pru laughed at the chairmen lining the sidewalk. "Lady Jemima may go by sedan chair, if she wants," she said. "I shall walk."

Max raised his brows as the footman closed the door after Lady Jemima had alighted from the carriage. "And . . . Lady Waverly? Is your sister not with you this evening?" he asked.

Pru slipped her arm through Max's. "Patience? Didn't I tell you? She could not come tonight. She had already accepted an invitation to a little reception at the American embassy. She asked me to make her excuses for her."

"Excuses?" Max said, a little sharply.

"Oh, she was excessively sorry not to be able to attend," said Pru, "but she could not disappoint Mrs. Adams, you know."

"I see," he said, tight-lipped.

"I am sorry if she has offended you," Pru said meekly. "If it were up to me, she would be here, but I can't make her do anything. She's as stubborn as an ox!"

A smile touched his lips. "True."

"We can do very well without her," said Pru, as they

drew close to the marble steps. "You have not forgotten that you promised me the first two dances?"

His mouth tightened again. "I have not forgotten," he said. "We have all been waiting for you to arrive to open the ball."

Patience was among the first of the guests to arrive at Number Nine, Grosvenor Square, and no one thought the worse of her for having arrived in a yellow hackney carriage, except, perhaps, the jarvey himself.

Louisa Adams, the pretty, English-born wife of the ambassador, received her very warmly.

"I see you have run the gauntlet at St. James's Palace, Lady Waverly," Mr. Adams said with a twinkle in his eye, "and lived to tell the tale! We read of it in the newspaper."

"Oh, sir!" Patience said, blushing. "It is not really a gauntlet, surely."

"It is of a kind," the ambassador replied. "Instead of striking their blows with sticks as the Iroquois do, they strike with hostile, contemptuous stares! When my father served as ambassador, my mother often complained of it. *Plus ça change, plus c'est la même chose,* as our French friends say. But, I forget, you are one of them, a baroness. A Peeress of the Realm. If you were a man, you would have a seat in the House of Lords."

"I am *not* one of them," Patience said quickly. "I hope you will call me Miss Waverly while I am here. No matter what I say, the English will call me 'my lady.' Even the servants refuse to be broken of the habit!"

Mrs. Adams smiled. "I had hoped to see both Miss Waverlys tonight."

"I beg your pardon, ma'am," Patience apologized. "My sister sends her regrets. But she had a previous engagement that could not be broken."

"Too bad," Mrs. Adams said graciously. "Young ladies are always much too scarce at my functions! I can never find enough partners for the gentlemen. But let me find a young man to look after you," she added, beckoning to someone with her fan.

Patience opened her mouth to protest, but closed it again as a tall, very good-looking young man detached himself from the small knot of gentlemen standing guard over the punch.

"Miss Waverly," he said warmly. "We meet again! I confess I had hoped to see you here."

"You know each other already," Mrs. Adams said, pleased. "If you will excuse me, I must go and rescue my poor husband from Mrs. Rush!"

She hurried off, leaving Patience with the young man. Fair-haired and blue-eyed, he was clean cut and very handsome, with classically sculpted features.

"You have me at a disadvantage, sir," Patience murmured in dismay. "I don't believe we are acquainted. I'm sure I would have remembered meeting a fellow American."

"I beg your pardon, ma'am," he said, reddening with embarrassment. "We have met before, but I am not surprised you do not remember. You were quite ill on the journey. It is Miss *Patience* Waverly, isn't it?" he added, looking at her curiously. "When you were ill, I had no difficulty telling you apart . . ."

"You saw me when I was ill?" she said, no less embarrassed.

"I had the honor of attending you," he quickly explained. "I too sailed from America aboard the *Seagull*."

Patience shook her head. "But the ship's doctor was a venerable old fellow called Reynolds! I am sure of it."

"I'm afraid a number of passengers fell ill on the journey. I was happy to help with those patients suffering only minor complaints."

"Minor!" she protested. "It did not feel at all minor to me, sir!"

"I'm sure it didn't."

Patience grimaced. "I fear you have seen me at my worst, sir."

"There's no need to be embarrassed, Miss Waverly," he said. "I am a physician. I have seen much, much worse."

"That is hardly a comfort, sir!"

He laughed. "Did your sister never happen to mention me?"

"Perhaps she did," Patience replied. "What is your name?"

"Forgive me! I am Roger Molyneux."

Patience frowned. "I'm quite sure she never mentioned that name."

"I see," he said gravely. "Is Miss Prudence here tonight? I would like to pay my respects."

"A prior engagement," said Patience. "Perhaps she did mention you," she added kindly. "Perhaps I do not remember it. I was quite done up when I arrived in England. I don't remember all that much. What brings you to England, sir?"

"I am here to complete my surgical training, Miss Waverly," he replied. "Oh, I beg your pardon! Do you prefer to be given your title? You are a baroness, I believe."

"Please, call me Patience," she said. "I hate my title. I have come here tonight to escape from it!"

"Roger," he said, and they shook hands. "I was very sorry to leave you at Plymouth, Miss—er—Patience. But I was obliged to find lodgings in London. I am dresser to Dr. Chandler these days. For the next eighteen months, I belong to him. I was very fortunate to be allowed to come here tonight. My life has been nothing but lectures since I came here."

"Oh, I quite understand."

"I'd be eternally grateful if you would dance with me."

Patience laughed. "Of course! That is just what I came to do!"

He led her onto the floor as the musicians played a lively jig.

"I am surprised my sister never mentioned you," Patience said frankly, as they were dancing. "You are exactly the sort of young man we most like to talk about, you see."

"You're very kind," he replied. "I believe your sister hardly noticed me. She thought of nothing but you, and your restoration to good health. It was all I could do to get her to leave the cabin for a little fresh air now and then. She never left your side unless I made her. Despite all my assurances, she was terrified that you were going to die."

"I had that fear myself, sir," Patience said, laughing.

"Miss Prudence is in good health, I trust?"

"Oh, yes," Patience assured him. "On Monday, she met the queen. Tonight, she is attending a ball at the Duke of Sunderland's house. And, yes, it is just as grand as it sounds. The ball is being held in her honor."

"Well, well!" he murmured. "She is happy, then, to be moving in such elevated circles! She would not care to waste her time here with us common folk. She told me she meant to marry a lord," he added, chuckling. "I don't suppose she has nabbed one yet?"

"I'm sure Pru was only joking with you," Patience told him. "She has not met anyone she likes well enough to marry."

"And you, Miss Patience?"

"Pshaw!" said Patience. "I don't care three straws for titles—not even my own, sir. I only accepted it because it was part and parcel with my inheritance."

"I meant, have you met anyone you like well enough to marry?"

"No, Mr. Molyneux," Patience answered. "But I have met someone I like well enough to dance with."

His blue eyes twinkled. "Will you dance another dance with a humble medical student, ma'am?"

"Yes," she said, giving him her hand.

A little after midnight, Isabella looked out of the drawing room window of her brother's house. They had attempted to crash the ball, without success. The duke had a sentry posted at the gates of Sunderland Square, checking each and every invitation. The earl had been obliged to take his sister home.

Across the way, the Americans at Number Nine were making a terrible noise as they always did when they had one of their interminable vulgar assemblies. They seemed incapable of doing anything quietly. They whooped, stomped, and clapped madly as they danced, and when they sang their horrid songs, they sang them at the top of their lungs, setting every dog in the neighborhood to barking. The rest of the street seemed deserted, however. Isabella guessed that all of their neighbors had been invited to the ball at Sunderland House.

"Someone really ought to do something about it!" she said angrily to her brother, who was dozing in the corner with one hand on the wine decanter. "Ivor! Go over there this instant, and tell them to be quiet! They are like a pack of wild Indians! They should not be here at all! This is Grosvenor Square! This is Mayfair! This is England!"

Milford was still smarting from the humiliation of having been turned away at the gates of Sunderland Square. He could not even look forward to a comfortable evening with his mistress, for he had broken his appointment with her in order to take his sister to the ball.

"They have a right to be there," said Milford, taking their part only because he was vexed with his sister. "It is their embassy. Everything between those four walls is considered the sovereign territory of the United States. There's nothing anyone can do about it."

"Coward!" said Isabella. In the next instant, however, she caught her breath. "Good heavens! What is he doing here? Good God, is he—? I do believe he is going over! He is going over! He is going in!"

"Who?" Milford asked, vaguely interested.

"It's about time somebody did something," said Isabella. "Now, perhaps, Grosvenor Square will be Grosvenor Square again!"

Milford was angry now, because his question had not been answered immediately. "Who has gone over?" he demanded.

"Mr. Purefoy!"

Milford hurried to the window, but he was too late to see Mr. Purefoy going into the American ambassador's house. "You're joking with me," he said. "Or else you are mistaken. What would Purefoy want with those barbarians?"

"I don't know," said Isabella. "But I am not mistaken. He did go in that house. And we shall wait right here, Brother, until he comes out again!"

Chapter 13

The fresh-faced young officer on duty at his ambassador's residence clearly had never heard of the noble family of Purefoy, and, as Max had no invitation, he was obliged to wait while the lieutenant dispatched a servant into the house with Mr. Purefoy's card. After a time, the servant returned to conduct Max into the house. The noise coming from the room beyond was almost deafening, but with effort, Max could hear the musicians struggling to rise above the sounds of raucous gaiety.

Mrs. Adams did not keep him waiting long. "Sir?"

Max offered her a bow, and, somewhat to his surprise, she responded with a very graceful curtsy. He opened his mouth to speak, but closed it again as he suddenly heard the sacrosanct strains of "God Save the King." The Americans, however, had invented their own lyrics:

> *My country 'tis of thee*
> *Sweet land of liberty*
> *Of thee I sing . . .*

As an Englishman, he found it quite unforgivably cheeky. Mrs. Adams hastily signaled to the servant to close the doors. "Are we making too much noise, sir?" she began nervously. "I do apologize. Our young men are in constant need of diversion, and, when given the chance, I'm afraid they can be quite boisterous. They need wives, of course, but, other than that, there's nothing really wrong with them. But we'll try to keep it down, sir. We do want to be good neighbors, you know. Would you care to come in for some punch? Mr. Adams makes it himself."

"Thank you, ma'am," he said.

The ambassador's wife blinked at him in surprise. "Oh, you would? How delightful."

Max had the impression that her hospitality was usually declined by his countrymen. She accepted his arm, again with an air of surprise, and together they made their way through the doors into the crowded, noisy ballroom.

He saw Patience instantly. Indeed, he could hardly have missed her, for she was wearing a low-cut gown of crimson velvet. She was dancing, if dancing it could be called, in the middle of the room. Her green eyes were sparkling, her cheeks were flushed, and her heavy black hair was slipping its pins. Her partner was a tall, grinning young man who seemed to think he was handsome. Hands clasped, the pair was spinning in ever-quickening circles while the crowd around them shouted their appreciation of the maneuver. Max had never seen Patience looking so happy as she smiled up into the bright blue eyes of her partner. They weren't even wearing gloves, which somehow made it worse.

Without realizing it, Max began to frown. "Who is that young man dancing with Lady Waverly?" he demanded of Mrs. Adams without thinking.

Mrs. Adams fluttered her fan. "Are you acquainted with Lady Waverly, sir?"

Glancing up, Patience saw Max coming down the stairs, and nearly tripped over her own feet. Her partner caught her with an efficiency that did not please Max at all. The young man's hands were much too quick. Patience seemed hardly to notice as she stared at the newcomer.

Max could easily read her lips: "Lord, what is *he* doing here?"

No one else paid the slightest heed to him. He might have been invisible as he slipped through the crowd. To Max, so accustomed to being fawned over wherever he went, it was a welcome respite.

Patience lost him for a moment in the crowd; while he stood head and shoulders above most of his own countrymen, there were a dozen or more American men in the room who matched or exceeded him in height.

"Are you all right, Miss Patience?" her partner inquired.

Patience felt out of breath and a little dizzy, but pleasantly so. "I think I see someone I know," she said, raising her voice to be heard. "Would you excuse me, please?"

Leaving her countryman, she plunged into the crowd in search of Max. Each was so determined to find the other that it was not long before they were face to face.

"Mr. Purefoy!" she said, laughing almost in disbelief. "I thought I saw you! What on earth are you doing here?"

He felt a foolish grin spreading across his face, but, before he could answer, she said suddenly, her eyes wide, "Is Prudence all right? Has something happened?"

"Your sister is perfectly well," he shouted over the din of the music and voices. "I came to see you."

"Me? Why?"

She seemed a little short of breath, probably from her exuberant dancing with Mr. Quickhands, Max thought sourly. But he forced himself to smile pleasantly.

"If the mountain won't come to Mahomet, Mahomet must go to the mountain!"

"What?" she cried, cupping one hand over her ear.

"I came here to dance with you!"

Her eyes widened. "Oh, no! Shouldn't you be at your own ball, dancing with Prudence? You promised her the first two dances, I believe."

"I have faithfully kept my promise," he shouted. "Dance with me! Prudence will never know."

He held out his hand to her.

For a moment, Patience stared at him. Max felt, absurdly, that everything depended on her answer. Then she said simply, "I will!" and he knew it was not absurd at all. Everything was perfectly all right, and nothing could ever be wrong again.

To his surprise, she caught hold of his wrist and began peeling off his glove. "In America, we don't need these!" she shouted. "We dance hand in hand, not hand in glove!"

"But this is England!" It was a protest in word only. She had already removed his gloves and tossed them aside.

"No, sir! This is America," she shouted back. "Like it or not, when you passed through those doors, you crossed the Atlantic Ocean. You're in my country now!"

For some reason, this delighted him. "I am at your disposal, Lady Waverly!"

She clucked her tongue at him. "Patience! None of your silly titles here, sir!"

"In that case, I am Max."

She laughed. "I know!"

The Americans lined up for the reel rather like civilized human beings, with gentlemen on one side and ladies on the other. The ladies curtsyed, the gentlemen bowed.

"A curtsy?" Max mocked his partner. "You swore you would not."

"Only as part of the dance," she said quickly, a frown drawing her dark brows together. "I suppose I ought to explain about court—about the diamonds—"

"No need!" he said, anxious to dispel her dismay. "I am well aware that Miss Prudence took your place."

"You are? How?"

He smiled. "She curtsyed," he replied. "You, of course, would never do that. Also, her hair is different. She has curls over her ears."

Patience felt oddly disappointed. For some reason, she had wanted to hear that he would know her anywhere, that he could pick her out amongst a thousand copies. If he had a twin, she wondered suddenly, would I know him? She smiled at him.

"Are you ready?" she called out.

He looked surprised. "For what?"

The musicians struck up a lively air, and, all at once, the two sides rushed at each other, and with roars from the gentlemen and whoops from the ladies, the dancing began in earnest and soon escalated to ferocity. Late to the start, Max was hard-pressed to keep up with his partner.

"Sir, you are too quiet," Patience complained. "In America, we do not dance with our mouths clamped shut!"

"Dance?" Max shouted in Patience's ear. "I thought the war had started up again."

"Only a skirmish!" she responded merrily. "This is nothing like the dancing you are used to at Almack's," she added.

"No, indeed!"

"English dancing is so elegant! So precise! Just like clockwork. Tick tock. Tick tock!"

The dance separated them, but they remained connected with their eyes until they could join hands again.

"Who is that young man staring at you?" he asked her as they met briefly between the two lines. "He is impertinent, I think."

Patience followed his gaze. Roger Molyneux, leaning against a pillar, was indeed staring.

"Oh, dear!" Patience cried. "Poor Roger! I forgot him completely."

"Roger!" Max exclaimed. "Is that his name?"

"Yes. He must be furious with me."

"Who is he? Has he some claim on you?"

She smiled. "*He,* sir, is *American* royalty."

Max frowned. "No such thing."

"We have an aristocracy," she told him. "But it is an aristocracy of talent, not birth."

"Oh, I see," Max said sourly. "The young man has talents! What, pray, are his talents? Besides pouting, I mean? You were dancing with him when I arrived, I believe."

Patience nodded. "Roger is a physician," she said. "He has come to London to finish his training. We came over on the same ship. He tended to me when I was ill."

Max did not like the sound of this at all. "And a wonderful job he did of it, too," he said. "As I recall, you arrived in the pink of health!"

"It's not his fault I was seasick," she protested. "Prudence got better almost at once. There's no predicting how it will go. Come! I'll introduce you," she added, tugging him by the hand.

"We are dancing," he said, resisting.

"By all rights, I should be dancing with Roger," she said. "I owe him an apology and an explanation, at the very least!"

Max did not think so, but he allowed her to drag him to the other man's position. At their approach, Molyneux abandoned his post and stood with his arms folded.

"Roger, I am so sorry!" Patience began. "I saw a—a friend. Mr. Purefoy, this is Mr. Molyneux. Mr. Molyneux, this is Mr. Purefoy. I was just telling Mr. Purefoy about your studies. Roger is working very hard."

"Oh, I can see that," Max said dryly. "Are you by some chance any connection to the Lancashire Molyneuxs?"

Molyneux gave a short, derisive laugh. "Try the Jersey Molyneuxs."

Max frowned, puzzled.

"He means *New* Jersey, Mr. Purefoy," said Patience, laughing behind her hand. "Roger's family is from Princeton, New Jersey. That's only about forty miles from Philadelphia."

"A very easy distance," Max said slowly.

"Actually," said Molyneux, "my family are settled near Pennsauken. I was schooled at Princeton."

"Pennsauken!" Patience exclaimed delightedly. "We're practically neighbors!"

"We're just on the other side of the Delaware," Molyneux agreed. "Not twenty miles from your door in Chestnut Hill, I daresay, Miss Patience."

"When we are home again, I hope you will visit us," Patience said impulsively.

"Perhaps I will set up my practice in Philadelphia," he said.

Max was liking this conversation less and less. "Very nice to have met you, Molyneux," he said curtly. "But, now, I think, Lady Waverly and I must finish our dance."

Molyneux raised his brows. "*Lady* Waverly?"

Patience was embarrassed. "It's nothing, Roger. A meaningless honorific."

"It is not meaningless," Max said coldly. "You are a Peeress of the Realm."

"Peeress of the Realm!" Molyneux snickered. "Patience Waverly of Twenty-six Cambridge Street, Philadelphia, Pennsylvania?"

"Baroness Waverly of Wildings, Number Seventeen Clarges Street!" Max said angrily.

"Stop it!" said Patience. "You are embarrassing me!"

"Yes, Molyneux! You are embarrassing her ladyship! You should apologize!"

"I mean *you*," Patience said angrily.

Max stared at her. "I? How so, ma'am? Indeed, how

could *anyone* be embarrassed at an assembly such as this? Am I not shouting loud enough, perhaps? Am I too precise? Do I dance too mildly?"

Patience was pale with shock. "Mr. Purefoy!" she murmured in dismay. "What is the matter with you?"

Max looked down at her coldly. "Nothing is the matter with me," he said sharply. "I am giving a ball tonight—in England, where gentlemen are scarce. I am sure more than one lady is in want of a partner. I must go back."

With a curt bow, he turned to go.

"Come, Patience," Molyneux said. "You don't want to dance with that cold fish anyway."

Without thinking, Max spun around and drove his fist into Roger Molyneux's face. Without a chance to defend himself, the young man went down.

"Roger!" Patience gasped, sinking to her knees beside him. "He's out cold!"

"You'll look after him, though, won't you?" Max sneered, as a group of young men appeared to drag him away.

Roger Molyneux sat up, shaking his head and feeling his jaw.

"How many fingers am I holding up?" Patience asked.

"I'm all right," he said, dragging himself up to his feet. "He sucker-punched me, by God! So much for fair play! Where is he? Where's the English bastard?"

"Don't worry about him," said Patience. "Our friends have thrown him out."

"I hope they kicked him around a bit first!" Molyneux said bitterly.

"Hush!" Taking her handkerchief from her décolleté, Patience dabbed at the blood trickling from the corner of his mouth. Molyneux tottered suddenly and had to sit down.

Mrs. Adams hurried over. "Are you all right, my dear?"

she asked Patience. "I should not have invited him in! But I thought he knew you. He seemed an English gentleman."

Suddenly, Patience was furious. "Will you look after Mr. Molyneux for me, ma'am?" she said, giving Mrs. Adams her handkerchief. "I would like to give that *English gentleman* a piece of my mind!"

While by no means gentle with Max, the Americans had refrained from kicking him around. They simply dragged him past the gates and threw him down on the hard cobblestones.

"And don't come back, you English bastard!"

From his new home in the gutter, Max could hear them dragging the iron gates closed.

"Wait!" cried Patience, running out into the street.

She almost stumbled over Max. "Oh! Did they hurt you, Mr. Purefoy?"

"No, Patience! I like it here in the gutter," he replied, sitting up.

"Lady Waverly, if you please," she said coldly. "We're back in England now. Perhaps that will help you remember your manners."

"Your friends were not very polite to me," he complained. "My stockings are quite ruined."

"Well, it serves you right, you brute!" Patience snapped. "You are rude and arrogant and—and just as vile as I thought you were! You could have hurt Roger!"

Max looked up at her, scowling. "You mean I *didn't* hurt Roger? That is a disappointment."

"You cold-cocked him when he wasn't looking," she accused him. "I ask you, is that cricket? And you call yourself an English gentleman!"

"Well, I am half Italian," he reminded her, getting up to

his knees. "It comes out when I am in love. He's lucky I left my stiletto in my other coat."

Patience caught her breath. "In love?" she echoed softly. "In—in love with *me, sir?*"

"No! In love with Roger," he snarled, now on his feet looking down at her.

One of the Americans chose this moment to call to her from the embassy gates. "Best come back in, miss, so we can close the gate. Best leave that varmint where he is."

Max surged forward. "Varmint? Who are you calling a varmint, my good fellow? You may find me at Jackson's boxing parlor in Bond Street any day of the week, good sir! Better yet, why don't you come out here and fight me now, you bloody Yankee-Doodle dandy?"

"Stop goading them," Patience snapped, following Max into the square. "It's not fair. You know they can't leave their post. It would cause a diplomatic nightmare for poor Mr. Adams!" She sighed, her anger dissipating. "I realize that you were—that you were jealous of poor Roger, but that is no excuse for behaving like an oaf."

He scowled at her. "Jealous of that—that boy?"

She raised her brows. "You were not jealous? I thought, perhaps, you were."

"No, indeed," he sniffed. "I hit him for the sheer pleasure of it."

"I'm glad," she said. "I'm glad you're not jealous, because I mean to dance with him all night!"

"You can go back to Pennsadelphia or whatever and *marry* the crown prince of New Jersey for all I care!"

That made her laugh. "If you do not admit this instant that you are jealous that's just what I'll do," she threatened.

Max gave the matter some thought. "Perhaps I was a little jealous," he admitted. "But the madness has passed, thankfully. I am myself again."

"Oh, Max, you are such an idiot," Patience said tenderly. Taking his face between her hands, she stood on tiptoe to kiss his cheek.

"What was that for?" he breathed.

"You know what it's for," she answered, twining her arms around his neck, and brushing her lips against his neck, her eyes closed as she gave herself up to a feeling of exhilaration.

Rather abruptly, he took her in his arms, and kissed her roughly. Patience gave him her mouth, pressing her body against him. "I think we have found something the English do with their mouths open," she murmured, laughing.

Lord Milford had fallen asleep with his head on the windowsill. Isabella's howl of rage woke him. "Wh-what?" he gasped, jumping up, a red hand printed on the side of his face.

"They are kissing," Isabella sobbed. "In full view of the street!"

"Who is kissing?" he asked, peering out into the square. He could see the lady's crimson gown, but not her face. Her companion was even more obscure. "Good God! A streetwalker! A streetwalker in Grosvenor Square."

"She came from the American ambassador's house! 'Tis one of the Americans! I saw her face as she ran after him!"

"What do you care if some American is kissing a streetwalker?" he said, amazed. "I'd rather they not do it in front of my house, too, but I ain't going to weep and wail and gnash my teeth."

"You fool!" she snarled. "It is Mr. Purefoy kissing one of the Americans."

"He did not stay long," Milford commented. "Do you recognize the lady?"

"It is Lady Waverly or Miss Prudence. I can't tell them apart!"

"It cannot be," said her brother, pressing his nose against the window. "They are all at Sunderland House tonight. Everyone is there, except us."

Isabella ignored him. "One of them must have attended the vile gathering at the American embassy," she murmured. "Instead of the ball. That is why he came here. He must have been furious to have his generosity thrown in his face."

"He doesn't look furious."

Isabella winced. "Is he still kissing her?" she whined.

"Oh, yes," he said appreciatively. "But is it Miss Prudence or Lady Waverly?"

"What does that matter?" she snapped. "Perhaps he means to have them both."

"Well, he can only marry one of them," Milford pointed out.

"There's no need to state the obvious," she said coldly. "Can't you do something?" she cried, stamping her foot. "I'd like to throw a bucket of cold water on them!"

Milford opened the window and leaned out, crowing, "Cock-a-doodle-do!" at the top of his lungs. "That's how we did it at university," he explained sheepishly to his bewildered sister.

Isabella hastily closed the window and put out the candle to preserve their anonymity, but she was glad to observe by the moonlight that her brother's outburst had achieved the desired effect.

"Good heavens!" Patience gasped. "What is that? A rooster?"

"A friend," said Max. "It means we have been seen. Run!"

"What?" she said, laughing. "I don't care who sees!"

"You will care very much when your sister reads about it in the newspaper," he said.

Patience started guiltily. "Pru! Oh, Max! Pru will never forgive me."

"You leave her to me," he said. "Hurry, my dear! Back to your embassy before the watch catches you."

"But, Max!" she protested. "Aren't you jealous?"

He grinned at her. "Should I be?"

"No!"

"Then go!" he commanded. "I will call on you to-morrow."

The following morning, Pru stumbled down to the breakfast table to find her sister scanning the columns of the newspaper. "Did you just get in?" Pru asked, bewildered. "Isn't that the same dress you wore last night?"

Patience blushed, self-consciously smoothing the neckline of her crimson velvet gown. To make it appropriate for day, she was wearing it over a high-necked muslin chemise with long, gathered sleeves. "Yes," she said. "I liked it so much I thought I'd wear it again."

"Crimson velvet is vulgar," said Pru.

"It's one of yours," Patience said, frowning.

"I bought it in Philadelphia, before I knew any better," Pru answered. "Red velvet is for curtains," Pru declared. "Curtains and courtesans."

"Dolley Madison wore a red velvet gown," Patience said coldly. "I'm sure you don't mean to criticize our First Lady!"

Pru got up to fill her plate at the sideboard. Trudging back to the table, she plunked herself down in her chair.

Suddenly, her green eyes widened. "Are you reading the *society pages*?" she asked incredulously.

Patience's face was bright pink. "I thought there might be some mention of Mrs. Adams's reception," she said.

"Is there?" Pru said doubtfully.

"No, there doesn't seem to be," Patience replied, trying not to show how vastly relieved she was about *that*. "It is all about the ball at Sunderland House."

"Well, of course it is. Who cares what happens at the American embassy?"

"Who, indeed," Patience murmured. "Did you enjoy yourself?"

"Oh, yes!" Pru said eagerly. "Even if Max only danced with me twice. He said it wouldn't be proper to dance with me a third time."

"You were not a wallflower, I trust?"

"Wallflower!" Pru said hotly. "No, indeed! I never lacked for a partner. But none of them were as agreeable as Max. I really do think I must love him—I miss him so much when he is not there."

Patience stared at her sister in unhappy silence.

"What?" Pru said at last.

"You can't be serious," said Patience. "In love with—with Purefoy? You never said you loved him before."

"I don't think I fell in love with him until he went away, just before Christmas," Pru said thoughtfully. "At least, I didn't realize until he had gone that I loved him. I'd grown so accustomed to him taking me out every day in his curricle."

Patience sighed in relief. "Is that all? I can take you out in a curricle, if that is what you want. You just get bored without someone to entertain you."

"Perhaps," Pru replied, with rare sense. "But last night, I was privileged to see him in his own element—master of Sunderland House."

"Was the duke not at home?"

"Of course he was," Pru said impatiently. "But he is nothing more than a dried up old bean in a chair! Everyone treats Max as if he were the duke already. You should have seen how they fawned over him! If I were his wife, I would be the Queen of London. They would fawn over me."

"If you were his wife—!" Patience exclaimed.

Pru bit her lip. "You would not stand in my way, would you, Patience?" she said anxiously. "By law, you are my guardian, and by law, I would need your permission to marry before my twenty-first birthday. You wouldn't make me wait, would you?"

"I don't know where all this is coming from," Patience said, taking a sip of her coffee in an attempt to soothe her rattled nerves. "Has Mr. Purefoy asked you to marry him?"

"Not yet, but he will." Pru seemed very confident.

"Was Lord Banville at the ball?" Patience asked.

"Oh, yes," said Pru. "I danced with him twice. He was extremely disappointed that you weren't there. He asked after you in the most *particular* way. He brought his mother with him, of course," she added, laughing.

After breakfast, Patience retreated to the drawing room. Taking out a sheet of paper, she took up her pen. She knew very well what she wanted to say—what, indeed she *must* say—but for several moments, she could not decide how to begin.

"Dear sir" would not do, of course. Much too cold. "My love"? Too hot.

"Dear Mr. Purefoy"? Perfectly ridiculous after the events of the night before.

"Dear Max"? As if she were addressing an old friend? Yes, that would have to do.

"Dear Max—"

Her hand trembled as she wrote, sending a fine spray of

ink across the page, but she soldiered on, dashing from one phrase to the next.

> *Do not come today— I cannot see you. Be assured my feelings remain unchanged— Pray, give me time to explain all to my sister. She will be greatly astonished when I tell her, and—I fear—none too pleased with me.*
>
> *Yours ever and always—*
> *Patience*

Blots were everywhere on the page, but, she thought, it was still legible. Setting it aside to dry, she found a wax wafer in the drawer and set her brass seal over the burner to heat.

"What are you writing?" Pru asked, coming into the room. "Not a love letter to Lord Banville, I trust?"

"Certainly not!" Patience said, laughing nervously. "Only a note to Mr. Bracegirdle. I have had good news," she added, turning to smile at her sister. "We have an offer on Wildings. Ten thousand pounds. I am going to his office this afternoon to meet with the land agent. Would you care to go with me?"

Pru made a face. "Leave Mayfair to go sit in a fusty old lawyer's office? Mr. Bracegirdle ain't even a barrister. He is merely a solicitor. Besides, I have to stay at home today. It's traditional for gentlemen to call on their dance partners the day after a ball."

Patience hastily folded her letter to Max, even though it was not quite dry. "I wonder if any of my dance partners will call on me," she said.

Pru scoffed. "I seriously doubt it. American men are all ill-mannered clodpoles."

"That is quite untrue," Patience said sharply. "There were many charming and agreeable young men at the embassy last night. I met someone you know, as a matter of fact."

"Who?" Pru demanded.

"A very promising young physician from New Jersey. He sends you his regards."

Pru scowled. "If you mean that Ronald Mollycoddle or whatever his name is—!"

"His name is Roger Molyneux."

"If you say so. I don't want his regards. Don't tell me you *danced* with him?"

"Several times. We cut quite a rug."

Pru made a face. "Really, Patience! He's nothing but a country doctor. And his *father* is nothing more than a country parson. You could do a lot better. Lord Banville, for instance!"

"I think Lord Banville is more your type than mine," Patience said. "You know he's much too handsome for me. And he seems to go everywhere with his mother."

"There's always Lord Milford, then," said Pru. "He is not too handsome! And, of course, Sir Charles Stanhope." Holding her stomach, she doubled over with laughter.

She was still giggling as Briggs came into the room bearing a card on his big, silver tray. Pru sat up and wiped her eyes. "Do you sleep with that tray, Briggs?" she asked irreverently, subsiding this time into soundless mirth.

"No, Miss Prudence," the butler replied.

"What is it, Briggs?" Patience asked, her tone apologetic.

Briggs cleared his throat. "The most noble Earl of Milford begs the favor of seeing Lady Waverly in private."

Pru burst out laughing. "Who? I'm afraid we're only acquainted with the *less* noble Earl of Milford," she roared. "I didn't know there were two of 'em!"

Patience stood up. "Oh, do be quiet, Pru!" she said

crossly. "You're giving me a headache. Tell his lordship I am not at home, Briggs, if you please."

"Don't send him away!" Pru said quickly. "This may be the only offer of marriage you are ever to receive."

"Marriage! Don't be ridiculous!"

"Of course he means marriage," Pru insisted. "Why else would he ask for a private interview? He has come to declare his love! If you send him away, he'll just keep coming back," she added. "Best get it over with now."

Patience sighed. "You're right. Very well. I will see his lordship in the book room downstairs," she told Briggs, rising from her desk.

"Would you like me to go in your place?" Pru asked solicitously.

"And wake up tomorrow engaged? No, thank you!" said Patience, moving for the door.

"Be kind!" Pru called after her sister. "Don't break his heart!"

Briggs followed his mistress from the room, closing the doors after him.

Pru went immediately to the desk. Something in Patience's manner had aroused her suspicions. Surely, a letter to the attorney would not inspire such blushing! No, it must be a note to Lord Banville—or possibly, even one to that clodpole Roger Molyneux. Pru picked up the letter, turning it over in her hands. It was sealed, but Patience had left the room without directing it. With the tip of a letter opener, Pru easily removed the wax seal, which was still warm and pliable.

Spreading open the page, she read the brief note through. At first, she could not believe her eyes. "Dear Max"! Patience was writing to *Max*? Why?

She read the few words again, their meaning sinking in slowly. Her hands began to shake. Cold rage swept through her body.

Patience was in love with Max. Patience, who had pretended for weeks that she didn't even like Max. And she was worried about telling her sister the truth?

She should be, Pru thought darkly. *She should be bloody terrified!*

Her first impulse was to rip the letter to shreds, and throw the bits in Patience's face when she returned to the room. But that, of course, would change nothing. Patience would still have Max. "Yours ever and always"! And Patience would never have written those words if the gentleman did not feel the same.

"You won't get away with this, Patience," she said through her teeth.

Snatching up her sister's pen, she scribbled a postscript. *This,* she thought with wild satisfaction, *will change everything.* Quickly, she folded the letter, found a fresh wafer, and sealed it again. Leaving it on Patience's desk, just as she had found it, she resumed her seat, and waited for Patience to return.

Chapter 14

Lord Milford swung around as Patience entered the room, and Patience was again struck by how large his head was in proportion to his body. With his short legs and tiny feet in tasseled boots, it was a wonder he didn't fall over. "Won't you sit down?" she said quickly.

Until this moment, Milford had clung to the hope that it had been Miss Prudence, not Lady Waverly, whom he had seen kissing Mr. Purefoy in Grosvenor Square. Now, of course, there could be no doubt.

"My God!" he exclaimed, goggling at her. "So it *was* you, after all! Don't deny it, madam! You're still wearing the same dress."

"I beg your pardon," said Patience.

"Cock-a-doodle-do!" he said coldly. "I trust I make myself clear, madam?"

Patience raised her brows, fighting the impulse to laugh. With his red face, red hair, and indignant expression, he actually did resemble the rooster he was impersonating. It was no good, however. She could not help laughing. "I don't understand you, sir! Is it not a bit early for a game of charades?"

"Cock-a-doodle-do!" he repeated very firmly. "Sometime after midnight, madam? Grosvenor Square? Cock-a-doodle-do!"

"Was that you, Lord Milford?" she asked, her fingertips at her lips. "Well! It seems I must thank you for acting as our lookout."

He blinked at her, which made him look even more like a rooster. His brain clicked rapidly. It did not seem likely now that he would win his bet with Lord Torcaster. But, if he played his cards right, then he might still win his bet with Mr. Purefoy. And he would need to win his bet with Mr. Purefoy, if he was to pay off his wager with Torcaster.

"I am here as your friend, my lady," he said. "As your friend, let me advise you that Mr. Purefoy is not to be trusted! I am sorry to pain Your Ladyship, but he does not love you. He only trifles."

Patience smiled incredulously. "I thank you for your opinion, sir. You need not worry about causing me pain, however. I know Mr. Purefoy, I think, better than you do."

"But he is a scoundrel, ma'am, a blackguard, an utter rascal!"

"That was his past," said Patience. "I do not regard it. I did not fall in love with him, sir, with my eyes closed. I love him in spite of his faults, just as, I trust, he loves *me* in spite of mine."

"Your Ladyship has no fault," Milford declared. "Unless it be a nature far too trusting."

"If anything, my nature is too suspicious!" said Patience. "Indeed, I can't help but wonder at your motives, sir."

"My motives are ever pure!" he said stoutly.

"Oh? Then you mean to marry your mistress?" Patience said politely.

"My what?" he said indignantly.

"The lady my sister and I saw you driving with in the park," Patience prompted him. "She is your mistress, is she not?"

"Certainly not! That was my—my cousin."

"Pardon me," Patience said contritely. "I did not know that Mrs. Philips, the actress, was your cousin. I look forward to seeing her in the new production of *Macbeth*. I have bought my tickets already."

"We were not speaking of me, madam," he said, becoming a little short with her. "We were talking of Purefoy—and his designs on you."

Patience only smiled. "Sir, I am well aware that your sister has designs on *him*. If Mr. Purefoy is such a blackguard, perhaps you should be having this talk with Lady Isabella."

"But he does not love you," Milford insisted. "You are deceived! He makes love to you, but that is only to win a bet!"

Patience, naturally, gave this statement no credence but it was bizarre enough to give her pause. "Sir—" she began.

He seized on her discomfiture eagerly. "It is true, my lady! If he does not marry you, then he must pay fifty thousand pounds. It is in the betting book at Brooks's club. There can be no escaping it."

"Go home, Lord Milford," she said coldly. "I do not believe you. I will never believe your lies. Save your breath."

"It is true, I tell you," he cried, seizing her hands. "He made the bet with me."

"May I see this betting book?"

"See the betting book?" he repeated impatiently. "Of course not. It is in the vault at Brooks's."

"Then you have no proof of what you say."

"I give you my word."

Patience shook her head in disgust.

"I tell you this not to hurt you," he said. "I tell you because I—I care for you, Lady Waverly. Indeed, I love you! I know you are infatuated with him at present," he went on quickly, "but in time you will see him for what he is. Then,

I hope, you will think of me more kindly. I only pray, dear lady, that it is not too late!"

"Sir, you are becoming ridiculous!"

He caught her roughly in his arms. "For you, I will make myself ridiculous," he said. "I still want to marry you. You have only to say the word."

"Let go of me," Patience said coldly.

"Not many men would stoop to marry you, not after seeing you forget yourself in the arms of another man," he went on, trying to find her mouth with his own puckered lips. "But I am quite run away by the violence of my feelings!"

"Cock-a-doodle-do, sir!" she said, looking at him dispassionately.

"What?" he said, scowling. At the same time, he felt a tap on his shoulder. Upon turning his head, he was immediately acquainted with Roger Molyneux's fist. With a moan, he slid to the floor. "You hit me," he whispered. "You hit me before I was ready. Not cricket!"

Patience frowned. "I said cock-a-doodle-do," she pointed out, "and Mr. Molyneux tapped you on the shoulder. You were warned, sir."

"Do you know who I am?" Milford said haughtily.

"Somebody important, I hope," said Molyneux, laughing at him.

Milford climbed to his feet, adjusting his lace cuffs and gathering his dignity. "I would challenge you to a duel, sir, but you are so decidedly beneath me in consequence, it would be an insult to my illustrious forebears. I see someone has already beaten you—for impertinence, no doubt," he added contemptuously.

Indeed, Molyneux's nose was swollen and bruised from his encounter with Max the night before. "You should try it," he said, reaching out to swipe at the blood on Milford's cheek with one finger. Terrified, Milford threw himself down on the floor, curled into a ball, and covered his head with his arms.

"Charades, is it?" said Molyneux, highly amused. "Hedgehog?"

"How dare you, sir," said a cold voice from the doorway. "How dare you offer violence to our noble visitor."

Darting into the room, Prudence helped Lord Milford to his feet. "Are you all right, my lord?" she said gently. "Did this big, stupid oaf hurt you?"

"Of course I hurt him," Molyneux said irritably. "He was taking liberties with your sister!"

"He really was making an ass of himself," Patience agreed.

"Patience can take care of herself," Pru snapped, helping Lord Milford to a chair. Putting her back to Molyneux, she took out her handkerchief. Dampening it with her tongue, she began dabbing at the blood on the earl's cheek.

Molyneux scowled. "Is he a friend of yours, Miss Prudence?"

"He is the Earl of Milford," she tossed over her shoulder.

Laughing, Molyneux turned to Patience. "Well, at least he's something in his own right, not like that fellow last night. Purefoy, as he calls himself! I found out later, he's nothing more than somebody's nephew. Imagine having nothing to hang your hat on but that! I'd be ashamed to be nothing more than somebody's nephew!"

Pru rounded on him furiously. "Mr. Purefoy is heir to the Duke of Sunderland!"

"Oh, well," he said coolly. "That makes all the difference, I suppose."

"It certainly does," said Pru. "Don't you have somewhere to go?" she went on rudely. "I thought you were in London to study medicine, not rampage about attacking your betters!"

"My betters are in the ground at Bound Brook and Baylor," he said hotly. "Not in the drawing rooms of Mayfair!"

"Sir," Patience said gently, her hand on Molyneux's arm, "perhaps you had better go."

"I'll go when the lordling is gone," Molyneux answered belligerently.

"I am going," said Lord Milford. "I will not stay another minute and be insulted by this impudent wretch."

"I'm sure I don't blame you," said Pru. "Anyway, you broke his nose, by the look of it. You have nothing to be ashamed of."

Taking his arm over her shoulder, she conducted him safely from the room. Outside, his groom helped him into his curricle.

Patience turned to Molyneux, wincing with embarrassment. "I'm so sorry," she said. "I won't pretend I'm not glad you were here to rescue me, but I am sorry for the insults. And my sister—I will explain to her what you did for me."

"No matter," he said quickly. "Nothing I do will ever be good enough for her, I know. I just came to return your handkerchief, Miss Patience."

Taking it from his pocket, he smoothed it out and handed it to her. "Freshly laundered and lightly starched, just how you like it."

Patience smiled at him. "Thank you, sir. You need not have gone to so much trouble."

Anxious to prevent a second meeting between Molyneux and Lord Milford outside, she tried to think of some excuse to keep the young man for a moment or two longer. "Your address! May I have your address in London, sir? Who knows? You may have another evening free. I'd be very glad if you would dine with us."

"I don't think your sister wants to dine with me," he said. "She'd rather dine with an English lord, I daresay, or even the nephew of an English lord."

Patience shook her head. "I can't understand it. Ever since we got here, she's had nothing in her head but titles and royalty! She was not like this in Philadelphia."

"You are nothing like your sister," he said warmly. "I don't have any of those fancy cards," he went on, "but if you ever want to find me, I'm at Twenty-one St. Saviour's Churchyard."

"Twenty-one St. Saviour's Churchyard," Pru said mockingly, coming back into the room. "Sounds about right for the son of a poor country parson!"

"It's convenient to Guy's Hospital," he replied curtly. "Where I'm due for a lecture in about twenty minutes," he added, after a glance at the clock. "Good-bye, Miss Patience!"

"Well!" said Pru, when he was gone. "What a rude young man! He didn't even say good-bye to me!"

"After the way you treated him," Patience said angrily, "are you surprised?"

"I am not surprised at all," Pru answered. "Given that he is an uncouth American bumpkin, one could not expect anything like manners from him."

Patience was almost bewildered by Pru's attitude. "I thought you would like him."

"Oh, no!" said Pru, her eyes narrowed. "You will not fob him off on *me*! I am going to marry Max! I am going to be a duchess! I am not going to be the wife of a poor country doctor from Pennsauken, New Jersey! If you like him so much, Patience, *you* marry him."

Patience began to argue. "I'm not trying to—"

"How does he know Mr. Purefoy?" Pru asked. "Did you see him last night?"

Patience paled a little. *This,* she felt instinctively, was not the right time to tell Pru the truth. If only Pru would take an interest in another young man! A royal duke, perhaps, or a foreign prince. Patience made a mental note to ask Max to find such a person. Once infatuated with someone else, Pru would not care if Max married her sister.

"I may have mentioned Mr. Purefoy last night while I was dancing with Mr. Molyneux," Patience answered vaguely.

Liar! Pru wanted to scream, but didn't.

"Don't forget to send your letter to Mr. Bracegirdle," she said sweetly instead. "You left it on your desk upstairs."

"Did I?" Patience hurried back to the drawing room.

"I would have sent it for you," said Pru, following her, "but I didn't know Mr. Bracegirdle's direction."

To Patience's immense relief, her letter was on her desk, exactly where and how she had left it. As Pru sat down on the sofa and took up one of her novels, Patience hurriedly directed her note and gave it to Briggs.

"You should send it by hand," Pru advised her, "for it looks quite urgent."

"Why do you say that?" Patience asked uneasily.

"Forgive me," Pru said innocently. "I couldn't help noticing all the blots. Nothing wrong, I hope?"

"No," Patience said quickly. "But it is fairly urgent. By hand, Briggs, if you please."

The Duke of Sunderland and his nephew were still at breakfast when Lady Waverly's page boy arrived. Max glanced over the lady's note impassively, ruffled the boy's hair, and said, "No reply."

"Very good, sir," said the boy, catching the coin Max tossed to him as he ran out of the room. "Half a crown, sir! Thank you, sir!"

The duke pushed his bowl of thin watery gruel away. "I'd give you half a crown for a steak and kidney pie," he muttered plaintively.

"You cannot have steak and kidney pie, sir," Max replied. Walking over to the fire, he fed Patience's note to it, and stood watching it burn. He had not been inclined to stay away from Clarges Street, as she requested, until he saw the postscript.

"I must see you, my love—I will come to you today as soon as I can steal away—Burn this—"

Blot after blot after blot, he thought, smiling. She must have been in quite a frenzy of emotion when she wrote. The thought of cool, collected Patience in a frenzy sent a warm glow through his limbs.

Notwithstanding his swollen face, Lord Milford returned home to his sister in good spirits. "What happened to you?" Isabella cried, alarmed. "Did you fight Mr. Purefoy?"

"Don't be silly," he said. "Purefoy is an English gentleman. Izzy, the most wonderful thing has happened."

"Did you see Lady Waverly?"

"See her? I proposed!"

Isabella gasped in delight. "And she accepted you? Oh, Ivor, that's marvelous! All that money, and the land, too! Then she was not with Purefoy last night? It was the other one."

"No, it was she," Milford replied. "In the flesh, so to speak."

"What do you mean, 'so to speak'?" Isabella said impatiently. "Was it Lady Waverly or not?"

"Oh, it was her all right! She even had the same crimson dress on."

Isabella wrinkled her nose. "Red velvet in the morning? How déclassé!"

"Quite," he agreed.

"When you are married you must talk to her about her clothes," said Isabella.

"I ain't going to marry her," Milford said impatiently. "After that disgusting display on the street? She is not fit to marry anyone. She is in love, if you please, with Purefoy. Even after I told her about his wager, she would not be shaken. Love is an ever-fixed mark that looks on tempests and wobbles not. She'll bear it out till the edge of doom, poor girl."

"Then why do you look so happy?" Isabella snapped. "How does this help me?"

"Well, it doesn't," he admitted. "It don't exactly help me either."

"Then why do you look so happy?" she howled.

"I'll tell you. You see my face? Well, I wasn't born this way. I was beaten! Beaten by a big, ugly American brute. He struck me with his fist."

"And this made you happy?"

"No, of course not. It bothered me considerably. But then who should come into the room but Miss Prudence! See? This is her handkerchief, with *my* blood on it!"

"Who was the American who beat you?"

"Nobody!" Milford sneered. "They're all nobodies, aren't they? Actually, now that I think of it, he was not alone. There were several of them together, traveling in a pack like the cowards they are. They fell on me from behind and hit me with clubs. I fought them to a draw, though I was outnumbered. They ran away."

"So I should think," Isabella said dryly.

"But, suddenly, there was Miss Prudence helping me to my feet. Like a tiger she defended me! Izzy, she is an angel!"

"Tiger! Angel! How does this help *me*?"

"It may not help you, but it helps me," he said. "Miss Prudence may not be my first choice, but she is just as rich as her elder sister. I'll marry her instead. With her money, I can cover all my bets, with a good deal left over. I might even provide you with a dowry, Isabella. You'll need it when Purefoy marries his baroness."

Isabella was not so sanguine. "You know what they say, Ivor, about chickens and eggs."

"No. What?"

"Don't count them before they're hatched!"

Milford laughed haughtily. "To which I say, strengthily, cock-a-doodle-do!"

Shortly after three o'clock that afternoon, Mr. Purefoy's flowers arrived in Clarges Street. Pru took the card and read it silently. "He isn't coming," she said. "He blames his uncle's poor health. I suppose the old man was quite done in by the ball. He says he is sorry he can't come, after having danced with me last night and all, but it couldn't be helped."

"If he is not coming," said Patience, "perhaps you would like to go to Mr. Bracegirdle's office with me, after all? We could go to Gunter's afterward."

"Bracegirdle's office!" Pru said scornfully. "Do you want me to die of boredom? Gunter's! Do you want me to get fat? No, thank you."

"The circus, perhaps," said Patience.

"I'm not a child," Pru said resentfully. "Besides, Lord Banville has not yet called. Go on to your meeting."

"Lady Jemima—" Patience began.

"Is taking a nap," said Pru. "I will call her when Lord Banville arrives. Don't worry! I shan't be alone with him for an instant. I know how little you trust me."

"I trust you completely," said Patience. "I don't trust *them*. Now, if you will need the carriage for anything, I'll be glad to take a hack."

Pru yawned, stretching her legs out on the sofa. "I shan't need it," she said quickly. "I will give Lord Banville one more hour, then I shall go to my room and lie down for a while. Don't forget we're going to the theater tonight."

"I haven't forgotten," said Patience. Kissing her sister's cheek, she left.

Pru instantly ran to the window and did not leave it until her sister's carriage was completely out of sight. Then she quickly rang for Briggs. When he appeared, she was scrambling for her bonnet and cloak. "Summon a hack for me, Briggs," she commanded. "No, you need not wake Lady Jemima. I have decided to go to the attorney's office with my sister after all. I shall return with her."

"Very good, Miss Prudence."

Less than a quarter of an hour later, she stepped out of the hack and walked up the steps to Sunderland House. Before she could touch the bell, the door opened. Venable said graciously, "Madam is expected. Please follow me."

He led her up an obscure flight of stairs to a small book room off the landing. Max was within, unpacking a crate of books. Pru slipped inside and Venable quietly closed the door.

"My love! I had to see you," Pru said breathlessly.

Max slowly rose from his chair. "What are you doing here . . . Prudence?"

"Prudence?" Pru laughed, but she could not quite keep the venom out of her voice. "No, my darling! It is I, Patience!"

"You should not be here, Miss Prudence," he said quietly. "Your sister will be worried."

Pru abruptly gave up all pretense. "My sister!" she said bitterly. "She wouldn't care if I jumped off a bridge like our dear, departed uncle!"

"That is not true," he said sharply. "Patience loves you very much."

"But she loves *you* more. Did you think I wouldn't find out?" she went on shrilly. "Did you think you could hide it from me forever?"

Max sighed. "Do not blame your sister. The fault is entirely mine. We did not mean for this to happen, Miss Prudence. We did not do it to hurt you. Patience, poor girl—I think she fought it as long as she could."

Pru snorted. "Oh, yes! To my certain knowledge, sir, you have met my sister only twice! Once, the night we arrived. And again, at Tattersall's. But, of course, you have been meeting secretly—behind my back!"

"It must seem that way to you," said Max. "But love cannot be fathomed. It cannot be anticipated. It cannot be defeated. One day, you will understand. The heart chooses, overruling the head. Nothing can stop it."

"*My* love is nothing to you then?" she said, her lower lip trembling. "*I* am nothing to you?"

"When I marry Patience, you will be my sister," he said. "I will be your brother."

Pru choked back a sob. "I don't want to be your sister. I want to be Mrs. Purefoy!"

"You don't love me, Prudence," he said. "You will see

that in time. You don't even know me. You only see what lies on the surface. You do not understand the man underneath."

"And *she* does, I suppose?"

"We understand each other, yes."

Sniffling, Pru groped for a chair. "The only men who seem to like me best are the trifling little fellows nobody cares about. And fortune hunters, of course."

"Lord Banville is no fortune hunter. He seemed to like you very well."

"All he talked about was Patience!"

"Never mind him then," Max said quickly. "Obviously he is not worthy of you. Please don't be angry."

Pru nodded glumly. "I'm not angry anymore," she said. "I understand that you could not help yourselves. I should not have come here. This was a terrible mistake."

He smiled at her. "Actually, I am glad you came. I know Patience has been dreading having to tell you. Now that you know, we can be married without a cloud over us."

Pru gave a pained smile.

"You will get over your disappointment very quickly, I promise you," he told her. "I have many faults. If you knew me better, you would not change places with your sister for the world."

Pru drew in a deep breath. "I want Patience to be happy, of course. And you, too."

"That is very generous of you, Prudence."

"Oh, my sister and I made a promise long ago never to let a man come between us," said Pru. "I will dance at your wedding, Brother. I hope one day, you will dance at mine."

"I will, of course," he said, smiling.

"I must go," said Pru. "Patience and I are attending the theater this evening. Will you send for a hack?"

"I'll do better than that," he said. "I'll drive you home in my curricle!"

"How very brotherly of you," said Pru.

* * *

Patience returned from the attorney's office a little after five in the evening. As the carriage pulled away, she was dismayed to see Lord Milford driving toward her in his curricle.

"Miss Prudence!" he hailed her, drawing up to the curb.

"Sir, it is I, Lady Waverly," she said impatiently.

Milford tossed the reins to his groom and descended to the pavement. "No," he said, striding up to her. "It is Miss Prudence, surely."

"Are we going to argue about it, sir?"

"No, of course not," he said. "It is Miss Prudence, though, is it not? I know it is, for I just saw Lady Waverly return to the house with Mr. Purefoy."

"You saw no such thing," she snapped. "I have only just returned this minute in my carriage alone. My sister has been at home all day."

He blinked at her. "Then it must have been Miss Prudence in the curricle with Mr. Purefoy. Very cozy they looked, too. Dammit! What is he playing at?"

"You saw *my sister* in a curricle with *Mr. Purefoy*? Sir, either you lie or your eyes deceive you. Either way, I am tired of you!"

Milford paid no attention to her. "I should have known it was she, for he was driving. Had it been you, you would have taken the reins into your own hands."

"Oh, go away!" Patience snapped.

Leaving him on the street, she went into the house. "Is my sister here?" she asked Briggs.

"Miss Prudence is in her room resting," came the reassuring reply.

Nodding, Patience went up to her own room to bathe and dress for the theater.

At half past seven, she knocked on Pru's door. There was no answer. "Pru!" she called, knocking. When there was still no reply, she became worried. Trying the handle, she discovered that it was locked. Now frightened, she hurried to her desk to find the keys. Opening the door, she discovered Pru on the bed, her eyes closed, a trickle of blood running down her arm. A wicked-looking letter opener, its tip stained with blood, had fallen to the floor.

With a scream that brought every servant in the house running, Patience ran to the bed.

Pru moaned faintly. "Let me die," she whispered.

Chapter 15

"Send for Dr. Wingfield at once," Patience cried, ashen-faced, flinging the words at the round-eyed servants in the doorway. As Briggs took charge of the servants, ushering them out of the room, Patience tore a strip of lace from the sleeve of her gown and used it to bind the source of the bleeding, a surprisingly small slash on Pru's forearm.

"Oh, what have you done to yourself?" she murmured, peppering Pru's cheeks with slaps.

"Pay?" Pru whispered pathetically. "Pay, is that you?"

"Of course it is," Patience answered quickly. "Lie still! I've sent for the doctor."

"I am betrayed," Pru said wildly. "Betrayed! Ruined! Compromised! He deceived me. He said he loved me. But I did not say he could do *that*. Truly I didn't!"

"What are you saying?" cried Patience. "No! Don't try to talk! The doctor will be here soon. He'll fix you right up."

"He isn't a doctor," Pru said, her voice sounding much stronger. "He's only a student."

"Mr. Molyneux?" Patience said, puzzled. "No—I—I sent for Dr. Wingfield. Mr. Molyneux is much too far away to be of use to us. Are you saying that *Roger Molyneux* has deceived you?"

"That clodpole?" Pru cried, sitting up. "I wouldn't let him near me, and he knows it!"

"Then I'm afraid I don't understand. You are talking very wildly."

Gently, Patience tried to ease Prudence back against the pillows, but Pru would have none of it.

"I am talking about Max!" she fairly shouted. "He did this to me!"

"Max cut your arm?" Patience said doubtfully.

"No! No! I did that to myself. But Max was the one who hurt me. Last night at the ball, he seduced me."

"Oh, nonsense," Patience said, her temper fraying. "Max was with—"

She broke off, frowning.

"With you last night?" Pru finished. "Well, before he was with you, dear sister, he was with me. He lured me away from the ball to an empty room in his uncle's house, and there—! Oh, must I say it? He wronged me!"

Patience sighed. "I think perhaps you are imagining things. This sounds quite a bit like the plot of one of your novels. And now that I think of it," she added, drawing away, "that cut on your arm is not very deep."

"I'm not lying!" Pru insisted, grasping her sister's arm. "He sent me flowers. Here is the note that came with them. He freely admits his guilt. Read it if you doubt me!"

Pru produced the note from under her pillow. Patience snatched it from her angrily, but whitened as she read it, her shoulders slumping.

Most abjectly, I am sorry for the events of last night. No lady should ever be exposed to such rude behavior. When I think that you may have come to grievous harm, I

*am deeply ashamed. Drunkenness, of
course, is no proper excuse for offering
violence and insult to a lady of quality.
I beg you will accept my profoundest
apologies. Please believe that I am, now
and forever, your most obedient servant
to command.*

It was signed "Purefoy."

Patience suddenly felt cold. She struggled to breathe. "I don't understand," she murmured. "What happened last night?" She looked sharply at Pru. "What exactly happened last night?"

"He left the ball for a time, and when he came back he was—I don't know—flushed with victory! He had been dull before, but suddenly he was full of gaiety and merriment. He danced with me. He told me he loved me. He said he would marry me. I thought—"

Patience was shaking her head.

"He did!" Pru insisted. "He told me he had a present for me upstairs—a betrothal gift. So we slipped away, laughing. By the time I realized what he really wanted to give me, it was too late. At first it was only kissing, which, I confess I liked very much."

Patience turned her face away, crushing Max's note in her hand.

"But then he started pushing his hands all over me and up my clothes," Pru went on, beginning to sniffle. "I did not like that. I broke free of him and ran to the door! It was locked!"

"This is not possible," Patience whispered. "There has been some mistake."

Pru did not heed her. "After that, what could I do? I tried to stop him, but he was too strong! His hands were everywhere. I started to cry, but he just said I was a silly girl, and that it would all be over in a moment. He promised to marry me and love me forever if I would be good. So I was good. I let him . . . I let him put his great ugly thing in me! It hurt! Oh, Pay! It hurt so much."

Patience could bear no more. Quickly, she jumped to her feet, but then stood frozen in indecision. What was there to do, really? What would running from the room accomplish?

"Won't you say something?" Pru begged.

Patience, overwhelmed by conflicting emotions, could not speak.

Pru burst into tears. "I knew you would say it was my fault! It *is* my fault, I suppose, for trusting him. Oh, Patience! I should have listened to you. Now he says he will not marry me."

Patience swung around. "When did he tell you that?"

"Today. I went to see him while you were out," Pru confessed. "I know I should not have gone to him, but the matter had been weighing on me so heavily. So I went to see him."

Patience listened in silence.

"His servant let me in. Max appeared. He took me up to the same room where he'd ravished me. He said I belonged to him now. I was happy, because I thought he would marry me. So I let him do it to me again. But, afterward, when I spoke of marriage, he laughed in my face. He told me I was his—his whore, and that he could do that to me any time he pleased. He told me—very roughly—to get dressed. Then he drove me home in his curricle as if nothing had happened! If you do not believe me, ask Lord Milford," she added. "He saw us."

Patience rested her forehead on her hand. "I know he did. He told me."

Sinking back down to the edge of the bed, she read Max's note again. Desperately, she tried to think of some innocent explanation for the words, but she could not. And Milford had seen them together! Max had been drunk, of course—he said so in his note—but that was no excuse. *He was not drunk when he was with me,* she thought. But, of course, he had gone back to the ball. Anything could have happened there . . . she had been asleep in her own bed by the time Pru returned home from Sunderland House.

In her hand was his admission of guilt.

Pru watched her curiously from the bed. "I was so distraught that I tried to take my own life. I suppose it is a good thing that I faint at the sight of blood."

"It is a very good thing!" cried Patience. Suddenly, she clasped Pru tightly in her arms. "Forgive me! I am sorry I ever doubted you, my love," she whispered, holding her twin close. "It was the shock of it, I fear. But I shall never doubt your word again. Say you forgive me." Drawing away, she held Pru's tear-stained face in her hands.

"I forgive you," Pru said generously.

"And do you promise never, never to try to hurt yourself again?"

"I promise," said Pru. "What are you going to do, Patience?"

Patience bit her lip. "I know that some people—many people—well, most people—would be inclined to think that marriage is the only possible solution," she said. "But, if it is not what you want, Pru, *I* will never force you to marry. If it is your wish to bring charges against him, I will bear the expense. I don't know the laws here in England, and I'm sure it will not be easy to bring a man like him to justice, but you will have me at your side. You will always have me at your side. And we have his confession in writing, do we not?" Hastily, she smoothed out the crumpled note. "The magistrate will want to see it, no doubt."

"Would it not be simpler to marry him?" Pru said anxiously. "I don't want to go to court."

"We might simply go home," Patience suggested. "Cut our losses here. The lawyers can sell the estate, settle Uncle's debts, and send us the remainder. And, now that Lord Banville has forgiven his debt, it could be a handsome sum."

Pru shook her head. "But I would still be ruined. No, Max should have to marry me. Don't you think? You're not going to let him get away with this, are you?"

Patience drew in a deep breath. "But, dearest, are you quite sure you want to marry a man like that? What sort of husband do you think he will make you?"

"I don't care about that. It's the only way to repair the damage to my virtue."

"Very well, then," Patience said wearily. "If marriage is what you want, I will make it happen. He shall marry you."

"What are you going to do?"

"Don't you worry," Patience said grimly. "I'll manage it."

Gently, she eased Pru's head down to the pillow and covered her body with the quilt. "I believe the doctor has arrived. I must go and speak to him."

"No! Don't leave me!" Pru cried, gripping her sister's hand. "Don't let him near me! I'm quite all right! It's only a scratch. It's stopped bleeding already. Please, Patience! I can't bear the thought of another man touching me!"

To allay her fears, Patience agreed. "Very well. But you must have a nurse. I will send for Mrs. Drabble. She took excellent care of me. I trust her completely."

"All right," Pru agreed reluctantly.

Lady Jemima was called to sit with Pru while Patience spoke to Dr. Wingfield.

"I am sorry to call you out for nothing, sir," she greeted him. "My sister is feeling a little—a little melancholy, but there is nothing really wrong with her. She is resting now. It seems I overreacted."

"Crossed in love, eh?" he said, smiling. "As long as I'm here, I might as well—"

Patience stepped in front of him. "Thank you, sir, but she is comfortable now. I'll send for you in the morning if she is no better. Please do bill me for your time."

Dr. Wingfield seemed insulted by the offer, and quickly took his leave, muttering under his breath.

By the time Mrs. Drabble arrived, all the servants save Briggs had gone back to bed and the house was quiet. Pru was resting comfortably with Lady Jemima watching over her. Patience, dressed to go out in cloak, bonnet, and gloves, met the nurse at the door. "Thank you for coming, Mrs. Drabble," she said, helping her out of her cloak. Quickly, she explained what had happened, with more candor than she had used with the doctor.

"No!" Mrs. Drabble gasped. "Not Max! I don't believe it!"

Patience shook her head. "I do not have time to argue, ma'am! I wish it were not true, but it is. My sister is in her room. Please be good enough to attend her. I must go out for a while."

Rather than go to the trouble of calling for her carriage, Patience simply took Mrs. Drabble's hack. "Sunderland House," she told the jarvey. Deep in thought, she hardly noticed her surroundings until the carriage lurched to a stop.

After a rather long wait, Venable opened the door to her. "Madam!" he said, startled.

"Baroness Waverly to see Mr. Purefoy," she said very quietly and firmly.

"Mr. Purefoy is not at home, madam. Was he expecting you this evening?"

"Where is he?"

"I cannot say, madam."

"Well, is the Duke of Sunderland at home?" she demanded. "Would you be good enough to let me in whilst you go and enquire?" she added, as Venable hesitated.

Stepping aside, he allowed her into the house and closed the door. While she stood, wringing her hands, he glided off.

Venable returned several moments later and conducted her to the drawing room. Huddled in his bath chair next to the huge marble fireplace, the Duke of Sunderland looked small and insignificant. His nurse stood behind him. "What do you mean coming here in the middle of the night?" he asked irritably. "I'm not at all well, you know."

"I'm very sorry," Patience replied. "I am Lady Waverly. I believe you are acquainted with my sister, sir."

"Acquainted? I gave her a ball, didn't I? Gave you a ball, too, though you couldn't be bothered to attend," he added resentfully.

"I did not ask you to give me a ball. I had a previous engagement. Sir, I have come to talk to you about my sister. My sister and your nephew."

"You're a haughty one," he observed. "Well, sit down, then. What about my nephew?"

"I will stand, thank you," said Patience. "I will be brief, sir, and blunt. Your nephew has compromised my sister. Now he must marry her."

He raised his brows. "Is that so, madam?"

"Yes, sir," she said coldly.

"I see. In what way has he compromised your sister?"

She frowned. "What do you mean *'in what way'*? He—he has seduced her. He has stolen her innocence."

He snorted. "You mean she has lost her virtue. How does that concern me?"

"Sir, it was your nephew who beguiled her with promises of marriage. Are you so jaded that the suffering of an innocent girl means nothing to you?"

"Max wouldn't be fool enough to promise marriage," declared the duke. "And there's no need for him to go about the place ruining virgins. He has a perfectly good mistress for all that sort of thing. The actress, Mrs. Tolliver. Perhaps you have seen her on stage? Very beautiful."

Patience's cheeks were flaming. "Was Mrs. Tolliver with him last night at your ball when he ravished my sister?" she said coldly. "Was Mrs. Tolliver with him this afternoon when he ravished her again in this house?"

The duke frowned. "What, here? This afternoon? Venable!"

The butler must have been listening at the door, for he appeared almost instantly. "Yes, Your Grace?"

"Was there a young woman here today with my nephew?"

"Yes, Your Grace. Miss Waverly visited briefly."

The duke stared. "What?" he cried. "Were they alone together?"

"Yes, Your Grace. Then Mr. Purefoy took the young lady away in his curricle."

"Thank you, Venable. You may go. This proves nothing," the duke added, glaring at Patience. "Your sister's always coming here uninvited—a family trait, it would appear!"

"I'm sorry to pain you, sir, but it's true. Your nephew has ruined my sister."

"You have no proof of anything."

"I beg your pardon, sir. I do have proof," Patience said quietly.

"What proof?" he demanded. "Dirty linen? Servant's tittle-tattle?"

"A letter, sir, written by your nephew to my sister."

He squinted at the paper she handed him.

"Did your nephew write it?" she said.

"It is his hand," the duke admitted, flabbergasted. "It does seem . . . Well! If the boy has done this terrible thing, I shall, of course, disown him."

Patience blinked at him. "Disown him, sir? Can you do that?"

"Very easily, too," he told her. "My brother Richard was only twenty when he married that girl out of the opera house. I'll simply have the marriage annulled. Max will be illegitimate, and so barred from the succession. My sister's grandson may then inherit. *His* bloodline is impeccable. And, as far as I know, he hasn't seduced any innocent girls. I shall meet with my attorney directly. Tonight! I wash my hands of the boy entirely."

"Good," said Patience.

"Good?" he repeated, surprised. "You realize what this means? Max will be penniless. He will never be Duke of Sunderland. If it is your sister's ambition to be a duchess, she had better cut line."

"How dare you," Patience breathed. "My sister gave herself to him because she loves him."

"Touching," he said dryly. "You want money, I suppose?"

"We don't care about your title or your money, sir," she said through gritted teeth. "We're not exactly paupers, you know."

"I will strip the boy even of his name," the duke warned. "I don't know that he has a name to give your sister— certainly none of distinction. Would your sister marry a nameless, penniless bastard? Well, that is love indeed. I'm glad I shall live to see it."

"Will you prevail on him, sir, to marry my sister?"

The duke shrugged. "How can I? From this moment on, I am nothing to him, and he is nothing to me."

"He is still your responsibility," said Patience. "You have let him run wild all these years. You have indulged him too much. Will you not lift a finger to help his victim?"

"You blame me?" the duke cried.

"Yes. If you have an ounce of decency, you will help my sister. We are far from home, sir. We have no friends here.

You are powerful—you can arrange these things with a snap of your fingers."

"That is true, I suppose," he said. "The Archbishop of Canterbury owes me a bit of a favor, now that I think on it. Would tomorrow morning suit you?"

"Suit me?"

"For the wedding, madam," he said impatiently. "It will have to be a small affair."

"Tomorrow," Patience repeated. "As soon as that?"

"When the cart has been put before the horse, the mistake should be rectified as quickly as possible. Would you not agree?"

"Yes, of course. Prudence will be very glad."

"Tomorrow, then. Six of the morning, shall we say? By law, a marriage cannot take place by night, so we must wait for the sun. Also by law, the thing must be done before noon. And, of course, it must take place in a church. Have you a church in mind?"

"No, sir."

"Let us say St. Bride's, then, in Fleet Street. No one I know attends there, but I know the rector. I will see to it that he has the special license. He will look for you at dawn."

"Thank you, sir. And—and the groom?"

"Oh, you won't have to worry about *him*," said the duke. "He'll meet you at the altar. Penniless, and without the protection of my name, he'll be hounded all over London by his creditors. I'll place the notice in tomorrow's paper. You have only to show it to him if he balks. Believe me, he will choose marriage over debtor's prison."

"Thank you, sir."

"You understand, of course, that I won't be attending the wedding." The duke signaled to his nurse, who began pushing his chair toward the door. "Good-bye, Lady Waverly."

Patience was left standing for a moment, then Venable came to show her out.

"Tomorrow?" Prudence echoed in disbelief, when her sister gave her the news. "As soon as that?"

Patience shrugged. "He's the Duke of Sunderland. Everyone hops to when he says so, even the Archbishop of Canterbury."

"St. Bride's Church?" said Pru, wrinkling her nose. "Couldn't he get Westminster Abbey?"

"A small, quiet service in an out-of-the-way little church will do nicely," said Patience.

"I suppose you're right," Pru said reluctantly.

Jumping out of bed, she ran to the wardrobe to look at her dresses. "Tomorrow morning! I can hardly believe it! What am I going to wear?" Turning away from the sight of her clothes, she went for the calf-bound fashion plates she had carelessly tossed in the window seat. "Really, Pay, I must have more time. Madame Devy can make me a gown in four days, if I pay double."

"Absolutely not!"

"But . . . I want Westminster Abbey! I want a golden coach drawn by four snow-white horses! I want a new gown—satin! It will take weeks to arrange everything properly."

"You will be married tomorrow morning, at St. Bride's Church," Patience snapped. "No! Not another word of this nonsense, Pru! If you are determined to marry this—this *libertine,* it should not be delayed. The world will know soon enough that you have been in the man's bed—the servants at Sunderland House know all about it already, and I don't expect they'll keep it to themselves."

With a sigh Pru closed her book of fashion plates.

"Was Max very angry with me for peaching on him? Did he rage and deny it all?"

"I didn't see him. I spoke to his uncle. But don't worry—he *will* marry you. I mean, he *shall* marry you. It's all arranged. Try to get some sleep; I'll wake you in plenty of time. We should leave here at dawn for St. Bride's."

Pru gave a shriek of dismay. "Sleep? I don't have time to sleep. If I don't start my hair now, I'll never be ready in time. Oh, where is my maid!"

Frantically, she rang the bell, then dashed to her dressing table. "Pass me the candlestick," she ordered Patience as she peered anxiously into the mirror. "Oh, I look a fright!"

Patience brought the candle, set it down on the table, and took up Pru's hairbrush.

"Which dress should I wear?" Pru fretted as Patience went to work on her tangles. "My court dress, do you think? Too much pomp and circumstance?"

"Your yellow sarcenet would seem more appropriate," Patience murmured.

Opening a jar, Pru rubbed cream on her face. "Married in yellow? Oh, no! There's a rhyme against that. Married in yellow, ashamed of your fellow."

"That's just what I was thinking," said Patience.

"That isn't helpful, Patience," Pru chided her, before rushing on. "There's no rhyme against being married in pink, is there?"

"Married in pink: no time to think."

"You made that up," Pru accused her, laughing.

Mrs. Drabble hurried into the room. "You rang, my dears?"

"Not for you," Pru said rudely. "I want my maid."

"But you should be in bed, Miss Prudence."

"No, indeed," said Pru. "I'm getting married in the

morning. You can go home, Mrs. Drabble. I shan't need you anymore."

"Married!" Mrs. Drabble cried in astonishment.

"I have seen the duke," said Patience. "He acknowledges his nephew's guilt."

Mrs. Drabble pressed her lips together. "Oh, he does, does he? Well, *I* don't acknowledge his guilt! Max is innocent!"

Pru laughed. "Who cares what you think? You're nothing but a servant—and an old discarded servant, too."

"Pru!" Patience laid a restraining hand on her sister's shoulder. "The duke is making the arrangements, Mrs. Drabble. Mr. Purefoy and Pru are to be married tomorrow morning at St. Bride's Church."

"That cannot be," Mrs. Drabble fretted, her face contorted. "Poor Max!"

"Poor Max!" Pru said indignantly. "He's lucky I've agreed to marry him at all. He don't deserve me."

"We agree on that much!" Mrs. Drabble said hotly. "You are lying about my dear boy. He never touched you. He wouldn't!"

"Did too!"

Almost in tears, Mrs. Drabble turned to Patience. "Lady Waverly, I beg of you! Don't listen to these wicked, wicked lies!"

Patience was trembling. "How dare you accuse my sister of lying!"

Mrs. Drabble bit her lip. "So that's how it is?" she said quietly. "Ah, well! They say blood is thicker than water. But we are friends no more, Lady Waverly, understand that."

"Oh, no!" Pru said sarcastically. "You mean her ladyship will be welcome no more at your pathetic little sewing circle hen parties?"

"Hush, Pru! I am sorry, Mrs. Drabble."

"So am I," Mrs. Drabble said, looking at Pru with loathing. Shaking her head, she stalked out of the room.

"Ring for that lazy maid, will you?" Pru said, supremely unconcerned.

As Mrs. Drabble was leaving Clarges Street, Max was pacing the rug in his uncle's bedroom. "She said I did what? That lying little minx."

The duke was propped up among the pillows. "Oh, I knew at once she was a liar."

Max dug his heels into the rug. "Not Patience. Patience is as honest as the day is long. Prudence! But how on earth did she convince Patience that I was a villain?"

"She had proof," the duke told him. "Some beastly note you'd written."

"I never wrote any letter!" Max snarled. "It was that lying little vixen! She wrote to me, pretending to be her sister! She bade me to stay at home today, which I did. But it was Prudence who showed up, not Patience. We had a nice little chat—"

"Nice little chat? She says you ravished her!"

"Rot!" Max said simply. "You don't believe it, do you, Uncle?"

"Dear boy! Of course not. You're a Purefoy."

"Could you not persuade her of my innocence?"

The duke shifted uncomfortably in his bed. "You know I hate talking to crazy people. I told her what she wanted to hear, and I sent her on her way. Good riddance to the pair of them, say I."

"My God!" Max muttered, shaking his head. "When I drove the girl home, I truly believed she was ready to accept me as her brother. I must go to Clarges Street at once. Patience must be brought to reason."

"Go to Clarges Street!" the duke repeated in alarm. "No,

no, dear boy! Lady Waverly expects you to meet her and her sister at St. Bride's Church in the morning. You are on the chopping block, sir! You will have to run away."

"Run away?" Max said scornfully.

"You must, dear boy. Lady Waverly will have your balls in a vise. I even threatened to disown you, and still she wanted marriage!"

Max's mouth twitched. "Not for herself, though."

"She swears her sister cares nothing for titles and money. She is in love with you. Lady Waverly will not be satisfied until there is a wedding."

"Then perhaps we should give her one," Max suggested.

"No," said the duke, when Max had explained what he had in mind. "You are my brother's son. I shan't disown you. I shan't call you a bastard."

"Let the *Times* do it for you. And the *Morning Post*. Oh, yes! We must have it in the *Morning Post,* too. And the marriage license. It should bear my mother's name, and not my father's, on the license. That will complete the charade. I'll send for your man of business."

"What if she marries you anyway?" the duke objected. "A fine mess you'll be in then!"

"We always said this is what we'd do if I got into trouble with some adventuress," Max reminded him.

"I'm telling you, she didn't bat an eye! She says her sister will marry a nameless, penniless bastard."

Max grinned. "She may believe it. I don't."

The duke shook his head. "You should run away, just in case. Join Freddie in St. Petersburg. Meet a nice Russian girl."

"I think *you* should join Freddie in St. Petersburg, Uncle."

"There's no need to be rude!"

"Not at all. When you disown me, Freddie becomes your heir. I hear St. Petersburg is lovely in the springtime."

"It's the dead of winter, sir!"

"All right. You needn't actually go to St. Petersburg. We'll just put it about that you've gone to Russia. You can go someplace sunny. Come to think of it, that's probably what Freddie's done."

The duke sighed. "You know I don't travel as well as I used to. Besides, you'll need me if you get into trouble."

Max thought it over. "You could stay here, I suppose. Have the servants take the knocker off the door and tell everyone you've gone. No one will expect you to want company after my disgrace. No one will be surprised to hear you have left London."

"I don't like it," said the duke. "What would your father say? He went to a good deal of trouble, you know, to make sure you were not born a bastard."

"My father would understand," Max assured him. "He was a great believer in marrying for love. That's what I mean to do, Uncle. I've found the girl I love. Now all that remains is to find out if I am the man she loves."

"Do you mean you are in love with the lying little minx?" the duke said incredulously.

"Of course not, you old fool," said Mrs. Drabble, coming into the room two steps ahead of a very flustered Venable. "He's in love with the lying minx's sister!"

"Julia!" the duke cried softly. "You've come back!"

She glared at him. "Don't think for a moment that I've forgiven you, old man," she snapped. "I'm only here because our dear boy is in trouble."

"How did you hear of it?" Max asked her.

"Miss Prudence made a holy show of killing herself," Mrs. Drabble answered, huffing with indignation. "Pity she didn't succeed."

"My poor Patience," Max murmured. "Oh, I could murder that girl!"

"So could I! Cheerfully!" Mrs. Drabble declared. "But it wouldn't do you a bit of good. She won't hear a word against her sister. As good as bit my head off when I called her a liar. But I'll try again tomorrow, Max."

Max shook his head. "I'm afraid that will be too late, Drabble. Tomorrow, I'm getting married. Would you be good enough to give us the wedding breakfast at your house?"

"Do something!" Mrs. Drabble said furiously to the duke. "Don't just lie there!"

"I lie here because my bones ache," he told her coldly. "And for your information, I *am* doing something. As soon as my man of business gets here, I'm going to disown my nephew. Then nobody will want to marry him."

"Don't say that," Max said mildly. "I hope someone will want to marry me! You won't forget gooseberry tarts for the groom, will you, Drabble? And cherry for the bride."

She looked at him, bewildered. "Cherry for the bride?" she repeated puzzled.

Suddenly her expression changed. Her eyes lit up and her cheeks turned pink.

"Oh!" she said.

Chapter 16

Prudence, her hair in curl papers, finally climbed into bed at one o'clock, falling asleep before her head hit the pillow. Patience ordered the exhausted maid to go to bed, then took up the candle and went to her own room.

A figure was bent over the hearth, poking the dying fire. "Leave it," she said wearily.

The figure straightened up, and she saw at once that it was Max.

"How dare you!" she gasped, the candlestick shaking in her hand.

"Careful! You'll burn yourself. Better put it down."

Patience was setting the candlestick on the table just as he suggested she do. She had to fight the childish impulse to pick it up again. "How did you get in here?" she asked coldly.

"Freddie gave me his key," he answered. "In case his tenants should need anything. I saw no reason to wake the servants. You look very tired," he added with a gentleness that made her bristle.

"I assume you have seen your uncle, Mr. Purefoy."

"Max! Please!" he protested. "We are to be brother and sister in just a few short hours."

"There is no such thing as a short hour," she snapped.

"What?"

"I have always detested that figure of speech."

"In that case, I withdraw it, with abject apology," he said glibly. "Where is the bride?"

Her eyes flew swiftly to his face. "You are here to see Prudence?"

"Of course. My blushing bride."

"Why? So you can rage against her for exposing you?" Patience snapped. "She is asleep, sir. I won't permit you to wake her."

Max clucked his tongue. "Poor little thing! She must be exhausted; she's been so very busy! Deceiving me, deceiving you, attempting suicide . . ."

"Prudence is not the deceiver, sir. You are!"

Max sat down in the chair beside the fire. "Will you at least hear my side of things?" he said, crossing one leg over the other.

"Save your breath. Prudence has already told me what you did to her!"

He stared at her. "You won't even listen to me?" he said incredulously. "What? Convicted without a trial?"

"Your guilt has been proved," she said. "There is not a shadow of a doubt."

"Oh, yes, of course. My uncle mentioned a letter. Obviously a forgery! I never touched Prudence! Even if I had, I would not be stupid enough to 'fess up to it in a letter! Why would I?"

"Because it is all a game to you," she said angrily. "You trifle with my sister, then you take up with me, then you trifle a bit more with my sister! But your trifling, sir, is at an end."

"Listen to me!" he said desperately, striding toward her. "She tricked me! She sent me a letter this morning. She asked to meet me alone at Sunderland House. She signed your name to it, then came to Sunderland House in your place."

"You lie," said Patience. "I did write to you this morning. But I asked you to stay away."

He nodded eagerly. "The page was covered in blots."

"That was my letter. I wrote it in a hurry. I did not ask to meet you anywhere."

"But there was a postscript," he insisted. "In the postscript, you wrote that you would come to me at Sunderland House."

"No," said Patience, frowning. "There was no postscript!"

"She must have added it when you weren't looking," he said.

"Impossible! You are flailing like a drowning man. There was no opportunity for anyone to add a postscript. I sealed the letter myself, and it was still sealed when I wrote the direction and sent it."

"I don't know how she did it," he said. "I tell you, there was a postscript! If I had not burned the letter, I could show it to you now."

Patience gave a laugh. "You burned it, of course! How convenient, sir. Well, I did not burn *your* letter." She took his crumpled note from her pocket and showed it to him. "You may call it a forgery until you are blue in the face—"

"It is not a forgery," he whispered, snatching it from her. "That little bitch! She is more devious than I thought."

"You admit you wrote it!" Patience exclaimed.

"Yes. But I wrote it to *you,* not your sister. *This,* dear girl, is my apology to you for throwing you over the balcony at my birth-night. I sent you flowers the next day, along with this note. White roses by the score."

"I have no memory of that," said Patience.

He scowled. "Well, you were rather ill. Don't you see?"

He took a step toward her, but Patience stumbled back toward the door.

"Prudence is jealous," he went on doggedly. "She knows that I love you. She knows that you love me. She wanted me for herself, and now she can't stand it."

Patience drew in her breath. "This conversation is futile. For my sister's sake, I will try to be civil to you. We are going to be brother and sister, after all."

A muscle twitched in his jaw. "Brother and sister! I don't think so, madam."

Dragging her into his arms, he kissed her mouth with desperate passion. Patience did not struggle against his superior strength. Instead, she remained unresponsive and turned her face away as soon as she could. "Fool!" he said, shaking her. "I am not going to marry that—that reeking mantrap you call a sister! I love *you*. I am going to marry *you*. You know me, Patience! I would never betray you. It is all malice. Lies. Don't let her come between us."

Patience broke away from him. Going to the bed, she felt under the pillow and pulled out a pistol. "My sister does not lie," she said, pointing it at him. "And no man shall ever come between us. Least of all you."

Max lifted his brows. "You sleep with a pistol under your pillow, do you?"

"One cannot be too careful," she replied. "It's loaded, by the way. Now get in the closet. Get in the closet, Mr. Purefoy, or I will shoot you."

"Don't be a fool," he said sharply. "I know you would never shoot me."

Her mouth curved into a smile, but her eyes remained

cold. "Of course I wouldn't," she said. "Not on purpose. But accidents do happen. I suggest you do as I say; it is the best way to avoid an accident."

Max held up his hands. "All right. Stop waving it around or it *will* go off."

Crossing the room, he entered the water closet and closed the door.

He heard the key turn in the lock. With no place else to sit, he closed the wooden lid of the privy seat and sat on top of it. "May I ask why you want me to go in the closet?"

"I am going to keep you locked up overnight so you can't run away," she explained.

"It's very dark in here," he complained. "May I have a candle, at least?"

"No," she answered.

"You condemn me to darkness, then?"

"I do."

"I think it very cruel of you," he remarked. "I'm sure Prudence will think it very cruel, too. By the way, have you told her that my uncle has disowned me?"

Patience made no reply. He thought, perhaps, she had withdrawn. But then he heard her moving about on the other side of the door.

"You didn't tell her, did you?"

"It wouldn't make any difference if I did," she said. "If she loved you enough to—to—"

"To what? Grant me the jewel of her innocence?" he said mockingly.

"Oh! You're disgusting."

"I was trying to be discreet. What I really wanted, of course, was the jewel of *your* innocence."

"Shut up!"

"Are you going to sit until morning with your pistol on your knee?"

"No," she said. "I will be going to bed soon. I am building a tower of books outside the closet door. At the very top, I am placing a china cupid. If you try to escape, the cupid will fall and break. The noise will wake me, and then I will accidentally shoot you."

"You have just given me a viable alternative to marrying your sister."

"The marriage would still take place," she said. "I wouldn't shoot you anywhere important. In the arm or, perhaps, the leg. I daresay the ride to church would be rather uncomfortable for you."

"And after the wedding?" he went on presently. "Shall we all live together in one house? You and Prudence and me?"

"Certainly not. Try to get some rest, Mr. Purefoy," she said coldly. "Tomorrow you begin your honeymoon. Where will you go? Paris? Venice?"

"Farnese."

"Farnese? Where is that?"

"It's my name," he told her. "I am Mr. Farnese now, not Mr. Purefoy. Farnese is my mother's name. Are you so very sure your sister wants to marry the penniless bastard of an Italian opera dancer?"

"There!"

"There?" he repeated, puzzled. "There where?"

"It was rhetorical," she explained. "I have finished stacking my books and the china cupid is in place. Now I am going to bed. Good night."

"Good night, Patience. Or should I say Pazienza?"

"Why on earth would you say that?" she asked crossly.

"That is your name in Italian," he explained.

"So?"

Max sighed. "Good night, Patience."

"Good night, Mr. Purefoy."

*   *   *

When Patience opened her eyes, sunlight was streaming into her room from the window. The chubby china face of a cherub looked back at her from the other side of the pillow. With a gasp, she sat up. The books she had stacked so carefully against the door of the water closet were still stacked against the door, but now the door was open. Somehow, he had pushed the door open without knocking them over.

Jumping out of bed, she accidentally sent the china figurine flying. It crashed to the floor and shattered to pieces. Paying it no heed, she ran to her sister's room.

Prudence was awake already and seated, half dressed, at her dressing table. Her maid was fixing her mistress's hair while Pru powdered her own bosom. "Good heavens, Pay!" Pru said, as Patience burst into the room. "You look simply awful. Didn't you get any sleep at all?"

"I fell asleep. I'm sorry, Pru! I lost him."

Prudence turned. "Who, Pay? Who have you lost?"

"The groom, I'm afraid."

Pru laughed lightly and turned back to the mirror. "Don't be silly, Pay. He's only just arrived. He is in the drawing room now, waiting for us. I've decided to wear blue," she went on, setting down her powder puff. "Married in blue: your love will always be true. Wait! Where are you going?"

"The drawing room," Patience answered. "I should not let him out of my sight until you are safely married."

"You are not fit to be seen," cried Pru. "Patience, I insist that you go to your room and splash a little water on your face. You look like death warmed over. Did you sleep in those clothes?"

Patience had not changed her clothes since dressing for

the theater the night before. "Yes," she said. Closing the door, she walked resolutely to the drawing room.

Max was standing against the fireplace, studying the various *cartes de visite* that Pru had displayed on the mantel like miniature trophies.

"I thought you had run away," she said.

He spun around at the sound of her voice. "You look awful," he said.

"How did you get out?" she demanded.

"I went out for the morning papers."

"I didn't ask *why* you went out," she said crossly. "I asked *how*. Oh, never mind! Prudence is almost ready."

"You'll be glad to know I reentered the house very properly by the front door. Briggs let me in. I assume you don't want the servants to know I spent the night locked in your privy?"

"I don't care," she said wearily. "I just want this over and done with."

"So do I," he said, producing a folded newspaper from behind his back. "I've taken the liberty of marking the pertinent columns."

"What is this?" she asked, taking it from him.

"The *Times*, I think, gives the most accurate account. If you would be good enough to read from here to here. And again, from here to here."

Patience did as he directed. "Your uncle has done it then," she murmured. "You are disowned. I am—I am very sorry."

He raised his brows. "You are sorry? I thought you were very much in favor of the idea."

"I am not sorry for *you,* Mr. Purefoy," she explained coldly. "I'm sorry for your uncle. He has some affection for you, I think. I'm sorry for Mrs. Drabble, too. The poor woman was distraught. I'm sorry for all the people you have hurt. But I am *not* sorry for you."

He regarded her impassively. "Would you be good enough to show the notices to your sister? She very well may change her mind about marrying me."

"She will not be pleased, I daresay," said Patience, "but nothing can change what has happened between you. You have put the cart before the horse, as your uncle put it. She is determined to marry you. If you are hoping to weasel out of it—"

"I was not aware that 'weasel' could be used as a verb," he said. "Let me put it another way," he went on as she glowered at him. "I will not marry your sister until she is acquainted with all the facts. If she still wants to marry me after you show her this, then, of course, I will marry her. She has the right to know whom she is marrying, surely. Why do you hesitate?"

"I will show it to her," Patience said coldly. "But it will not make any difference."

With newspapers in hand, she marched back to her sister's room. Pru was now fully dressed in a gown of ice blue satin.

"Lord, Patience!" she exclaimed irritably. "You look worse than you did before."

"I have news, Prudence," Patience said. "It concerns your husband-to-be. Would you like to read it for yourself?"

"What about Max?" Pru said sharply. "Tell me at once."

"Very well. His uncle has disowned him, has declared him illegitimate."

"What?" Pru cried, snatching the newspaper from Patience's hand.

"His parents' marriage is null and void," Patience went

on dully. "He is stripped of his name, fortune, and any hope he had of becoming Duke of Sunderland."

Pru took up the story, her eyes glued to the newspaper. "The duke is no longer responsible for his nephew's debts! His grace gives him no allowance. From this day forth, he refuses to acknowledge his brother's natural son. He is ruined. Max is ruined."

She looked up from the newspaper, round-eyed. "But I never meant for this to happen! Ruined! He is not to inherit? Not the title, not anything?"

"Not a penny," Patience answered. "Of course, this changes nothing for you. You still have to marry Mr. P— Mr. Farnese."

"Mr. who?"

"Farnese. That is his mother's name. The only name to which he has any claim now. He wanted to make sure you knew before the wedding."

"Wedding?" Pru gasped. "There isn't going to be any wedding!"

"Now, Pru," Patience admonished her. "I know it's a shock, but the carriage is waiting to take us to St. Bride's. There's no reason to delay the wedding."

"What wedding? You keep talking about a wedding!" Pru angrily tore silk flowers from her elaborate coiffure. "You said you would never force me to marry against my will. You said we could bring charges against him. I've given the matter some thought. And I think we *should* bring charges against him, just like you said."

Patience shook her head. "I was angry. I spoke foolishly. Of course you must marry him. You have had intimate relations with him. There may be a child, you know."

"There is no child," said Pru. "I never had intimate relations with that man."

"What?" cried Patience.

"He never touched me. Now get me out of this dress!" Pru snapped at her maid, who stood rooted to the spot, listening with great interest.

"You would not tell such a wicked lie, surely," Patience said slowly.

"Was I lying then, or am I lying now?" said Pru. "I guess you'll never know!"

"Are you saying you made the whole thing up?" Patience said angrily. "You lied to me!"

"You lied to me first," Pru returned. "You *stole* him from me. All I did was steal him back. Well, I don't want him now. You can have him."

"But he confessed in his letter," Patience said slowly.

"Oh, that! He wrote that to me months ago. I kept his note for sentimental reasons. I didn't expect it to be so useful. Of course, I never expected my own sister to betray me."

"That note was his apology to *me*," said Patience. "The roses were for *me*."

Pru scoffed. "Oh, Pay! Not everything is about *you*. Although, when you think about it, all of this really is your fault. If you hadn't stolen him from me, I would never have retaliated, and none of this would be happening. His uncle would not have disowned him."

Too weary for anger, Patience closed her eyes. "And my note? You added the postscript, didn't you?"

"Yes, I read your note," Pru said, her face twisted by pent-up fury. "That is how I found out what was going on behind my back! It was the easiest thing in the world," she boasted. "When you left the room, the seal on your note was still warm. I simply peeled it off and put a new one in its place when I was finished. I could not believe my eyes when I read it! When I think of how you pretended to hate him—! And all along, you wanted him for yourself!"

"No," Patience protested. "It wasn't like that at all. I never meant to hurt you, Pru."

Pru became shrill. "Never meant to hurt me? You knew I liked him!"

Patience stared down at her hands. "You are right," she said, after a moment. "I should have been honest with you. Mr. Purefoy has been making love to me since I met him that day at Tattersall's. I should have told you, but I didn't. I am sorry."

Pru snorted, but did not otherwise respond.

"But it doesn't change the fact that what you did was very, very wrong, Pru," Patience went on. "Mr.—Max could sue you for slander. Could sue *us* for slander," she added miserably. "We will have to make peace with him."

"He would not dare!"

"Think of what he has lost because of us!" Patience said. "Yesterday, he was the Duke of Sunderland's heir. Today, he is penniless. If I were he, I would sue. We will have to negotiate some sort of settlement with him. But, first, we must beg his pardon."

Pru bristled. "Beg his pardon! No! Never! He should be begging *my* pardon, as you did. I am the wronged party."

"Your revenge was perhaps a trifle disproportionate," Patience said dryly.

"I don't care if he sues us," Pru declared. "I would rather die than apologize to him. Anyway, he should be too ashamed of his own behavior to sue anybody."

"Bitterness is no defense, my dear. *He* has not broken any laws. In a court of law, we would be at his mercy. And think of your reputation, Pru! It would be better for us, certainly, to settle with him now."

"If he *dares* to sue me, I shall stand up in court and accuse him all over again!" Pru declared.

"Prudence!" said Patience, shocked. "You will do no such thing!"

Pru's eyes flashed. "I shall! He's not going to get away with what he did to me. If he sues me, I shall defend myself."

"Prudence, you cannot mean what you are saying. It is against the laws of God as well as man to bear false witness against your neighbor."

"He's not my neighbor."

"Of course he is," Patience snapped. "It's not meant to be taken literally, you know."

"Well, if it's not meant to be taken literally, what is there to worry about?" Pru wanted to know.

"Oh, my God," Patience muttered under her breath.

"Now you're taking God's name in vain," Pru chided her. "Isn't that like pointing out the mote of dust in your neighbor's eye or something?"

Patience controlled her temper with difficulty. "He is waiting in the drawing room. We must go and tell him something."

"You go," Pru said carelessly. "I have nothing to say to him. This is all your fault, anyway. Who should clean up the mess but you?"

Patience frowned at her. "You know, Prudence, if this goes to court, I am not going to lie for you. I will tell the truth."

"You would not give evidence against me," Pru said confidently. "Not for *him*. He used you, Patience! Remember what Lord Milford told you! Max only pretended to love you to win a bet. For that alone, he deserved to be ruined."

Patience flinched. "I had nearly forgotten that," she said quietly.

"Oh, dear," Max said, as Patience entered the room. "Is it as bad as that?"

Patience could not meet his gaze, she was so mortified.

"Let me guess," Max said quite cheerfully. "She doesn't want to marry me, after all?"

The lightness of his tone brought her eyes up to his face briefly. To her amazement, he seemed quietly amused. His gray eyes were definitely twinkling.

"I don't know what to say to you, sir," she said, her voice hollow. "My sister has admitted— She has admitted—"

"That she lied?" he said helpfully.

Sick at heart, Patience nodded. "She has admitted to everything."

"I expected as much. Yesterday, she would say anything to ensnare me. Today she'll say anything to be free of me."

Patience stole another doubtful glance at his face. "I shall, of course, speak to your uncle at the first opportunity. Perhaps something can be salvaged?"

"My uncle has already left London," Max replied. "He has gone off to St. Petersburg."

"St. Petersburg?" she repeated, baffled. "St. Petersburg, *Russia*?"

"He has gone there to fetch Freddie. My cousin, you know. On his mother's side, he is a Purefoy. Which, of course, I no longer am," Max added thoughtfully. "Now that I am disowned, Freddie is my uncle's rightful heir."

Patience blinked back sudden, unwelcome tears. "I'm so very sorry. I thought you were guilty. I could not see how you could be innocent. I will write to your uncle at once. I will tell him you are innocent. Perhaps my letter will overtake him. If there is any way to restore you to your rightful place, I'm sure he will do it. You must not despair, Mr. Purefoy."

"Farnese," he corrected her gently. "You may write until you are blue in the face. It will change nothing. My parents' marriage is dissolved. I am now a bastard."

She winced. "Are you quite certain it is irrevocable?"

"Oh, yes," he replied. "It says so in the *Times*."

"Well, even if it is, which I hope it is not," she said quickly, "your uncle, when he hears that you are innocent, will certainly acknowledge that you are his brother's child. You may be excluded from inheriting the title, but you need not be penniless."

"You think I would take money from him, after what he has done to me?"

"But it is my fault," she protested. "He only did it because—because I persuaded him that Pru was telling the truth. Do not blame your uncle. It is my fault."

"I rather think it is your precious sister's fault."

"No, sir. It begins and ends with me," Patience said firmly. "I should have told her of your—your interest in me. We have never kept secrets from each other before. When she found out about—about us—she was so hurt and angry that she struck out at you—at us—blindly. Please forgive her. She did not know what she was doing."

"I beg your pardon!" he said. "She knew exactly what she was doing!"

"She did not think of the consequences. She did not know your uncle would disown you."

"How can you defend her even now?" he asked incredulously.

"She is my sister," Patience said helplessly. "She has done wrong but I cannot turn my back on her. What will you do?" she asked, after a slight pause.

"What do you suggest? I have no name, no money, no home. My fiancée has deserted me. I don't suppose you would care to take her place?"

"Is that a serious offer?" she asked quietly.

Max's expression grew sober. "Yes. I'm sorry. It must have sounded quite facetious. Patience Waverly, will you marry me?"

"Yes," she said.

He blinked in surprise. "You will?"

"If you had asked me yesterday before all this happened, I would have accepted you. I can't very well reject you now, can I?"

"It would indeed be hypocritical," he agreed, laughing softly with relief. "Do you know, I thought it would take a bit more persuasion."

He would have kissed her, but she turned her face away. "We are not married yet," she reminded him. "I do have one or two conditions," she added.

"I thought you might," he said jovially. "I am excessively fond of conditions."

"You must do nothing to harm Pru. You will not sue her. You will never speak of this—this unfortunate incident. When you are reconciled with your uncle, you will persuade him to keep silent as well. Nor will you seek to exact any sort of private revenge."

"Agreed."

"Second: my money is my money. You will not touch it."

"Fair enough."

"Third: you will get a job."

"What?" he said sharply.

"You must do something with yourself. Now that you are penniless, you will need an income. Perhaps you could go into business for yourself."

He was scowling. "What sort of business?"

"That would be up to you," she replied. "You should think of your reversal of fortune, not as a defeat, but as an opportunity to make something of yourself. My grandfather arrived in America with nothing but the clothes on his back. Twenty years later, he was the richest man in Philadelphia. You might do as well, if you apply yourself to something."

"I don't want to be the richest man in Philadelphia."

"Those are my conditions."

"I suppose," he said slowly, "I might— For many years now, I've had a special interest in amateur theatricals. I suppose I could get a job down at the theater."

Patience's eyes narrowed. "My fourth condition is that you go nowhere near the theater."

"Which one?"

"You are not to go near any of them!" she said crossly. "You're to have nothing to do with plays or—or actresses. You might do something with horses," she went on quickly. "You're good with horses."

"I'm good with actresses," he said.

"No actresses."

"I thought you liked the theater. At least, you were looking forward to going."

"The rector will not wait forever," she told him. "Have we an agreement?"

She stuck out her hand, and, after a moment, he shook it.

"Very well, madam. I agree to your terms."

Patience nodded. "Give me but a moment to splash a little water on my face," she said. "I will meet you downstairs."

"You can splash water on your face when you are married," he said. "Let's to church."

"But my dress," she protested weakly. "I must change my dress."

She had slept in her theater gown. It was now crushed and wrinkled, and the lace at one sleeve had been torn away to make a bandage for Pru's arm.

"No one will see it," he assured her. "'Twill be under your cloak."

"But—"

"That is *my* condition," he said. "We must hurry; the rector won't wait forever."

Taking her by the arm, he propelled her out the door.

Chapter 17

It hardly seemed worth the trouble of arguing. Patience did not feel like a bride, so it mattered little to her that she did not look the part. At least her hair, which must have been in a frightful mess, was as hidden by her bonnet as her dress was by her cloak.

"I hope you don't mind," he said, as he handed her into his curricle. "I dismissed your carriage. Would you like to drive or shall I?"

Patience pulled the fur rug over her knees. "I wouldn't know the way to the church."

"Perhaps on the way back," he suggested lightly.

"Perhaps," she answered, marveling at his cheerful mood.

Despite the gloomy sky overhung with dark clouds, Max seemed pleased with the world and everything in it, especially her. Most especially her. It was as if nothing unpleasant had taken place at all. As he drove, he kept picking up her hand and kissing it, to keep it warm, he said, for she had left the house without her gloves.

"This job of mine," he said suddenly. "Whatever it is, it will have to be lucrative. I've acquired a taste for the finer things in life. I fully intend to cover you in jewels."

"Sounds rather heavy," Patience said. "Covered in jewels, I might drown if I fell in a pond or something."

The bells were ringing as they drew alongside the church. The groom jumped down to take the reins from his master, while Max handed Patience from the vehicle himself. Patience stood for a moment with her head tilted back, admiring the church's beautiful, white, tiered spire as it cut into the gray sky.

"Why did your uncle choose this church?" she asked.

"You don't approve of the church?"

"It's very pretty," she replied. "I suppose he chose it because it was far away from Mayfair. I don't suppose it is frequented by the fashionable set."

"I'll have you know that I was baptized here," he said. "When I was born, my mother was living in poverty just a few streets away. As you know, my father was disowned by the mighty Purefoys when he married my mother. They had a rather hard time of it. My father even had to get a job— a black fate for a gentleman in those days. He built and painted sets at the opera where my mother danced."

"My grandfather disowned my mother when she married my father," Patience told him.

Max smiled. "Your grandfather did not approve of the younger son of a baron?"

"No, he just hated the English," Patience explained. "He got to know them when they occupied Philadelphia during the War of Independence."

"War of Independence? Oh, yes; that is what you Americans call your Revolution. But he relented . . . your grandfather, I mean," Max added. "He forgave your mother?"

Patience shook her head. "Not while my parents lived. Even after they died— Well, he took us in because it was his duty. And he left us his money because he had no one else. But he never relented. My father gave music lessons.

He never seemed to have time to teach us. He was so tired in the evenings."

Max held out his hand to her. "You can tell me all about it when we are married," he said. "We have kept the rector waiting long enough, I think."

Mrs. Drabble was waiting for them inside. The ribbons of her lace cap fluttered as she hurried down the black-and-white-patterned floor and kissed Patience. "My dear," she said, a little breathlessly. "I was beginning to think you weren't coming!"

"What are you doing here?" Patience blurted out in amazement.

"I took the liberty of asking Mrs. Drabble and Miss Haines to be our witnesses," Max explained. "That's all right, isn't it?"

Miss Haines waved her handkerchief gaily from the front of the church.

Mrs. Drabble beamed. "The rest of the ladies are at my house putting the finishing touches on the wedding breakfast."

Patience frowned at Max. "You are very sure of yourself, sir!"

"Of course he is," said Mrs. Drabble. "He knew, as I knew all along, that he was innocent. But I'm in your way," she hurtled on before Patience could utter a word, "and the rector is in *such* a hurry!"

As she bustled back toward the altar where an austere clergyman waited in his white robes, Max took Patience's hand and tucked it in the crook of his arm. "You see? Not everyone has disowned me," he murmured.

"I'm glad," she said, her eyes fixed on the altar.

"This is a Christopher Wren church, is it not?" she said, as they started down the aisle. "Your English churches are funny."

"How so?" he asked politely.

"In America, all the pews face the front. Here they face each other."

"You're talking more than usual," he observed. "Not nervous, are you?"

"No," she said, then clamped her lips together.

"Shall I tell you why the pews face each other?" he asked. When she made no reply, he went on, "It makes it easier for the gentlemen to ogle the ladies. It's the only reason men come to church. And, of course, the ladies only come to see what the other ladies are wearing."

"That is dreadful," Patience murmured, whispering because they had drawn near to the altar and the clergyman was looking at her with piercing dark eyes.

"I do not speak of myself," he protested. "These days I only go to church to get married. And only then because it is the law."

"Hush!" she pleaded. "He will hear you."

Miss Haines pressed her lace handkerchief in Patience's hand. "Something new," she whispered. "I made it myself. And your cloak is blue. But you must have something old. Something old, and something borrowed, or it is very bad luck."

Mrs. Drabble quickly took off her wedding ring. "Take it," she said, closing Max's fingers around the plain gold band. "It's old *and* borrowed. You can give it back to me when you have bought her a proper ring."

"You're very kind, Mrs. Drabble," Patience said, moved by the gesture. "Thank you, Miss Haines."

The rector cleared his throat impatiently, and they all snapped to attention.

After ferreting out that the bride had no middle name, the clergyman ran through the service as if his tongue were on fire. Patience wondered at the amazing capacity of his lungs. He hardly gave the bride and groom time to repeat their vows, and he scarcely paused as Max placed Mrs. Drabble's wedding ring on Patience's finger.

And then it was over.

Weeping, Miss Haines ran forward to kiss Patience. "I know it's silly," she said, tears streaming down her wrinkled cheeks. "But I always cry at weddings."

"Better take this, then," said Patience, giving her back the handkerchief. "I think you need it more than I do."

"I see what you mean," Miss Haines said, dabbing at her eyes. "You *will* not be crying."

Mrs. Drabble had been congratulating Max. Now the two ladies changed places.

"We have laid a fine wedding breakfast for you," Mrs. Drabble said. "Four tiers to the wedding cake! And, Max, of course, would have my gooseberry tarts. There's cherry for you, as well. Mrs. Bascombe's recipe."

The rector cleared his throat again, and Max hurried to place his name and the name of his bride in the register. Everyone signed the marriage certificate, the rector cleared his throat for a third time, and they all hurried out of the church to discover that it was raining.

Max summoned a hackney coach for Mrs. Drabble and Miss Haines while his groom raised the top over the curricle. While Patience waited in the curricle, Max sent the jarvey on his way to Wimpole Street. "Happy?" he asked, joining Patience in the curricle.

"I am content," she answered.

He frowned. "Well, I am happy," he declared. "I have wanted to marry you since I kissed you in Hyde Park."

"As long as that?" she said lightly. "But two weeks? Three perhaps?"

"It seemed like an eternity to me," he said, his tone reproachful.

"And was that before or after you made your bet?" she asked politely.

His hand must have jerked the reins for his horses gave a sudden start. Max quickly got them under control, but his face was grim. "Made my *what*?" he said sharply.

"Wager, if you prefer," she said. "You did make a wager that you would marry me, did you not? Forgive me, if I am mistaken."

"You are not mistaken," he said, after a pause. "I did make a wager, but that was—that was a moment's foolishness only. Pray, do not regard it. I was in my cups. The Earl of Milford was annoying me."

"So it is true, then. I wasn't sure."

"You're not going to tax me with this," he said curtly. "On our wedding day? I tell you, it was nothing. I haven't the slightest intention of collecting, if that makes it any better."

"Oh, do you think I am angry?" she asked. "Not at all, I assure you. I think it's a good thing that you made this bet. In light of recent events, a very good thing. If you are going to start out in business, you will need capital."

Her pragmatic tone set his teeth on edge. "May I ask how you know about this bet?"

"Lord Milford told me."

"Of course he did," Max said angrily. "He made a bet of his own—that *he* would marry you. He has no business discussing the betting books outside of our clubs!" Max said indignantly. "I could have him blackballed for this."

"Please do not give *my* feelings another thought," Patience said coldly.

He frowned, puzzled. "You said you weren't angry."

"I'm not," she snapped. "I'm *glad*. I'm glad you made a wager that you would marry me."

He sighed. "You are angry."

"Not at all," she insisted. "I'm very glad you've won your bet; I helped you do it. My conscience will never be *truly* clear until I'm able to contact your uncle, but, at least

I've done all I can to make amends to you. You're not completely penniless."

Cursing under his breath, he pulled his horses to the curb and checked them. "I told you, madam," he said coldly, "I haven't the slightest intention of collecting on that asinine wager. May we please drop the matter? Our wedding breakfast awaits us."

"Under the circumstances," Patience said primly, "I don't feel right about attending a wedding breakfast."

"What circumstances?" he growled. "We've just had our wedding; we've not yet had our breakfast. Those are the circumstances. It would seem to me to be an ideal time for a wedding breakfast."

"But those ladies think we are really married," Patience protested. "They think it is a happy occasion. They don't suspect that I only married you so that you could collect on your wager. Mrs. Drabble has gone to a lot of trouble."

"*What* did you say?" he demanded.

"I said Mrs. Drabble has gone to a lot of trouble."

His gray eyes narrowed as he stared at her. "Before that," he drawled. "Do you mean to say you only married me so that I could win a bet?"

"Well, I felt terribly guilty about your uncle disowning you. You will need something to live on. With fifty thousand pounds, you could live in style."

"Fifty thousand?"

"Yes. That was the amount of your wager, was it not?"

He smiled tightly. "Not quite, my sweet. You have been misinformed. I gave Milford odds of five to one."

"What does that mean?"

"It means that I hazarded fifty thousand pounds. He only hazarded ten."

"Oh. Well . . . ten thousand pounds is a handsome sum, too. For your sake, I wish it were more."

"For the last time, I have no interest in the money. I will never collect on that bet. Never."

"Don't be foolish. Of course you must collect. You cannot afford to be proud. Remember, you agreed never to touch my fortune. Where will you live? How will you eat? How will you look after your horses? I bet they eat a lot. How will you pay your groom?"

"I will live with my wife," he answered. "I will share her food. My horses will be kept in her mews. My groom will work for nothing, because he is loyal."

Patience was shaking her head. "That will not be possible. You cannot live with me. I live with my sister. It doesn't bear thinking about. I married you so you could collect your money, but there it ends, I'm afraid."

"Just a moment—" he began hotly.

"We wronged you, Prudence and I," she interrupted him. "I am very sorry for that. But you—you wronged us, too, did you not?"

"Did I?"

"You devoted yourself to my sister for weeks. Your attention to her even received notice in the newspapers! Then you made your bet with your friend, Lord Milford. Suddenly, your interest in my poor sister withered away, and you began to pursue me. We both know why."

"Are you insinuating that I married you for a mere ten thousand pounds?" he demanded. "I? Maximilian Tiberius Purefoy?"

"I think, when you made that bet, it was a game to you," she said calmly. "Life, I daresay, was a game to you. But it isn't a game now. You're not Maximilian Purefoy. You're Maximilian Farnese—and you're poor!"

"How could you misunderstand me so completely?"

"But I do understand," she argued. "There's no need to be so defensive. I am not angry. But if you think you're going to—to have your cake and eat it, too, you are very much mistaken."

"What cake?" he said sullenly. "My cake is at the wedding breakfast."

"Let me be perfectly plain," she said. "You can have the money. Take it with my blessing! But you cannot have me. This marriage will be annulled as soon as I can make the arrangements. In fact, I would be grateful to you, sir, if you would drop me at my attorney's rooms. They are not far from here, in Chancery Lane. Do you know it?"

"This is my town," he said coldly. "Of course I know it."

Clicking his tongue, he brought his team of grays back to life and turned them smoothly back onto the cobbled street. "May I ask," he went on presently, "on what grounds do you propose to annul our marriage?"

"I should think it quite obvious," she said sharply.

"Nothing about this is obvious to me," he returned.

"We are not man and wife. Nor shall we ever be."

"I see. You are aware, I suppose, that, as your husband, I have certain rights, should I choose to exercise them?"

Patience colored slightly, but not nearly as much as he had hoped. "You won't do that," she said confidently. "If I thought you were that sort of man, I would never have married you."

"I think you will find that getting an annulment is a rather complicated affair."

"No. It's perfectly simple. The marriage will never be consummated. It must be annulled."

"I don't know how you do things in America, of course," he said, rather snidely, "but here we take 'what God hath joined' and all that rot rather seriously, I'm afraid. You can't just tell the Church you want an annulment and *presto!* The Church has to make an investigation."

"Investigation!" she exclaimed. "What is there to investigate?"

"First, you will have to prove that the marriage has not been consummated. I suppose they have a physician examine you, or, perhaps the bishop does it himself. I'm not really clear on that point."

"You are lying!" she said angrily.

"There's more. By law, a man has the right to consummate his marriage—or not, just as he chooses. You can't be granted an annulment simply because your husband does not choose to exercise his marital rights. You will have to demonstrate to the court that I am *incapable* of performing in the bedchamber."

"Demonstrate? How?"

"In such cases, the courts will be obliged to appoint a woman to examine me, which should make for some interesting evidence."

"That is ridiculous," she said, though more than a little taken aback by his apparent knowledge of a process of which she was entirely ignorant.

"Oh, let the bishops have their fun," he said tolerantly. "God knows they lead dreary lives. Did I mention, before you can proceed with the annulment, we shall be obliged to share a bed for a period of not less than three years?"

"This can't be true," she said.

"Your attorney will tell you. What's his name, by the way?"

"Bracegirdle."

"Ah, yes. He'll tell you. But don't look so glum," he added. "We can always apply for an annulment on the grounds of *your* incompetence, rather than mine."

"I am not incompetent," she snapped.

"You are not yet twenty-one," he said. "In the eyes of the law, that *is* incompetence. And we won't have to share a bed for three years—or even at all. Your attorney can begin the process right away."

"Why didn't you say so in the first place?" she said furiously.

"I was simply pointing out the folly of your little idea of accusing me of impotence," he replied. "Then I offered you the correct solution to your problem. You should be thanking me."

"If it *is* the correct solution, my lawyer will tell me the same thing. You need not have bothered."

"I wish you had told me you were only marrying me to atone for your sister's sins," he said, after a long, uncomfortable silence. "I could have saved us both a good deal of trouble."

"Meaning you would not have married *me,* I suppose!"

"No," he answered shortly.

Stung, she retaliated. "If I had known you wouldn't take the money, I would not have married you either!"

As he drew up to the attorney's building in Chancery Lane, she opened the door and jumped out before either he or his groom could assist her. "You *will* end up collecting on that wager!" she told him. "You won't have a choice. You wouldn't last a day in a world where you had to earn your own keep. You're too lazy to work at anything, and too dissipated to do anything worthwhile with your money even if you could earn any!"

Max's eyes glinted. "Would you care to make a wager on that?"

Shaking her head in disgust, Patience turned on her heel and walked into the building.

He had already started off when he heard her calling out to him. Hastily, he pulled the team to a stop. "Yes?" he said quickly as she ran up to the car.

"Please be good enough to return this to Mrs. Drabble," she said.

Instinctively, he held out his hand. Into it, she dropped the widow's plain gold band. By the time he had dropped it into his pocket, she was gone.

Mr. Bracegirdle closed the door to his office and listened to his client in silence, taking notes from time to time with his goose-quill pen. When Patience had finished, he asked her a series of particular questions. Where had the marriage taken place? Who had officiated? Names of the witnesses? He asked to see the license, and sighed when Patience told him it was in the keeping of the man she had married.

He shook his head. "I do wish Your Ladyship had consulted me first."

Patience leaned forward in her chair. "But can you get me out of it, Mr. Bracegirdle?"

"It won't be easy," he said. "It will take time. These witnesses—Miss Haines? Mrs. Drabble? Are they women of good character?"

"Excellent character!" Patience said emphatically. "Mrs. Drabble is a respectable widow, and Miss Haines's father was a colonel in the army, I believe."

"Too bad," he murmured. "The annulment of a legal union is by no means a simple matter, you must understand."

"But I cannot stay married to him, Mr. Bracegirdle!"

"Yes, I understand his uncle has disowned him," the attorney said sympathetically. "How very disappointed you must be. You thought you were getting a duke's heir. Instead, he turned out to be nothing but a fortune hunter. I'm sure the court will be sympathetic."

Patience was on her feet. "What? No! Good God! Is that what you think? I don't want an annulment because his uncle disowned him. He's not a fortune hunter, and neither am I. I married him so that he could collect on a wager."

He stared at her. "You mean you knew he was penniless when you married him? You knew that he had no expectations?"

"Yes, of course. He didn't deceive me, if that's what you're getting at."

He shook his head, the candlelight glinting on his spectacles. "Too bad. The court would have been very sympathetic. You realize, of course, that your husband is within his rights to take control of your fortune."

"Not at all. He has promised never to touch my money."

"He has relinquished all claims to your inheritance?" Mr. Bracegirdle said incredulously.

"You have this in writing?"

"No, not in writing. He gave me his word."

Mr. Bracegirdle looked very grave. "Oh, dear. This *does* make it difficult."

"But it can be done?" she said anxiously, striding about the room. "I don't care what it takes. I don't care how much it costs. I can't stay married to him. It—it hurts too much!"

"I beg your pardon," he said, startled. "I did not realize the marriage had already been consummated! I'm afraid that does change the . . . er . . . landscape considerably."

Patience pressed her hands to her hot cheeks. "No, Mr. Bracegirdle! We came straight here from the church. What I meant was: it hurts to look at him. His face is so—so—"

"He is rather swarthy, perhaps," Mr. Bracegirdle conceded. "But I understand his mother was Italian, and no better than she should be."

"How dare you!" Patience said angrily. "My husband is the most beautiful man in the whole of creation. I have never had the honor of meeting his mother, but I'm quite sure she is exactly what she ought to be. Now, perhaps, you understand why I can't stay married to him. I love him too much!"

"I understand, of course. I'm not sure the court will."

"But he doesn't love me. He only wanted to marry me to win a stupid bet. Before that, he was practically engaged to my sister. I cannot possibly spend the rest of my life married to a man who does not love me!"

"I quite understand. Perhaps if Your Ladyship were to use your feminine arts, you could make him love you," the attorney suggested. "I daresay it would be a good deal easier than obtaining an annulment from the Church of England."

Patience glared at him. "If he is too stupid to love me," she declared, "then he doesn't deserve me. Feminine arts, indeed! I'd sooner punch him in the nose! Now do you understand?"

"Yes, my lady."

"Good! Then kindly stop babbling and get me my annulment!"

"Yes, my lady," he said, but she had already swept from the room.

The effect was rather spoiled, however, when she was obliged to return to ask him to send for a hackney to carry her back to her house.

In Clarges Street, she found her carriage waiting at the curb. Lady Jemima, dressed to go out, ostrich plumes adorning her golden turban, was coming down the stairs as Patience entered the house. "Lady Waverly! Where have you been? You are not dressed! Hurry! For it is the Torcasters' ball this night."

The trill of excitement in her voice made Patience feel quite weary. She went up the stairs to Pru's room. Prudence was dabbing French perfume behind her ears. "Where on earth have you been?" she cried. "We were just about to go without you."

Patience sat down on the bed, which was covered in

gowns—Pru's obvious rejects. "You will have to go without me," she said. "I've just come from Mr. Bracegirdle's office."

"Oh?" Pru twisted around, studying the view of her rear in the cheval glass. As cross as Patience was, she could not help but notice that the back of her sister's gown was as heavily decorated with flowers as the front; Pru obviously did not mean to sit down at the ball. "I borrowed your pearls. You don't mind, do you?"

"You have pearls of your own," Patience objected.

"A single strand! I should be ashamed to wear only a single strand," Pru said scornfully. "What did old Bracegirdle want?"

"Nothing. I went to seek his advice about—about Mr. Purefoy."

"Mr. Farnessi or Farinelli, you mean."

"Yes."

Pru seemed only mildly interested. "Does Mr. Bracegirdle think he will sue us?"

"He won't sue us," Patience said slowly. "I—I've settled with him."

Pru frowned. "I hope he was not unreasonable! I hope his terms were not too high. I do hate having to pay blackmailers."

"You will kindly not refer to Mr.—Mr. Farnese as a blackmailer!" Patience said sharply.

Pru shrugged. "I shan't refer to him at all. How is that?"

"Thank you," Patience said dully.

"How do I look?" Pru demanded.

"The back of your gown will be crushed in the carriage," Patience said, "if that matters."

Pru smiled at her triumphantly. "No, it won't," she said. "I shall lift it up before I sit down and sit on my petticoats. Is that not scandalous?" She laughed, and went dancing out of the room without waiting for Patience to reply.

Chapter 18

"I don't understand!" the Duke of Sunderland said angrily.

All morning he had sat in his bath chair in Mrs. Drabble's—to him—tiny drafty parlor, surrounded by a gaggle of old women, and when Max finally arrived, the hour was ridiculously late and his nephew was alone. Mrs. Drabble, after one look at the bridegroom's face, had sent the old ladies away. Tactfully, she and Jane had carried the wedding cake out of the room, leaving the uncle alone with his heir.

Max sat down and began eating gooseberry tarts. They tasted like ashes in his mouth, but he continued eating them just the same. "I don't completely understand it myself."

"Well, where is she?" the duke demanded. "Doesn't the silly girl know we have been waiting here all day? Does she know I had to be carried up those poky little stairs? Did you tell her you're not really disowned?"

"If I thought it would make a difference, I would have," Max murmured. "She is with her lawyer now, planning the annulment."

"What annulment?" the duke cried, horrified.

Max lifted his shoulders and let them fall. "She wants

an annulment. She only married me so that I could collect on a bet."

"Oh?" the duke said, with a sneer. "Madam wants an annulment, does she? Good riddance, say I! I'll see that she gets it, too! I'll send to the archbishop directly! Twenty thousand pounds ought to do the trick."

"You'll do no such thing," Max said sharply.

The duke waved a hand. "Dear boy! I don't care about the money. You're better off without this—this American wench. We'll find you someone much, much better. I'll get you a Spanish princess, if that's what you want."

"I don't feel better off," Max said, taking another tart from the plate. "And even if I am better off, who says I want to be better off?"

The duke threw up his hands. "You don't mean to say you still want her?" he said incredulously.

"Would it distress you to hear that I now want her even more?"

"Distress?" His uncle shrugged. "More perplexing than distressing, I'd say. But I have always said you may marry where you will. I vowed never to interfere in your choice— though I have watched many sweet and pretty creatures marry themselves to far inferior men than my nephew. But I say nothing. I do not complain. I do not nag you. Perhaps I should have. Lady Amelia would never have left you on your wedding day. She would not make you miserable."

Max smiled faintly. "She couldn't."

"Quite so," said the duke, utterly mistaking his nephew's meaning. "But you did not want Lady Amelia, and so she married somebody else."

"Lord Irving. She makes *him* miserable."

The duke frowned. "Perhaps," he conceded. "But she would not have made you so. Bah! I thank God my health never permitted me to marry. Take me home now, Max. I am tired. Tomorrow we'll have the newspapers print a full retraction. We'll forget all about this unfortunate incident."

Max was shaking his head. "No! No, let there be no retractions. If she finds out I am still your heir, I will lose her forever. She'll never come back to me."

"Pshaw! She'll crawl through the streets to you on her hands and knees. Remember, I could fall dead any day now, and then she would be a duchess."

"You don't know her, Uncle. She would fear being thought a mercenary, and I would lose her forever. No, we must wait. I must have time to—to persuade her."

The duke scowled. "No woman can be worth all this trouble!"

Mrs. Drabble came back into the room with the tea tray.

"Is that so, Your Grace?" she asked, her blue eyes narrowed.

"No *American* woman," he said, hastily redefining the parameters of his declaration.

"She is my choice, Uncle, whether you like it or not," said Max. "She is my choice whether *she* likes it or not," he added under his breath.

"That's the spirit!" said Mrs. Drabble.

"Yes, indeed," the duke agreed heartily. "You young people these days! You give too much thought to what the woman feels or likes! Bah! You have only to order her to go home with you, and the thing is done. By law, she is your property, boy. She should be treated as such."

"That is odious!" cried Mrs. Drabble, slamming down the teapot. "Don't listen to him, Max!"

"It may be odious," the duke responded, "but it is the law. Don't tell me Mr. Drabble would have put up with such nonsense."

Her plump cheeks were quite red. "Mr. Drabble," she said indignantly, "was the kindest, gentlest, dearest soul who ever lived! If there were any justice in this world, he would have been born a duke, and *you* would have been born in the gutter."

The duke blinked at her in surprise. "I didn't know Drabble was born in the gutter."

"He wasn't!" she snapped. "But *you* should have been, with a mind like yours."

"What did I do?" he wondered innocently. "I was only explaining the law to the boy. A married man has rights!"

Max held up his hand for peace. "Uncle, if I thought it would answer, I would take your advice. But I know very well it won't answer," he added quickly, as his former nurse began to squawk.

"Well, what are you going to do?" the duke demanded. "You can't let her get away with this. Her conduct is disgraceful."

"Oh, do be quiet," Mrs. Drabble said impatiently.

"Don't tell me to be quiet," he snapped.

"I'll say what I like! It's my house!"

"Who paid for it?"

Mrs. Drabble balled up her fist and shook it at him. "I earned every penny of that money, looking after you for a dozen years and more!"

"Please!" said Max, holding up both hands.

Mrs. Drabble composed herself. "You must forgive your uncle," she said, handing him a cup of tea. "He's always crotchety at this time of day. What *are* you going to do?" she went on quickly, before the duke could retort, effectively giving herself the last word.

"I'm going to get a job."

The duke was so shocked, he completely forgot his argument with Mrs. Drabble. "A what?" he cried in utter disbelief.

"A job," Mrs. Drabble said loudly, as if the duke were going deaf, when, in fact, she was quite as amazed as Max's uncle. "He said he's going to get a job."

"I heard what he said!" the duke snapped.

"It means employment for financial remuneration."

"Yes, I know what it means," he shouted at her. "But why is he—?" Breaking off angrily, he turned to Max. "Why would you do such a thing?"

"I must earn a living," Max replied.

"Why?" the duke wanted to know.

"Because *she* thinks I can't!" his nephew explained.

The next morning, Pru dressed very carefully, in anticipation of receiving visits from all the gentlemen with whom she had danced the night before. "Lord Torcaster himself took your sister in to dinner," Lady Jemima told Patience at breakfast. The chaperone quivered with delight, her pinkish hair almost glowing in the morning sunlight.

"Is he not a married man?" said Patience, frowning.

"La, Patience!" Pru said derisively. "Don't you know anything? Husbands never escort their wives to dinner! Why, they would have to sit next to each other. And who would want to sit next to Lady Torcaster? She's so frumpy! And her father was in trade."

Patience set down her coffee cup. "You should show more respect for your hostess," she said reproachfully. "And need I remind you that your own fortune comes from trade?"

"Only on our mother's side," Pru protested. "Our *father* was a gentleman. If he were alive today, he would be Baron Waverly."

"If he were alive today, he would spank you," Patience muttered.

If her companions heard this remark, they gave no sign of it. After breakfast, they repaired to the drawing room. Patience sorted through her correspondence, handing all invitations to Prudence, then settled down to read a lengthy report from Mr. Campbell, the estate manager at Wildings. Mr. Campbell urged her to accept the offer of ten thousand pounds for the property, citing numerous proofs that it would cost more to turn the place to account: the cottages were broken down, the tenants fleeing, the sheep were dying of some mysterious disease, and the roof was missing quite a few slates. There was scarcely a window that hadn't been broken.

"Sounds charming," Pru sneered when Patience gave her the gist of it. "Sell it!"

"I should like to see it before I sell it, but Mr. Campbell says the roads are flooded. I wonder how his letter reached me if the roads are flooded."

"It's much too cold to go to Wildings," said Lady Jemima. "Besides the Season is in full swing!"

"We are invited to Princess Esterhazy's musicale!" cried Pru, waving an invitation engraved in gold on an elegant purple card. "She is the wife of the Hungarian ambassador, you know."

Patience showed a spark of interest. "I suppose Mr. and Mrs. Adams will be invited, too."

Lady Jemima gave a trill of laughter. "One hardly thinks so, Lady Waverly. Only persons of distinction are invited to the Princess's gatherings."

"Then I shall write to her at once and explain that we are nobodies."

"You will do nothing of the kind!" Pru was already arranging the invitation on the mantel. She was still admiring it when Briggs came in with his tray.

"Lord Banville," Pru read from the card. "And his mother, of course! This is a compliment to *you,* Patience. Banny and his mama were most anxious about you at the ball last night."

"Why should he be anxious?" Patience asked.

"I told him you had the headache. If you do not appear

at Princess Esterhazy's musicale, I shall have to give you something much more dreadful—scarlet fever or something. It will be a great insult to the princess if you do not attend."

Patience shrugged. "She should not snub my ambassador."

Lord Banville escorted his mother into the room.

"Hallo, Banny," Pru drawled. Sauntering over to the viscount, she offered him her hand.

"Miss Prudence," he said, bowing over her hand. "How nice it is to see you again."

"But you did not come to see me, surely," she laughed. "As you can see, my sister is quite recovered."

Lady Mortmaigne had spied the purple card on the mantel. "You have your invitation from Princess Esterhazy, I see!" she exclaimed. "We got ours yesterday."

"So did we," Pru lied.

The lady's son, meanwhile, approached Patience, who was standing somewhat awkwardly beside her desk. "How do you do, sir?" she said politely.

"Very well, my lady," he returned, rather too warmly for her comfort. "I need not inquire after Your Ladyship's health," he went on. "You are blooming."

"Am I?" she said, flustered. She could not, in good conscience, receive his attentions. She was, after all, a married woman! She blushed to think of it, and blushed even more as she realized that Lord Banville must think her blushing was for his sake.

"I have been thinking, sir, about your IOU," she said quickly. "As kind as it was of you to relinquish it, I fear I cannot accept your generosity after all."

He blinked at her in surprise. "I don't understand."

Rummaging through the pigeonholes of her desk, she found the card he had given her. "You see I have not burned it. Please take it," she said quietly, holding it out to him.

"The debt will be paid as soon as I can manage it. I must insist, sir. You would not argue with a lady," she added, mustering a smile.

"No, indeed." Taking the card from her, he put it in his pocket.

"I hope I do not offend you," she said anxiously.

He smiled. "Not at all, ma'am. May I at least know the identity of my rival?"

"Rival?" she repeated blankly.

His eyes widened. "I see," he said gravely. "The gentleman has no rival! Fortunate man."

"What are you talking of over there, Banny?" Pru demanded, coming to claim the viscount. "Never mind! Come and tell me which ball I should attend on the nineteenth."

He smiled down at her as she led him away. "All of them, of course!"

After staying the requisite twenty minutes, Lord Banville and his mama departed, only to be replaced by Lord Milford and his sister. While not precisely pretty, Isabella looked radiant in a saffron gown and emerald green redingote that emphasized her auburn hair. To Patience's dismay, Prudence and Isabella suddenly appeared to have become as thick as inkle weavers: Pru exclaimed over Isabella's dress, and Isabella went into raptures about Pru's hair.

Lord Milford favored Patience with only the briefest of greetings, which surprised her very much since, according to Max, he had wagered a good deal on winning her affections. Perhaps he has given up, she thought happily.

For her part, Isabella chatted away with Pru for several moments before deigning to take any notice of Patience whatsoever.

"My dear Lady Waverly!" she said suddenly, cutting Pru off as the latter was sneering about the lace on Lady Torcaster's gown. "I did not see you there at your little desk! You are always so quiet. But, tell me, how *are* you bearing up?"

Patience found Isabella's concern wholly unconvincing. "I don't know what you mean, Lady Isabella."

"I am talking of Mr. Purefoy, of course," Isabella said, shaking her head sadly. "Mr. Fusilli, I should say, or whatever his name is. I don't speak dago."

Patience turned in her chair and skewered the other woman with her green eyes. "Farnese," she said coldly.

Isabella lifted her finely plucked brows. "Is *that* what his name is? I was sure *you* would know, Lady Waverly. He was *interested* in you at one time, was he not?"

"The duke should have annulled his brother's unfortunate marriage long ago," declared Lady Jemima. "It was an affront to all decent women—the younger son of a duke marrying a girl out of the opera house!"

"I suppose they loved each other."

"Nonsense! Lord Richard only did it to stick his thumb in his father's eye," Lady Jemima scoffed. "And ended up dying of pneumonia in some garret in the city or Cheapside or whatever. The mother went back to her ragtag gypsy people. I, for one, never believed the child was actually Lord Richard's."

"You go too far, madam," Patience said.

"One has only to look at him to see he is not of the blood," Lord Milford declared. "His features are too coarse. It's fairly obvious his father must have been a blackamoor. But who can say for certain, when the mother is an actress?"

"Ivor!" Isabella admonished him.

"His hands, Bella!" her brother pursued. "They are the hands of a blacksmith! They are not the hands of a gentleman. Surely you noticed."

"I cannot say that I did," his sister replied, laughing

lightly. "I could scarcely be bothered to notice the man's hands."

"You seemed to like him well enough when you were driving with him in the park," Patience said softly. "He was quite a favorite of yours at one time, I believe. Now you laugh at him."

"A favorite of mine?" Isabella looked bewildered. "Whatever can Your Ladyship mean?"

"You know exactly what I mean," Patience snapped. "When he was heir to a dukedom, it was your ambition to marry him!"

Isabella stared. "I? Marry with that—that *mongrel*? But I am engaged to Sir Charles Stanhope," she added haughtily. "Here is my engagement ring."

Thrusting her hand under Patience's nose, she showed a ruby the size of a man's thumb.

"Sir Charles Stanhope?" Pru echoed, wrinkling her nose at the man while giving his ruby its due. "That old fossil?"

"Sir Charles is a worldly man of wisdom and experience," said Isabella. "His father was the fourth baronet, and his mother was perfectly unexceptional."

"And, best of all, he is rich," said Lord Milford.

Patience laughed shortly. "Yes, I *do* think you have been hardest hit, Lady Isabella."

Isabella smiled coldly. "My dear Lady Waverly! I am very sorry for you, I'm sure, but one cannot rewrite history! Don't forget that my brother and I saw you with Mr. Faradiddle in Grosvenor Square—" Isabella's eyes fell demurely. "But I shall remain silent on that score."

"Indeed you will!" her brother said furiously. "No good can come of speaking of that regrettable incident."

"Why?" Pru cried. "What happened in Grosvenor Square? I demand to know!"

"Your sister did not tell you?" Isabella said, wide eyed. "Ivor, I think it is time we go."

Pru could hardly wait for them to leave. "What happened in Grosvenor Square?" she demanded, as the door closed.

Patience sighed. "You already know I saw Mr. Purefoy at Mr. Adams's house on the night of your ball. Pru, how can you bear the company of such poisonous hypocrites? I should have left the room, except I shudder to think what they might say if I were not here to check them. And you, madam!" she went on, turning to Lady Jemima. "It is my understanding that Mr. Purefoy brought you to this house. Your patron has fallen on hard times; take care you do not meet with the same fate."

Lady Jemima's mouth worked helplessly, but Pru came to her defense. "It is important that we blacken his name, Pay! Before he blackens ours! Who knows what the man may be saying about us right now? It could be anything. He is Italian, after all."

"Whatever he is saying," Patience replied, "I'm sure it's no more than we deserve."

And, as Briggs came in to announce the next round of callers, she made her escape.

Two weeks passed without Patience hearing anything from the man she had married, though she did manage to hear a good deal *about* him, mainly from Lady Jemima. The shocking misdeeds of his past, now seemingly newly discovered, were the talk of the town. Tales of drunken routs, lewd balls, and scandalous escapades swept through London like wildfire.

"But, considering his descent, one could not expect better," was Lady Jemima's constant refrain.

That he owed money all over London did not surprise Patience in the least. But no one, including his creditors, seemed to know where or how he was living. "If the bailiffs catch him, he'll never see the outside of Fleet Street Prison," Lady Jemima said gleefully. "That's how much he owes."

Another week passed without any fresh news. Made uneasy by all the rumors swirling around, Patience drove to Wimpole Street to see Mrs. Drabble. She had not seen Max's former nurse since her wedding at St. Bride's Church, and she dreaded having to face the other woman. Jane opened the door to her, but said, her face full of disapproval, that she would see if her mistress was at home. Patience was left waiting in the little hall so long that she nearly went away again. Finally, Mrs. Drabble herself appeared, and invited her up to the parlor for tea.

Patience was so obviously filled with anxiety that her hostess took pity on her. "We have missed you at our meetings, my dear," she said kindly.

Patience blushed at what must have been a fib. She could just imagine Miss Haines's hurt and bewildered look when she realized there would be no bride at the wedding breakfast they had all worked so hard to prepare. Mrs. Bascombe would probably have strangled her. The others would have been less demonstrative, perhaps, in their disapproval. They would have clucked their tongues and shaken their heads, at least. "It's very kind of you to say so, Mrs. Drabble," she said. "But I'm sure you must have thought me very rude."

"Yes," Mrs. Drabble said simply. "But Max says we are not to be angry at you."

"You have seen him?" Patience said eagerly. "Where is he? I—I must speak to him, Mrs. Drabble. 'Tis said his debts are so great that he will soon be arrested."

"Would you care if he were?" Mrs. Drabble asked, her blue eyes suddenly alert.

"Of course I would care," Patience said indignantly. "I don't know what he has told you. I daresay you think me quite heartless, but I have no wish to see him condemned to debtor's prison. I would not wish such a fate on my worst enemy. Will you not tell me where I can find him?"

"How do I know you wouldn't lead the bailiffs straight to him?" Mrs. Drabble asked.

Patience gasped. "You think I would betray him?"

Stung, she rose to her feet. "If that is what you think of me, I will take up no more of your time, Mrs. Drabble. But . . . if you should see him . . . Tell him he must collect on his wager. Let not his foolish pride stand in the way. Nothing could be worse than the shame of going to prison!"

"Forgive me, Lady Waverly," Mrs. Drabble said quickly. "I did not mean it. Of course, you would not betray him. Please stay."

Patience resumed her seat, but said, frowning, "I would *not* betray him," as if Mrs. Drabble had argued against her. "I wish him no harm. I *want* him to collect his money. But he won't do it. He is stubborn."

"But, my dear," Mrs. Drabble said gently, "do you not realize that it is entirely within your power to take him out of danger, if he is too pigheaded to do it himself?"

"Is it?" Patience exclaimed. "How?"

"You have only to insert a notice in the newspapers that you have married him, and his creditors will be at *point non plus*. Honor will do the rest."

Patience shook her head. "Honor? I don't understand."

"These gentlemen and their clubs! They do have their code of honor. The wager will be paid or that gentleman will be drummed out of all good society."

"I'll do it," Patience said eagerly, jumping to her feet.

She was halfway to the door before she realized she was still carrying her teacup.

The following morning, she rose very early, making sure to collect all the newspapers in the house and disembarrass them of the society page before Pru saw them. She need not have worried. After another late night at some ball or other, Pru did not trudge into the breakfast room until half past nine.

"Why will the servants not serve me breakfast in my room?" she sullenly demanded as she slid into her chair.

"They have their pride, I suppose," Patience answered.

Pru grunted. "Was I in the paper?" she asked Lady Jemima. "Everyone said I was the prettiest girl there, and the most graceful dancer."

Lady Jemima looked askance. "My dear, it is a very curious thing. I have looked through all the papers, but they all seem to be missing the most critical part: the society pages."

Pru scowled. "But there could be a sketch of me!"

Patience, who was, in fact, sitting on the missing pages, said quickly, "Never mind, dearest. We can send out for more newspapers. There is something I must tell you. Something rather important."

Pru was instantly diverted. "You have discovered the secret of transforming lead into gold!" she guessed, her green eyes dancing with merriment. "I didn't even know you were trying."

"I'm quite serious, Pru," Patience said quietly. "I meant to tell you yesterday, but by the time I returned to the house, you'd already gone out. I must have fallen asleep waiting for you."

"I was home by four in the morning," Pru said indignantly. "You can't complain about *that*."

"I'm not complaining at all," Patience protested.

"If you would but *go* to one ball," Pru went on heedlessly, "you would understand how impossible it is to leave early, even if you wanted to. It takes a full hour just to get to the top of the stairs, and another hour to get back down—unless of course, you take a *short cut,* like poor Mrs. Malahide!"

Lady Jemima laughed appreciatively, but Pru laughed even louder.

"Poor thing! She fell head over end down the staircase at Arundel House, and, Patience, she hadn't any drawers on!" Pru collapsed into helpless giggling.

"For heaven's sake, Pru!" Patience snapped, not at all interested in Mrs. Malahide's tumble down the stairs.

Pru held her sides, where the seams of her gown were in danger of splitting. "But wait! I haven't told you the very best part!" she wheezed. "I have since learned that her Christian name is—you will not credit it—indeed, you will not—Fanny!"

In spite of herself, Patience could not help laughing.

All three ladies were still laughing when the door opened. For a moment, they hardly noticed the tall, broad-shouldered man standing on the threshold; after all, servants were forever coming and going. But this man was not dressed as a servant. He was dressed as a gentleman, in a burgundy coat and buff-colored pantaloons. Lace cuffs and a wondrously intricate cravat completed the look. Patience gasped as he sat down at the table.

"Good morning, my lady," he greeted her politely. Tapping the belly of the silver coffeepot on the table, he proceeded to ask, quite calmly, if there was any chance of a fresh pot.

Lady Jemima uttered a silly little shriek of dismay. Pru choked back her laughter, staring at him, round eyed.

"This one seems to have gone cold," the gentleman went on in the same congenial tone. "Though to be fair, I *am* a trifle late for breakfast. I trust I am forgiven?"

Patience stared into his gray eyes. "What do you think you are doing?" she stammered, slowly rising from her chair. "Who let you in this house?"

Max looked at her in surprise. "Briggs, of course."

"Well, he can let you out again!" Pru said loudly. "Who do you think you are? You can't just waltz into other people's houses and order more coffee!"

"I wouldn't dream of it, my dear. I don't waltz."

"Patience!" Pru said shrilly. "Do something!"

"Sir," Patience began nervously, "what are you doing here?"

Max lifted his brows. "Don't you read the papers, my lady? It seems we are married. I live here."

Chapter 19

Pru made a disgusted sound. "You forget, sir, that I chose *not* to marry you, after all."

"Wasn't talking to you," Max retorted.

Pru's eyes flew to her sister's white face. "Pay!"

Patience bit her lip. "This is what I wanted to tell you, Pru . . ."

"You haven't told her yet?" Max drawled, leaning back in his chair.

"You married him?" Pru shrieked. "*Him,* of all people? Oh, please, tell me it's a lie!"

"It is no lie, Sister," Max said.

"I am not talking to you!" Pru shouted, jumping to her feet with her fists clenched.

"I am sorry, Pru," Patience said softly. "I did marry him. But that does not explain what you are doing here," she went on, turning to Max. "I told you you couldn't live here."

"That was before someone splashed the news of our marriage all over the newspapers," he replied. "And it wasn't I, in case you were wondering."

"No, I—I did it," she said.

He stared at her for a moment. "Did you?" he said

finally, a faint smile touching his lips. "Why would you do that, I wonder?"

"It was not to summon you here!" she cried. "You may be assured of that!"

"Well, you have made it impossible for me to live anywhere else," he said. "A man who does not live with his wife is a laughingstock."

Pru's face contorted with fury. "Allow me to inform you, sir, that you are already a laughingstock!"

"No, they hold me in contempt, perhaps, but they do not laugh at me."

"Oh, don't they?" Pru sneered.

"Prudence, please!" cried Patience, her fingertips pressed to her temples.

"Either *he* goes or I do!" Pru shrieked, stamping her foot.

"Sit down!" Max commanded her sharply. "You're not going anywhere. Not without my permission."

"Permission?" Pru repeated incredulously.

"You do realize that, when I married your sister, I became your legal guardian, don't you?"

Patience uttered a sharp cry and clapped both hands over her mouth. Slowly, she sank down into her chair.

"What are you talking about?" Pru snarled. "Patience, what is he talking about?"

Max answered, apparently enjoying himself. "The law gives me complete control over you—your person, your money. I can send you to the other side of the earth if you displease me."

Without thinking, Patience touched his arm. "Max, you promised—"

Taking her hand from his arm, he kissed it before she realized what he meant to do. "I promised I would take no revenge upon your sister," he said.

"Is this not revenge?" cried Patience.

"No, madam. This is breakfast," he said. "Of course I shall *punish* her when she is naughty, but that is hardly revenge. I would be a very poor guardian if I did not discipline my ward. But it will be for her own good, and she will thank me for it later."

"Patience, are you going to let him talk to me like that?" Pru howled.

"I wasn't talking to you," Max told her. "I was talking to my wife. The first thing I'm going to do is cancel her allowance."

"You can't do that!" Pru screamed.

"I am still talking to my wife," Max said curtly. "Then, I think, she should not be allowed to leave the house unless she can prove to me that she has spent at least two—nay, three—hours employed in some useful exercise."

"What!"

Max shrugged. "I don't know. You might darn my socks, or plant a garden."

"Oh, do stop provoking her," Patience pleaded.

Max tightened his grip on her hand. "She is too old for tantrums."

"I will not stand here and be treated like this!" Pru cried. Tossing her head, she stalked out of the room.

Patience immediately got up to follow her, but Max still held her hand. She looked at him unhappily. "You cannot stay here," she whispered.

"Where would you have me go?"

Although he whispered, too, Lady Jemima had no difficulty hearing every word.

"Where were you before?" asked Patience.

"Oh! Here and there. The gutter, mostly."

She shook her head. "That coat did not come from the gutter," she said dryly. "Let go of my hand, sir. Let me go to my sister."

He leaned toward her, still whispering. "If you did not

want me to come, why did you announce our marriage to the world? You could have kept it a secret."

"I did not—" she began quickly, but he silenced her by kissing her hand again.

"You did not mean to summon me like a demon from hell. Yes, I heard you. I know why you *didn't* do it. I would like to know why you did."

"Mrs. Drabble suggested it. She said it would put off your creditors."

He released her hand abruptly. "My creditors?"

"They say you owe money all over town," Patience told him. "They say you are but two steps ahead of the bailiffs."

"Is that what they say?" he drawled. Patience could not interpret his expression. "Yes, I suppose the news of my marriage will put off my creditors. And you had no other reason?"

She shook her head. "No, Max. Of course I didn't."

He sighed. "Will you at least admit that you are glad to see me?"

"I am *not* glad to see you," she protested. "This is a catastrophe!"

"Mildly pleased to see me?"

"Please just go! Leave!"

But she was the one who hurried from the room.

Lady Jemima, finding herself alone with Max, pushed back her chair and stood up.

"Oh, let her go, Jemmie," Max said. "She'll be all right."

"How dare you address me in that offhand manner?" Lady Jemima said haughtily.

Max looked at her in surprise. "Et tu, Jemmie?"

"Lady Waverly has asked you to leave this house," she rasped.

His eyes narrowed. "I don't think I care for your tone, Jemmie. You and I both know Lady Waverly cannot make me go."

"If you were a gentleman—!" she began. "But, of course, you are *not* a gentleman," she added maliciously. "You were born on the wrong side of the blanket."

"As you say, I am not a gentleman."

"I will not stay another moment under the same roof with the likes of you, sir! I will be gone within the hour."

Satisfied with her grand, if rather self-contradictory, declaration, she swept from the room.

Max calmly signaled to the footman. "More coffee."

The footman looked startled. "Very good, Mr.—sir! Master!"

Max leaned back in his chair as the cold coffeepot was carried out. "Master," he murmured. "I like the sound of that."

Several hours later, Patience came to him in the drawing room, where he was setting up the chessboard. "I had hoped you would be gone," she said, looking at him with anguish.

Her distress nearly unmanned him, but he managed a cool shrug. "I believe Lady Jemima has left you. I could not deprive you of all your company at once."

"Max!" she murmured, lingering near the door.

"I assume that gentle Prudence has locked herself in her room?"

She nodded glumly.

"Good," he smiled. "It saves me the trouble of doing it for her."

"You would not dare—!" she began hotly, then bit her lip.

"I have all the keys."

"Why are you doing this?" she asked. "You will make all three of us miserable, if you do this. Please just go."

He frowned. "Of course, I will go if you ask me to—"

"I have just done so!"

"Then I'm afraid I cannot do as you ask!" he snapped.

"You are my wife, and now the whole world knows it. I will not be made a laughingstock. You will not shame me by putting me out of this house! I am a tolerant man, God knows, but I will not tolerate *that*. I don't know how it is in America, but here in England a man lives with his wife. You have done enough to me, I think, without making me the butt of a thousand jokes!"

Patience was horrified. "It was never my intention to shame you. I wanted to help you, that's all."

"I know it wasn't your intention," he said gruffly. "If I thought you were *that* sort of woman, I would never have married you. I don't like this talking at each other back and forth across the room," he added impatiently. "I feel I ought to cup my hands around my mouth, like the master of the hunt! Come and sit down with me. I'm not going to bite you."

Patience hesitated for a moment, then crossed the room. The pieces on the chessboard rattled as she sat down, bumping into the table.

"Do you play?" he asked her.

She looked at him blankly.

"Chess," he said, calling her attention to the red and white pieces. "The game of kings. Do you play?"

Patience mutely shook her head.

"Backgammon? No? Cards, then. Cribbage? Fox and Geese? Jackstraws? Why do you have all these games, if you don't play any of them?" he said, exasperated.

"I've never seen them before in my life except the chessboard. It stands in the corner usually."

"I prefer to play at fireside," he said. "The others I found in the japan cabinet. Surely you play cards, at least?"

Patience was a little disconcerted that he apparently had been rifling through the japan cabinet, which stood between the two long windows, but, apart from the accounts and correspondence she kept in the desk, she stored no personal items in the drawing room. Nor did Pru, to her knowledge. She had often admired the cranes painted on the cabinet but she had never looked inside. "These games must have been here when we took the house," she said impatiently. "And no, I don't play cards. I believe gambling is immoral."

"Do you really?" he said. "Curious! But I hardly think of cardplaying as gambling. It's not dice or roulette. It requires skill. And we must have something to do in the evenings before we go to bed."

She jerked to her feet, upsetting a few pieces on the board. "We're not going to bed!" she blurted out in a horrified whisper, her cheeks stained scarlet. "If that is what you think—!"

"My dear girl," he protested, laughing. "You cannot imagine that I would presume to share Your Ladyship's bed? I have not come here to impose on you, if that is what you fear. Inconvenience you I must, but I would by no means injure you. Despite what you may have heard— despite what you *have* heard—I am not in the habit of forcing myself on women."

"I know that," she said quickly. "I am not afraid of you." Slowly, she sank back into the chair.

"Then what is the trouble?" he asked, resetting the pieces on the board.

"You know what it is! It's Pru! You'll be at each other's throats."

"I daresay it will be contentious at first," he conceded. "You are not firm enough with her, my dear. She stamps her foot, and you let her have her way. A few tears, and you are reduced to a jelly. She will not find *me* so easy."

Patience frowned at him. "You know nothing about my sister. My grandfather was very hard on her. Very hard."

"Not hard enough, if you ask me."

Patience shook her head. "You would not speak so

lightly of it if you had known my grandfather," she said fiercely.

All traces of humor vanished from his face. "Was he unkind, really?"

"He was a tyrant."

"Forgive me! I had misunderstood; I rather thought you admired your grandfather."

"Oh, I did," she said. "I do. I admire his success. I am truly grateful to have inherited his wealth. But, I must confess, I never had any affection for him. He was a cruel man. Pru always had the worst of it, because she was the more rebellious. She did go a bit wild when my grandfather died, but that is to be expected after all she suffered at his hands."

"Did you suffer at his hands?" he demanded.

Patience looked down at the chessboard. "He was not cruel to me, but only because I did my best to meet his expectations. As I said, Pru had the worst of it. My sister will not do as she's told, not even if what she's told to do is perfectly reasonable."

"I had noticed that," he said dryly, earning a faint smile from Patience.

"If you are going to stay here—and—and I suppose you are—you must promise to be kind to her."

Max looked away, unable to bear the sight of tears in her eyes. "Is she going to promise to be kind to me?"

Patience choked back a laugh. "I shouldn't think so!"

"I'm to be her whipping boy, then, is that it?"

She reached across the table and touched his hand. "Don't let her provoke you, and don't provoke her," she pleaded softly. "Promise me!"

In that moment, he would have promised her anything, but, unfortunately they were interrupted. "Don't let me interrupt you!" cried Pru from the doorway.

Patience jumped up, knocking the chessboard and all

the pieces to the floor. "Pru! How—how long have you been standing there?"

"I didn't mean to spoil your *tender moment,*" Pru said scathingly as she sailed into the room.

Patience blushed. "What? We were just playing chess." Bending down, she began picking up the pieces.

Pru snorted. "You don't even play chess! If you *must* touch him, I wish you would do it in the drawing room. Respectable people come here to see me." With her fan she made a sweeping gesture that included all the cards and invitations displayed on the mantelpiece.

"Do any of them ever return for a second visit?" Max asked very politely.

"Don't be sarcastic," Patience pleaded, slapping a handful of chess pieces into his hand.

Pru chose not to hear. Flouncing over to the sofa, she spread out her skirts and flopped down. "Patience, would you be good enough to tell that man to leave the room?" she said haughtily, addressing her sister. "I attended a ball last night, and I am expecting callers."

"If any of your beaux turn up, I shall be happy to leave the room," Max offered, giving Patience no chance to humiliate him by asking him to go. "Laughing all the way."

"What do you mean *if*?" Pru snapped, looking at him with loathing. "Of course they will turn up! Gentlemen *always* call the next day. Except *you,* of course," she added scathingly. "*You* only sent flowers."

Patience resumed her seat at the game table and watched as Max set up the pieces.

"Tell him to go, Patience!" Pru insisted shrilly. "His face is annoying me."

"I cannot help my face," Max protested.

"You could put a bag over it," Pru suggested sweetly.

Silently, Max appealed to his wife.

"Prudence, that is no way to talk to your brother," Patience scolded her belatedly.

"Brother!"

"And there is no need for him to leave the room," Patience went on. "This is his house, too, after all. Your beaux cannot object to finding your brother-in-law in the drawing room."

"I'll lay odds none of them show up today," said Max.

Pru looked around for something to throw at him. "Are you going to let your *husband* insult me like that?"

"Max! Apologize at once."

"I meant no offense," said Max. "The news of your sister's marriage will not have escaped the notice of your friends, Miss Prudence. As much as they may like you, I am sure they dislike me more."

"You will not keep them away," Pru said, tossing her head. "I am too popular!"

As if to settle the matter, the bell on the front door rang just moments later. Pru smiled triumphantly, and smoothed her skirts in anticipation, but the visitor whom Briggs brought up the stairs to the drawing room had come to see Patience.

"Mr. Molyneux!" Patience exclaimed, a little flustered as the young man bounded up to her and shook her hand vigorously. "This is a welcome surprise."

Molyneux's cheeks were red from being outside in the cold wind, and there were a few specks of snow on the shoulders of his blue coat, but his smile was as warm as ever. "I read in the newspaper, ma'am, that you'd married. I am come to congratulate you."

"Thank you," Patience said. "I believe you already know my—my husband."

"Oh, it's you, sir!" said Molyneux. "I didn't recognize the name in the paper. Did they get it wrong?"

"They do sometimes," Max said coolly. "I see your face has recovered from our last meeting?"

Molyneux laughed. "Yes, sir. Suffice it to say, I understand *now* how I offended you."

"Won't you sit down, Mr. Molyneux?" Patience said quickly. "I'll send for some tea. Or would you prefer coffee?"

Molyneux sat down on the sofa next to Pru, inadvertently sitting on her skirt, to which she instantly objected. "Don't tell anyone, Mrs. Farnese, but I've grown accustomed to English tea," he said, when the situation on the sofa had been rectified.

"I prefer coffee," said Pru.

Patience asked Briggs to bring both.

Max turned his chair to face the sofa. "And so, Mr. Molyneux, you came all the way from Southwark to congratulate my wife?"

"Not at all," Molyneux replied. "*You're* the lucky one, from where I sit. I've come to congratulate *you*."

Max smiled briefly. "She remains Lady Waverly, by the by," he said. "Not Mrs. Farnese. When the lady outranks her husband, she keeps her title and her name."

"Does this mean you are now Lord Waverly?" Patience asked him.

"Alas, no. I am merely Your Ladyship's consort," he answered, and was amazed to see her face turn bright pink. He could not imagine that he had said anything untoward.

"It was very good of you to call on us, Mr. Molyneux," Patience said quickly. "I know you must be very busy with your lectures."

"I was lucky today," he replied. "Dr. Chandler sent me to Harley Street with a message for one of his colleagues. He sometimes uses me for that purpose."

"I suppose he does not think you are fit for much else," Pru sniffed.

Molyneux glanced at her. "Tomorrow I'm to assist him in surgery. We're going to attempt to repair a cleft palate. Von Graf has had some success with his protocol at the University of Berlin. We hope to duplicate that success."

"*Attempt* to repair? *Hope* to duplicate?" Pru mocked him.

"It's a very complicated and delicate business," he told her. "You would not understand."

She made a face at him. "With so much on your mind, I wonder you have time to read the social columns!"

"I don't usually," he retorted. "I take but little interest in people so wholly unconnected to me as Miss W—— and Mr. P——. But I was obliged to wait for Dr. Wingfield's reply to Dr. Chandler, and so I picked up the newspaper and glanced through it while I waited."

"Was it Wingfield you went to see?" Max said, pleased. "How is the old buzzard?"

Molyneux blushed. "I did not actually see Dr. Wingfield, you understand. My message was carried to him by his clerk."

Pru snickered.

"If you ever *do* get the chance to talk to Dr. Wingfield," Max said suddenly, "you must ask him to give you his famous lecture on the diagnosis and treatment of chlorosis."

Mr. Molyneux ducked his head quickly, but could not quite hide his laughter.

"Why, what is chlorosis?" Pru demanded, suspecting quite correctly that Max and Molyneux were sharing a private joke at her expense.

"Dr. Wingfield has made a study of it these last twenty years," Max said blandly. "It's a type of anemia peculiar to young females."

"Patience had anemia," Pru said. "I don't see anything funny about that."

"This is a different type of anemia," Max explained. "The symptoms of chlorosis are very distinct. Those young ladies so afflicted are invariably bad tempered, mean spirited, and thoroughly disagreeable. Their skins are tinged a greenish gray, and there is only one cure for it."

"Is that so?" Pru snapped, her eyes narrowed.

Molyneux suddenly looked very grave. "I think perhaps I had better go," he said, climbing to his feet. "Thank you for the tea, Mrs.— er—Lady Waverly."

"But you hardly touched your cup," Patience protested. "Perhaps I made it wrong?"

"It isn't that," he hastily assured her. "I must get back to Dr. Chandler. I've been away too long as it is."

Max rose to shake his hand. "You must come to dine with us soon, Mr. Molyneux."

Molyneux glanced at Pru's angry face and said, regretfully, "Thank you, sir, but I—I keep a schedule of odd hours. I could not tell you when I might be free again."

Max shrugged. "You will always be welcome at my table," he said. "We dine at eight o'clock every night. Come any night you can, and we will be pleased to see you."

He walked with the young man to the door, but when he returned to his chair, he found two sets of angry green eyes fixed on him. Pru's anger was to be expected, but Patience's puzzled him.

"What have I done?" he asked.

"How dare you invite someone to dinner without speaking to me first?" Patience snapped.

"I thought you liked Molyneux," he said, surprised.

Her eyes snapped. "What will I tell the cook if people start showing up at dinnertime?"

"I'm quite sure we can accommodate one guest, my dear," he said mildly. "I will speak to Cook myself."

"I wonder you would want him around," Pru said sullenly. "He so obviously has eyes for your wife. I should think you'd be jealous."

Patience scowled, but Max suddenly felt almost fond

of Pru. Her last remark had brought him to a better understanding of his wife. Patience, too, thought he should be
jealous of young Molyneux, and clearly, she was none too
happy that he was not.

"Oh, do be quiet, Pru," Patience said with uncharacter-
istic violence.

"Sounds like someone else has a touch of chlorosis,"
said Pru. "Pray, what *is* the cure for it, Brother?"

"You'll find out," Max assured her, "when you are
married."

Silent for once, Pru stared at him, round eyed.

"I seem to have rendered our sister incapable of speech,"
Max said lightly.

Patience glared at him. "I wish you would not make
vulgar jokes!" she snapped.

But he only smiled at her slyly.

Chapter 20

The three of them sat in the drawing room all afternoon, but there were no more visitors. For lack of anything better to do, Patience agreed to let Max teach her the game of chess, but she was able to concentrate less and less on the game as Pru's agitation grew. She glanced at the clock almost as often as her sister did, and fidgeted in sympathy as Pru paced around the room, or looked out the window in the hope of seeing someone she knew on the street outside.

The arrival of the afternoon post ought to have been a welcome diversion.

"Nothing for me?" Pru asked as Patience went through the letters. "Nothing? Ten different gentlemen danced with me last night! I have never been used so ill."

"Then you are very fortunate," Max remarked.

She turned on him angrily. "This is all your fault!"

"Cheer up," he told her. "They will like you again when the marriage is annulled."

Patience looked up from her letters. She had not mentioned the annulment, and she did not much like him bringing it up, either, he could tell.

"You do still want the annulment?" he asked quietly.

"Of course," she said immediately. "I have written already to my solicitor in America. He is the closest thing Pru and I have to a guardian. He will be able to supply everything necessary to prove my age. Then we can begin the process."

"That will take months!" Pru complained. "The Season will be over."

"These things have been known to take years," Max told her.

"I was supposed to go to Almack's tonight! But, now, of course, I have no chaperone! Pay? I don't suppose you would take me?"

"Certainly not," Patience said, carrying her letters over to her desk. "You don't really want to go, do you? All the young men you danced with last night who snubbed you today will be there."

"They would not snub me at Almack's," said Pru, throwing herself down on the sofa. "I'm the most popular girl of the Season. Everyone says so. I've done nothing wrong! *I'm* not the one who married *him*."

"You had your chance," Max taunted her.

"Mr. Campbell writes again," Patience said loudly, from her desk. "He says his buyer will pay a premium of one thousand pounds if I will close within thirty days."

Max frowned. "Who the devil is Mr. Campbell?"

"The estate agent for Wildings," Patience told him, delighted to divert his attention from his argument with Pru. "He has an offer for ten thousand pounds—now eleven—but only if I close directly."

"How many acres has Wildings?"

"Twenty-six thousand. Do you not think it a good offer?"

He shrugged. "Why must you close in thirty days? What's the hurry?"

"I think you should sell," Pru declared.

"I think we should at least see the place before we sell

it," said Patience. "And so I told Mr. Campbell in my last letter."

"Now he offers you a thousand pounds *not* to see the place?" said Max. "One smells a rat. Perhaps we should take a trip?" he suggested.

"Mr. Campbell tells me the roads are still flooded."

Leaning back in his chair, he laced his fingers behind his head. "The rat grows fatter and smellier! We must definitely take a trip. I must meet your Mr. Campbell."

"I can't stay here by myself," Pru protested.

"No," he agreed.

"And I'm not going anywhere with *you*!"

"I think it would be very good for you to get out of London, Pru," said Patience.

"This is so unfair," Pru whispered, shaking her head. "What have I done to deserve this?"

Patience was losing her temper. "Shall I tell you? You slandered Max. Have you forgotten already? This should be a lesson to you not to tell lies!"

"Nobody knows about that except us," said Pru. "Or do they?" she added, scowling at Max. "You blabbed, didn't you? You told everyone that I—you told them what I did!"

"Oh, I never blab," he answered. "Anyway, who would I tell? None of my former acquaintances are at home to me these days, thanks to you. I've even been thrown out of all my clubs; it seems they have no member named Farnese."

"Oh, Max," Patience murmured sympathetically. "I am sorry."

"Oh, Max!" Pru mimicked her cruelly. "Have you forgotten that he made you the object of a disgusting bet? Have you forgotten that he tried to drown you in the ballroom? Not to mention all his trifling with me—I know *that* makes no difference to you!"

"You were the one who jilted me," Max snapped. "You

liked me very well until you found out I had no money. Until you found out you would never be a duchess!"

"You're quite wrong," Pru shouted back. "I never liked you! You could have been a *king* and I still would never have married you. Never! For I can't conceive of a worse fate than being your wife! I would rather die a thousand deaths than be touched by you. You nauseate me."

Max's eyes narrowed to slits. "You insufferable baggage," he said softly. "Go to your room. Go to your room, or by God, I shall drag you there myself."

Pru whirled to face her sister. "Are you going to let him talk to me like that?"

"Go to your room, Pru," Patience said wearily. "I—I will talk to him," she added quickly.

"You'd better," said Pru. Sweeping out of the room, she banged the door closed.

Patience turned on Max with a fury that surprised him. "I thought you were going to make an effort to get along with her! Calling her names is no way to go about making friends."

"I should be congratulated on my restraint," he said indignantly. "I've never wanted to spank anyone so much in all my life! As for calling her names—she *is* an insufferable baggage. Why shouldn't I say so? I thought you Americans believed in freedom of speech."

"I'm sorry your friends have abandoned you," she said. "But, perhaps, they were not true friends."

"Possibly," he said dryly.

"I am sorry you have been thrown out of your clubs," she went on. "But if you cannot make peace with my sister, you will have to go. I will not have discord in my house."

"You cannot make me go," he pointed out.

Her eyes flashed. "And you cannot make *me* stay!"

He stared at her. "You would leave me?"

"I cannot live like this," she whispered. "I must have peace."

As the words were leaving her mouth, a loud boom was heard, reverberating through the house, rattling the crystals in the chandeliers and causing a card or two to topple from the mantelpiece.

"What the devil is that?" Max demanded, leaping out of his chair.

Patience laughed faintly. "It's only the dinner gong. I find it very jarring, but Briggs insists on banging it every night."

"Does he indeed?" Max murmured, glancing at the clock on the mantel. Its face, fortunately, was not obscured by any of Pru's prized invitations. "No wonder your nerves are so frayed, my dear. But it's only six-thirty. I told Molyneux we dine at eight."

"Well, you should have asked me first," she said, moving to the door. "We always dine early when Pru is going out. Though I don't suppose she will be going out tonight," she added.

"Do you change your dress for dinner?" he asked, getting to his feet.

"I never do." She paused at the door. "There is a washroom on the landing, if you don't mind cold water," she said, before slipping away to her own room to wash her face and hands.

Max was seated at the dining table when Briggs sounded the gong for the second time. Patience slipped into her chair at the other end of the table a few minutes later. "Prudence is going to have a tray in her room," she explained. "You may bring the soup, Briggs."

Max shook his head at the butler, effectively stopping the soup. "Nobody eats off a tray unless he is sick," he announced. "Miss Prudence will come down and eat with her family or she will not eat at all. Tell her if she is not at table in three minutes, we shall start without her."

"Very good, sir," Briggs said smoothly.

"Max!" Patience protested.

Max ignored her. "And from now on there will be no more dinner gong," he informed Briggs. "It rattles her ladyship's nerves."

"Very good, sir."

Patience tried again as Briggs faded from the room. "Don't you think it would be best to let Prudence stay in her room?"

He snorted. "And have your heart and mind with *her* while your body sits empty here with me? I don't mind cold water, but a cold shoulder I won't tolerate."

Patience sighed. "You're just going to argue."

"Not I," he assured her. "For your sake, I am determined to get along with her. We are brother and sister now, after all."

Taking two wads of cotton out of his pocket, he inserted them into his ears. "You will never truly have peace," he said, very loudly because he could not hear himself, "until her mouth is fitted with a cork, but at least I shan't be provoked."

Patience shook her head, but could not help laughing.

Hunger conquered pride, and a few moments later, Pru swished sullenly into the room to take her place at the middle of the table, halfway between her sister and Max.

Max rose from the table and bowed to her. "Good evening, Prudence," he shouted.

"I am not talking to you," she informed him loftily.

He only smiled sweetly. Resuming his seat, he shouted for the soup.

Patience's shoulders shook from the effort of not laughing.

"I am not talking to you, either," Pru told her coldly.

Together, they shared a very peaceful meal. Afterward, Pru swept back to her room, still not speaking to anyone. Max pulled the cotton out of his ears, and Patience burst out laughing.

"You are dreadful," she gasped, finishing her wine.

"It seemed the simplest way to make peace with her."

"She was giving us the silent treatment tonight," said Patience. "It won't be so easy when she starts talking again."

"I'll lend you some of my cotton wool," he promised. Pushing his chair back, he held out his hand to her. "Shall we?"

Patience stared at him uncertainly. "Shall we what?" she asked nervously.

"Another lesson in chess, I thought," he said. "Or there's backgammon, if you prefer."

Patience rose from the table. "I don't think I'll be good at these games," she said. "I usually do my mending in the evenings. Also, I must write to Mr. Campbell to tell him that we are coming."

Taking her by the elbow, Max guided her from the room. He felt her body tense for a moment, then a little shudder went through her, as if her knees had buckled. "Would it not be better to surprise him?" he murmured, studying the hollow behind her left ear—as ideal a spot for a kiss as he had ever seen. "If he is up to no good, we may catch him at it."

In the drawing room, she immediately went to her sewing basket.

He sat on the sofa and stretched out his long legs, regarding her intently. "Shall I thread your needle for you?" he offered.

Patience smiled faintly. "No, thank you. You might read a book, if you are bored."

Max picked up a book from the table. *"A Vindication*

of the Rights of Woman," he read somewhat dubiously. "This you did not find in the house," he guessed.

"No, I bought it. The bookshops of London must be the envy of the world. Do you know the book? Mrs. Godwin has some interesting ideas, I think. I would be interested to know your thoughts."

Max set the book down carefully. "I think *Vindication* would be an excellent name for a horse," he said. "Or, possibly, a yacht. No, a race horse, I think."

Patience pulled her needle through the hem of the petticoat she was mending. "Mrs. Godwin argues that men and women are born equal. They only seem unequal because of a gross inequality in education. What do you think of that argument?"

"*Equality* would also make a good name for a horse," said Max. "Though some might find me guilty of a pun, *Equus* being the generic epithet of the horse."

"You have no opinion?" she pressed him.

"I do not accept the author's premise," he replied. "We are each of us, male and female, born unique—even you and your sister. By no stretch of the imagination was she born your equal, and no amount of education could ever make her so. You are her superior in every category."

Patience could hardly be displeased with such an answer, but she did try to appear unimpressed. "You did not always think so," she reminded him. "When we first met, as I seem to recall, you mistook me for the Medusa!"

He groaned. "Pray, do not remind me of how I behaved then! I'm ashamed of myself."

"Have you never had a friend who would tell you when you had gone too far?" she asked curiously. "Did your uncle never correct you?"

"My uncle!" he exclaimed. "You may be sure I never let my poor uncle see me in such a state. As for my friends— for them, I could never go far enough!"

"And your mistresses?" she said, looking down at her work very diligently. "Didn't they mind your—your indiscretions? Your mermaids?"

Max squirmed uncomfortably.

She stole a glance at him when he did not answer, and was surprised to see that his face was red. "I'm not embarrassing you, am I?"

"A little," he admitted. "But, no, my mistresses never objected to anything I did. If they did, I would simply get rid of them. But I always gave them a handsome settlement."

"How very generous of you," she said tartly. "Did you give *Mrs. Tolliver* a handsome settlement? Or is she still in your good graces?"

"Mrs. Tolliver!" he exclaimed. "Who have you been talking to?"

"Your uncle mentioned her name. I have not had the opportunity to see her on stage, but I understand she is very beautiful. She may object to your being here now."

"I doubt it," he said dryly. "She likes her gentlemen plump in the pocket. Sadly, I no longer meet her requirements. But I hear she has landed on her feet—on her back, I should say—in a very soft bed. It's as if she never loved me at all."

"I'm so sorry," she said primly.

He laughed aloud. "You're a terrible liar! But, then, I have always thought that an excellent quality in a wife."

"Oh, I've had just about enough of your flattery," she began lightly, but her eyes widened as he got to his feet. "Where are you going?"

Max stretched his arms over his head. "It's a bit early, I know, but I think I'll go to work now. A walk in the cool air will do me good. Dinner always makes me a bit sleepy."

"*Where* are you going?" she asked, not sure she had heard him correctly.

"To work," he repeated. "You *did* make me promise to

find some employment," he reminded her. "You needn't look so shocked. How do you think I've been surviving all these weeks? I have joined the working class."

"But what could you possibly be doing at this time of night?" she demanded.

"A great many things," he told her. "For example, I might be shifting cargo at the East India Docks. I might be a barber or a night watchman or even a Bow Street Runner. I might be delivering coal or clearing horse dung out of the streets. But, of course," he went on quickly as she stared at him in horrified fascination, "I'm not doing any of those things. Too much like work, I suppose."

"What *are* you doing then?"

"I run the faro bank at the Black Swan," he replied. "It's a thoroughly disreputable gambling hell, so, of course, I know everyone there, staff and patron alike. I do enjoy taking money from my former friends, and they seem to enjoy sneering at me. My table gets more traffic than anyone—except Big Sally, of course, but her breasts *are* the largest in London."

"You are *gambling*?" Patience said, distressed. "That's not exactly what I had in mind!"

"I am not gambling," he protested. "It's the punters who gamble. *I* play for the house, and the house always wins. The owner lets me keep five percent of the profit."

"I don't like it," said Patience.

He smiled. "You may not like it, my love, but you cannot accuse me of breaking my promise to you. I'll leave you a chess problem to solve, if you like."

She watched in silence as he quickly set up the chessboard using less than half the pieces. "Checkmate in seven moves," he told her. "If you cannot solve it, I will help you tomorrow. Don't stay up too late."

"When are you coming back?" she demanded.

"You will see me at breakfast," he promised. "I will not be late."

Patience could not resist going to the window to watch him go down the street. He glanced up, as if he knew she would be there, and, by the light of the street lamp, saluted her once before the night swallowed him up.

Patience went to bed an hour or two later, but it was not until after midnight that she drifted off to sleep. She did not hear her husband return to the house, but, as he came into the dark room he had the ill fortune to bump into her dressing table, knocking over a bottle of perfume.

"Is that you?" she murmured sleepily. Her voice, coming from the bed, sounded like a child's, thin and reedy.

"I told you I would not be late for breakfast," he whispered, creeping over toward the bed and cracking his shin on a footstool.

Patience sat bolt upright, listening to his muffled curses. "Max?"

Fumbling in the drawer, she found matches and lit the candle on the bedside table. He was hopping around on one foot. "I was trying not to wake you," he began, then stopped short and caught his breath.

"What is it?" she whispered, throwing back the coverlet.

"How beautiful you look," he said softly, "with your hair down around your shoulders, with the candlelight in your eyes."

Patience wore her nightgown loose at the neck and it had slipped from one shoulder. Hurriedly, she pulled it back into place and tightened the string. "What are you doing in here?" she whispered. "This is not your room. Yours is at the end of the hall."

"You're joking," he said.

"I certainly am not!" she said, jumping out of bed and scrambling for her dressing gown, which she belted tightly around her thin body.

"Don't shame me in front of the servants," he pleaded. "It's already after seven; your girl will be coming to wake you any minute now. I'll be good," he added. "I won't even undress."

Going over to her bed, he climbed in and pulled the covers up to his chin.

Patience giggled suddenly. "You look ridiculous in that hat!"

He tossed it onto the bedpost. "Better? Now, lay down beside me, and pretend to be asleep," he invited her. "I'll do the same. I promise I'll be good," he said, as she stood rooted to the spot. "You won't even know I'm here."

Shaking her head, she hurried over to her dressing table and righted the perfume bottle he had overturned. "You spilled half of it," she complained.

His reply was a soft snore. Patience could hear the servants stirring in the house, footsteps on the stairs, the heavy tread of the girl carrying the coal scuttle. Hastily, she tore off her dressing gown and jumped into the bed. The man next to her groaned; turning toward her, he nestled his head against her breast, his hand splayed across her belly. His hand was obscenely warm. She felt as if it were burning through her nightgown. She would have pushed him away, but the girl's steps were almost to the door.

Instead, she murmured, under her breath, "What am I going to do with you?"

He stirred in her arms, his cheek brushing against the nipple of her left breast. Again, her nightgown seemed to offer no protection at all. "Shall I tell you what I would like you to do with me?" he whispered, his breath warm on her neck.

As he spoke, his arm tightened around her, but, curiously, she made no effort to escape him. Encouraged, he inched upward, until he could whisper in her ear.

"Scoundrel," she whispered back languidly, lying quite still with her eyes closed.

"Then I would like you to—"

"Hush!"

Max was content to be silent. Slowly he pulled the drawstring of her gown and slipped his hand inside, cupping her small, perfectly formed breast. As the girl came in to build the fire and open the curtains, they lay perfectly still, hardly breathing, only their heads above the coverlet. The door closed softly, and Patience opened her eyes.

He had propped himself up on one elbow and was looking down at her. Sunlight streamed through the windows, making him a red-tinged silhouette. The coverlet was down to her waist, and her nightgown very nearly was too. His hand looked very brown against her pale skin as he covered one breast. Instinctively, she covered the other with her own hand.

"What am I going to do with you?" he murmured, a contented smile playing on his wide mouth.

"Max," she whispered, rather helplessly.

Bending down, he nibbled at her mouth.

"You mustn't," she murmured, but her eyes were full of consent, even longing.

"Mustn't what?" he asked, but her voice refused to work.

"Please," she mouthed soundlessly, as he lifted his hand from her breast. He could not resist fastening his mouth on the sharp little nipple. Patience offered no resistance, and after a moment or two, he felt her hands on his back, but only remotely, through the layers of his clothes. He had not even removed his coat, a cursed encumbrance as he tried dragging her gown up to uncover her legs.

Here was another stumbling block: Patience wore

drawers. He could not recall the last time he had made love to a girl wearing modest drawers under her nightgown, and he was less than pleased to find that he was doing so now. Never had he felt so many buttons under a woman's skirts: twenty at least! Never had he felt so clumsy as he began to work on these ridiculously tiny, cursedly numerous buttons. Worse yet, Patience seemed to grow unsure again, and actually murmured fretfully that they should not—they must not—and it took a great deal of kissing to fill her eyes with consent again. She cried out weakly as at last his hand found its way in to claim the soft, warm mound between her thighs, but it was only helpless surrender. His middle finger rested quite rightly along the outer lips, but he did not separate them, not yet. He knew she would be wet and welcoming, but for the moment, he wanted simply to possess the prize, and he wanted her to feel him possessing her.

She stared up at him with huge eyes, seeming not to care in the least that both her breasts were exposed. "Am I . . . all right?" she whispered.

It seemed to him an odd question. "I should be asking you that. Would you like me to pleasure you?"

"What do you mean?"

Slowly, he opened her with his finger, caressing the silky hair of her mound.

Patience caught her bottom lip between her teeth, but not before another faint cry escaped her lips. "I don't think I can bear it," she whispered.

"If you want me to stop, I will," he panted, but, in truth, he did not think that anything could have stopped him.

He was quite wrong. He was stopped quite effectively when the door banged open and his sister-in-law sailed into the room. "I hope you are happy now!" she shouted, in a tone that suggested quite the opposite. "My vouchers to Almack's have been revoked!"

Her eyes widened as she caught sight of Max. "Oh, my God!" she shrieked, her voice curdled with disgust. "You *let* him in your bed?"

Patience, frantically trying to make herself decent, was crimson with shame. For that alone, Max could cheerfully have strangled Prudence.

"Get out of here, brat!" he said, leaping out of bed and chasing her to the door. "In the future, you will not enter this room without knocking."

Pru stumbled back, afraid of him, but managed a weak and shrill, "You're disgusting—both of you!" before he shut the door in her face.

Patience was out of bed by now, with her robe belted on, and, of course, there would be no getting her back in the mood now. Max sighed. "I'm sorry. I should have locked the door."

She could not meet his gaze. "I'm glad she interrupted us," she said. "We were about to make a terrible mistake. Oh, God! What a mess! I wish I had never met you!"

"If I thought you meant that, it would break my heart," he said quietly.

That brought her eyes swiftly to his face, but they fell again. "Everything was so simple before you came along," she said unhappily.

"That I do believe."

He would have taken her in his arms, but she would not allow it. "I must see what Pru is upset about now," she said. Pushing past him, she hurried out of the room.

Max went down to breakfast with but one thought in his head:

Prudence Waverly must go.

Chapter 21

As to how the twins were to be separated, short of murder, he had no idea, so it was just as well that Pru came up with a plan of her own. Neither sister joined Max in the breakfast parlor. After breakfast, he went to bed, not in his wife's bed, but in the room the servants had prepared for him at the end of the hall. He did not emerge until luncheon.

"You're still here," Pru greeted him as he came to the table.

"I am," he answered civilly. "And so are you."

Patience could not look at either of them without blushing. Fortunately, the china pattern on her plate was sufficiently interesting that there was no real need to look at anything else. It did worry her, however, that her husband seemed not to have taken the precaution of plugging his ears with cotton.

"But, Max," Pru said sweetly, "I live here."

"And so do I."

Her eyes narrowed. "I wonder how long it will take you to spend my sister's fortune."

Patience could not allow this insinuation to pass unchallenged. "Prudence, you know perfectly well that Max is not a fortune hunter. And, if he is, it is only because you have reduced him to it with your lies."

"Thank you, my dear," Max said dryly. "I did not *feel* reduced until you spoke, but I suppose it would be useless to deny that my fortunes have waned. No matter! I must set about building them up again."

Patience set down her fork and stared at him. "You have a plan?"

"I promised I would not touch your fortune, and I won't. But I don't see why I shouldn't help myself to Pru's money."

"What?" Pru snarled. "You cannot *touch* my money. My money is held in trust until my thirtieth birthday, and even then no one can touch it but me."

"I shall try not to borrow against it too much," he said. "I would not have you on my conscience when you are thirty."

"Max, you are not serious!" Patience began.

"Do you see what you have done?" Pru cried, turning on her with a vengeance. "Do you see what you have married? Well, I don't see why *I* should be made to suffer just because my sister is a fool! I am leaving." She stood up from the table.

"Leaving?" Patience repeated. "Don't be silly, Pru. Max is only joking. Aren't you, Max? He is not a thief. He wouldn't steal from you."

"No," Max agreed reluctantly. "But I could, if I wanted to."

"I see." Pru smiled triumphantly as she resumed her seat. "I must tell you, Max, I don't care for idle threats."

Max smiled at her. "You prefer *real* threats, do you?"

"Personally, I never make threats," she said airily. "I prefer to strike without warning."

"I remember."

"Good," she said, robbing him of the last word.

To her annoyance, Max ignored her. What was the good

of getting in the last word in an argument, if your opponent simply ignored you and changed the subject?

"I have been thinking, Pazienza," he said, looking down the length of the table at his wife. "We should get to Wildings sooner rather than later, if, as you say, your buyer wants to close in thirty days. Would the day after tomorrow be convenient?"

Patience stared at him. "What did you call me?" she asked breathlessly.

"What did I call you?" he murmured. "Pazienza, I suppose. That is your name in Italian. Patsy, for short."

"Pazienza is lovely," she said.

"What is *my* name in Italian?" Pru demanded.

"Prudenza. It suits you, don't you think?"

Pru scowled at him.

"You were talking of Wildings," Patience said quickly, before another argument could erupt. "I suppose we ought to go soon. But what about—what about the Black Swan? Will they let you go?"

"I fear the novelty of finding Max Purefoy at the faro table may have worn a bit thin," Max said ruefully. "The first week, I was all the rage. Now it seems I am old hat. I scarcely managed ten quid last night. I doubt they'll notice I've gone."

Pru snorted and laughed at the same time, almost choking. "Do you mean you have been *working*?" she exclaimed in disbelief.

"Yes, in a gambling hell. Your sister made me promise to get a job, else she would not marry me."

Pru laughed. "Then she has done more to ruin you than I ever could! Patience, don't you know anything? Gentlemen do not work. Your husband is now well and truly sunk, and it is your fault, not mine. He will never be admitted into society again. He brings the stink of trade with him wherever he goes."

"Is this true, Max?" Patience's face was very white.

"I was on my way down, anyway," he said. "My dear Patsy, don't let it trouble you."

"It's being called Patsy that should trouble her," Pru muttered.

"Be quiet, Pru," Patience snapped. "If I'd known it would ruin you, I wouldn't have—have asked it of you," she said contritely to Max. "I thought it would be good for you to make your own way in the world for a change."

"Your uncle will never forgive you," Pru chimed in. "Dukes are very proud, you know. He'll never take you back, even if Pay manages to convince him that you are innocent."

Patience was truly grieved. "Oh, Max!"

"Oh, Max!" Pru mimicked her. "Have you forgotten that he only married you to win a bet? And you let him in your bed! Don't you feel ashamed?"

"Shut up, Pru," Max said quietly.

"I hope you enjoyed it, Pay, because you can be sure it meant nothing to *him*. He must make dirty little wagers like that all the time."

Patience looked up. For the first time, she was able to meet Max's eyes with her own. "If so, he would not have been a bachelor when I met him," she said.

"He—" Pru broke off, frowning. "If he had made the same bet about me, he would be my husband now."

"I only make bets I care to win," said Max. "You may be sure I never bet against my own interests."

The color rose in Patience's cheeks, but she said as calmly as she could, "In any case, Pru, you swore you would not have him. You don't even like him."

"I hate him!"

Patience actually smiled, though her head was lowered so that Pru could not see it. "But we were talking of Wildings," she said, after a slight pause. "Yes, Max. The day after tomorrow would be very convenient. Tomorrow would be convenient. In truth, I'd be happy to leave London directly after lunch."

"Well, you needn't think that *I* am going with you," Pru declared. "The Season is just getting started."

"Of course, you must come with us," said Patience.

"The Season is over for you anyway," Max told her brutally. "Your vouchers to Almack's have been revoked, remember? No one will touch you now."

Pru sniffed. It was true that the morning post had brought no new invitations. "That is only because *you* are here," she explained. "Once you are gone, I shall be as popular as ever. Society isn't going to punish me because my sister has made a bad marriage."

Patience shook her head, but did not argue the point. "You cannot stay here by yourself. If Max and I go, you must come with us."

"I shall have Lady Jemima back. No, not her, for she abandoned me in my darkest hour. I shall find some other lady to chaperone me."

"It won't answer," said Max. "No respectable female will set foot in this house, and I shall never consent to leave you in the care of any other kind."

"No, indeed," Patience murmured in agreement.

Pru glowered at him. "I should think *you* of all people would be glad to be rid of me."

"Glad? I should be ecstatic. You must have made some friends while you've been here."

"Friends?" Pru echoed. "Of course. I have many friends."

"Perhaps one of them will take pity on you, and invite you to stay with her."

"Take pity on me!" Pru said angrily. "I have many friends in London who love me!"

"Then, by all means, write to them."

"I shall!"

Pru stormed out of the room.

"I don't think this is a good idea, Max," Patience said.

"What is your objection?" he asked mildly. "Prudence will not be happy if we take her away from all her friends. You want her to be happy, don't you?"

"Well, of course I want—"

"Then we are in perfect accord," he said, smiling.

"I don't know," Patience said uneasily.

"She will not be happy if we make her go," he repeated. "And she will make *us* miserable. I don't care to be miserable on my honeymoon."

Patience blushed to the roots of her hair. Mindful of the servants in the room, she said, "I daresay no one will invite her, and then her feelings will be hurt."

"Then she will come peacefully with us to Wildings," he replied.

Patience looked doubtful, but kept her thoughts to herself.

Despite her claims, Prudence had no friends in London. Of beaux she had plenty, but she had never much bothered with the members of her sex. There was really only one person to whom she could write.

Lady Isabella Norton received her letter that afternoon, and read it over with much scornful laughter. "What is so funny?" her brother asked gloomily, as he came into the room to be given his tea. Isabella lost no time in telling him, but, to her surprise, he did not laugh.

"What are you waiting for?" he said, sitting up in his chair. "Ask her to stay with you! Is her page boy still here?"

"No, I sent him away," she replied, staring at him. "Why should you want me to invite *her*? Now that her sister has married you-know-who, the Waverlys are far beneath our touch, surely!"

"Now that I have lost my bet, no single female of large fortune is beneath my touch," he said bitterly.

"Your bet," she said impatiently. "How much did you wager? A monkey? Send him one and see if he laughs."

"Ten thousand pounds I wagered," he replied.

Isabella stared at him in horror. "Ten thousand! Have you lost your wits?"

"If I do not get me an heiress soon, I will lose more than my wits, dear Sister! Send to Miss Prudence at once."

Isabella shook her head. "Only consider, Brother, if she is under our roof, her sister may visit her! No, it is not to be borne. And what, pray, would I say to Sir Charles?"

Milford frowned at her. "You should worry less about what you will say to Sir Charles," he said. "You should worry what *I* might say to him if you do not obey me!"

"What can you mean by that, sir?" she said indignantly.

"I may say something to him about the six months you spent in Ireland," he replied. "How fat you were when you left England. And how thin you were when you got back."

"Ivor, you wouldn't!" she whispered.

"Do not try me, Isabella," he replied.

Prudence brought Isabella's note to her sister the moment it arrived. Max had set Patience another puzzle at the chessboard in the drawing room, and Patience was doing her best to solve it before he returned.

"Isabella Norton!" she exclaimed in surprise.

"She has such lovely handwriting, don't you think?"

"I don't trust her," said Patience. "I don't even like the *idea* of you staying in London without me, but I especially don't like the idea of you staying with Isabella. There must be someone else you could ask."

"Of course, there are several other young ladies who have asked me to stay with them," said Pru, "but Isabella is my particular friend. And you know she is engaged, so there can be no jealousy between us. Really, Pay! And, if I get into trouble, I'm just up the street from the American embassy."

Patience did not smile. "I still say you had much better come to Wildings with me."

"I would go to Wildings with *you,* but I will not go with *him*! Where is he anyway, your lord and master?"

"If you mean Max," Patience said rather coldly, "he has gone to make the arrangements for the journey."

"I should like to be gone before he gets back," said Pru. "Isabella says I may come to her as soon as I wish. My maid can follow with my trunk."

"There's no need for such haste, surely," Patience protested. "We won't be leaving for a day or two. You might change your mind."

Pru shook her head. "I have already accepted Isabella's invitation. May I have the carriage?"

"I'll drive you in the curricle," Patience offered.

"No," Pru said quickly. "I must go alone, for I cannot ask Isabella to receive you. It wouldn't be fair to her. May I have the carriage?"

The carriage was sent for, and the sisters parted, Pru congratulating herself on having escaped social death, and Patience as offended as she was hurt.

Max returned to the house for his dinner. "Are we waiting for Prudence?" he asked, finding Patience in the drawing room.

Patience wished she had solved the chess problem, but she had not. She rose from the chessboard. "Prudence is gone," she told him, almost defiantly.

His eyes widened. "You got rid of her for my sake?"

Smiling, she shook her head. "She went of her own

accord. But she went with my consent, and my blessing, and my carriage."

"Gone?" Max spoke with the air of one who cannot believe his good fortune.

"She wanted to go," Patience said. "I could not make her stay. She's not a child. She can make up her own mind."

"You are not her keeper," he agreed, pleased.

"No, indeed."

"You're *my* keeper," he added. "But you are not to worry. I won't give you any trouble. I'm really quite . . . docile."

"If I believed that, Mr. Farnese," she said, "I think I would be disappointed."

"I would not on any account disappoint you, my lady," he said softly.

The next day, they left London before sunrise and Patience did not care if she ever saw the place again. "Max, did we *really* do all those things last night?" she asked, whispering as she snuggled in his arms in the coach and four he had hired to take them north to Wildings.

"Perhaps not all of them," he replied, enjoying the feel of her in his arms. "Not *quite* all of them, perhaps. But some of them," he went on as Patience began to giggle uncontrollably. "Yes, I believe we must admit, my dear girl, that some of those things *were* done, and, what is more, we did them."

Patience caught her breath. "I am glad we did not do *all* of those things," she said. "Some of them were very wicked."

With his forefinger, he lifted her chin. In the dim light of the carriage lamps he could just make out the green of her eyes. "I am not sorry," he murmured, "but if you are, gladly will I bear all the blame."

"Liar," she teased him. "You want all the *credit* for yourself. Perhaps you do deserve the lion's share of it, but I rather think that my contribution, however small—"

She was not allowed to finish, his kisses making it rather impossible to think, let alone talk.

The morning sun was just skimming the clouds overhead as the streets of London gave way to the vast, green fields of the countryside. The interior of the coach seemed ridiculously large for just two people, but Max had insisted that a smaller carriage would not be equal to the rugged roads they would encounter as they moved north. Patience pulled her cloak around her, settled back into her husband's arms, and let the motion of the carriage rock her to sleep.

The noises of a roadside inn awakened her some time later. The carriage had stopped. Looking out the window, she saw that the sun was directly overhead. The inn looked charming, but not half as charming as the tall, gray-eyed man walking toward her. He had bought her a bottle of lemonade and for himself a bottle of beer. Opening the door, he placed them in the compartment.

"Where are we?" she asked him as he resumed his place next to her.

"Redbridge."

"Redbridge!" she exclaimed in surprise, reaching for her guidebook. "This is not the way to Wildings."

"I know a shortcut. It's only a day or two out of our way. Surely, you can spare a day or two for your husband?"

"How can it be a shortcut if it takes us a day or two out of our way?" she said primly.

"All right; it's not exactly a shortcut. It's more of a scenic detour. But I'm afraid I must insist on having my way. After all, I let you have your way last night," he added, with a wolfish grin. "I was extremely flexible. Did I not do everything Your Ladyship required of me?"

"Oh, hush!" she said angrily.

He would not be silenced. "*I* was good. *I* wanted to wait," he declared. "But you said you would not grant me the jewel of your innocence in a public bed in some dirty roadside inn where thousands of travelers have made the beast with two backs. You insisted you be laid in your own bed. I merely gave in to your demands."

"I have never in my life said anything so indecent!" she protested, laughing.

"Yes, I was obliged to translate your maidenly stammers into plain English," he agreed. "Mind you, some of these places along the Great North Road *are* quite well traveled. I would not have you rise from a night of love covered in flea bites. So perhaps it is as well you were so impatient to have me."

"I was not impatient—" she began, but the carriage suddenly made a hard shift as the driver resumed his seat. Patience bit her lip as the carriage rolled forward upon Max's knock.

"Admit it!" he continued loudly as she tried in vain to shush him. "You could not wait to get me into bed. Exhibit A: You refused to play chess with me after dinner."

"I don't like chess," she said.

"Pity," he said, "for you are extremely adept at mating. Your little queen," he went on, despite her pummeling him with her fists, "swooped down on my poor king like the hawk seizing the sparrow! Really, I thought she would break his poor neck!"

"Shut up! or I shall break *your* neck!" she said, covering his mouth with her hand.

Catching her glove in his teeth, he pulled it off. "There is a better way to silence me."

"Oh, yes? How?"

"You know how," he replied, pointing to his mouth.

Patience shook her head, but kissed him.

"Put your hand in my pocket," he invited her.

"Why?" she said suspiciously.

Taking out a velvet jewel box, he presented it to her.

"What is it?" she asked shyly.

"It's your wedding ring, if you want it."

Her face clouded. "I hope you didn't spend too much on it."

"I spent nothing on it," he replied. "'Twas hazarded and lost at my table last week at the Black Swan. It's only topaz."

Satisfied, Patience opened the box and caught her breath as she stared at the ring nestled in the velvet lining. "It certainly sparkles like a diamond!" she exclaimed softly.

"Yes, it's very well cut," he said. Impatiently, he placed it on her finger. "I am sorry 'tis only a topaz. You deserve the finest of all diamonds."

"No, indeed," she said indignantly, admiring the large stone on her hand. "I love my topaz. I shall never take it off."

"You understand what this means, of course."

Patience threw her arms around him and kissed him. "Of *course* I know what it means!"

"It means that, in all probability, it will turn your finger green."

"It means I am yours forever," she told him reproachfully.

"That too, of course."

At half past four, they stopped for tea at another small inn catering to travelers. Afterward, Patience fell asleep in her husband's arms, and did not wake until the sky was quite dark. Discovering that Max had fallen asleep, too, she quickly shook him awake. "Max! It is night! The roads are not safe after dark. We must stop somewhere."

Yawning, he stretched his arms over his head. "What do you fear?" he asked, smiling. "Highwaymen? Let me assure you this road is very well patrolled by militia, and, anyway, the coachman has a pistol. So have I, if it comes to that."

"So do I, of course," she said. "But think of the horses. Tell the driver we must stop at the very next inn. Here it is now," she added, relieved as she saw the lights of a hostelry up ahead. "Tell him."

Looking out the window, he made a face. "That place? I wouldn't kennel my dog there. There's a much nicer place, just a little further ahead, if you will be patient."

"It's beginning to snow," she said worriedly.

He glanced out. By the glow of the driver's lantern, he could see snowflakes floating like feathers in the air. "Don't concern yourself," he said. "It never sticks."

"I think we should stop now, even if the place does have fleas," she said.

"I am eager, too," he said, nuzzling her neck. "The place we're going is but two miles past the Flea's Rest."

"It is the *Angler's* Rest," she corrected him, laughing.

"Trust me, you would be better off resting with fleas than with anglers," he said. "Come away from the window. You'll catch cold. Come away, or I shall begin describing at the top of my voice all the many things I intend to do to your poor body as soon as we are alone."

Shocked, Patience covered his mouth with her hand.

"This is the longest two miles I have ever known!" she declared some time later. "It will be dawn by the time we get there."

"It just seems that way because you are dying to get your hands on me."

Patience punched him in the ribs. "Hush! Someone might hear you."

He laughed. "It's just past this clump of trees."

"What clump of trees?" she wanted to know, pressing her nose to the cold glass. "It's black as pitch."

Just as she spoke, a gravel drive flanked by dozens of flickering torches appeared around the bend. Patience could make out the looming outline of a very large house at the end of the drive, its windows full of golden light.

"Is this it?" she asked, surprised by the size of the place. "It's rather big for an inn, isn't it? It's like a palace."

"It was once an abbey," he replied. "Confiscated by King Henry the Eighth."

"I wonder they can stay in business in this lonely part of the world," Patience murmured, watching curiously as a number of servants came out of the house to greet them.

"During the racing season the house is always full," he told her. "There are several race courses nearby. But I daresay, we are their only business tonight."

Patience made a face. "I hope they don't cluster around us. I don't think I will ever get used to having so many servants as you do here in England. I prefer to fend for myself wherever possible."

"I daresay they will leave us alone once we explain to them that all we want is a bed for the night."

"You cannot tell them that!" she protested, horrified. "They will think—! Well, you know very well what they will think! At least we must have supper first."

"I would prefer to have supper *after*."

"Max! I am quite serious. It is one thing to talk like that when we are alone, but, I beg of you, do not shame me in front of these people."

"No, indeed," he said gently, as the carriage rolled up to the front steps.

Before the carriage steps were let down, Patience's trunk was on its way inside. Max climbed out first and hailed the tall, dignified woman who seemed to be in charge of the servants. Despite the lateness of the hour, she looked exceedingly tidy and clear eyed. Patience took her to be the landlady.

"Mrs. Oliver! I hope we have not kept you up too late."

"No, indeed, sir," she warmly replied. "We are very happy to see you, as always. The room you requested has been prepared for you."

"Excellent! Here is Lady Waverly," he said, handing Patience out of the vehicle. She had put on her bonnet in haste and it showed. Blushing, she clung to Max's arm.

Mrs. Oliver curtsyed. "Your Ladyship is very welcome."

"Lady Waverly is very tired. We'd like to go directly to bed, if that's all right."

"Max!" said Patience, in a horrified whisper. "You promised!"

Max chuckled. "It seems my wife is also hungry," he said. "But there's no need, Mrs. Oliver, to open the dining hall just for us. Send something up to the room, if you please. And we will want a hot bath."

"Two," Patience said in a small voice. "Two hot baths."

"One will suffice," he said firmly.

The landlady curtsyed again. "Of course, sir. If you would be good enough to follow me? John has already brought your trunk up to the room."

They followed Mrs. Oliver at a discreet distance to the end of the hall and up the big staircase. Patience whispered to Max, "Is this a respectable place?"

He glanced at her sharply. "Why on earth would you doubt it?"

"Mrs. Oliver seems to know you very well."

He laughed aloud. "In that case, it cannot be respectable."

"And she didn't even ask us to prove that we are married! For all she knows, you are not my husband, and I am not your wife. I think we should go back to the little inn we passed. It may have fleas, but at least it is respectable."

"I will show her the marriage certificate, if you like."

"That isn't the point. The point is she didn't ask to see it!"

Mrs. Oliver stopped at one of the doors on the long upstairs hall. She opened it for them, sinking to a curtsy as they passed through.

Patience went at once to the huge, elaborately carved marble fireplace, putting her back to the enormous bed with purple velvet hangings. It was the largest bed she had ever seen, and she could not look at it without blushing. The coverlet was turned down to show snow white linen sheets and more than four fluffy white feather pillows.

"I trust everything is to Your Ladyship's satisfaction?" Mrs. Oliver said, sounding a little anxious.

"Yes, thank you," Patience said quickly.

Mrs. Oliver beamed at her. "And may I say, Your Ladyship, we're all very glad to see the young master married at last."

"Young master?"

"That is what we call that rogue you have there," Mrs. Oliver said fondly.

"Mrs. Oliver, you make me blush," Max said.

"May I ask how you know we are married?" Patience asked.

Mrs. Oliver looked surprised. "Sure, didn't we read it in all the London papers?"

Patience felt very foolish. "Oh, I see. Yes, of course."

Stopping at the door, Mrs. Oliver curtsyed again. "I'll leave you to it then." She backed out of the room, closing the door.

Max slowly pulled the ribbons of Patience's bonnet. "Well, my dear," he said gently. "Shall we bathe before . . . or after?"

Patience glanced around to make sure they were alone. "After," she said, shamefaced.

He tossed her bonnet aside, and she did not care where it landed. "Shall we eat before or after?"

"After," she said, reaching for him.

Laughing softly, be bent to fasten his mouth to hers, walking her backward to the bed until she fell through the slight opening in the bed curtains onto the deep feather mattress, dragging him with her.

Chapter 22

In the warm darkness behind the bed curtains, Max undressed himself swiftly and expertly while Patience was still fumbling with the clasp at her cloak.

"Hurry up!" he said, stretching out beside her.

"It's not a race," she said primly.

"Slowpokes always say that," he complained, rolling onto his back.

"You're on my skirts," she said, tugging.

"I should like to be up your skirts," he muttered.

"Good things come to those who wait," she told him sweetly.

Catching her by surprise, he hauled her across his naked body. "I know how to get good things without waiting," he said roughly. Patience protested weakly as his hands searched under her skirts for the buttons of her drawers. "Let me have you, just like this," he whispered. "All I need is one tiny opening, a little . . . Ah! There it is."

He sighed deeply as with one finger he delved into her warmth. "Shall I thread your needle for you?" he asked, making Patience laugh.

"Yes, please."

In the darkness, he took her swiftly. The urgency of

his lust excited her, but it was over too soon to bring her satisfaction. At the end, he was content, and she was still panting. A very sorry state of affairs, as he himself observed.

Leaving the bed, he opened the curtains. Patience had not been shy in the darkness, but now she kept her eyes averted from his body until he found a dressing gown.

"What shall we do now? Bathe or eat?"

Patience was horrified to see that their supper had been laid on the table before the fireplace. A bottle of champagne was chilling in a silver bucket. "That wasn't there before!" she exclaimed. "Max! The servants must have brought it in while—while we were—!"

He shrugged, already easing the cork from the champagne bottle. "What of it? The curtains were closed. We were very quiet. Well . . . *I* was very quiet. How else were they to bring us our supper?"

Patience was red in the face. "Has no one in this establishment heard of privacy?"

Max brought her a glass of champagne. "I'll speak to them about it," he promised. "Come and eat. We have roast chicken and strawberries and asparagus tips and every good thing."

Somewhat mollified, she let him lead her to the sofa. After two glasses of champagne, she let him undress her. He threw off his dressing gown and they ate their supper on the rug in front of the fire, as naked as two savages. Then he took her slowly and gently, postponing his pleasure until she with sharp, wild cries found hers.

After a little more champagne, Patience groggily stumbled for the closet. As she opened the door, a maidservant scrambled to her feet beside the steaming copper bath, dropping into a deep curtsy.

Patience screamed. Running naked to the bed, she dove

behind the curtains and would not come out until Max assured her that they were quite alone.

"What kind of place is this?" she wanted to know.

"It's her job to make sure the bath water stays hot," Max told her.

Patience clutched the sheets. "Max, she saw me naked!"

He sighed. "For the life of me, I cannot understand why you are so ashamed of your body. Don't you know you're beautiful?"

"It's called modesty," she said crossly. "I don't suppose you've ever heard of it!"

He hadn't even bothered to cover himself. She could not help looking at his body. She resented the effect the sight had on her. Wrapping the sheet around her, she went into the closet and closed the door.

The busy servant had unpacked her trunk. Her night-gown was hanging up for her.

Patience bathed quickly, terrified that servants were going to burst in on her at any moment. Safely in her nightgown, she found her hairbrush and carried it with her to the bed.

Max bathed while his bride brushed her hair, emerging from the closet as naked as he had gone in. "Where is your nightshirt?" she asked, exasperated. "You'll catch your dead."

"I'm warm natured," he assured her, slipping into bed. "I'm as good a bed warmer as you are apt to find anywhere in England."

Still damp and hot from his bath, he smelled of fresh soap and something deeper that could not be washed away: his own dark, warm smell, woodsy and animal at once. Patience took a deep breath to steady herself. Surely he could not want her a third time?

But, yes, he did. Grunting, he pulled her hard against him, covering her with the warmth of his body. Patience kissed him eagerly, wrapping her arms around him tightly.

The entire staff of this peculiar inn could have paraded across the room and she would not have noticed or cared.

"I am so happy," she whispered in his ear as he nuzzled her neck.

He was tender, and sleepy, his mood mirroring her own. Her hand moved possessively across the fine dark hair that covered his chest. "I can feel your heart beating."

He felt it only proper to return the gesture. "I can feel yours," he said, taking her small breast in his hand and caressing it through her gown. The next moment, his hand was inside her gown.

The first time he had touched her so intimately, she had been as one paralyzed. Hardly had she dared to breath. The sensation still was so exquisite as his warm fingers played with her nipple that she could hardly bear it. Taking his hand, she pressed it to her cheek. "I want you inside me now," she whispered. "Now, my love! Don't make me wait."

He laughed softly. "You are the strangest creature! One minute you are shy, and the next you are begging me to bed you quicker. Is there no pleasing you?"

"Hurry up," she explained. "I'm dying."

"So impatient!" he laughed. "But I think I will make you wait a little."

"You shall not!" she said fiercely.

Roughly, she pushed his head lower down, forcing his mouth to her breast. Groaning, he pushed her nightgown up over her thighs. Opening her with his hand, he placed himself at the entrance.

"Not like that," she panted. "All at once. I want to feel you as far inside me as you can go."

He did as instructed, with good result. Slowly, he withdrew until only the very tip of his member still touched her. Then all at once, he drove his full length into her. "We call that heel to toe," he informed her as she flung her head back and gasped.

"Never mind what you call it," she said harshly. "Do it again!"

With a low animal moan, he fell upon her, taking his pleasure from her open body, his mouth against her sweet-smelling neck, her fingers digging into his back instinctively.

Collapsing into her arms, he lay as still as death.

"My love," she repeated helplessly, holding his wet body against hers. "My love, my love."

She drifted in pleasure for a long time, her fingers lazily playing in his hair. When at last he lifted his head and kissed her, she was hungry again. She jumped out of bed, her nightgown somehow still clinging to her, and ran to the table. He watched her with half-closed eyes, his body glowing in the firelight, as she selected a plum and slowly returned to the bed.

She bit into the fruit, and was dismayed when the juice ran down her chin and stained her fingers. With a strange growl he pulled her to him.

"Again?" she giggled, proud that he wanted her so much.

The plum rolled away as he slowly devoured her fingers, then lapped at her chin. Finally, he drove his tongue deep into her flavored mouth.

In the early morning, he woke her by stroking her naked breasts and belly. Patience was exhausted and sore and a bit hungover and happier than she had ever been in her life.

"Imagine," she said softly, snuggling against him, "sharing a bed for three years without touching!"

Max was rather taken aback. "Come now! It wasn't that bad. I think you even liked it a little."

Chuckling, she turned in his arms to face him. "You told

me if we were to get an annulment, we would have to share a bed for three years without—without touching. I was thinking how impossible it would be."

"Thank God. You frightened me."

Sitting up, she stretched her arms over her head. "Do you think it is safe to go into the closet now? Or do you think there is a servant lurking there?"

"I've spoken to Mrs. Oliver. We will not be disturbed. They will leave all our meals outside the door. You will not see another servant as long as we are here."

Climbing out of bed, she stifled a yawn. "Of course, we will not be here very long," she said. "We must get on to Wildings."

"I thought we might stay here a day or two," he said.

"Heavens, no!" she exclaimed. "We must leave here at once!"

"Don't you like it here?" he protested.

"No, not at all," she said vehemently.

"But . . . it is a handsome house, is it not?"

"Yes, very handsome," she conceded. "But, Max, I'm sure the servants must have heard us last night. We were not very discreet. They all know what we've been doing in here. And, don't forget, that girl saw me naked. No! I shall be very glad when we are on the road again."

"One more day," he pleaded. "Your bottom must be sore. You should not travel on a sore bottom."

Patience blushed, but said firmly, "Another day and I won't be *fit* to travel! Go and pay the bill. We must leave directly after breakfast. Do you need money?"

Max swung his feet out of bed. "No. The rates are very reasonable here. You'd be surprised."

* * *

Three days later, as the sun was just beginning to set in the west, they reached the ivy-covered gatehouse of Wildings.

No one answered the coachman's call, so he was obliged to stop at the gate. It was soon discovered, however, that one of the gates had rusted off its hinges, and they were able to pass through with relatively little trouble. The path beyond, overgrown with weeds and brambles, led in a roundabout way to the house, tall, but not very wide, its windows choked with ivy.

"Good heavens!" Patience exclaimed in dismay.

Max eyed the structure with an air of profound doubt. "Your Mr. Campbell wasn't lying about the state of the house, at any rate."

"No," she sadly agreed. "I wouldn't feel right taking ten thousand pounds from an unsuspecting buyer. We shall have to clean it up and make repairs. Even then, I doubt it could be worth ten thousand pounds."

"You're forgetting the land," said Max. "Good, fertile land is hard to find. In America, I know, 'tis only three cents an acre, but we are an island."

"Only two working farms; scarcely any rents. Most of it seems to be rather mountainous terrain. The shooting is said to be very good."

"Who has made the offer?"

"A Squire Colebatch. He owns the adjoining property."

"Perhaps the squire is a sporting gentleman," Max suggested. "But it seems a shame to sell something that has been in your family for so many years."

"I promised Prudence I would sell it and split the profits with her," Patience said.

As she spoke, the carriage jerked to a stop. Max let the window down to speak to the driver, who had jumped down from his box to examine one of the wheels. "A stone has wedged itself in the works," he reported to Patience. "The wheel is jammed. It's but one or two hundred yards to the house. Shall we walk?"

Leaving the coachman and the two footmen to deal with the horses, the couple waded through the weeds up to the house. Patience's skirts were wet to the knee and studded with burrs as they came up to the ivy-covered porch. A dog was barking within.

"That is a good sign," Patience said, ducking under the hanging ivy to seize the door knocker.

"That will depend on the dog," he said dryly. "He sounds rather annoyed."

The door opened before Patience could knock, and a stooped little man wearing a dirty shirt, and dirtier, torn breeches swung a lantern in her face. "What yer want?" he said roughly.

His terrier was less friendly. Leaping up, it seized a mouthful of Patience's skirt and refused to let go, twisting and growling with all its might as it hung on.

"Mr. Moffat?" Patience said, doing her best to remain polite as she struggled to rescue her skirt from the dog. "I am Patience, Lady Waverly. The new owner of Wildings This is my husband, Mr. Farnese."

The lantern swung from one face to the other.

"Would you be good enough to call off your dog?" Max said sharply.

The little man did so, eyeing them with resentment.

"You *are* Mr. Moffat, aren't you?" Patience asked, checking the damage to her skirts as the dog was banished to the recesses of the house.

"I'm Archie Moffat. What yer want?" he repeated suspiciously.

"Her ladyship has explained it to you already," Max said

angrily. "Now stand aside, my good man! We have had quite enough of this nonsense."

"You don't mean yer coming in?" he said, apparently amazed.

"I do mean it," Max said curtly. "Our vehicle is bogged down in your lawn—in your weeds, I should say. Send someone this instant to collect my lady's trunk."

"Ain't no one here but me," said Moffat, thrusting his jaw out fiercely.

"Then *you* go!" Max snapped. "Quicker, please! And direct my men to the stables. Thank you!" he added, dragging the man from the doorway and sending him on his way down the path. The terrier, no longer restrained by his master's foot, lunged at Patience again.

Ignoring him, Max lifted his bride in his arms and carried her over the threshold with the terrier still attached to her skirt, which was beginning to tear.

It was extremely dark within, despite the modest fire in the big hearth. The furnishings were sparse, namely a pair of worn wooden settles and an age-blackened table in the inglenook. The stone floor was strewn with leaves that seemed to have blown in from the outdoors. In the farthest corner of the room, a milk cow stood in a mound of straw, placidly chewing her cud. As Max and Patience stared at her, she greeted them with a dull moo.

"We seem to have found the stables," Max said, setting Patience on her feet. Kneeling down, he pried the terrier's jaws apart and freed her skirt. Tucking the dog under his arm for safekeeping, he climbed to his feet.

"You mean this is not the house? Oh, thank God!"

"No, this is the house," he told her apologetically. "This is the house *and* the stable."

"Oh, dear," she said, looking around in dismay. "I think the cow has been eating the curtains."

"I think you are right," he said. "Have a seat by the fire," he added, handing her the dog. "Dry your skirts. I'll see if there's anything to eat in this cursed place. I am hungry, but not hungry enough to eat the curtains."

Patience carried the squirming dog to the inglenook while Max lit a candle and went off to find the kitchen. The table between the two benches in the nook was covered with books, old newspapers, and shoe-black. Mr. Archie Moffat, she supposed, had been polishing his boots when they arrived. Patience sat down on one of the benches and removed her bonnet, setting it on the bench next to her.

It was a mistake. The terrier instantly seized it and ran off. Patience gave chase, pursuing him to the stairs, shouting, "You rascal! Come back here!"

At the staircase, she caught the newel post and skidded to a stop as the dog darted up the stairs and dropped her bonnet at the feet of the tall, spare gentleman on the landing. As Patience stared, the tall man stooped to retrieve her bonnet.

"His name is Rufus," he said. "He is indeed a rascal."

Patience stared at the man in disbelief. He was much older than she remembered, but his eyes were a clear green without a trace of hazel and his features were finely sculpted.

"My God!" she gasped, pale and struggling to breathe.

"No," he said, coming down the stairs toward her, with his little dog on his heels. "I must insist his name is Rufus. I know, you see; I named him."

"I beg your pardon!" Patience stammered. "For a moment, I thought you were someone else. Who—who are you?"

"Who am I?" he repeated. "Don't you know, child? I know who you are."

"But . . . it can't be," she whispered. "You're dead."

"No, child," he said, drawing nearer. Slowly, he reached out and placed his thin hand on her shoulder.

Patience looked into his green eyes, and, for the first time in her life, she fainted.

When she came to, she was lying in the inglenook, on one of the settles, and Max was hovering over her with a look of concern on his dark face. "Oh, Max!" she said, throwing her arms around him. "I have seen a ghost."

"Drink this," he said calmly. Helping her sit up, he handed her wine in a cracked glass. As she took the glass, he wrapped a blanket around her shoulders. It smelled strongly of shoe polish and tobacco. "There's no such thing as ghosts," he told her firmly.

"I know that," she said. "But I have seen one all the same. My father is here. I mean, his spirit is here. He has come back from beyond the grave! He must have something very important to say to me."

"No, Patsy," he said gently, again pressing her to drink from the glass.

"He is here!" she insisted. "Max, I tell you: I saw him! I am not mad."

"I'm not your father, child," said another voice. Its owner sat down on the other side of the table. "I am your uncle, Ambrose Waverly. I'm sorry I gave you a fright," he added.

Patience shook her head rapidly. "No! You're dead."

"So is your father, if it comes to that," said Ambrose Waverly. Impatiently, he looked at Max. "I say! You told me she was a sensible young woman."

"I am a sensible young woman," Patience said indignantly.

"Well, then!" he said. "Cease your prattle! Arthur is

dead, I suppose, but *I* am very much alive. Heavens! Did Arthur never tell you he had a twin brother?"

Patience shook her head. "My father never mentioned you," she said. "He never spoke of his family at all."

Ambrose, Lord Waverly, grunted. "No? Well, he wouldn't, would he? We never got on. I suppose he blamed *me* for having been born first."

"That does not sound like my father," Patience murmured.

He looked at her keenly. "You have a twin sister, I believe, or so Campbell tells me. Does *she* ever resent *you*?"

"No," said Patience, glaring at Max, who could not help rolling his eyes. "Of course she doesn't."

Lord Waverly grunted.

"I beg your pardon, sir," Patience said tentatively, "but if you are not dead, sir . . ."

"Of course I'm not dead!" he snapped.

"Then who was it they pulled out of the river?" she asked. "Who is buried in your grave?"

"An excellent question," said Max, sitting next to her on the settle.

Lord Waverly looked annoyed. "How should I know? Whoever he was, he was a thief, and I'm not sorry he's dead. Why should I be?"

"If you don't know him, how do you know he was a thief?" Patience asked reasonably.

"He had my watch in his pocket, didn't he?" said her uncle. "That's what it said in the newspapers, anyway. Well, I didn't *give* my watch to him. Ergo, he must have been a thief. Still, he did me a favor. I was very glad to hear that I was dead. My debts had become quite tiresome!"

"Yes, I know," Patience said dryly. "As your heir, I was called upon to pay them!"

"As my heir, I'd say it was the least you could do!" he retorted.

"So you decided to play dead in order to escape your creditors," said Max. "It would appear the jig is up, my lord. What now?"

"What do you mean the jig is up?" Lord Waverly squawked. "You ain't going to peach on me, are you?"

"We can't go on pretending that you're dead, Uncle," said Patience.

"I'd liefer be dead, if you don't mind," he replied. "Look here, you can keep the title. Just sign the sale papers."

"I see," said Max. "The sale was your idea."

"I can't sell something that doesn't belong to me!" Patience protested. "Why don't you sell the place yourself? It's your property, not mine."

He looked at her as if she were an imbecile. "I can't sell it; I signed an entail when I was just a nipper. My hands are tied. *You* haven't signed any entail, have you?" he asked sharply.

"No."

He beamed at her. "Good girl! Then you can sell it and give me the money."

"Uncle! That would be fraudulent."

His eyes narrowed. "Oh, I see! You want a piece of the action. Well, I won't give you more than five percent."

"I don't want money," Patience laughed.

"Well, of course you don't," he said. "You're an heiress, aren't you? And your husband is rich as Midas, too. Why do you begrudge me a mere ten thousand? I must have something to live on."

"You must have something to live on because you are alive," Patience pointed out. "Be glad of that, Uncle."

He made a face. "No, I must stay dead. I owe Sir Charles Stanhope more than this place is worth."

"Sir Charles!" Patience said scornfully. "He doesn't even have an IOU."

Lord Waverly chuckled. "Yes, I tricked him proper, didn't I? He thought I'd gone over to the writing desk to give him my vowels. But, in fact, I wrote in plain English: "Kiss mine arse"! By the time the old fool read it, they were pulling me out of the river!"

"Oh, Uncle!" Patience chided him, though she could not help laughing.

"I was not so clever with Lord Banville," he muttered.

"That was only twenty-five hundred pounds," said Patience. "I will pay it."

"That is good of you," he approved. "But it still doesn't give me anything to live on."

Patience frowned. "Have you no income from the estate?"

"A pittance!" Slyly, Lord Waverly looked at Max. "You see how it is, don't you, Purefoy? I'm not a greedy man, I hope. Ten thousand pounds would set me up forever!"

"Uncle!"

"Surely that is not too much to ask?" Lord Waverly said belligerently. "After all, I am giving you my favorite niece. What say you, Purefoy?"

Patience put her hand on Max's arm. "I'm afraid you misunderstand the situation, Uncle," she said coolly. "My husband is not as rich as Midas. He can give you nothing. Even if he could, I would forbid him to do so. I am not to be purchased like a head of beef!"

"You talk nonsense, baggage," Lord Waverly snarled at his favorite niece. "Is he not nephew and heir to the Duke of Sunderland? I daresay his income sits pretty at ten thousand a year! Of course he shall pay. And you are not yet twenty-one, I believe."

"What has that to say to anything?" Patience said angrily. "Do not presume that you are my guardian!"

"I do so presume, you brazen hussy! You *will* be purchased like a head of beef, if I have anything to say about it. I shall be paid, or, by God, I've a mind to challenge this marriage. I'll have it annulled, so I will."

Max held up his hands for peace. "Let us come to an understanding," he said quietly. "My lord, we have no quarrel with you. Ten thousand pounds is more than reasonable. I will pay."

"What?" cried Patience. "Even if you had that kind of money, which you don't—! Max, I forbid you to give him so much as a penny!"

"A penny! 'Tis no more than you're worth, too, little saucebox!"

"You're barking up the wrong tree, Uncle," Patience told him coldly. "My husband is the Duke of Sunderland's nephew, but he's not his heir. Not anymore. The duke had his parents' marriage annulled. He's not even a Purefoy anymore. His name is Farnese. And, since I am no more Lady Waverly, that means I am Mrs. Farnese."

"Mrs. Farnese! What nonsense is this? This is the son of Lord Richard Purefoy and his lawful wife. There's no annulling *that* marriage; 'twas attempted at the time. Even if it could be annulled, Sunderland wouldn't do it. He's a sentimental old fool, fond of the boy."

"But Max's father was not twenty-one when he married," said Patience, glancing at Max. "I know it is painful for you, my love, but you must tell my uncle you are not the golden goose he thinks you are!"

"Not twenty-one!" Lord Waverly snorted. "True enough, I suppose. He was four and twenty at least. I should know, for we were at school together. Somebody's sold you a bill of goods, my girl! I shouldn't be at all surprised to find that your marriage is a sham through and through."

"Max!"

"Don't be absurd," Max said angrily. "Of course it is not a sham. Patience is my wife."

"Is she?" Lord Waverly wondered. "She doesn't appear even to know her husband's name. What did she call you? Farzini?"

Max's eyes narrowed. "Continue in this vein, sir, and you may well find yourself drowning in the Thames, after all!"

Lord Waverly assumed an injured air. "You threaten me, sir? You marry my poor niece under a false name, and you threaten me? You have injured this sweet, innocent child—innocent no more, alas! You will pay dearly for her maidenhead, by God!"

Patience dug her fingers into Max's arm. "Max, what is he saying?"

Lord Waverly clicked his tongue. "My poor honey! It's the oldest trick in the book, dear girl. He only pretended to marry you. It was all to get you into bed. I don't suppose you would have let him have you otherwise."

Patience was on her feet. "Don't be ridiculous, Uncle! Max, tell him he is wrong. Tell him we are married. Tell him, for God's sake!"

"Of course he's wrong," Max said angrily. "You're my wife. Good God, you don't actually think—!"

Overwhelmed with relief, Patience threw herself into his arms. "Of course not! Of course, I'm you're wife. I won't listen to any more of this poison!"

Max's arms tightened around her protectively. "We'll fix everything when we get back to London, I promise."

He felt her stiffen in his arms. Slowly, she drew away from him. Her green eyes were stormy with doubt. "If we are married, what is there to fix?" she asked slowly.

He cupped her face with his hand. "It's true, Patsy, that my uncle has not disowned me."

"What!"

"He couldn't disown me even if he wanted, which I trust

he does not. 'Twas all pretense, to get rid of your sister, which it did."

"Oh, ho!" said Lord Waverly. "Had your sister as well, did he? The cad."

"Shut up!" Max snarled.

"How dare you talk to my uncle like that!" said Patience, disentangling herself from Max. "So it was all pretense, was it? Our marriage *is* a sham!"

"No," he said violently. "I was going to tell you on our wedding day, but you would not go to breakfast with me. You went to your attorney instead."

She stared at him. "And after?" she snapped. "When I took you in, when you had nowhere else to go? Of course, you had somewhere to go! You had a palace! Why did you not tell me then? You must have been laughing at me the whole time!"

"I couldn't tell you then. You would never have let your-self love me. But you . . . you loved me even when you thought I had nothing."

"So it was a test!" she cried, infuriated. "You have been testing me all this time?"

"That is not what I meant. You are twisting my words."

"How could you do this to me?" she railed. "Your own wife? Oh, but of course, I am *not* your wife, am I? If I am not your wife, what am I to you?"

"Don't be silly!" he snapped. "Of course you're my wife. It's simply a matter of getting the right name on the right documents."

She shook her head. "Which you did not care to do *before* you married me! You lied to me, Max! You de-ceived me."

Her anger he could bear easily, but this weary resigna-tion frightened him. "It's only a piece of paper," he said, trying to laugh it off.

She stared at him, horrified. "Do you truly believe that?"

"Of course," he assured her. "We'll have the whole thing sorted in a trice when we get back to London. My uncle knows the Archbishop of Canterbury personally. This won't be a problem."

"Your uncle is used to fixing your mistakes."

"Yes. You're going to feel very foolish for making such a fuss about nothing."

"I feel like a fool already," she said bitterly. "Uncle, I would like to go to my room now. Suddenly, I'm very tired."

"Of course, my dear," Lord Waverly said, jumping up from his seat to take her arm. "You can sleep in the room next to mine. Moffat will build you a nice fire. You can have Rufus with you, too, for extra protection."

"I am all the protection she needs," Max declared.

Patience turned on him furiously. "Think again, Mr. Purefoy! You can sleep with the cow in her bed. She's as much your wife as I am! That is what you have made of me," she added bitterly, "a poor, dumb beast!"

"Oh, that is ridiculous!" Max snapped.

"So now I'm ridiculous?" she said shrilly. "Were you ever going to tell me? Were you going to let me live my whole life in sin with you?"

"Of course, I was going to tell you."

"Oh? Why? According to you, it's nothing. Why tell me at all, if it's nothing?"

"Exactly!"

Lord Waverly patted her hand. "He would have told you when he tired of you," he declared, laying his arm across her shoulders. "Then he would have put you away quietly. That's the advantage of a sham marriage, you see."

"Don't listen to him, Patsy," Max pleaded. "Our marriage is not a sham!"

"Are you sure of that?" she asked.

"Well, I am not a barrister," he said roughly. "But it seems to me—"

"It seems to *me* you don't care! 'Tis only a piece of paper, after all! A sham either way, is that it? And if our children are all bastards, what of it? Obviously, I'm just being ridiculous!"

Max bit his lip. "I will make this right for you, Patsy. I swear!"

Patience trembled with rage. "Stop calling me Patsy!" she howled at him.

Breaking free of her uncle, she ran upstairs. Entering the first room she came to, she banged the door so hard that a chunk of soot was dislodged in the chimney downstairs, landing with a crash in the fireplace and sending sparks flying.

Max turned on Lord Waverly. "You and your poisonous tongue!" he said furiously. "Now look what you've done!"

"It's no good blaming me, boy," the baron replied. "You're the one who put the cart before the horse. Now you have to pay. I think it's only fair to tell you my price has gone up . . . considerably."

Chapter 23

Lord Waverly enjoyed the journey to London immensely. He sat on one side of the carriage with his niece and his terrier, while Max sat brooding on the opposite seat. Patience stared pointedly out the window, cold and unforgiving.

"What a delightful conveyance!" exclaimed his lordship, bouncing on the seat. "So well sprung! One of your uncle's, I suppose?"

Patience turned accusing eyes to Max. "You told me it was hired."

"Oh, no, my dear," Lord Waverly assured her. "If you look at the door in full sun, you can see where the crest has been painted over."

"Is there anything you haven't lied to me about?" Patience demanded, glaring at Max.

Max sighed. "I never lied about the important things," he said wearily.

"Just your name," she sniffed. "Our marriage! Nothing important!"

"I do hope we can spend at least one night at Breckinridge," Lord Waverly said eagerly.

"No," Max said shortly.

"But, surely it is not so very much out of the way," Lord Waverly insisted. "And so convenient to London! I cannot believe you did not take my niece to Breckinridge on your way to Wildings. These roadside inns can be quite sordid. I suppose you were too ashamed to take her to Breckinridge."

"I *did* take her to Breckinridge, as it happens," Max said tightly.

"No, you didn't," said Patience.

"Of course I did. We spent the night there. The first night of our journey."

Patience stared at him. "You told me that was an inn! And Mrs. Oliver? Was she not the landlady?"

"She is the housekeeper."

Patience slowly turned red, thinking, he was sure, of the night they had spent there together. "Does she know we are not married?"

"For the last time: we are married."

"We most assuredly will not be staying *there*," Patience said vehemently.

Max bit back a curse. "We can certainly change horses and drive through the night."

"It's two hundred miles to London!" Lord Waverly protested.

Max shrugged. "What's two hundred miles in a well-sprung vehicle? We'll be there in two days."

Patience suddenly had a thought. "And my topaz?" she asked, tearing off the glove on her left hand.

Max had the grace to look ashamed. "I'm afraid it *is* a diamond. But only ten carats," he added quickly. And then, even more quickly as she began pulling the ring over her knuckle, "You swore it would never leave your finger!"

Patience contented herself with glowering at him.

"I can get you a topaz, if you want," he offered. "I'd have

to buy it, however, and would that not be a false economy? That ring has been in my family for three generations."

Patience refused even to smile at his attempt at humor.

They did travel through the night, but, at the end of the next day, Lord Waverly was moaning so piteously on account of his carbuncles that they were obliged to stop for the night at Saint Albans. Three rooms were not to be had for the three travelers, and Max spent the night in front of the fire in the taproom.

The following morning, they rolled into London, Lord Waverly floating in a cloud of laudanum, the boils on his bottom freshly lanced and dressed.

The road brought them first to Sunderland Square.

"I will take my leave of you here," said Max, his fingers on the door handle. "I will consult with my uncle and his attorney. I will call on you this afternoon."

Patience shrugged. "It will be good to see my sister again," she said.

"Oh, yes; do give Prudence my love," he said sourly.

He got out and closed the door, but turned back full of hope as she opened the window.

"Max?"

Instantly, he caught the gloved hands clutching the windowsill. "Yes, my love?"

"You w-will call on me, won't you?" she said, a slight tremor in her voice.

Max was so relieved, he almost laughed. "Of course I shall! Now kiss me good-bye; there's a good girl."

With a backward glance, to be sure her uncle was still in a drugged stupor. Then, leaning out the window, she gave Max her mouth.

"It *is* more than just a piece of paper, you know," she said reproachfully. "It is a sacrament. Think of our children. What would become of them if our marriage is on shaky ground?"

"I will make this right, Pazienza. Just have a little patience with me," he added, with a faint smile. "And don't listen to your bloody uncle! He thinks I'm as bad as he is."

"And you're not?" she said, arching an eyebrow.

"You know I'm not," he said softly.

Sitting back, she closed the window, and Max sent the driver on his way.

Patience felt almost happy. On impulse, she decided to stop in Grosvenor Square to surprise Prudence. Lord Waverly hardly stirred as the carriage stopped outside Lord Milford's house.

Patience went up the steps alone, but, before she could knock, she heard an upstairs window opening. "Patience!" Prudence hissed at her.

Looking up, she saw her sister's head and shoulders leaning out the window.

"Prudence!" she called happily. "I was just about to—"

"Don't!" It would have been an urgent scream if Prudence had not been whispering. "Don't ring the bell! I'll come down!"

"Don't be silly," Patience began as Prudence disappeared from the window. In the next moment, Pru's bare feet came over the window ledge, startling Patience.

"What are you doing?" she cried, alarmed. "When you said you were coming down, I thought you were going for the stairs!"

"I cannot stay in this house another instant!" Pru declared.

"That much is obvious!"

Prudence was standing on the window ledge. The fact that her sister was wearing nothing but a thin nightgown suddenly impressed itself on Patience. "Go back inside at once!" she gasped. "At least put on your dressing gown!"

Pru ignored her. "If your coachman would move up a

little, do you think I could jump onto the roof of your carriage?"

"Certainly not!" Patience cried, alarmed.

The coachman, however, seemed to think it was an excellent notion. Slowly, and carefully, he began backing up his team, angling the coach over the curbstone.

By this time, they were attracting attention in the street, which, fortunately, was not very busy at this early hour of the morning. The door of Lord Milford's house opened and a man whom Patience took for his lordship's butler came running down the steps. He looked up at Prudence in horror, his periwig slipping over his bald head.

"Don't just stand there, man!" Patience snapped. "Get a ladder!"

From inside the house, a hand reached out to grasp Prudence's ankle. She shrieked in surprise and nearly fell. Patience could not see her sister's would-be rescuer, but Pru did not react well. "Let go of me, you brute!" she screamed.

"No, don't!" Patience shouted to the unknown hero. "Don't let go of her, I beg of you! She'll fall! Will someone please get a ladder?"

With her free foot, Pru stomped on the hand of her rescuer. Howling, he let her go. This time, she did fall, or rather, she jumped, to Patience's horror. The coach was not ideally placed, however, and she did not land on the roof. Instead, she struck the side, but managed to grab hold of the brass railing of the luggage rack. From there she was able to drop into the arms of the footman who had jumped down to assist her.

Lord Milford leaned out the window. "I—I had to grab her," he stammered, looking down at Patience with a very red face. "She was going to fall!"

"Thank you very much, sir!" Patience shouted. "I will take her home now, I think."

"No! Wait!" His lordship withdrew into the house.

"Patience!" Pru cried. "Take me away from this place! Hurry!"

She was already in the carriage, beckoning wildly to her sister. "Thank you," Patience told the butler with what dignity she could muster. "I don't think we'll be needing the ladder after all."

Hastily, she got into her carriage. "What on earth—?" she began furiously, as the footman closed the door.

The carriage lurched to one side as the wheels descended from the curb. Then it righted itself, and they were off, moving briskly toward Clarges Street.

"Prudence, what is the meaning of this?" she began again. "I'm sure your friends must think you're mad!"

Pru's teeth were chattering as she hugged herself. "They are not my friends," she said tearfully. "I'm so c-cold!"

Hastily, Patience wrapped her up in the carriage rug, pulling it off the inert form of their uncle. "Of course you're cold!" she scolded her. "You're still in your nightgown, you silly girl! What do you mean by climbing out the window? You could have broken your neck!"

"I can think of worse things," Pru said darkly.

Patience sighed. "What have you done now? Did you quarrel with Isabella?"

"I haven't done anything," Pru said shrilly. "You always blame me! Is it my fault that I was locked in a room for days with no clothes, no shoes, no fire, nothing to eat? I don't even know what they did with my maid! It's a wonder I'm alive at all!"

Patience could hardly believe her ears. "What are you saying?"

"Lord Milford has been holding me a prisoner in his house," Pru told her. "He said I could not have anything to eat unless I promised to marry him."

"What?"

"If it were not for Isabella, I would have starved," Pru declared. "I suppose you got her note? She promised she would send one to you. *She* at least is not the monster her brother is."

"I received no note," said Patience. "But we have been traveling . . . I stopped here before going home on the merest whim. My God, Prudence! If you have been injured— Are you all right?"

"No, I am *not* all right!" said Pru, the words half obliterated by a powerful sneeze. "I got tired of waiting for you to come and get me," she went on crankily, when she had made use of her sister's handkerchief. "I was so c-cold and so hungry that I—that I— Well, finally, I told him I *would* marry him! I had no choice!"

Patience took Pru to her, rubbing her arms to warm her. "Darling, I'm so sorry!"

"I thought perhaps R-Roger would see the notice in the newspaper. I thought he might come to c-congratulate me."

Again, she sneezed. Patience quickly opened her cloak and gathered her shivering sister into its folds.

"He c-came so quickly to congratulate you," Pru continued, sniffling. "I was watching from the window in case he should come. When I saw you get out of the coach—! Oh, Pay! I've never been so happy to see anyone in my life!"

"I knew that Isabella was not to be trusted," Patience said grimly.

"It's not Bella's fault," said Pru. "If she hadn't smuggled food into my room, I would have starved."

"She should have let you out of the house!"

"I won't hear a word against Bella," Pru insisted. "She did the best she could. He—he was going to come into my room and—and— Well, *you know*. But Bella wouldn't let him. She said the appearance of my having been compromised would be sufficient for his purposes."

"We must be grateful to her for that, at least!" Patience

snapped. "What on earth could his purpose be? Has he gone mad?"

"He is not the wealthy lord we thought him," said Pru. "He needs money desperately. And I went right to his house like a lamb to the slaughter! The instant we are married he means to start borrowing against my inheritance."

Patience hugged her tightly. "Never mind, dearest. You're quite safe from him now. Oh, I should have insisted on taking you with us to Wildings! It was—it was selfish of me to leave you behind."

"It was," Pru whimpered. "It was selfish of you. I s-still can't believe you chose him over me. He's not even all that good looking. Quite swarthy!" she added with a shudder.

"I didn't choose him over you," Patience protested. "You mustn't think that. You will always be my sister. And now you are his sister as well. Max will be furious when I tell him. He will make Lord Milford very sorry, I can assure you!"

Pru snorted. "Of course he will; but do you think he will ever wake up?" She jerked her chin toward the sleeping figure on the opposite seat.

Patience laughed. "Oh, that's not Max! That is our uncle, Lord Waverly. It turns out he isn't dead, after all."

"Just sleeping, then?"

"He's a scoundrel, Pru! He's been at Wildings all this time, hiding from his creditors. The sale was his idea. He was going to abscond with the money. Disappear and never come back."

Pru sighed. "Then we have come all this way for nothing! Do you think *he* will ever wake up?" she added, doubtfully eyeing Lord Waverly.

"Poor man," Patience murmured. "The doctor at Saint Albans gave him laudanum. He has carbuncles on his—on his behind. Don't laugh, Pru. It's very painful, I understand." She sighed. "I must warn you: he's not a very nice man. He may look like our father, but he's nothing like him in character."

"Nor in carbuncles!" said Pru, making her sister laugh. "I suppose," Pru went on after a short pause, "dear Max is at Clarges Street already?"

"He *is* dear to me, Pru," Patience said quietly. "I wish you would try to get along with him for my sake. You're brother and sister now."

Pru groaned.

"He's not waiting for us in Clarges Street, as it happens," Patience went on. "He is . . . he is with his uncle at Sunderland House. There is . . . There is some slight problem with our marriage."

"What do you mean?" Pru said sharply.

"It— it may not be valid," Patience confessed.

"Patience!"

"Oh, Max assures me it's nothing to be concerned about," Patience said quickly. "But, when he married me, he used the name Farnese."

"I know that already. But what is the problem?"

"Farnese is not his name, as it turns out. His name really is Purefoy. It has never been anything but Purefoy. He was not disowned. His parents' marriage could not be annulled. I don't think the duke even attempted it. It was all . . . a mistake."

"A mistake! He deceived you!"

"No, it wasn't like that."

"Well, is your marriage valid or not?"

"I don't know," Patience admitted.

"Well, if you are not married," Pru declared, "I will get a pistol, and I will force him to marry you!"

Patience thought of the kiss she had shared with Max that morning. "I don't think that will be necessary."

"I'm quite serious! If he tries to weasel out of it, I'm

getting a pistol! No one trifles with my sister and gets away with it!"

"He did not trifle with me," Patience protested. "We are married. I'm sure of it. And if we are not, Max will make it right. I have—I have faith in him. It's only a piece of paper, after all."

If Briggs was at all startled by the sudden, unannounced return of his mistress and her sister, he gave no sign of it. However, it cannot be denied that as Lord Waverly was carried inside the house, the butler's brows were slightly elevated.

Patience tended to Prudence herself. First, Pru had a hot bath. Then she was bundled up into a flannel nightgown and put to bed, where she ate an enormous breakfast. As she was eating, a letter arrived by hand from Grosvenor Square. Patience took it from the servant who brought it up to her sister's room. "He has a lot of nerve sending you a message!"

"What does he have to say for himself?" Pru asked. "I'm too tired to read anything."

Patience broke the seal. Slowly she sank down to the bed as she read it.

"What does it say?"

Patience glanced up. "It is not from Lord Milford," she said. "It's from Isabella. She says her brother has your letters, but she knows where he keeps them. She thinks she can get them for you. If you can meet her at the bridge in Hyde Park tomorrow at dawn, she'll return them to you. Pru, what letters?" she demanded, frowning. "What is she talking about?"

"I haven't the slightest idea," Pru said with far too much innocence to be credible.

"Prudence! Tell me you didn't write letters to Lord Milford! Love letters? If so, my dear, the joke was in very poor taste! Is it any wonder if he took them as a sign of encouragement?"

Pru scowled. "I never wrote any letters to Lord Milford!"

"Then what is the meaning of Isabella's offer to restore them to you?"

"If you must know, she refers to some letters that I wrote, not to Milford, but to Max!"

"Max," Patience repeated blankly. "What? My Max?"

"He was mine before he was yours," Pru said, scowling. "You cut me out."

"I could not have cut you out if he hadn't liked me best," Patience replied with some irritation. "Anyway, I believe you said you never liked him seriously."

"No, indeed!" said Pru. "You're very welcome to him, I'm sure."

"And yet you wrote some letters?"

"It was a long time ago," Pru said defensively. "When he went home to his uncle for Christmas, I wrote him a— a few times. They were very silly letters, I do admit. But I didn't mean any of it. I plagiarized most of it. I was just . . . just bored, really."

"And how did Lord Milford get his grubby paws on some letters you wrote to Max?"

"Well, they were there," Pru explained, "at Breckinridge. Bella and her brother, I mean. They were invited to the Christmas Ball. I don't know how he got my letters exactly; he must have stolen them. That's all I can think. But we must get them back, Patience!"

"Just how silly are these letters?" Patience asked, frowning.

"Very. You would blush."

"I'm sure I wouldn't," Patience said. "I don't regard it in the least. You were not serious. If Milford tries to blackmail us, we'll just laugh in his face."

Pru pushed her food away. "It's all well and good for you!" she said. "I'm glad you don't care! But if . . . if *Roger* were to see those letters, he would never forgive me!"

"Roger?" Patience repeated blankly. "Roger Molyneux? What does *he* have to do with you and your letters?"

"Nothing."

Patience was hardly credulous. "Prudence!"

Pru sighed. "We *were* sort of secretly married, but it's over now. I don't even know why he suddenly popped into my head. I just thought—"

"What?"

"I haven't thought of him in donkey's years. He didn't even care that I was engaged to another man. I'm sure he won't care that I wrote some foolish love letters to my sister's husband."

"Are you saying that you are *married*?" Patience broke in. "To *Roger Molyneux*?"

"Not married-married," said Pru. "It happened in the middle of the Atlantic Ocean, for heaven's sake. The captain married us; he's not even a clergyman. I realized at once that it was a horrible mistake. Well, almost at once. Before we married, he was so gentle and kind and thoughtful. But after . . ." She sighed heavily. "It was as if I didn't matter at all!"

Patience sat gaping at her. "Married! Why didn't you tell me?"

"I was too ashamed to tell anyone!" cried Pru. "Anyway, it was all a sham. He just wanted to get me into bed. You know what they're like."

"I don't believe it," said Patience. "Not Roger! He's from Pennsauken! His father's a clergyman!"

"I might have known you'd take his side," Pru said bitterly.

"I'm not taking sides! Tell me what happened."

"We had a terrible fight on our wedding night," Pru

went on. "Of course, he waited until *after* to show his true colors!"

"What did he do?"

"All I said was he'd have to quit his medical studies now that we were married. I mean, I can't be a doctor's wife; I'm an heiress. *He* said he wouldn't disappoint his parents. He said they'd sold off the back acres just to send him to Europe, whatever that means. But I don't want to be a doctor's wife, I told him. Too bad, he said. I want a divorce, I said—you know, quite reasonably, not shouting—you know I never shout. And *that's* when he told me we weren't really married. Well, thank God! I said, and I meant it, too."

"Prudence, if the captain married you, then you *are* married," Patience told her. "He has that authority when his ship is at sea. I'm sure Roger must know that."

"But I'm not yet twenty-one," Pru protested. "I can't get married without permission from my guardian."

Patience shook her head. "That is true in England, but you were married on an *American* vessel. American law applies. You only have to be sixteen to marry."

Pru stared at her. "You mean I'm married to that—that *clodpole*?" she cried.

It took some time to convince Pru, but, finally, the awful truth took hold. "Why, that stinking liar! No wonder he didn't come to congratulate me on my engagement!"

Patience rose from the bed wearily. "This has been quite a morning! I'm too tired even to think. If you don't mind, I'll go to my room now. I want a bath and a hot breakfast, too. You should rest."

Pru looked at her in astonishment. "What about my letters?" she demanded. "If Roger sees them, he'll divorce me! Will you come with me to meet Bella?"

"No," Patience told her. "You already have a cold. I'll go in your place."

Pru sighed with relief. "Thank you, Pay."

Patience kissed her sister's cheek. "Get some rest."

Pru was asleep before her sister was out the door.

After she had bathed and eaten, Patience too tried to sleep, but, with one eye on the clock, she could not relax. Noon came and went. Pru slept through lunch. A tray went up to Lord Waverly's room, and came back out picked clean. Alone in the dining room, Patience picked at her food. By two o'clock, it was plain that Pru had not emerged from Milford's house completely unscathed; she had developed a nasty cough. Max still had not appeared.

Dr. Wingfield was summoned, but, though he recommended complete bed rest for a day or two, he did not seem unduly concerned about Pru's condition.

By the time Max finally arrived in Clarges Street the street lamps were being lit outside, and Patience's nerves were completely frayed.

"You certainly took your time!" she greeted him sharply as he came into the drawing room.

"Well, I've had quite a day," he replied. Ignoring her frown, he kissed her lightly on the mouth. "You'll be glad to know it's all been sorted."

"We're married?" she said softly.

Max hesitated.

"We're not married!"

"Of course we're married," he said, reaching for her.

"But?" she said, eluding his grasp by neatly stepping behind a chair.

Again, he hesitated. "According to the lawyers, it is not unassailable. Of course, no one will ever dare dispute that we are married—not while I live. But, as my widow, you would not be secure. Our children—if we are so blessed— would not be secure."

"Oh, God!"

This time she allowed him to take her in his arms. "There is a very simple solution," he told her. "Tomorrow morning, we marry again—very quietly. No one need ever know we botched it the first time. *I* botched it the first time," he corrected himself quickly as she glanced up. "My uncle has arranged for the Archbishop of Canterbury to marry us at Sunderland House."

"I thought we had to be married in a church," she objected.

He smiled. "Apparently, the archbishop *is* the church. Or, at least, he brings it with him everywhere he goes like a tortoise with his shell. All the lawyers agree it will answer," he added, "and we can rely on the discretion of his excellency."

"Well . . ." she said. "If you're sure you want to marry me again . . ."

"Quite sure," he said softly, making her feel warm all over.

"Then I will come to you tomorrow at Sunderland House," she said.

His arms tightened around her. "You don't understand," he said, laughing. "I have come to take you home tonight—now! Mrs. Drabble will sit with you all night to make certain everything is done properly," he added quickly. "You will not be molested—until tomorrow night. Then, I'm afraid, Mrs. Drabble won't be able to help you."

Patience squirmed away, laughing. "But I can't go with you tonight," she told him. "Pru has a cold, and it's not getting any better."

All traces of humor vanished from his face. "She has come home, then, has she?" he said, with noticeable disdain. "I daresay her friends could not get rid of her soon enough!"

"That is not fair, Max!" Patience said. "You don't know what she's been through. She's had a terrible time!"

"Should I be sorry for her?" he asked dryly.

"Yes!" she answered vehemently. "Lord Milford has

been keeping her a prisoner in his house! He has forced her to agree to marry him!"

"Indeed? How did he do that? Dangle his title in front of her nose? She will like being a countess."

"You don't understand," Patience said. "He took away her maid. He took her clothes, her shoes, everything. He starved her! Locked her in a room! She had to escape by climbing out a window. She could have broken her neck!"

Max seemed unimpressed. "Did she tell you all that?"

Patience scowled at him. "You think she is lying?"

"Now, why would I think that, I wonder?"

"I saw her climb out the window with my own eyes! Lord Milford tried to stop her."

"I should bloody well think so!" he retorted. "She could have broken her neck."

Patience sighed. "You think because she told a little fib about you—"

"Little fib!"

"It doesn't mean she is lying now. I believe her."

"You believe all her little fibs," he scoffed.

"No, I don't. But I do believe this one!"

He sighed.

"That is not what I meant!" she said angrily. "You're twisting my words. Are you going to do something about Lord Milford or not?"

"Forgive me if I don't feel inclined to accuse a gentleman of kidnaping on the word of a proven liar," he drawled. "I know how it feels to be falsely accused."

"Max!"

"Unless you have some proof . . . ?"

"My sister's word is enough for me," she said stubbornly.

"We are not going to agree on this subject," he said.

Patience shook her head. "No," she said sadly. "I won't trouble you about it anymore. I will deal with it myself."

"Good," he said.

Patience frowned. "She is not lying about having a cold at any rate," she said. "Dr. Wingfield has been to see her. I suppose you accept *his* word as proof? So I cannot go with you tonight. And, if she grows any worse, I may not be able to meet you tomorrow either."

His eyes flashed. "What? You certainly *will* meet me tomorrow! Tomorrow is my wedding day."

"If my sister is too ill for me to leave her, the wedding will have to be postponed," said Patience. "Surely, you can see that."

"No, I don't see that!" he retorted. "Why should my wedding be postponed because your sister has a cold?"

"Well, it's not my fault you botched the first wedding," she shot back. "Nor is it my sister's fault."

"I must be mad," he said, gritting his teeth, "to submit to a lifetime of having *that* thrown in my face!"

"You needn't!" she told him.

He jabbed his finger into the air imperiously. "Understand this, my girl: if you are not at Sunderland House by seven o'clock tomorrow morning, I shall come back here and rain holy hell down on you! I will drag you bodily from this house to mine."

"If my sister—" she began.

"I don't care if your sister is *dead* come morning!" he shouted. "You *shall* marry me!"

Turning on his heel, he stormed out of the room.

Chapter 24

Pru did not die in the night. In the morning, she was perhaps a little better, though not, in Patience's judgment, well enough to leave the house. Patience drove to Hyde Park at the appointed time. Leaving Hawkins with the curricle, she went on foot to the rendezvous.

The fog was deepest down by the river. Patience foolishly craned her neck, as if that could help her eyes penetrate the heavy gray fog enveloping the bridge up ahead. Anything or anyone could be hiding within it, she suddenly realized. Reaching into her reticule, she found her pistol. Its weight reassured her.

Up ahead on the bridge a solitary, slim-shouldered figure in a hooded cloak paced back and forth. Suddenly, it stopped and lowered its hood. Patience recognized Isabella's auburn hair at once. Isabella beckoned to her impatiently, holding up a packet of letters in one hand.

Patience hurried forward. As she set foot on the bridge, a heavyset figure detached itself from the shadowy bank and leaped on her, catching her from behind. A handkerchief doused in ether was pressed roughly over her nose and mouth. After a brief struggle, she slumped in her attacker's arms. She never had the chance to use her pistol.

Isabella signaled for her brother's carriage as Lord Milford carried Patience across the bridge. "I suppose you know this is kidnaping!" Isabella fretted as the carriage flew out of the park.

Lord Milford was busy binding Patience's hands. He had already gagged her with his cravat. "Don't be silly," he said impatiently. "I am engaged to Miss Prudence. If you can't kidnap your own fiancée, then what's the point?"

"Very well! You've kidnaped her," Isabella snapped. "What do you plan to do now?"

"I shall take her to my country estate, of course," he replied. "The vicar of Milford owes his living to me. He will marry us or I'll turf him out. I've the special license in my pocket."

"And how is the bride to make her vows with her mouth full of your necktie?"

"There are some things," he told her, "that go without saying. Besides, I shall have witnesses who will swear they heard her speak her vows."

"Well, I shall not be one of them," Isabella declared. "Sir Charles has pledged to take me to Gunter's this afternoon. You will have to set me down at Grosvenor Square, or he may think that *I* have been kidnaped."

Her brother grumbled.

"You needn't be afraid of detection," she said. "No one is following us."

"I am not afraid," he said sharply.

She smiled. "Of course not. How silly of me. Then you will set me down in Grosvenor Square?"

She kept on smiling until, grumbling, he knocked on the little sliding door that separated him from the driver. "Home!" he said gruffly.

* * *

"You're wearing a hole in my rug," the Duke of Sunderland complained.

"I'll buy you another one," Max snapped, suppressing the sudden urge to knock every ornament from the mantelpiece, including and most particularly, the French clock that had the temerity to show the correct time.

"There's no need to bite my head off," the duke said. "It's not my fault you are stood up again."

"I am not stood up!" Max said angrily. "Her sister must have gotten worse."

"Then why does she not send a message?" the duke asked sensibly.

"It is only a little after the appointed time," said Max.

"It is half past seven," the duke said firmly. "Charles Manners-Sutton cannot wait any longer. He has a funeral to meet at Westminster Abbey. War hero and all that sort of thing. Big to-do. He can't be late. Shall we send round to Clarges Street for her?"

"No," Max said grimly. "I shall go."

"Something must be wrong," Mrs. Drabble insisted.

"For her sake, I hope her sister is dead!" Max retorted. "I will accept no other excuse for her tardiness!"

His curricle was brought up and he set off for Clarges Street at once, arriving there just as Hawkins was returning to the house with Freddie Broome's curricle.

Max called out to him, throwing the reins to his own groom and jumping out of the vehicle.

Hawkins was relieved to see him.

"Where is your mistress?" Max demanded. "What keeps her? I have been waiting for her at Sunderland House all morning!"

"I cannot tell you, sir," Hawkins replied. "We drove out to the park very early."

"The park!" Max interrupted. "At this hour? Why?"

"My mistress did not say, sir."

"Well, where is she now?"

Hawkins shook his head. "My mistress bade me leave her at the gates."

Max blanched. "You left her in Hyde Park? On foot?"

"I did not like to, sir, but she insisted . . ."

Max bit back a curse. "Then what happened?"

"Nothing, sir. I waited for her for an hour. I searched, but there was no sign of her."

"So you left?" Max said incredulously.

"Begging your pardon, sir! I thought— I rather had the impression that her ladyship had gone to meet someone. Yourself, possibly. When I could not find her, I thought, perhaps . . ."

"No," Max said curtly. "She did not go there to meet me."

Hurrying up the steps, he hammered on the door with his fist. "Did you see no one else in the park?"

"Not a soul, sir," Hawkins said. "I'm very sorry, sir."

"So you should be!" Max said sharply. "Send to Bow Street at once. I want every inch of that park searched. If my wife has met with some accident, you will answer for it, Hawkins!"

Pushing past Briggs, who had come to answer the door, he entered the house. The butler tried to take his hat, but Max rebuffed him. "Have you seen your mistress this morning?"

"No, sir," Briggs replied. "That is, not since her ladyship went out."

"She went to the park, I believe, to meet someone?"

Briggs looked helpless. "Did she, sir?"

Max sighed impatiently. "Whom did she go to meet, Briggs? I will have answers!"

"I'm sure I don't know, sir. Perhaps Miss Prudence may be of some assistance."

"Have her brought to me," Max commanded, walking briskly up the stairs. "On second thought: I shall go to her. She is still abed, I suppose?"

"Sir!" the butler protested, but Max paid him no heed.

Pru was indeed still in bed, but she was sitting up. She opened her mouth to scream as Max burst into her room, but her surprise was overtaken by a round of violent sneezing.

"Where is Patience?" he demanded as she blew her nose. "Where is my wife?"

Pru's eyes were streaming and her nose was very tender and red. "Is she not with you?" she asked, wheezing pathetically.

"Would I be *here* if she were?" he snapped. "She went out to meet someone hours ago. She has not returned. Whom was she meeting?"

"Is it so late?" Pru mumbled, rubbing her temples.

"It is *very* late!"

"She should be back by now," said Pru, squinting at the clock on her mantelpiece. "That is, I thought she must have gone on to Sunderland House to marry you. Hawkins did not bring her back from the rendezvous?" Pushing back the coverlet, she set her feet on the floor.

"I have had enough of this!" Max said angrily. "Who was she meeting in the park? Tell me at once or I shall throttle you."

Pru climbed unsteadily to her feet and hobbled over to the wardrobe. "You needn't threaten me," she said irritably. "She's my sister! I want her back as much as you do. She went to meet Isabella," she added.

"Isabella *Norton*?" he said in disbelief. "Why?"

Pru opened the wardrobe door. Standing behind it,

she began pulling on her blue walking habit over her nightgown.

"Why, Prudence? Tell me at once or I shall wring your neck!"

"She went to get my letters, if you must know," Pru snapped.

His lip curled. "*Your* letters! I might have known it was something to do with you! What letters?"

"*You* should have been more careful with them," she accused him. "They were private! But you let Milford, of all people, get his hands on them."

Max flinched. "Not . . . not those absurd schoolgirl letters you wrote to *me*?"

"I suppose you gave them to Milford! I suppose you both had a good laugh at my expense!" she said bitterly.

"Certainly not," he said coldly. "I stopped reading them after a time. I threw them away."

"Then he must have stolen them from the rubbish," said Pru. "You should have burnt them!"

"I'd like to burn you," he growled. "And Patsy went to get them back for you? How like you to get her to do your dirty work for you!"

"She wouldn't let me go," Pru protested. Dressed now, she banged the wardrobe shut. "She was going to ask *you* to go with her, but I gather you were not interested in helping *me*. I would have gone with her, but she wouldn't let me. I am sick!"

"She never said a word about any of this to me! Just a lot of nonsense about Milford holding you prisoner."

"It was not nonsense!"

Max suddenly groaned. "You don't suppose she *read* your stupid letters? She wouldn't take them seriously! She wouldn't—She wouldn't blame *me*?"

"No," Pru said reluctantly. "She'd never blame *you* for

anything. In her eyes you are perfectly wonderful. No. If she hasn't come back here, and she hasn't gone to Sunderland House, then something must have happened to prevent her from doing so."

"I have sent to Bow Street," said Max. "The park will be searched. In the meantime, it would be worth speaking to Isabella. If she has returned home, that is," he added. "It could be they are both missing."

"Or perhaps she never made it to the rendezvous at all," Pru suggested. "Maybe her brother caught her trying to leave the house."

"I will call in Grosvenor Square," said Max.

"I am going with you!" cried Pru, running after him as he hurried from the room.

"Absolutely not!" he told her firmly. "If anything happened to you, Patsy would never forgive me. I know that much."

"She's my sister," Pru insisted. "I'm going with you whether you like it or not! Is this really a good time to argue about it?" she added quickly as he began to object.

"At least put on your cloak," he said gruffly. Taking it from the servant, he tossed it to her.

Less than five minutes later they arrived in Grosvenor Square. Max was shocked to see a uniformed officer of the foot patrol standing guard at Lord Milford's door.

"What has happened?" he demanded as the patrolman barred his way to the door.

"And what is your business here, sir?" the patrolman responded in kind.

"Nothing to concern you," Max retorted. "My business is with Lady Isabella Norton."

Pru pushed past him. "Sir, my sister has gone missing! Lady Isabella was the last to see her. Won't you let us in?"

"You're the missing lady's sister?" the patrolman cried,

opening the door for her. "Why didn't you say so? Go right in! Mr. Morton of Bow Street is here already. You'll find him in the drawing room with his lordship."

Isabella gasped as Max came into the room with Prudence in tow. Lord Milford was seated at the fireside holding a raw steak to his face. A meticulously dressed gentleman got to his feet, his brows raised slightly as he regarded the new arrivals.

Max was surprised to find the runner so gentlemanlike. "Mr. Morton of Bow Street, I presume?"

Morton bowed. "And you are . . . ?"

"I am Purefoy," Max said simply. "Lady Waverly is my wife."

"Liar!" cried Isabella, jumping to her feet. "You are not a Purefoy! Your name escapes me at the moment. Though I will allow that he *is* married to Lady Waverly," she added grudgingly.

Morton bowed to Prudence. "My lady! You may be assured that we are doing all we can to find your sister."

Pru stared at him. "You think that *I* am Patience?" she asked.

"I understand that you are impatient to have your sister back," he replied.

"You think that *Prudence* was kidnapped?" Max interrupted.

"Well, of course she was kidnapped!" snapped Isabella. "It happened right before my eyes! We had just gotten back to the house, when, suddenly, *he* was there! He *beat* my poor brother and carried off my sweet friend as if she had been a rag doll!"

Morton cleared his throat. "Perhaps now Your Ladyship will explain how you came to be returning to the house at such an hour? Where had you been? And why was Miss Waverly with you?"

"How dare you question my sister!" Lord Milford said angrily. "We are the victims!"

"It's all right, Ivor," Isabella told him. "I will answer. Miss Prudence, I'm sorry to say, was running away from her brother-in-law, that man there!" She pointed her finger at Max. "When she told me of his cruelty to her, I could not help but pity her. My brother and I rescued her."

Pru's mouth fell open. "That is a lie!" she cried. "My sister went to meet you in the park to retrieve some letters!"

"It is *you* who are lying, Lady Waverly," Isabella answered. "Your husband has been in your sister's bed, and the poor child could bear it no more."

"What did you say?" Pru gasped.

"Considering his descent, one could hardly have expected any better. His mother was an Italian opera dancer, you know," she told Mr. Morton.

Pru's face was red. "I am *not* Lady Waverly! I am Miss Waverly!"

Isabella's mouth curved into a cruel smile. "Indeed? I did hear a rumor that Lord Waverly still lived. He only pretended to be dead to escape debtor's prison. What a family! How could I not take pity on poor little Prudence?"

"I thought you were my friend," Pru said bitterly. "But you were part of his plan all along, weren't you? You only pretended to help me."

"I don't know what you mean, Lady—er, what is your name? Mrs. Fusilli? I'm sorry about your sister, but it is not our fault she was kidnapped. My brother and I were only trying to help her."

"Could this be true?" Morton gravely asked Pru. "Could your sister have run away?"

"No!" Pru said violently. "Everything *she* just said is a beastly lie! My sister went to the park to meet Isabella! If they brought her here it was against her will!"

"I don't believe for an instant she has been kidnapped twice," Max declared. "I believe she is still in this house. Have you searched it, Mr. Morton?"

"If we were holding a girl prisoner, we would hardly have summoned Bow Street," Isabella sneered. "The fact is, my brother was attacked, and Miss Waverly was carried off into the fog by that—that brute!"

"You *know* who took her?" Max roared. "Who was it?"

Lord Milford eyed him resentfully with his one good eye, the other still being hidden behind the raw steak. "I know exactly who it was," he declared. "It was that boy who was always hanging about Lady Waverly's house! You know: the American! He's attacked me before. Lady Waverly can attest to that."

"You mean *Roger*?" cried Pru. "*Roger* beat you up and kidnapped my sister?"

Max breathed a sigh of relief. "Oh, that's all right, then!" he exclaimed. "I was terrified something awful had happened! Well, Mr. Morton!" he went on, actually smiling. "You can call off the search. Wherever she is, I know she's perfectly safe."

Morton stared. "You *know* the young man who attacked his lordship?" he said slowly. "You would trust him with your wife's sister?"

Max gave a laugh. "No, indeed," he said. "But I believe I can trust him with my wife! You kidnapped the wrong girl, my lord," he added, growing cold as he gazed at Lord Milford. "You thought you were taking Prudence, but you were wrong. The lady who went to the park to meet your sister, the lady whom you brought here against her will, was, in fact, *my* wife!"

The raw steak fell from Lord Milford's eye and slapped the floor.

"What are you talking about?" Isabella demanded, white faced. "There is your wife!"

Pru stuck out her chin. "No, I am Prudence. Patience went in my place because she is a good and loyal sister. I would never run away from her. She would never hurt me, and—and neither would Max! What you said about him was quite disgusting!"

"Not to mention slanderous," said Max.

Morton frowned. "So the missing woman is not Miss *Prudence* Waverly? She is Mrs. . . . ?"

"Purefoy," Max told him. "She is Mrs. Maximilian Purefoy."

"You are not a Purefoy," Isabella spat, "however much you would like to pretend. Your uncle has disowned you! You are *nothing*!" She turned to Mr. Morton. "You will not take their word over ours, surely? *He* is nothing but a by-blow, and she—*she* is an American!"

"But this young lady *is* Miss Prudence Waverly?" said Morton.

"I suppose so, yes," said Isabella. "Yes! Miss Prudence wears curls on her brow. Her sister does not."

"Then it was Mrs. Purefoy in your carriage this morning," Morton said. "Why? Was she running away from her husband?"

Isabella stared at him, unable to think of any plausible lie.

"My lady?"

"It was *his* idea!" she cried, pointing her finger at her brother. "I only went along with it because he—he bullied me! He was going to take her to Milford and make her marry him. He's desperate to get his hands on her fortune!"

"Why, you—!" Lord Milford flung his raw steak at her before Morton could get him under control. The patrolman was summoned to haul his lordship from the room.

"And you as well, my lady," Morton told Isabella.

"I?" she cried. "What did I do?"

"Kidnapping, blackmail," Morton began.

"No! No!" She protested. "It was my brother who kidnapped her! He doused his handkerchief in ether and he grabbed her from behind! I was just the decoy or the bait or whatever. I did nothing! As for the blackmail . . . I never blackmailed anyone! I was going to *give* those letters back! Honestly, I was!"

"Perhaps Your Ladyship would be good enough to retrieve them now," Morton said gently.

Isabella did so eagerly. Taking the packet from her cloak, she handed it to Morton.

Morton glanced at the direction. "These are addressed to you, sir," he said to Max. "Allow me to return your property to you."

"Thank you," said Max, pocketing them without looking at them.

"There is still the matter of your missing wife, of course," said Morton. "Bow Street is at your disposal, sir. We'll find the young man."

"He said something," Isabella said quickly, suddenly eager to be helpful. "The American. He said he was taking her back to America!"

"America?" Morton said doubtfully.

Max laughed aloud. "It's closer than you think, Mr. Morton!" he said. "In fact, it's just up the street."

"Of course!" said Pru. "Mr. Adams's house!"

As Morton led Isabella out to the hackney coach where her brother was waiting, Sir Charles drove up. "What the devil is going on?" he demanded. "Who are you, sir? Where are you taking my fiancée?"

"She's being arrested for kidnapping my sister," Pru told him. "Her *and* her brother. They're going to prison for a very long time!"

"Sir Charles!" Isabella cried. "Help me!"

Without another word, the baronet drove away.

Max and Pru continued on to Mr. Adams's house. Mrs. Adams did not keep them waiting long. Conducting them upstairs, she led them into a cheerful little room. Roger Molyneux was bent over the bed, taking his patient's pulse. Nodding curtly to Pru, he spoke to Max.

"You got my note, I see? The instant we got her bonnet off, I knew, of course, who it was. I sent for you at once."

Max sank down to his knees at the side of the bed, and took Patience's cold hand in his. "I must have gone already to find her," he murmured, his eyes on Patience's face. "Can we not wake her up?"

"My guess is the bastard etherized her," Roger answered, stepping back from the bed. "But all her vital signs are good. She'll be back with us soon."

"What a good thing you were there, Molyneux," said Max. "I'm truly grateful to you."

Pru slipped to her knees on the other side of the bed and smoothed Patience's hair back from her brow. "Why *were* you there, Roger Molyneux?" she asked.

"I was in the neighborhood," he replied.

"Oh?"

He frowned. "I heard you were engaged to the big lord," he said sullenly. "I wanted to congratulate you."

Her eyes gleamed. "You thought it was *me,* didn't you?" she said softly. "You came to rescue *me!*"

"No," he retorted. "I was going to kidnap you."

Pru jumped to her feet and ran to him. "Oh, Roger! You *do* care! I wish it *had* been me," she went on, snuggling in his arms. "But Patience said I wasn't well enough to get out of bed, let alone—"

"Why? What's the matter with you?" Roger said sharply.

"Nothing! Just a trifling little cold," she assured him.

"There's no such thing as a trifling little cold," he said sternly. "You could have pneumonia! I shall have to examine you."

"Yes, doctor," Pru said meekly. "I think you should."

When Patience opened her eyes some time later, there was no one else in the room but Max. "Hello," he murmured, looking down at her tenderly.

"Where am I?" she murmured in confusion.

"You're at the American embassy," he told her. "You're safe now. How do you feel?"

"A slight headache," she replied, sitting up. "The embassy?" she repeated.

"Yes. What's the last thing you remember?"

Patience had to think. "I was going to meet Isabella," she said, concentrating. "I saw her on the bridge. But, just as I was going to meet her, someone pounced on me!"

She frowned at him. "Max! Max, how could you?"

He blinked at her. "What?"

"You kidnapped me!" she accused him.

"Kidnapped you! I?"

"You," she said softly. Taking his face in her hands, she kissed him gently. "How romantic! Though not at all necessary," she added. "I didn't mean what I said. Of course, I was going to marry you again. I would not have missed our wedding for anything."

"But we *have* missed it," he pointed out. "It's afternoon. But we can try again tomorrow."

"Try again tomorrow!" she mocked him. "As though I could wait another day!"

"What would you have me do? I can't turn back the clock."

"This is America, Max. We don't have all your silly rules. We are a free people. We can get married any time we like, day or night. Ask Mrs. Adams if we can borrow the chaplain."

"But I don't have the license," he said. "I left it at Sunderland House."

"In America, we don't need a license," she told him. "But you know that, of course. It's why you brought me here, isn't it? We don't even need my uncle's permission!"

Her eyes clouded suddenly. "I just wish my sister could be here," she said sadly. "Then everything would be perfect."

"Then everything *is* perfect," he told her. "Prudence is waiting outside."

"Truly?"

He smiled. "Truly."

Patience flung her arms around his neck. "Thank you, Max," she said simply.

Epilogue

By the time his nephew returned to the house that afternoon, the Duke of Sunderland had given up on the marriage entirely. The archbishop had left hours ago, the other guests had been dismissed. The cake had been given to an orphanage, and the servants had eaten the breakfast. His grace's gout was troubling him, and he was in the drawing room soaking his feet in a bath of Epsom salts.

"So you decided to come, after all?" he said irritably as Max led Patience to him. "That is very good of you, madam."

Patience was too happy to take umbrage at his less than welcoming tone. Bending at the waist, she kissed his cheek. "How do you do, Uncle?"

"Uncle, is it?" he said gruffly. "Well, it's too late for you to be married today."

"But I am presenting my wife to you, sir," Max told him. "We were married at the embassy."

"Embassy? *What* embassy?"

"*My* embassy, sir," Patience told him, smiling. "I am married to your nephew. I am very glad to see you again. It was not very pleasant the last time we met. I am sorry for that."

"So you should be," he rasped. "But, Max, I don't like this embassy business. You should be married by the archbishop, as we planned. I'll ask him to come again tomorrow."

Patience laughed. "I'll marry your nephew as many times as you like, sir."

"Very generous of you, madam, I'm sure," the duke said sourly. "But you needn't look so pleased with yourself! I'm not as frail as I look. If I were, I'd have died years ago. You will have to wait a good long while to be a duchess."

"Oh, I hope so, sir," Patience replied. "And, you know, I might never be a duchess. It is possible that, in the years to come, England will do the sensible thing, and abolish the aristocracy. Wouldn't that be wonderful, sir?"

The duke glared at her. "I trust, madam," he said frostily, "I shall never live to see *that* day!"

6'. 1/2016

GREAT BOOKS, GREAT SAVINGS!

When You Visit Our Website:
www.kensingtonbooks.com
You Can Save Money Off The Retail Price
Of Any Book You Purchase!